'Pelevin's all-out attac[k on] [contem]porary culture so[unds] [oppres]sive society, consume[...]

'There are some excel[lent] [?] and [the imag]e [of vam]pires decanting the m[...] [the] [...] [...] livestock, and the cor[rupt as] beauty of the revealed world will have some readers purring with pleasure . . . the superb translation means it's always exquisitely written'   *SFX*

'Trust me, *Empire V* is unlike anything else you'll read this year. Pelevin creates this complex vampire mythology in order to skewer modern-day corruption, cruelty, greed, and authoritarianism'
                                                            SF Signal

'Really strikes a cord whether you're au fait with contemporary Russian history or not'   *Sci-Fi Now*

'Invention bubbles out of every paragraph; metaphors are pushed until they fall over; pantomime slips into nuanced parody and back again... there are so many good jokes, and conceits and notions'   M. John Harrison, *TLS*

Also by Victor Pelevin from Gollancz:

S.N.U.F.F.

EMPIRE V
The Prince of Hamlet

Victor Pelevin

Translated by Anthony Phillips

First published in Great Britain in 2016
by Gollancz
an imprint of The Orion Publishing Group Ltd
Carmelite House, 50 Victoria Embankment
London EC4Y 0DZ
An Hachette UK Company

1 3 5 7 9 10 8 6 4 2

A CIP catalogue record for this book
is available from the British Library.

ISBN 978 1 473 21308 1

Typeset at The Spartan Press Ltd,
Lymington, Hants

Printed and bound by CPI Group (UK) Ltd, Croydon, CR0 4YY

MIX
Paper from
responsible sources
FSC® C104740

www.orionbooks.co.uk
www.gollancz.co.uk

CONTENTS

Empire 'V'

The locomotive is an ingenious construction, a
   quality of which the locomotive is not itself aware.
Would anyone even think of making a locomotive
   without an engineer to drive it?

Fr. Mitrofan Srebryansky

BRAHMA

When I came to, I found myself in a large room full of old furniture, antiques perhaps. I could see a mirrored sideboard encrusted with fretwork stars, an elaborate escritoire, two nude life-studies and a small picture of Napoleon on horseback in the heat of battle. One wall was taken up by an elegant floor-to-ceiling filing cabinet in Karelian birch, its drawer-fronts embellished with variously coloured labels and insignia. Next to the cabinet stood a stepladder.

I became aware that I was not lying flat, as would be expected of a person recovering consciousness, but was upright. The reason I had not fallen down was that my arms and legs were firmly strapped to Swedish exercise bars attached to the wall. I deduced that the structure was a set of parallel bars – I could feel the outline of a wooden crossbeam through my fingertips. Other bars were pressing into my back.

On a small red divan against the opposite wall sat a man wearing a red dressing-gown and a black mask. The mask was like a top hat coming down over the head as far as the shoulders, or perhaps the cardboard Stahlhelms worn by the Teutonic Knights during the Battle on the Ice in the film *Alexander Nevsky*. A sharp protuberance marked the area of the nose; the eyes looked out through two oval holes; while a rectangular slit had been cut out round the mouth and covered by a piece of black material. The overall effect was something like mediaeval doctors one sees in engravings of the Black Death in Europe.

This was way over the top. So much so that I wasn't even scared.

'Good day to you,' said the man in the mask.

'Hello,' I replied, ungluing my lips with difficulty.

'What is your name?'

'Roman,' I said.

'How old are you?'

'Nineteen.'

'Why have you not been called up into the army?'

Assuming he was having me on, I ignored the question.

'I must ask you to excuse a certain theatricality in the setting,' continued the man in the mask. 'If you have a headache, it will soon pass. It comes from my having sprayed you with a special gas.'

'What sort of gas?'

'The kind that is used against terrorists. Nothing to worry about – it's all over now. I advise you not to try calling for help. There is no point and it will do no good. The only outcome will be that I shall develop a migraine, which will spoil our conversation.'

The unknown man had a deep, confident voice. The cloth covering his mouth fluttered when he spoke.

'Who are you?' I asked.

'My name is Brahma.'

'Why are you wearing a mask?'

'Several reasons,' said Brahma. 'But in any case it is to your advantage. Should our relationship fail to progress to a satisfactory outcome, I shall be able to release you without any difficulty since you will not know what I look like.'

The prospect of eventually being allowed to go free was a relief, certainly. But the words might contain a trap.

'What is it you want from me?' I asked.

'My desire is that a vital interest within a very important part of my body, and simultaneously of my spirit, should be stimulated in your direction. But this, you see, can only come about if you are a person of noble and aristocratic lineage...'

Man's a maniac, I thought. *Main thing is not to upset him. Better distract him by talking...*

'Why must I be of noble and aristocratic lineage?' I asked.

'The quality of the red liquid in your veins plays an important role. There is little chance of it, however.'

'And what do you mean by a vital interest?' I enquired. 'Is the idea that I should be alive when this takes place?'

'I can see I shall get nowhere with you by trying to explain it in words,' said Brahma. 'You need a demonstration.'

Rising from the sofa, he came towards me, folded back the black cloth covering his mouth, and leaned towards my right ear. Sensing a stranger's breath on my face I shrank back, anticipating something loathsome.

What a fool I've been, I thought. *Whatever possessed me to come here?*

But nothing happened. Having breathed into my ear, Brahma turned away and went back to the sofa.

'I could have bitten you on your arm,' he said. 'Unfortunately, however, your arms are numb as a result of having been bound. The effect would not be the same.'

'I suppose it was you who bound them?'

'Yes,' sighed Brahma. 'No doubt I should apologise for my actions. I see that they must appear strange and reprehensible. Nevertheless, all will soon become clear.'

Settling himself on the divan and staring at me as though I were an image on a television screen, he studied me for several seconds, now and then clicking his tongue. 'Don't be alarmed,' he said. 'I am not a sex maniac. You may rest easy on that score.'

'Well, what are you?'

'I am a vampire. Vampires are not perverts. They may sometimes pretend to be. But their interests and goals are entirely other.'

No, this is no common or garden pervert I'm dealing with here, I thought. *This one's insane as well. I must keep him talking to distract his attention.*

'A vampire? Do you drink blood?'

'Not by the glassful,' replied Brahma, 'and it is not the basis of my self-identification... Although in a sense you are correct.'

'So why do you drink it?'

'It is the best method of getting to know another person.'

'How so?'

The eyes visible through the oval holes blinked several times. Then the mouth behind the black cloth said: 'There was a time when the two trees growing on the wall, a lemon tree and an orange tree, were more than trees – they were gates to a secret, magic world. And then something happened. The gates vanished, to be replaced by nothing but two oblong pieces of canvas hanging on the wall. Not only did the gates disappear, so did the world to which they led. Even the dreaded flying dog that stood guard over the entrance to the world reverted to being a wicker fan bought in some tropical resort or other...'

To say I was impressed by this account would fail utterly to describe its effect on me. I was stunned. What to any ordinary person would have been complete gibberish, to me was the secret code unlocking my childhood. Even more astounding, the only person in the world capable of formulating it was myself. Even though I was lost for words, after a while I could restrain myself no longer.

'I don't understand. I suppose I might have said something

about the pictures while I was unconscious. But I could not possibly have said anything about the magic world on the other side of the gates, because that was not how I thought of it. Nevertheless, now you put it like that, I can see that, yes, that is exactly what it was...'

'But perhaps you don't know why it happened as it did?'

'No, why did it?'

'The enchanted world in which you formerly lived was the invention of a grasshopper hidden in the grass. Then along came a frog, and the frog ate the grasshopper. From that moment on, even though nothing changed in your room, you no longer had anywhere to live.'

'Yes!' I cried, taken aback. 'That's true as well. You have told it exactly as it happened.'

'Please think of something,' said Brahma, 'anything that comes into your head, as long as it is something only you know about. Then ask me a question about it, the answer to which only you would know.'

'All right, I will,' I said, and plunged into thought. 'Well, for instance... there was a fan hanging on the wall at home – you've already mentioned it. How was it attached to the wall?'

Behind the holes in the mask, Brahma closed his eyes.

'It was glued. And the glue had been applied in the shape of the letter X. Not a conventional cross, but specifically an X.'

'How...?'

Brahma raised his hand. 'Just a moment. You glued the fan to the wall because you had come to believe it was really a vampire dog which would come down at night and bite you. Such an idea is, needless to say, not only arrant nonsense but an insult to true vampires.'

'How do you know all this?'

Brahma rose from the sofa and came over towards me. Lifting the black cloth with one finger, he opened his mouth, revealing large, strong, nicotine-stained teeth. So far as I could see there was nothing unusual about the teeth, except perhaps that the canines were a little whiter than the others. Brahma raised his head to give me a view of his palate. In the middle was a peculiar, corrugated, orange-coloured membrane, as if a fragment of dental bridgework was adhering to it.

'What's that?' I asked.

'That is the *Tongue*,' said Brahma, carefully enunciating the word, making two syllables of it and freighting them with emphatic deliberation.

'Tongue?' I echoed.

'Not a human tongue. It is the soul and essence of a vampire.'

'Is it the Tongue that allows you to know things?'

'Yes.'

'But how does it do that?'

'There is no point in trying to explain. If you want to understand, you will have to become a vampire yourself.'

'I'm not sure I want to do that.'

Brahma returned to his seat on the sofa.

'You see, Roma,' he said, 'for all of us, what is to be is decided by fate. You came here yourself. And I have very little time.'

'Are you going to be my teacher?'

'No. Teaching is manifest not in the person of a vampire, but in his nature. Initiation consists in the vampire biting his student. However, it does not follow that a person has merely to be bitten by a vampire to become one. As they say in bad films, ha ha, *that* only happens in bad films...'

He chuckled at his own little joke. I too essayed a smile, but it was not a success.

'There is one particular bite,' he went on, 'of which a vampire is capable only once in his life. And then only if the Tongue wills it. By tradition, this can take place on the day of the summer

6

'solstice. And here you are. My Tongue is about to transfer to you.'

'How do you mean – transfer?'

'In the literal sense. Physically. But I must warn you, the experience will be painful, both at first and later on. You will feel unwell, as though you had been bitten by a poisonous snake. You should not worry – it will pass.'

'Could you not have found someone else to instruct?'

Brahma paid no attention to the question.

'You may lose consciousness for a while. Your body will become numb. Possibly you will be visited by hallucinations. Possibly not. But whatever happens there is one effect you are certain to experience.'

'What is that?'

'You will recall everything that has happened in your life. The Tongue finds out and familiarises itself with your entire past life – it must know everything about you. Something similar is said to happen when a person drowns. But you are a young man and your drowning will not take long.'

'And what will you do while this is going on?'

Brahma made a peculiar, strangled noise in his throat.

'Don't, er, worry about me. I have a meticulously worked out plan of action.'

With these words, he took a step towards me, grabbed hold of my hair with his hand and bent my head down to my shoulder. I thought he was going to bite me, but instead he bit his own finger. Blood immediately flowed over his wrist.

'Keep still,' he said. 'It will be better for you.'

The sight of blood unnerved me, and I obeyed. He brought his bloodied finger up to my forehead and wrote there something with it. Then without warning he sank his teeth into my neck.

I tried to cry out but could manage no more than a half-choked moan: the angle at which he was holding my head made it impossible for me to open my mouth. The pain in my neck was unbearable, as though a crazed dentist were jabbing his electric drill into my jaw. For one second I was sure that the hour of my death had arrived, and I was reconciled to it. Then, suddenly, all was over. Brahma let go of me and leapt backwards. I felt blood on my cheek and on my neck, and saw that his mask and the cloth over his mouth were smeared with it.

I realised the blood was not mine but his own. It flowed out of his mouth down his neck, across his chest, down the red dressing-gown and splashed to the floor in viscous drops. Something appeared to have happened to Brahma; it was as though he, not myself, was the one to have been bitten. Swaying on his feet he returned to his red sofa, sat on it, and began to shuffle his feet agitatedly to and fro on the parquet.

There flashed into my mind Tarkovsky's film *Andrei Rublyov*, the scene where a time-hallowed punishment is being inflicted on a monk, the pouring of molten metal into his mouth. The whole time leading up to his execution the monk lets fly at his torturers with a continuous stream of the most hideous curses, but from the moment when they begin pouring the metal down his gullet he utters not another word, while his whole body continues to jerk and twitch mercilessly. This silence was the most dreadful thing of all, and in the same way it was the silence of my interlocutor that now caused me the greatest terror.

Still shuffling his feet, he reached into the pocket of the dressing-gown, produced a small nickel-plated pistol, and shot himself in the head through the side of the cylindrical mask that covered his face. His head rocked from side to side, the hand holding the pistol slumped to the sofa, and he lay still.

At that moment I felt a kind of faint movement in my neck, just beneath the jaw. It was not exactly painful, more as though I was feeling it through an anaesthetic injection, but it was deeply unpleasant. Not long after I began to lose consciousness, so that my memory of what then took place is confused. I was being drawn inexorably towards sleep.

Brahma had spoken the truth. My past life began to appear in a series of trance visions, as though someone was screening in a small, intimate cinema inside my head a documentary film of my childhood. *How strange*, I thought, *my greatest fear was always vampires...*

CITY OF THE SUN

From the time of my birth, I lived with my mother in Moscow. Our flat was in a building belonging to the Professional Dramatists Union, not far from the Sokol Metro station. It was a multistorey beige brick structure, built in a vaguely Western style and enjoying Soviet Category A status – the sort of building usually inhabited by Central Committee *nomenklatura* and select echelons of the Soviet intellectual elite. Black Volga cars with flashing beacons were always to be seen around the building, and one could not fail to notice that the cigarette ends that littered the staircase and elevator landings were those from the most coveted American brands. My mother and I occupied a small two-room flat of the kind known in occidental lands as a 'one-bedroom'.

My formative years were spent in this one bedroom, which had clearly been envisaged as such by the architect. It was small and elongated, with a tiny window overlooking a car park. I was not permitted to arrange it according to my tastes: my mother chose the colour of the wallpaper, decreed the location of the bed and the table, and even the pictures on the walls. This last was the subject of many disagreements: after I once called her a 'little Soviet tyrant' we were not on speaking terms for a week.

For my mother, no more offensive accusation could have

been imagined. A 'tall, thin woman with a faded face', as a playwright neighbour once described her to a policeman, she had in her youth been associated with various dissident circles. In memory of this affiliation she often used to play to visitors a tape recording of a baritone with a reputation for defying the establishment. This man was reading some heretical verses, to which my mother's voice could be heard contributing a sarcastic commentary from somewhere in the background. The baritone declaimed:

> Your nickel's in the Metro slot
> And two plain-clothes cops are on your tail...
> While queuing for another vodka shot
> You know they'll haul you off to jail.

At this point my mother's youthful voice intruded itself: 'Why don't you read the one about Solzhenitsyn and that cunt with the bushy eyebrows?'

It was the first time I heard the kind of obscene word that well-brought-up children in the era of *perestroika* usually learned from sniggering peers in the kindergarten dorm. My mother, whenever she played this tape recording, felt it necessary to explain that the obscenity was justified by artistic necessity and by the context. As for me, I found the word 'context' even more puzzling than the word 'cunt' since the whole scene was dimly suggestive of the mysterious and threatening grown-up world towards which the winds of change issuing nightly from the TV were imperceptibly wafting me.

My mother's pro-human-rights cassette had been recorded many years before I was born. It would seem that marriage, a state of life crowned by my appearance in this world, was the cause of her abandoning an active role in the struggle. But her propinquity to revolutionary democracy, which irradiated my

11

childhood with a romantic glow, went apparently unremarked by a regime already sliding into its dotage.

On the wall to the right of my bed were two small identically sized pictures. Forty centimetres wide by fifty centimetres high, they were the first objects I measured with the ruler in the geometry set that I received as a gift in my first grade of school. One picture depicted a lemon tree in a tub, the other a similarly planted orange tree. The only difference between them was the shape and colour of the fruit: the yellow ones elongated and the orange ones spherical.

Directly above the bed hung a wicker fan in the shape of a heart – purely decorative because it was too large to be of any use. In the hollow between the two knoll-like ventricles was a round knob, making the whole thing resemble a gigantic bat with a tiny head. In its middle was a blob of red lacquer paint.

I was convinced that this fan was actually a flying vampire-dog (a creature I had read about in a magazine called *Around the World*) which during the day was at rest on the wall but came to life at night. As with a mosquito's abdomen, I could see through his skin the blood he had drunk: this would be the origin of the red stain in the centre of the fan.

The blood, I assumed, was mine.

I realised my terrors were an echo of stories I had heard at summer camps (they tended to be repeated unchanged for years on end). Despite this, I was regularly visited by nightmares from which I would awaken in a cold sweat. Eventually, so concrete did the presence of the vampire-dog spreadeagled against the wall become, and so afraid of the dark was I, that I had to switch on the light to make the dog once again assume the form of a fan made of palm leaves. I knew it would be no good confiding my terrors to my mother. The only thing I could think of was to fix the fan firmly to the wallpaper with superglue. Once I had done that, the terror left me.

Another idea I took from those summer camps was my earliest conception of the physical world. At one of them I saw a remarkable fresco. It showed the earth as a flat disc resting upon three whales swimming in a pale blue ocean. Trees grew upwards from the earth, telegraph poles poked skywards, and there was even a jolly red tram bowling along between a higgledy-piggledy jumble of identical white buildings. Round the front edge of this terrestrial disc were spelt out the letters U S S R. I knew that I had been born in the USSR, and that sometime later it had disintegrated. This was very puzzling, because whereas the houses, trees and trams were still where they always had been, the solid ground on which they stood had evidently vanished... However I was still very little, and my mind accommodated itself to this paradox as it did to hundreds of other imponderables, all the more so as I was already beginning to grasp the true bottom line of the Soviet economic catastrophe: a country that finds it necessary to have two police officers in civilian clothes spying on people who would, in a normal society, be receiving unemployment benefit, could hardly be expected to end otherwise.

But these were vague, phantom shades of childhood. The moment at which my childhood came to an end was my first truly personal memory. It occurred while I was watching an old cartoon film on television, *Dunno in the City of the Sun*. Marching across the screen was a column of cheerful, tubby little midgets from Soviet comics. Waving their arms in glee, they sang:

> And then along came Mr Frog,
> His tummy brightest green,
> His tummy brightest green.
> He swallowed up a grasshopper,
> Who had no time to think, no time to guess,

What was about to come,
What was about to come,
That all would end like this...

I knew without a doubt who was the grasshopper they were singing about, the tiny insect Russians for some reason call the 'little smith'. He was the muscular forger of the new world, seen on all those old posters, tear-off calendars and postage stamps, swinging his hammer high in the air. The jolly little midgets were waving a final salute to the Soviet Union from the safety of their City of the Sun, the road to which the Soviet people had so miserably failed to find.

Seeing the beaming faces of the diminutive marchers, I burst into tears. My grief had nothing, however, to do with nostalgia for the USSR, which I barely remembered. No, the tiny figures marching along through enormous bluebells half as high again as they were, reminded me of something simple that I knew to be of fundamental significance, although I could no longer remember what it was.

The loving, gentle world of my childhood, where every object seemed as huge in scale as these giant flowers and where there were as many happy sunlit paths as in the cartoon film, now lay forever in the past. It was lost in the long grass that had been home to the grasshopper, and now I knew that henceforth it would be the frog I must deal with. The longer this went on, the more indissoluble would be the relationship.

The frog's belly was indeed green, but it had a black back and on every street corner an armour-plated outpost known as an *exchange bureau*. Grown-ups believed implicitly in the frog, and only in the frog, but I had a feeling that at some time in the future the frog would betray them too, and then there would be no bringing back the little smith...

The cartoon midgets were the only people who were concerned

14

to bid farewell to the ridiculous country in which I had been born. Even the three whales on whose backs it had rested now pretended that they had had nothing to do with it, and opened a furniture store which they advertised with an endlessly repeated TV jingle: 'Three whales, three whales, they're the best, forget the rest...'

Of my own family's history I knew precisely nothing. But some of the *Lares* and *Penates* with which I was surrounded bore the imprint of something dark and mysterious.

First, there was an old black and white print of a lion-woman with a languorously thrown back face, naked breasts, and paws armed with powerful claws. This print hung in the hallway, below a wall light reminiscent of an icon lamp. The feeble illumination it provided in the half-darkness caused the image to take on a fearsome, magical aspect.

In my imagination some such creature must lie in wait for people beyond the 'threshold of the grave'. This expression, frequently to be heard on my mother's lips, I learnt by rote before I had any notion of what it meant: to imagine a concept as abstruse as ceasing to exist was beyond my powers. My idea of death was of being translated to another location, probably the place at the end of the path that led up between the paws of the Sphinx in the black and white print.

Another message from the past was contained in the silver knives and forks emblazoned with a crest consisting of a bow and arrow and three cranes in flight, which I found one day in the sideboard my mother usually kept locked.

Once she had done bawling me out for inquisitiveness, my mother informed me this was the family crest of the Baltic Barons von Storckwinkel, the stock from which my father was descended. My own surname was the rather less aristocratic Shtorkin. According to my mother, during the years of War

Communism it was common practice to have one's name surgically operated on, in the hope of concealing its social origins.

My father left the family hearth immediately after I was born. Despite all my efforts, this was the only information I succeeded in gleaning about him. I had only to touch on the subject for my mother to turn pale, light a cigarette and repeat the same phrases, quietly at first but gradually rising to a scream:

'Get out of here, do you hear? Be off with you, you loathsome scum! Leave me alone, you criminal!'

I assumed that her reaction was connected in some way with a dark and mysterious secret. But when I entered the eighth grade, I learnt more about my father as a result of my mother having to resubmit the paperwork for our living accommodation.

He was a journalist on a leading newspaper. I even found his column on the Internet: a bald man with an ingratiating smile lurking behind gig-lamp specs. The gist of the article was that Russia could not hope to become a normal country until her people and the powers-that-be recognised other people's property rights as deserving of respect.

As a concept it made complete sense, yet for some reason it failed to inspire me. This may have been because my father was overfond of using expressions I did not at the time understand ('plebs', 'responsible elites'). The smile on the paternal visage was obviously addressed not to me but to the 'responsible elites' whose comfortable substance I was being exhorted to respect.

Approaching the end of my school days, I began to think about a profession. Glossy magazines and advertisements vaguely indicated the direction I should take to succeed in life, but the nature of the recommended steps that would lead to the achievement of my goal remained, so far as I could see, a closely guarded secret.

'If the quantity of fluid passing through a pipeline per unit of time remains static or increases only in a linear progression,' my physics teacher was fond of intoning during lessons, 'it is only logical to assume that it will take a long time for the number of people with access to the pipeline to increase.'

The theorem had the ring of plausibility, but rather than encouraging me to join the lemming rush towards the pipeline in question, it made me want to distance myself as far as possible from it. I decided to enter the Institute of African and Asian Countries, to learn some exotic language and work in the tropics.

The course of study needed to gain admittance to the Institute was expensive, and my mother categorically declined to pay for tutors. I appreciated this was due not to simple miserliness but to the lack of money in the family budget, and did not make too much of a fuss. A suggestion that I might approach my father precipitated the usual row, my mother declaring that a real man ought to be able to make it from scratch on his own.

I would have been happy to make it from scratch on my own, but the problem was that I could not see how, or where, to start scratching. The thick fog all around was not in itself the problem: I simply had no idea in which direction I should set off in search of sun and money.

I failed at the first hurdle, an examination essay. The exam was, for some reason, based in the physics faculty of Moscow State University, and the subject was: 'The Image of the Motherland in my Heart.' I wrote about the cartoon film in which the small tubby characters had sung about the grasshopper, about the sliced-up hockey puck labelled 'USSR', and about the smart, conniving whales... Needless to say I knew in my bones that in any attempt to enter such a prestigious Higher Education establishment it would be suicidal to speak the truth, but I had no choice. What sealed my fate, so I was informed, was a phrase in my essay: 'Despite everything, I am a patriot: I love our cruel, unjust society living in conditions of permafrost.' The word 'society', apparently, should have been followed by a comma.

On my way to the final interview with the entrance application panel, I caught sight of a drawing on the door depicting a happy-looking snail (its smile, as with the photograph of my father on the Internet, directed at someone else). Below it was a verse from an ancient Japanese poet:

Oh snail!
When climbing to the top of Mount Fuji,
there is no need to hurry...

Taking out a pen, I added:

There are enough snails
on the top of Mount Fuji
as it is.

The rejection letter was the first real reverse of my life. My response to fate's decree was to take a job as a lorry unloader at the supermarket not far from our house.

For the first few days I felt as though I had sunk to the very dregs of existence, below the level at which the laws of Social Darwinism could begin to operate. But I soon came to realise that no chasm, no ghetto, could be deep or isolated enough to insulate one against these laws, because any individual cell in the social organism functions according to principles identical to those of society as a whole. I even recall the circumstances in which this became clear to me (I was at the time teetering on the brink of clairvoyance, although this was to become clear only much later.)

I was watching an English film, *Dune*, in which interstellar travel is accomplished by beings called Navigators who routinely consume a special narcotic that transforms them into a creature halfway between man and pterodactyl. The Navigator would spread his membranous wings, in so doing shrinking space and enabling a flotilla of cosmic ships to transport itself from any part of the cosmos to any other... It occurred to me that somewhere in Moscow a similarly evil species of web-winged creature had spread its wings over our world. People did not notice but continued ant-like to crawl about, preoccupied by their own affairs without realising that they no longer had any affairs to speak of. Excluded from the loop, they had no idea they were already living in another universe where different laws applied.

These laws operated in the world of the unloaders. There was an accepted level of stealing (neither too far below nor too far above the norm) and a common fund of stolen goods from which distributions were made in equitable proportions. One had no choice but to fight for a place nearer the invisible sun – to fight, moreover, not just any old how but according to the prescriptions of a time-honoured choreography of body movements. All in all, it was a place with its own Mount Fuji, however paltry and vomit-spattered.

Here also, I should mention, my social origins were against me. Supervisors took to assigning me to consecutive night shifts, night after night on the trot, and dropping me in it with Management. The prospect of ending up as a loser even among unloaders was intolerable, and the second summer after leaving school I quit the job.

While it lasted, the money I had earned from the supermarket – including my ill-gotten proceeds, which amounted to a tidy sum – left me in a position to maintain a reasonable degree of independence from my mother and to restrict contact with her to a minimum. For all practical purposes, this was confined to a single ritual exchange: every now and again my mother would stop me in the hallway and say, 'Well, go on then, look me straight in the eye!'

She was convinced that I was using drugs and believed herself capable of determining at any given time whether I was stoned or not. As a matter of fact I did not use any illegal substances at all, but in my mother's eyes I was under the influence of a whole cocktail of narcotics almost every day. Her assessments were based not on any objective measurements such as the dimensions of the pupil or the condition of the whites of the eyes, but on certain specific indices known only to her – which helpfully prevented me from learning techniques to conceal them. For this reason it was impossible to contest my mother's expertise in this field. It was a contest that in any case I declined, aware that the only result would be to provide yet more evidence to support the justice of her attitude. ('It's dreadful how aggressive you get when you've taken drugs!')

In addition to these gifts, my mother possessed remarkable powers of hypnosis. It was enough, for instance, for her to say, 'See, there you go again, gabbling your words,' for me to begin doing exactly that, although I had not hitherto even known what the expression meant. Therefore, whenever my mother got too much for me, I would clam up and leave the house for hours at a time.

One summer's day we had our usual row about my taking drugs. On this occasion, it was unusually stormy and I felt I absolutely had to get out of the house. As I went through the door, I lost control and said: 'That's it. I won't live here any longer.'

'Good news,' replied my mother from the kitchen.

Needless to say, neither of us really meant it.

It was nice in the centre of town, quiet and not too many people around. I wandered through the little streets between Tverskoi Boulevard and the Garden Ring. I was not thinking very clearly, but it occurred to me that the reason Moscow in summer is so beautiful owes less to its streets and its buildings than to the obscure promise of escape it harbours. This promise was all around – in the breeze, in the fluffy white clouds, in the puffballs floating down from the poplar trees that this year had flowered early.

Suddenly my attention was attracted to an arrow drawn in green chalk on the pavement. Beside it, written in the same green chalk, were the words

Your chance to join the elite
22.06 18:40–18:55
A genuine unrepeatable opportunity

My watch showed a quarter to seven. Also, it was 22 June, the day of the summer solstice. The arrow, already all but erased by the feet of passers-by, was obviously part of a game someone was playing. But whoever the instigator was, it was a game I felt drawn to play.

I looked around. The few passers-by were absorbed in their own affairs and no one paid any attention to me. Neither was there anything of interest to be seen in the windows of the nearby buildings.

The arrow pointed towards a shabby archway into a court-yard. I went through and saw another green arrow pointing to the farthest corner, this time with no accompanying inscription. I went on a few paces and saw a small, depressed-looking yard with two old cars, a large waste container and a back door in the middle of a painted brick wall. On the asphalt in front of the door was another green arrow.

There were more arrows on the staircase. The last was on the fifth floor, and it pointed towards a steel-reinforced back door to a large flat. The door was half-open. Holding my breath, I looked through the crack and immediately recoiled in fright.

A man was standing in the semi-darkness behind the door. He held in his hands an object that looked like a blowtorch but I saw no more because something he did caused everything to go black.

At this point, my memory of what had occurred reached a point which was in such close alignment with the present that I remembered where I was – and came back to myself.

MITHRA

I was standing upright at the Swedish parallel bars. I desperately needed to go to the toilet. Also, there was something odd about my mouth. Inspecting it with my tongue, I discovered that the upper incisors had been extracted and in their place were two holes in the gum. I must have spat out the teeth while unconscious, because there was no trace of them in my mouth.

I sensed vaguely that the room contained another living creature besides myself, but since my eyes refused to focus I could see nothing in front of me except an indistinct smudge. The smudge was trying to attract my attention, uttering muffled sounds and repeating the same movements over and over again. Suddenly my eyes regained their focus and I saw before me a man I had never seen before, dressed in black. He was passing his hand in front of my face, testing whether I reacted to the change in light. Seeing that I had come back to my senses, the stranger inclined his head in a gesture of welcome and said: 'Mithra.'

I assumed that was his name.

Mithra was a tall, scrawny young man with a piercing gaze, a pointy Spanish-style beard and barely detectable moustache. A faintly Mephistophelean air hung about him, one which might, however, perhaps have undergone a recent upgrade, increasing the level of tolerance. This particular devil would not necessarily shrink from a good deed provided it had a reasonable prospect of accelerating progress towards his evil goal.

'Roman,' I croaked in reply, and turned my eyes to the sofa along the wall opposite.

It no longer supported a corpse. The blood on the floor had also vanished.

'Where is ...?'

'They've taken him away,' said Mithra. 'A tragic event, alas, that took us completely by surprise.'

'What was his mask for?'

'The deceased had been rendered unsightly as a result of an accident.'

'Why did he shoot himself?'

Mithra shrugged. 'No one knows. The deceased left a note to the effect that you are to succeed him.' He measured me up and down with a thoughtful look. 'And that seems to be the case.'

'I do not want to,' I said quietly.

'Do – not – want – to?' repeated Mithra, stretching out the words.

I shook my head.

'I don't understand,' he said. 'By rights you should be extremely happy. After all, you are an advanced young man. You must be, otherwise Brahma would not have chosen you. You just haven't yet understood how fortunate you are. Forget all your doubts. In any case, there is no way back ... You'd do better to tell me how you are feeling in yourself?'

'Bad,' I said. 'Head hurts terribly. And I need to go to the toilet.'

'Anything else?'

'Some of my teeth seem to have fallen out. The upper incisors.'

'We'll check everything out now,' said Mithra. 'One second.'

In his hand appeared a short glass test tube with a black stopper. It was half filled with a clear liquid.

'This vessel contains some red liquid from a man's veins diluted with water. The concentration is one part to a hundred...'

'Who was the man?'

'You'll see.'

I did not understand what Mithra meant by this.

'Open your mouth,' he directed.

'Is there any danger?'

'None at all. Vampires are immune to any diseases transmitted by red liquid.'

I did as I was told, and Mithra carefully deposited on my tongue a few drops from the test tube. I could detect no difference between the liquid and ordinary water: if there was anything alien it, it had no taste.

'Now rub your tongue against your upper gum, inside the teeth. You will see something after this. We call it the personality map.'

I touched the palate with the tip of my tongue. Now I could feel something extrinsic. It was not painful, more of a slight tingling, as if from a low-powered electrical current. I took my tongue several times round the palate, and suddenly...

Had I not still been strapped to the bars, I would have lost my balance. Without warning I experienced a blindingly powerful sensation, unlike anything I had previously known. I was seeing, or more accurately feeling, another human being from the inside, as if I had myself become him, as sometimes happens in dreams.

Inside the aurora-borealis-like cloud within which the apparition presented itself to me, I could distinguish two contrasting zones, repulsion and attraction, dark and light, cold and hot. The zones overlapped at multiple points forming overlays and archipelagos so that the intersections sometimes resembled islands of warmth in a frozen sea, at other times icebound lakes in a temperate landscape. Everything in the zone of repulsion was unpleasant and painful – all the things this person did not like. The attraction zone, by contrast, contained all that gave him reason to live.

I was looking at what Mithra had called his 'personality map'. Indeed, I could sense an invisible path threading through both zones, hard to describe but nevertheless palpable, like rails along which, insensibly and involuntarily, the attention slid. It had been formed by traces of the mind's habitual pathways, a furrow worn by repeated thoughts, a meandering trajectory of the mind's daily cognitive processes. By studying the personality map for a few seconds it was possible to penetrate the subject's most salient characteristics. I did not need Mithra to explain this to me; it was as if I had known it all along.

This particular individual worked as an IT engineer in a Moscow bank and harboured a multiplicity of secrets, some of them shameful, which he kept from other people. But the most insidious, the most secret and humiliating of all his problems, was his inadequate grasp of Windows.

He hated it, and had been hating many a version of this operating system for more than a decade already – as a long-term convict in the camps learns to hate several generations of guards. The depth of his hatred verged on the comic, to the extent that when Windows Vista came on stream he would be upset by hearing the Spanish expression 'hasta la vista' when he went to the cinema. Everything connected to his line of work was to be found in his zone of repulsion, and in the centre of this zone fluttered the flag of Windows.

At first I thought that sex was the nodal point of the zone of attraction. But when I looked more closely, I saw that the chief source of joy in this particular life was, in fact, beer. Stated simply, the man lived to drink good German beer immediately after sex, and for this was ready to endure all the horrors of fate. He may not have known himself what for him was the key to life, but to me it was as clear as day.

I cannot claim that the stranger's life was opened to me in its entirety. It was more as though I stood at the half-open door of a darkened room, tracing by the light of a torch the images depicted on its walls. Whenever I allowed the light to linger on a particular picture it would momentarily expand and then dissolve into hundreds of others; this pattern was repeated again and again. Theoretically I could have accessed every single one of the memories, but there were simply far too many of them. After a while the images faded, as though the battery in the torch was exhausted, and everything grew dark.

'Did you see?' asked Mithra.

I nodded.

'What did you see?'

'A computer specialist.'

'Describe him.'

'Like a set of scales,' I said. 'Beer on one side, Windows on the other.'

Mithra showed no surprise at this strange phrase. He took a few drops of the liquid into his mouth and for a few seconds moved his lips back and forth.

'Yes,' he assented. 'Windows Ex Pee...'

The response did not surprise me. It was one of the ways our computer expert had demonstrated his special loathing of this particular version of the operating system marketed as XP.

'What was I seeing?' I asked. 'What was it?'

'What you have been experiencing was your first degustation, your first tasting. In the weakest possible concentration. Had the solution been at full strength, you would have lost all knowledge of who you yourself really are, and if that had happened everything would take much longer to accomplish. Until you get used to it, it can produce a severe psychic trauma. But you will

27

only have as strong a reaction as that in the initial stages; later you'll get used to it … In any case, my congratulations. You are now one of us. Or at least, almost one of us.'

'Forgive me for asking,' I said, 'but who are you?'

'I am your friend and comrade. I'm a little older than you. I hope we are going to be friends.'

'In the light of our future friendship,' I said, 'might I ask you to do me a friendly service in advance?'

Mithra smiled. 'But of course.'

'Could you untie me from these wall bars? I need to go to the toilet.'

'By all means,' said Mithra. 'I ask your pardon, but I had to be certain that everything in the procedure had gone according to plan.'

When the straps binding me fell to the floor, I attempted to take a step forward but would have fallen over had Mithra not caught hold of me.

'Steady on,' he said. 'You may have problems for a while with your vestibular apparatus. It takes a few weeks for the Tongue to take root fully … are you able to walk? Shall I help you?'

'I can walk,' I said. 'Where is it?'

'Down the corridor on the left. By the kitchen.'

The bathroom appointments were consistent with the style of the rest of the apartment: a museum of Gothic sanitaryware. Sitting on a black throne with a hole in the middle, I tried to compose my thoughts. But in this I was unsuccessful: my thoughts simply refused to be corralled into any sort of coherence. It was as if they had vanished somewhere. I felt no fear, no excitement, no concern for what would happen next.

Emerging from the toilet, I realised that no one was keeping guard over me. There was no one in the passage, nor in the kitchen. The back door through which I had entered the apartment was only a few paces from the kitchen. But the strangest thing of

28

all was that the idea of flight did not occur to me. I knew that I was going to return to the room and continue my conversation with Mithra. *Why have I no desire to escape?* I thought.

The reason was that in some way I knew that to do so would not be right. In my efforts to understand why this should be so, I discovered something very odd indeed. My mind seemed to have developed a centre of gravity of its own accord, a kind of black sphere implanted so ineradicably that nothing could threaten the balance of a soul so equipped. Located in this sphere was the faculty of reviewing and assessing all possible options for acceptance or rejection. The prospect of flight had been weighed in the balance and found wanting.

The sphere wanted me to return, and this being what the sphere wanted, I complied. It was not an instruction; all the sphere had to do was tilt in the direction of the desired decision, and I followed the inclination.

So that was why Mithra allowed me to leave the room, went through my mind. *He knew I would not run away.*

I deduced that the source of Mithra's knowledge was his possession of a similar sphere.

'What is it, exactly?' I asked when I returned to the room.

'What are you referring to?'

'I've got some kind of nucleus inside me. Everything I try to think about now passes through it. It's as though I have lost my soul.'

'Lost your soul?' Mithra asked. 'What do you need it for, anyhow?'

Evidently, confusion was written all over my face. Mithra burst out laughing.

'Is your soul the same thing as you, or is it not you?' he asked.

'In what sense?'

'In the literal sense. Is what you call your soul you, or something else?'

'I suppose it is myself... or maybe not – perhaps it is something separate.'

'Let's look at this logically. If your soul is not you but something other, why should you bother about it? But if it *is* you, how could you possibly lose it, when here you are?'

'Yes,' I said. 'I see you can talk anybody into anything.'

'And we'll teach you to do so, as well. I know why you're in such a stew about it.'

'Why?'

'Culture shock. According to human mythology, anyone who becomes a vampire loses his or her soul. That is nonsense. You might just as well say that a boat loses its soul when it is fitted with an engine. You haven't lost anything. You have only gained. But you have gained so much that everything you knew previously has been so compressed as to become virtually non-existent. That is why you feel you have lost something.'

I sat on the sofa that only a short while ago had supported the corpse of the masked man. Normally I would feel most ill at ease sitting in such a place, but the heavy black globe inside me was quite indifferent.

'It's not actually a sense of loss,' I said. 'I don't even feel that I am I any more.'

'Correct,' replied Mithra. 'You are not you now, you are another. What you sense as a nucleus is your Tongue. Before you it lived in Brahma. Now it lives in you.'

'I remember,' I said. 'Brahma told me that his Tongue would transfer to me.'

'But don't run away with the idea, please, that you have Brahma's Tongue. Brahma was the servant of the Tongue, not the other way round.'

'Whose Tongue is it now?'

'You cannot say it is anyone's. It belongs to itself. The vampire's person is divided between the head and the Tongue. The head is the human side of the vampire, the social person with all his or her accumulated baggage and impedimenta. But the Tongue, the other centre of the personality, is the more important. It is the Tongue that makes you a vampire.'

'But what, exactly, is it?'

'The Tongue is another living creature, one from a higher plane of nature. The Tongue is immortal and moves from one vampire to another, or rather from one person to another, like the rider of a horse. But it can exist only in a symbiotic relationship with a human brain. Take a look at this.'

Mithra pointed to the picture of Napoleon mounted on horseback. The Emperor looked a bit like a penguin, and if you felt like it you could see the picture as a circus number: a penguin riding a horse in the midst of a firework display.

'I don't feel the Tongue with my body,' I said, 'but somehow differently.'

'Quite right. The trick is that the Tongue's consciousness elides with the consciousness of the host in whom it has taken up residence. Just now I compared the vampire with the rider of a horse, but a truer analogy would be a centaur. Some people say that the Tongue subordinates the human mind to itself. But it would be more accurate to see the relationship as the Tongue raising the human being to its own higher level.'

'Higher level?' I queried. 'My feeling is just the opposite, I'm at the bottom of some kind of pit. If this is higher, why does everything seem so dark to me?'

Mithra hesitated.

'Darkness can be under the earth, and also high in the heavens. I know how you feel. It is a difficult time both for you and for the Tongue. You might think of it as a second birth – metaphorically for you, literally so for the Tongue. For the Tongue it is a new incarnation, as all the human memory and experiences that have accumulated in a former vampire host evaporate when it moves to a new body. You are a blank sheet of paper, a newborn vampire who must study, study, study.'

'What do I have to study?'

'Your job is to become, in a short space of time, an individual of high culture and exceptional refinement, significantly superior in intellectual and physical capacity to the great majority of humankind.'

'How am I supposed to achieve this in a short space of time?'

'We have special methods, very quick and effective ones. But the most important things the Tongue will teach you. You will cease to feel it as something alien. You and it will become one.'

'How does that work? Does the Tongue absorb part of my brain?'

'No. It replaces the tonsils and makes contact with the prefrontal cortex. In effect it adds a supplementary element to the brain.'

'And I remain myself?'

'In what sense?'

'Well, will I suddenly become someone else?'

'Look, whatever happens, tomorrow you will be different from what you are today, and the day after tomorrow even more so. If something is destined to happen, let it happen to your advantage. Is that not so?'

I got up from the sofa and took a few steps around the room. Each step was difficult to accomplish and inhibited my ability to think. I felt that Mithra was manipulating the conversation, or perhaps laughing up his sleeve at me. But in my present state I was in no position to argue with him.

'What am I supposed to do now?' I asked. 'Should I go home?'

Mithra shook his head.

'In no circumstances. You live in this apartment now. The deceased's personal belongings have all been removed. Whatever remains here is your inheritance. You have work which you must get down to.'

'What at?'

'You will have private tuition. Make a start on getting used to your new status. And to your new name.'

'What new name?'

Mithra took me by the shoulders and turned me around so that I was facing the mirror on the sideboard. I looked terrible. Mithra pointed with his finger to my forehead, where I observed a brown-coloured inscription, already drying out and cracking, and remembered that before Brahma died he had written something there in blood.

'A-M-A-T,' I began spelling out the letters backwards. 'No, A-M-A-R...'

'Rama,' Mithra corrected me. 'According to ancient custom, vampires take the names of gods. But all gods are different. You will have to think deeply about the meaning of your name. It is a lamp which will illuminate your path.'

He fell silent, evidently anticipating another question. But I had no more to ask.

'That is the way we speak of it – the lamp, I mean,' explained Mithra. 'It's another of our traditions. But to be honest, you won't get lost even without the lamp, because for a vampire there is only the one path. And with or without a lamp there is only one direction for you to travel.'

He broke into laughter.

'Now it is time for me to go,' he said. 'We shall meet again at the time of the Great Fall.'

Must be some kind of a joke, I decided.

'What on earth is that?'

'It's a sort of examination to become a vampire.'

'I'm not much good at exams,' I said. 'I usually fail them.'

'You must never blame yourself when the blame should be

33

put on the system. That essay you wrote was very good, full of freshness and candour. It also testified to your literary gifts. Your only problem was that there were already too many snails on the summit of Fuji.'

'You got that from biting me, I suppose?'

He nodded, thrust his hand into his pocket and withdrew a narrow glass tube, about the dimensions of a cigarette, with a plastic stopper at either end. The phial contained several drops of blood.

'This is your personal material. Others will acquaint themselves with it – our superiors.'

He raised his eyes upwards in an expressive gesture.

'Now let's deal with a few practical problems. You will find money in the escritoire. I expect you will need some. Your meals will be brought up from the restaurant downstairs. A cleaning lady will come in twice a week to tidy up. If there is anything you need, just go out and buy it.'

'Where could I possibly go, looking like this?' I asked, nodding towards the reflection of my ravaged face in the mirror.

'That will soon clear up. I'll arrange for you to be brought everything you need, in the way of clothes and shoes.'

'Shall I tell you my size?'

'No need,' he answered and clicked his tongue. 'I already know it.'

ENLIL MARATOVICH

As a child I was always hungry for miracles. I would have unhesitatingly jumped at the chance to become a flying Tibetan yogi like Milarepa or to study with a famous magician, as Carlos Castaneda and Harry Potter did. Even a less illustrious destiny would have done for me: to become a hero of the cosmos, to discover a new planet, or to write one of those great novels that shake the hearts of men, forcing critics to grind their teeth and fire their turd projectiles from the depths of their stinking pits.

But to become a bloodsucking vampire...

At night I was plagued by bad dreams. I saw my friends weeping over my misfortune, telling me how sorry they were that they could not help me. Towards morning I dreamt of my mother. She was tearful and tender in a way I could hardly ever recall her being in life. Dabbing her eyes with a handkerchief embroidered with the Von Storckwinkel crest, she whispered: 'Romochka, my spirit watched over you as you lay asleep in your cot. But you fixed me fast to the wall with superglue and there was nothing I could do to help you!'

I did not know how to answer her, but my Tongue came to the rescue; it was viewing my dreams along with me (presumably for the Tongue there was little difference between dreams and reality).

'Excuse me, you are not his mama,' the Tongue announced in my voice. 'The only thing his real mother would have said would be to accuse him of sniffing the glue.'

Then I woke up. I was lying in an enormous bed beneath a baldaquin embroidered in brown and gold. A blind of the same heavy material covered the window; all the furnishings of the room were in Gothic style. On the bedside table was a 1950s black ebony telephone.

I got up and dragged myself into the bathroom. Catching sight of myself in the mirror, I shuddered. Half of my face was covered in black and violet bruises round the eyes, which made me look as if I had been brutally concussed. They had not been visible the day before, but now they looked awful. For the rest, however, it was not too bad. I had washed the blood off the previous evening; all that could be seen on my neck was a small dried up hole just below the jawline, like the trace left by a nail that had broken the skin at that point. No blood oozed from it and it no longer hurt. It was hard to believe that such an insignificant wound could have been the cause of such excruciating pain.

My mouth had resumed its normal appearance, except for the thick orange patina that had appeared on my swollen palate. The area round it was slightly numb. The cavities from which my incisor teeth had disappeared itched horribly, and in the black orifices could already be seen the sugar-white tips of new teeth, which seemed to be growing at an implausible rate.

The kernel inside me, though ever-present, no longer troubled me. During the night I had become almost completely accustomed to it. I experienced a feeling of phlegmatic detachment, as if whatever took place concerned not me but another individual whom I was observing from a fourth dimension. The sensation induced a feeling of relaxed freedom and a pleasing absence of obligation, even though I was still in too feeble a state to attempt anything like self-analysis.

I took a shower and set about inspecting my new flat. Its size and air of gloomy luxury made a great impression on me. Besides the bedroom and the room with the filing cabinet there was a home cinema room with a collection of masks on the wall: Venetian, African, Chinese and some others that I could not identify. There was also a kind of drawing room with armchairs, a fireplace and, in the place of honour, an antique radio set in a mahogany case.

Finally, there was a room whose purpose I could not divine at all. It was actually more like a large store cupboard, its floor covered with thick, soft cushions. The walls were draped in black velvet decorated with stars, planets and the sun. All the heavenly bodies bore human faces, sombre and impenetrable. In the middle of the room there was an object resembling a huge silver stirrup: a horizontal bar attached to a curved metal rod hanging by a chain from the ceiling. From the wall protruded a metal valve wheel, which raised or lowered the rod above the cushions. What the purpose of this apparatus was I could not imagine, unless it were to accommodate a giant parrot with a taste for solitude... Also on the walls of the storeroom were some small white boxes resembling alarm sensors.

The room with the filing cabinet, where Brahma had shot himself, was at least more familiar to me as I had spent some considerable time in it. I therefore felt entitled to inspect it in greater detail.

It had clearly served its former owner as a study, even though it was hard to determine what sort of work he had done there. Opening at random some of the drawers in the cabinet I found plastic racks supporting clips of test tubes, sealed with black rubber stoppers. Each of them contained two or three cc's of clear liquid.

I guessed what they were. Mithra had given me my experimental 'Windows Ex Pee' preparation from just such a test tube. Evidently, the filing cabinet contained what was in effect a vampire's library. The test tubes were all labelled with letters and numerals. There was also a label on each drawer front, consisting of letters and numbers. Presumably somewhere there must be a catalogue of the library's contents.

Two pictures of nudes hung on the wall. In the first of them, a young naked girl of about twelve years of age was sitting in an armchair. The effect was rather spoilt by the fact that her head was that of a balding, no longer young Nabokov, the join in the region of the neck masked by a spotted bow tie of an overtly bourgeois design. The picture was entitled 'Lolita'.

The other picture showed a very similar girl, except that her skin was extra white and her breasts completely undeveloped. Nabokov's face in this picture was distinctly old and flabby, and the bow tie masking the join disproportionately large and garish with comets, colourful cockerels and geographical symbols. This picture was entitled 'Ada'.

There were some differences in the physical details of the two childish bodies, but it was disagreeable and even frightening to look at them too closely, because in a masterful effect the un-known artist had contrived to make the eyes of both Nabokovs stare at the viewer with a penetrating, faintly affronted intensity.

I suddenly became aware of a barely perceptible movement of air around my neck.

'*Vladimir Vladimirovich Nabokov als Wille und Vorstellung,*' said a resonant bass voice behind my back.

Startled, I turned round. A metre from me stood a short, portly man wearing a black jacket over a dark polo-neck sweater. His eyes were hidden behind black mirror glasses. In appearance he was between fifty and sixty years old, with bushy eyebrows, a hooked nose and a high, bald forehead.

'Do you know what it was the artist intended to convey with these pictures?' he enquired.

I shook my head.

'Nabokov's novels *Lolita* and *Ada* are variants of the triple bed. Vladimir Vladimirovich, like Lenin in the olden times, is always with us. That is the meaning.'

I looked from Lolita to Ada, and noticed that the latter's milk-white skin was rather flyblown.

'Lolita?' I queried. 'Does that come from LOL?'

'I'm not with you,' said the stranger.

'"Laugh Out Loud",' I explained. 'Internet terminology. Like "IMHO" or "ASAP". So a "LOLita" would be a girl who laughs a lot.'

'Ah, yes,' sighed the stranger. '*Autres temps, autres mœurs*. Sometimes I feel that I'm a museum exhibit... Do you read Nabokov?'

'I have done,' I lied.

'What do you think of him?'

'Bullshit,' I declared confidently. 'Who cares what that old clown had to say?'

I had long realised this was the sort of opinion that conferred immunity from looking foolish. You could never be in error with judgments like that.

'Old clown? Bingo, your starter for ten!' said the stranger and smiled. 'I see how you get there. *Look at the Harlequins*, right? And those lilac lozenges on Pnin's socks... Has to be more than just a coincidence...'

I remembered that the back door was always left open. Evidently that was how this madman had got into the flat.

'All this,' continued the stranger, 'can definitely be traced back to the glass pavilion in Vyra, with its coloured lozenges at which the terminally bored future writer would stare during some French or English lesson. Isn't it incredible that such a tiny seed produced so powerful a shoot?'

He may not be mad, after all, I thought.

'I don't quite understand,' I said politely. 'What made you describe these novels of the writer Nabokov as a triple bed?'

'Because whenever you come across lovers in his books, you always find him lying between them. Every now and again he drops in a subtle aside which draws attention to himself. This can seem rather discourteous to the reader's sensibilities, unless, of course, he happens to be a gerontophile... Do you know what my favourite erotic book is?'

The intensity with which the stranger spoke was quite staggering.

'No,' I said.

'It's *Dunno on the Moon*, the third book in the trilogy about the midget people from the City of the Sun. It hasn't a single word of erotica in it, that's why it is the most erotic text of the twentieth century. Read it, and just think what those little guys must have got up to in their rocket during their long flight to the moon...'

No, definitely not mad. On the contrary, a very intelligent man.

'Yes,' I said. 'I used to think about that too, when I was a little boy. But who are you?'

'My name is Enlil. Enlil Maratovich if you prefer to be formal and call me by my name and patronymic.'

'You startled me.'

He held out to me a paper napkin. 'There is a wet patch on your neck. Wipe it with this.'

I could not feel anything, but did as I was told. Two tiny spots of blood showed up on the paper towel. I realised why he had started talking about the little people from the City of the Sun.

'You as well... yes?'

'Outsiders do not come in here.'

'Who are you?'

'In the world of people I would be regarded as top brass,'

replied Enlil Maratovich. 'In vampire speak I am simply the co-ordinator.'

'Ah, now I get you,' I said, 'although at first I thought you were just mad. Lozenges, Nabokov on the Moon... It's your way of distracting attention, isn't it, to keep one from noticing the bite?'

Enlil Maratovich smiled wryly. 'How are you feeling?'

'Not too good.'

'I must say you don't look very well, not to put too fine a point on it. But that is par for the course. I have brought you some cream. You must rub it into your bruises at night. By morning they will all have gone. And I'll also get some calcium tablets for you. You should take fifteen each day, for the teeth.'

'Thank you.'

'I detect,' said Enlil Maratovich, 'a certain lack of enthusiasm for what has befallen you. Don't pretend otherwise; there is no need. I know. It's quite normal. Not only that, it's admirable. It shows you are a good person.'

'Does a vampire need to be a good person?'

Enlil Maratovich's eyebrows shot upwards into his forehead. 'But of course,' he said. 'How could it be otherwise?'

'But surely...' I began, but trailed off without finishing. What I had meant to say was that I saw little necessity to be a good person in order to suck the blood of another – rather the reverse, but then thought it would be impolite.

'Rama,' said Enlil Maratovich, 'you have no understanding of what sort of creatures we really are. Everything you think you know about vampires is false. Now I want to show you something. Come with me.'

I followed him into the room with the fireplace and the easy chairs. Enlil Maratovich went over to the fireplace and pointed to a black and white photograph of a bat hanging above it. The photo had been taken from very close up. The bat had small, beady black eyes, erect ears like a terrier's, and a wrinkled up pig's snout of a nose. It looked like a cross between a piglet and a dog.

'What is that?' I asked.

'*Desmodus rotundus*. The vampire bat. It is found in the Americas on both sides of the equator. It feeds on the red liquid in the bodies of large animals, and lives in big families in old caves.'

'Why did you want me to see it?'

Enlil Maratovich sank into one of the chairs and motioned me to sit opposite him.

'If you listen to the legends they tell in Central America about these tiny creatures,' he said, 'you would think there is no more fearful being on the planet. They will tell you that this bat is the devil incarnate, that it can assume the form of a man to entice its victims deep into the forest, that flocks of them can tear a lost wanderer to pieces. And a mass of other equally fantastic nonsense. Whenever they find a cave that is home to vampire bats, they smoke them out or destroy them by dynamiting them...'

He looked me as if inviting some kind of response. But I could not think of anything to say.

'For some unknown reason human beings consider themselves to be the unique repositories of goodness and light,' he continued, 'while vampires represent the blackest progeny of hell. But if you look at the facts... Try giving me just one justification for thinking people superior to vampire bats.'

'Perhaps,' I hazarded, 'because people help one another.'

'Only very rarely. Vampire bats, on the other hand, help one another constantly. They share any food they bring home. Something else?'

Nothing else came to mind.

'Man,' said Enlil Maratovich, 'is the cruellest and most senseless killer on the planet. He has never done any good to any of the living creatures by whom he is surrounded. And as for harm... would you like me to enumerate instances?'

I shook my head.

'And this tiny animal, chosen by man to be the emblem of his own secret terrors, never kills another creature. It does not even cause serious harm. It punctures the skin with its front incisors and then takes its two cubic centimetres, neither more nor less. What harm could that possibly do to a horse or a bull? Or a man? Medically speaking, letting a small quantity of red liquid from the veins is considered beneficial. There are documented reports, for instance, of a bite from a vampire bat saving the life of a Catholic monk who was dying of fever. But' – and here he raised an admonitory finger – 'you will find no documented instance of a Catholic monk saving the life of a bat dying of fever.'

It was difficult to argue with this.

'Remember this, Rama. All the ideas human beings have about vampires are false. We are very far from being the monsters of evil that we are depicted...'

I studied the photograph of the bat. Its furry face truly did not appear threatening: rather it was intelligent, nervous and a little frightened.

'Then what are we?' I asked.

'You know what a food chain is? Or, as it is sometimes called, a feeding chain?'

'You mean, like McDonald's?'

'Not exactly. McDonald's is a *fast*-food chain. A food chain is a sequence of plants and animals linked to one another by the relationship of food to consumer. Such as the rabbit to the boa constrictor, or the grasshopper to the frog...' He smiled and winked at me. 'Or the frog to the Frenchman. Or the Frenchman to the worm in the grave. Human beings believe they are at the apex of the pyramid because they can eat whomever they

43

like, as often they like and as much as they like. This belief is the basis of human self-esteem. But in reality there is a higher stage in the food chain, a stage of which the majority of human beings have no conception. And that is us – vampires. We are the penultimate link.'

'What is the ultimate link?' I asked.

'God,' replied Enlil Maratovich.

To this I made no reply, but shrank deeper into my chair.

'Vampires are not merely the highest link in the food chain,' continued Enlil Maratovich, 'they are the most compassionate. The link representing the highest moral standards.'

'And yet it strikes me,' I said, 'that to be a parasite living on other creatures is not good.'

'Do you really think it better to deprive an animal of life in order to eat its meat?'

To this I could find no answer either.

'Which is the more humane,' Enlil Maratovich pursued his questioning, 'to milk cows in order to drink their milk, or to kill them in order to produce cutlets?'

'Milking is more humane.'

'Certainly it is. Even Count Tolstoy, who has had a great influence on vampires, would agree with that. That is how vampires behave, Rama. We don't kill anything. Not, at least, for gastronomic purposes. The vampire way of life is more akin to dairy husbandry.'

I began to detect, as I had done with Mithra, a tendency to special pleading.

'These things are not truly comparable,' I said. 'People breed cattle for specific purposes. Also, cows are raised in an artificial environment. They would not have developed as they did in a pure state of nature. After all, vampires did not raise human beings specially, did they?'

'How do you know?'

'You mean to suggest that vampires did breed human beings for specific purposes?'

'Yes,' said Enlil Maratovich. 'I mean exactly that.'

I thought he must be joking. But his face was perfectly serious.

'How did they do that?'

'You won't be able to understand, until you study Glamour and Discourse.'

'Study what?'

Enlil Maratovich laughed. 'Glamour and Discourse. They are the two principal vampire studies. You see, you don't even know what they are, but you're already trying to discuss complex issues. When you have acquired a sufficient education, I will myself enlighten you as to the history of creation, and how vampires exploit human resources. At the present juncture, we would simply be wasting time.'

'So when am I to begin studying Glamour and Discourse?'

'Tomorrow. Your course will be undertaken by two of our best specialists, Baldur and Jehovah. They will visit you tomorrow morning, so you should retire to bed early. Do you have any questions?'

I thought for a while. 'You said that vampires raised human beings for specific purposes. Why, then, do people regard them as evil monsters?'

'It obscures the true state of affairs. And then, it's more entertaining that way.'

'But, after all, humanoid primates have existed on Earth for many millions of years. And *Homo sapiens* for hundreds of thousands of years. How could vampires have raised them?'

'Vampires have lived on Earth for an immeasurable length of time. Human beings are by no means the first species to have provided them with nourishment. But, as I have already said, it is too soon for us to talk about this. Do you have any more questions?'

'I do,' I said. 'But perhaps you will again say it is too early to discuss them. I don't know.'

'Try me.'

'Can you explain how a vampire is able to read the thoughts of another person. Is it by sucking his blood?'

Enlil Maratovich winced. 'By sucking his blood – yuck! You must remember, Rama, that is not how we refer to it. Not only it is vulgar, it can offend the sensibilities of some vampires. With me it is all right. I sometimes use such language myself, for effect. But others' – he shook his head – 'might find it hard to forgive.'

'How do vampires speak of it?'

'A vampire would say "while engaged in a degustation".'

'All right, then. How is a vampire able to read the thoughts of another person while engaged in a degustation?'

'Is it the practical method that interests you?'

'I already know how degustation is carried out,' I said. 'What I should like is a scientific explanation of how it works.'

Enlil Maratovich sighed. 'Look Rama, any explanation can only be a function of concepts that already exist. If the explanation is a scientific one, it depends on concepts that already exist in science. In the Middle Ages people believed that plague was transmitted through the skin of the body. At that time it was good prophylactic practice to prevent people taking baths, because they open the pores. Today, scientific opinion is that the plague infection is transmitted by fleas, and people are recommended to take frequent baths as a prophylactic measure. When concepts alter, so do the conclusions. Does that make sense?'

I nodded.

'In the same way,' he went on, 'today's science lacks concepts on which to base a scientific answer to your question. Such concepts do not exist. The only explanation I can offer is to suggest an analogy from another discipline, one with which you are familiar. You know quite a bit about computers, don't you?'

'A little,' I said modestly.

'No, you are pretty competent, I've seen that for myself. Do you understand the difference between keeping information on your hard drive and on the net?'

I shrugged my shoulders in amusement.

'Sure I do. In the first case you keep all your data in your room. In the second, the user makes a connection to the Net and by putting a password gains access to the particular cell housing his information.'

'There you are!' exclaimed Enlil Maratovich. 'Exactly so. I would have struggled myself to formulate the difference with such clarity. Now imagine that the human brain is a computer, about which almost nothing is known. Scientists today see the brain as resembling a hard disc on which is written everything its human owner knows. But it may not be so. It could be that the brain is no more than a modem connected to the Internet, and all the information is stored there. Can you imagine it like that?'

'In principle, yes,' I said. 'Absolutely.'

'Well then, once we have reached that stage, everything follows quite simply. The user deploys a password to connect with his information cell. If a third party is able to intercept that person's password, he can make use of that person's information cell just as if it were his own.'

'You mean the password is a kind of information code which is stored in the blood?'

Enlil Maratovich blenched and recoiled. 'Please, do not use that word. Erase it from your vocabulary from the very outset. Get this into your head – you may use the B-word in writing as

47

much as you like, that is normal practice, but orally to a vampire it is indecent language and not acceptable.'

'What is one supposed to say in place of the B-word?'

'Red liquid.'

'Red liquid?' I echoed. I had heard the expression several times already.

'It's an Americanism,' explained Enlil Maratovich. 'Anglo-Saxon vampires talk about "red liquid", and we have copied them. It's a long story. In the nineteenth century they talked about "fluid". Then that word began to have questionable overtones. When electricity became all the rage, the word "electrolyte" came into use, and eventually was shortened to "electro". After a while that too began to seem too crude, and people started to talk about a "preparation". In the nineties it became a "solution". Now we have "red liquid"... It's all a lot of nonsense, of course. But one cannot swim against the tide.'

He glanced at his watch. 'Any more questions?'

'Please tell me,' I asked, 'what is that store cupboard for, the one with the apparatus hanging down from the ceiling?'

'That is not a store cupboard,' replied Enlil Maratovich. 'It's a hamlet.'

'Hamlet? From Shakespeare?'

'No,' said Enlil Maratovich. 'It's from the English word for a small place, not big enough to have a church. It is, so to speak, an unconsecrated refuge. To us a hamlet is everything. It is connected to a slightly shameful and very, very magical side of our life. But you will learn all about it later on.'

He rose from his chair.

'Now it really is time for me to leave you.'

I accompanied him to the door. As he got there he turned, bowed to me ceremoniously, looked me straight in the eye, and said: 'We are happy that you are back with us.'

'Goodbye,' I muttered.

The door closed behind him. I realised that the last phrase had not been directed at me. It had been addressed to the Tongue.

BALDUR

The cream Enlil Maratovich left acted with improbable speed: by morning the bruises below my eyes had disappeared as if I had merely wiped some make-up from my face. If one discounted the two missing teeth I now looked exactly as I had done before, and this did wonders for my mood. The teeth were also growing; my gums were irritated as if I were teething like a baby. Not only that, but my voice had lost its croak and reverted to its former timbre. After taking the prescribed dose of calcium, I decided to telephone my mother.

She enquired where I had disappeared to. This was her favourite pleasantry, signalling that she had been at the brandy bottle and was in a mellow mood. This question would, as night follows day, be followed by the next observation: 'I suppose you know, don't you, that sooner or later you'll disappear for good?' I allowed her to say it, and came up with a cock-and-bull story about having met an old school friend and gone out of town with him to a *dacha*, which did not have a telephone. Then I told her I had found a flat to rent and would soon call in at home to collect my things. My mother delivered a chilly warning that drug addicts do not generally live beyond thirty years of age, and hung up. Thus were my family circumstances disposed of.

Not long after, Mithra rang.

'Are you asleep?' he asked.

'No,' I said, 'I've been up some time.'

'You made a good impression on Enlil Maratovich,' he informed me. 'So you can regard yourself as having passed the first test.'

'He told me some teachers would be coming to see me today.'

'That's right. Study hard and don't think about anything else. You can only become a vampire once you have absorbed the best that the human intellect has produced...'

The moment I put down the telephone receiver, the doorbell rang. Peering through the spyhole I observed two men dressed in black. They were carrying black valises such as obstetricians use.

'Who's there?' I asked.

'Baldur,' said one voice, deep and thick.

'Jehovah,' added the other, lighter and higher.

I opened the door.

The men I saw standing on the doorstep looked like old-timers from some former KGB unit. I envisaged them fit, ruddy and athletic, driving expensive foreign cars, living in handsome apartments in dormitory suburbs, getting together every once in a while in some out-of-town *dacha* to booze and play dominoes. All the same, there was a glint in their eyes that did make me wonder whether this mellow exterior might not be camouflage for something else.

I noticed one odd thing about the pair straight away, although exactly *what* I was to realise only later when Baldur and Jehovah came to see me separately from one another. They were at the same time both very like, and very unlike, one another. Seen together, they seemed to have little in common. Yet when I met them separately, I had difficulty telling which was which, despite the fact that they were of quite different builds and facial appearance.

Baldur taught Glamour, Jehovah – Discourse. The full course

in these disciplines occupied three weeks. The scale and range of knowledge that had to be absorbed was comparable to a full university degree course followed by a Masters and a PhD.

It must be admitted that at this time I was a bright young man and inclined to be glib, but there were still a good many words whose meanings I did not properly know. Continually hearing the terms 'Glamour' and 'Discourse', I dimly imagined the latter to be something wise and hard to understand, the former as chic and expensive. Furthermore, the words seemed to me very like the names of card games played in prison. As it turned out, this was not so far from the truth.

Once we were acquainted, Baldur said:

'Glamour and Discourse are the two main skills a vampire must master. The essence of them is disguise and control, and therefore power. Do you know how to disguise and control? Do you know how to exercise power?'

I shook my head.

'We are going to teach you how.'

Baldur and Jehovah settled themselves on chairs in either corner of the study, and told me to sit on the red sofa. This was the sofa on which Brahma had shot himself, and to begin with I felt most uncomfortable sitting on it.

'Today we are going to instruct you simultaneously,' began Jehovah. 'Do you know why?'

'Because Glamour and Discourse are in fact one and the same thing,' continued Baldur.

'Yes,' agreed Jehovah. 'They are the twin pillars of contemporary culture which come together in an arch high above our heads.'

They fell silent, expecting me to react.

'I don't really understand what you are saying,' I confessed. 'How can they be one and the same if they have different names?'

'They only *appear* different at first glance,' said Jehovah.

'"Glamour" comes from a Scottish word meaning witchcraft. It came originally from the word "grammar", and "grammar" in turn gives us "*grammatica*". In the Middle Ages this word had various meanings relating to aspects of erudition, and one of these was occult practices, which were associated with literacy. In this sense, the meaning is almost the same as "discourse".'

I found this interesting. 'What is the derivation of the word "discourse"?'

'In mediaeval Latin one finds the term "*discursus*", literally "running hither and thither", "flight forward and back". Carefully peeling off the etymological layers, you find it comes from the verb "*discurrere*". "*Currere*" means to flee, and "*dis*" is a negative-signifying prefix. "Discourse", therefore, is *forbidding flight*.'

'Flight from what?'

'If you wish to understand that,' said Baldur, 'we had better begin from the beginning and proceed in order.'

He dived into his holdall and produced a glossy magazine. Opening it at the centrefold he turned it towards me.

'Everything you see in these photographs is Glamour. The columns of type running between the photographs are Discourse. Clear?'

I nodded.

'You can put it another way,' said Baldur. 'Everything a person says is Discourse ...'

'And how he looks while saying it is Glamour,' added Jehovah.

'But this explanation only holds good as a starting point ...' said Baldur.

'Because in reality the meaning of the concepts is much wider,' finished Jehovah.

I began to feel as though I was sitting in front of a stereo system with two brisk, black-garbed revenants taking the place of the loudspeakers. It was like a retro experience from the sixties, a psychedelic sensation much prized by the early pioneers of rock, who used to chop the wall of sound in two in order to overwhelm the listener with the maximum stereophonic effect.

'Glamour is sex expressed as money,' said the left-hand speaker. 'Or, if you prefer, money expressed as sex.'

'While Discourse,' came the response from the right-hand speaker, 'is the sublimation of Glamour. Do you know what sublimation is?'

I shook my head.

'Then,' continued the left-hand speaker, 'let us put it like this: Discourse is sex, which is lacking, expressed as money, which is absent.'

'In extreme cases one may find sex having exceeded the brackets of Glamour,' said the right-hand speaker. 'Money, expressed as sex, may be seen as money expressed as sex expressed as money, which comes to money being expressed as money. The same applies to Discourse, only with a necessary correction for the hypothetical nature of the factor outside the brackets.'

'Discourse is the flickering play of the inconsequential concepts produced from Glamour simmering in the furnace of black envy,' said the left-hand speaker.

'While Glamour,' came from the one on the right, 'is the scintillating glint of insubstantial images produced from Discourse evaporating in the fire of sexual excitement.'

'Glamour and Discourse together stand in the relationship of yin and yang,' declared Left.

'Discourse encases Glamour and acts as an exquisite frame for it,' elucidated Right.

'Glamour infuses the breath of life into Discourse and prevents it from drying up,' added Left.

'Think of it like this,' advised Right: 'Glamour is the Discourse of the body...'

'...while Discourse is the Glamour of the spirit,' finished Left.

'The point where these two concepts meet is the genesis of all contemporary culture,' said Right.

'Which thus reveals itself as the dialectical unity of Glamorous Discourse and Discursive Glamour,' concluded Left.

Baldur and Jehovah pronounced both 'Glamour' and 'Discourse' with the accent on the wrong syllable, which lent them a sort of pseudo-professional air – much as veteran Gazprom sharks, for instance, like to talk about 'pet*rol*' rather than '*pet*rol'. It was intended to inspire confidence in their knowledge and admiration for their experience; however, the confidence and admiration I felt did not prevent me from rapidly falling asleep.

They did not wake me up since, as I was subsequently informed, intellectual matter is assimilated four times more quickly as a result of irrelevant mental processes being blocked when one is asleep. Several hours passed before I awakened. Baldur and Jehovah seemed tired, but content. I had absolutely no recollection of what had occurred during this time.

Subsequent lessons, however, were very different.

Talking was kept to a minimum. Very occasionally my teachers would dictate to me something that needed to be written down. At the start of each session they laid out on the table identical plastic racks reminiscent of DNA testing equipment in a laboratory. The racks housed short test tubes with clear liquid and elongated black stoppers, and the tubes were labelled with stickers giving either a description or a number.

These were the *preparations*.

The procedure was simple. I applied two or three drops of the clear liquid to my mouth and added to them another clear, bitter-tasting liquid known as the 'fixative'. The result was that my memory was invaded by an explosion of hitherto unknown information – something like a cognitive aurora borealis or a firework display of self-unpacking data. The process was similar to my first tasting, the difference being that the knowledge was

55

now retained in my memory even after the initial effects induced by the preparation had worn off. This was the contribution of the fixative, a complex distillation that acted on the chemistry of the brain. It was damaging to health to be exposed to its influence for long; this was why instruction had to be restricted to sessions kept as brief as possible.

The preparations that were the subject of my tastings were an elaborate cocktail of red liquid from a great number of people, the eidolons of whose personalities overlaid one another in my perception like a crystalline chorus singing various kinds of information. Along with this I was burdened with often distasteful and boring details of their personal life. The secrets thus revealed provoked no interest in me – rather the reverse.

The way I absorbed the information contained in the preparations was different from the way in which a student absorbs a chapter of a textbook or a lecture he attends. I was drinking from a source more like an endless television programme in which instructional material coalesced with soap-opera realism, family photograph albums and amateur pornography usually of a repulsive nature. On the other hand, the manner in which any student assimilates useful knowledge is inevitably accompanied by approximately the same proportion of irrelevant trimmings, so my training could be regarded as essentially similar.

In itself, this swallowing of large quantities of information added nothing to my store of wisdom. But I found that when I started to think about any given issue, new facts and perceptions would rise up unexpectedly from my memory, and as my thought processes developed, they led me to places I could not have imagined. The sense of what happened is best conveyed by a Soviet song I used to hear at the very dawn of my days (my mother had a standing joke that its last line was a reference to Brezhnev's memoirs about World War Two):

Today I shall rise before dawn
And walk through the wide, wide field –
Something has started in my memory,
I remember everything that happened not to me...

At first this process was extremely unpleasant. Ideas familiar from childhood blossomed with new angles I had not known before, or at least had not thought of. It all happened quite suddenly, resembling one of those cognitive chain reactions when random impressions bring to the surface a long-forgotten dream that instantly infuses everything around with a special meaning. I already knew that similar hallucinations can be symptoms of schizophrenia. But as the days went by the world grew more and more interesting; I soon lost my fear and eventually began to take pleasure in what was happening to my mind.

For example, I was in a taxi one day going along Warsaw Prospect. I happened to look up and see an image of a bear on the wall of a building – the emblem of the 'United Russia' party. It suddenly came to me that the Russian word for bear – 'medved' – is not in fact the true name for the animal but a substitute. The primeval Slavs invented it because they were afraid that uttering the animal's real name – 'ber' – might inadvertently bring one into the house. And the literal meaning of the word 'medved' is itself revealing: 'the one who is after the honey'. This thought sequence took place so quickly that at the moment when the true meaning shone blindingly through the emblem of the victorious bureaucracy, the taxi was still approaching the wall. I began to laugh, and the driver, thinking I was expressing pleasure in the song that was playing at the time, stretched out his hand to the radio in order to increase the volume...

The main problem I found at the beginning was that I lost my former verbal orientation. Until memory succeeded in restoring order to my ability to focus, I could completely lose my way. A synoptic became a sinful optician; a xenophobe someone allergic to the ubiquitous TV celebrity Xenia Sobchak; a patriarch a patriotic oligarch. A prima donna turned into an old lady smelling of Prima cigarettes, and an *enfant terrible* – Tsar Ivan IV at a tender age. But the most radical of my distorted insights was this: I interpreted 'Petro-' not as relating to the city and palaces founded by Peter the Great but as indicating a link to the oil industry. In accordance with this, 'Petrodvorets' signified not the great Peterhof Palace on the shores of the Gulf of Finland but the sumptuous offices of an oil company. Mayakovsky's well-known First World War line 'In that never-to-be-forgotten hour / Our Petersburg became Petrograd' was transmogrified into a prophecy – a bitter one, but true.

This confusion extended to foreign words, for example the expression 'Gay Pride'. I remembered that in English 'pride' was the name given to a social grouping of lions, and before the lights came on in my memory to illuminate the word's primary meaning, the quality of 'being proud', I imagined a pride of homosexuals (presumably refugees from homophobic regions of Europe) roaming the African savannah: two lop-eared senior males lying in the parched grass near a desiccated tree surveying the expanse of prairie and now and again languidly flexing their muscles; a slightly younger male pumping his triceps in the shade of the baobab tree while around him frisk and frolic the young cubs, irritating their grown-up companion with their fussing and squeaking until with a roar he sends them scattering for safety...

I developed quickly and without particular effort, but at the same time lost my sense of inner space. Jehovah warned me that my studies would make me older, since the true age of a person is determined by the sum of his knowledge. The acquisition of vicarious experiences must be set against the loss of my own inexperience, which is to say of my youth. But in those days the changes I was undergoing caused me no regret, because my reserves of this capital seemed to me inexhaustible. Parting with some of it was like jettisoning unwanted ballast while an invisible aerial balloon was raising me high into the sky.

Baldur and Jehovah assured me that my study of Discourse would reveal to me the hidden essence of contemporary social thought. An important element in the programme was concerned with human morality, conceptions of good and evil. However, our approach to the subject was not extrinsic, an investigation into what people were saying on the record, but internal, via an intimate acquaintance with what they actually thought and felt. Needless to say, this investigation severely shook my faith in humanity.

Looking at a wide variety of human minds, I noticed one interesting general characteristic. Every individual possessed within him his own personal court of moral judgment, to which the mind would unfailingly appeal whenever a dubious decision needed to be taken. This personal moral court malfunctioned on a regular basis – and I began to understand why. This is what I wrote in my notebook on this subject:

People have long believed that in this world evil triumphs while good receives its reward only after death. For a while this equation produced a kind of balance, providing a link between earth and heaven. In our time, however, the balance has become imbalance because the idea of heavenly reward has come to be seen as an obvious absurdity. At the same time no one has succeeded in challenging the hegemony of evil on earth. As a result, any normal human being seeking the positive here on earth will naturally incline towards evil: a step as logical as becoming a member of the ruling political party. The evil to which the person has thus affiliated himself is contained exclusively within his head. But when everyone has enlisted in

the ranks of evil, which is located nowhere else but in the head,
what need has evil of any other victory?

The concept of good and evil inevitably ran up against religion. But what my lessons had to teach me about religion (a 'localised cult', Jehovah called it) genuinely surprised me. As revealed by the preparations I imbibed from the rack of test tubes labelled '*Gnosis+*', at the dawning of Christianity the God of the Old Testament was regarded by the new teaching as a devil. Subsequently, in the early centuries of our own era, the interests of strengthening Roman hegemony and political correctness led God and Devil to be united in a single object of veneration to whom the orthodox patriot of the declining Empire was obliged to bow the knee. Primary texts were chosen, transcribed and painstakingly redacted to conform to the new genius, while all those not so selected were, as is customary, burnt.

I wrote in my notebook:

Each nation, as each individual, must work out its own religion and not simply continue wearing out the rags of others, swarming as they are with the lice from which all diseases come... The peoples who are on the rise in our own time – Indians, Chinese and so on – import no more than technology and capital; their religions are purely local products and they keep them that way. A member of these societies may be quite sure that the gods he is praying to are his own loony deities, not the latest totemic importations, scribe's misreadings or mistakes in translation. But for us... to base our world view on a mishmash of texts written by unknown hands in unknown places at an unknown time is equivalent to installing a pirate Turkish version of Windows 95 in a crucially important computer with no upgrade available, completely unprotected against spyware, Trojans and viruses, and with the added bonus – courtesy of an unknown geek – of

a fucked-up dynamic *.dll library which causes the computer to
crash every two minutes. What people need is a free, uncluttered,
open-source architecture of the soul. But Judeo-Christians are
extremely crafty and have succeeded in branding anyone who
advocates any such architecture as the Antichrist. Truly, to
continue crapping so far into the future from a fraudulent arse
stuck in the distant past must be counted the most impressive
of the miracles wrought by Judeo-Christianity.

Naturally, some of these maxims may strike the reader as somewhat overconfident for a tyro vampire. In my defence I can only
say that these sorts of concepts and ideas never meant much, if
anything, to me.

I mastered Discourse quickly and easily, although it set me on
a generally misanthropic course. Glamour, however, presented
me with difficulties from the very start. I understood almost
everything up until the moment when Baldur said:

'Some experts state that there is no such thing as ideology
in contemporary society, because none has been formulated in
an unequivocal manner. But this is a delusion. The ideology of
anonymous dictatorship is Glamour.'

I was instantly gripped by a sense of terminal bewilderment.

'But what is the Glamour of anonymous dictatorship then?'

'Rama,' said Baldur, visibly irritated, 'this is where we began
in the first lesson. The Glamour of anonymous dictatorship is
its Discourse.'

The words spoken by Baldur and Jehovah were always in
themselves models of clarity, but it was hard for me to understand how images of bimbos with diamond embellishments to
their silicone-enhanced tits could represent the ideology of a
regime.

Happily, there was an effective method of seeking clarification for knotty questions of this sort. If I could not understand

something Baldur said, I would ask Jehovah at the next lesson, and get an alternative explanation. And if something Jehovah said was not completely clear, I asked Baldur. The result was that I forged upwards like a rock climber jamming his feet alternately against the walls of a chimney.

'Why does Baldur say that Glamour is an ideology?' I asked Jehovah.

'Ideology is a description of the invisible aim which justifies visible means,' he replied. 'Glamour may be regarded as an ideology because it provides an answer to the question: "In the name of what was all this done?"'

'What do you mean by "all this"?'

'Look at your history textbook and read through the chapter headings.'

By this stage I had absorbed enough concepts and terminology to be able to carry on a conversation at an acceptable level.

'How then would you define the core ideology of Glamour?'

'Very simple,' said Jehovah. 'Disguise. Masking.'

'Disguise? Changing clothes?'

'Yes, but "changing" has to be interpreted in a wide sense. Change embraces such things as moving from one part of town to another, say from Kashirka to Rublevka, or from Rublevka to London, transplanting skin from the buttocks to the face, changing sex, all transformations of that sort. In the same way, all contemporary Discourse leads merely to a repackaging of those few topics that are permitted to be discussed in public. This is why we say that Discourse is a variant of Glamour and Glamour is a variant of Discourse. Do you understand now?'

'Not very romantic,' I said.

'Well, what did you expect?'

'Glamour seems to me to promise something miraculous. Didn't you yourself tell me that the original meaning of the word was "sorcery"? Isn't that why people place such value on it?'

'Yes, Glamour does promise miracles,' said Jehovah. 'But the promise obscures the complete absence of the miraculous in life. Changing clothes, disguise and concealment through masking are not merely technology, but the unique content of Glamour. And of Discourse as well.'

'Are there, then, no circumstances in which Glamour is able to produce a miracle?'

Jehovah thought for a while.

'As a matter of fact, there are some circumstances.'

'What are they?'

'For example, in literature.'

This seemed very strange to me. Literature was as far removed from the sphere of Glamour as it was possible to imagine. Also, as far as I knew, it was a field in which no miracles had occurred for a very long time.

'After the writer today finishes a new novel,' explained Jehovah, 'he devotes a few days to trawling through glossy magazines in order to incorporate brand names of expensive motor cars, neckties and restaurants. The result is that his text assumes a reflected simulacrum of high-budget expenditure.'

This exchange with Jehovah I transmitted to Baldur:

'Jehovah says that this is an instance of a Glamour miracle. But what is so miraculous about it? It seems to me a classic piece of masking.'

'You didn't understand what he said,' replied Baldur. 'The miraculous transformation takes place not in the text but in the author. We have transformed engineers of the human soul into unpaid advertising agents.'

I found I could apply this bipolar questioning technique to almost any query. But sometimes it produced more, rather than less, confusion. Once I asked Jehovah to elucidate the meaning of 'punditry', a word which I was coming across almost every day on the Internet, reading about some 'media pundit' or other.

'Punditry is neurolinguistic programming in the service of the anonymous dictatorship,' intoned Jehovah.

'Come, come,' grumbled Baldur, when I appealed to him for comment. 'It's a good, resonant phrase. But in real life it's very hard to say who serves whom – punditry serving the dictatorship or the other way around.'

'How is that?'

'The dictatorship, even though it is faceless, pays hard cash. But the only tangible result of neurolinguistic programming is the salary earned by professors of neurolinguistic programming.'

The following day I was to regret bitterly having asked my question about 'punditry': Jehovah brought in to the lesson an entire rack of test tubes labelled 'Media Pundits Nos. 1–18', every one of which I was forced to sample. I wrote in my notebook in the interval between tastings:

Any intellectual today, peddling his 'expertise' in the marketplace, is doing two things: sending out signals, and prostituting meaning. These activities are in fact dual aspects of a single act of will, which is the sole raison d'être of any work by any philosopher of today, or any culturologist, or expert of any description. The signals announce the expert's readiness to prostitute meaning, while the prostitution of meaning is the means whereby the signals are sent out. The new generation intellectual often has no idea who the future commissioner of his work is going to be. He is like a plant growing on the pavement whose roots feed on unseen sources of moisture and nourishment and whose pollen is dispersed beyond the limits of the monitor. The difference is that the plant does what it does without thinking, but the new generation intellectual believes that he is being awarded life-giving nourishment in return for his pollen, and engages in complicated schizophrenic double-entry

accounting. Such calculations are the true roots of Discourse –
damp, grey, moss-covered, stagnating in stench and darkness.

Before many days passed I knew the word 'culturologist'. True, I did not really know what it meant: I thought it must refer to a urologist whose knowledge of the human urinary–sexual system was so detailed that he had earned cult status and the right to pronounce on spiritual matters. This in itself did not strike me as particularly strange; after all Academician Sakharov, inventor of the hydrogen bomb, had become a universally accepted authority on humanitarian issues, and much the same happened with many other scientists or doctors.

In short, my brains were well and truly scrambled. But this hardly seemed a tragedy to me, since previously they had contained very little of anything.

It was not long before my involvement with Glamour turned sour (much the same had happened to me with Organic Chemistry in school). Sometimes I exhibited nothing short of terminal stupidity. For instance, it took me a very long time to understand what a 'vamposexual' could be, and this was a core concept of the course. Baldur advised me to understand the term by analogy with 'metrosexual', and I experienced a slight but distinct shock when I discovered that this was not a person who enjoyed having sex while travelling on the Metro.

Baldur explained the meaning of the word 'metrosexual' as follows:

'A metrosexual is a person who dresses like a queer, but in fact is not one. That is to say, he may in fact be queer, but it's not necessary.'

This was rather confusing, and I appealed to Jehovah for elucidation.

'Metrosexuality,' said Jehovah, 'is just another packaging of "conspicuous consumption".'

'What?' I asked, and at once remembered information gleaned from a recently swallowed preparation. 'Oh, I know. Consumption for show. A term introduced by Thorstein Veblen at the beginning of the last century.'

I waited until the next Glamour lesson to repeat this to Baldur.

'Why does Jehovah feel he has to mess with your head like that?' muttered Baldur crossly. '"Conspicuous consumption", indeed! Why use an English expression? Everything should be called by its proper Russian name. I've already told you what a metrosexual is.'

'Well then, what is a vamposexual?'

'A vamposexual is what you must become,' replied Baldur. 'There is no precise definition; everything depends on your own intuition. It is what you have to become in order to catch the pulse of the times.'

'And what is that?'

'Exactly what the pulse of the times is,' said Baldur, 'no one knows, because time possesses no such attribute. All there is, really, is a collection of op-ed columns on the pulse of the times. But when enough of the op-ed pieces agree the pulse of the times to be such and such, then everyone starts to repeat it because they want to stay in step with time. But that is absolutely impossible because time has no legs.'

'Surely normal people don't believe what editorials and op-ed pieces say?'

'When did you last meet a normal person? In our country there are not more than a hundred of them left, and they are all under close FSB surveillance. Things are not that simple. On the one hand there is in reality no pulse of the times, nor anything to be in step with. But on the other hand, everyone tries to get a handle on the pulse of the times and to be in step with it, because the corporate model of the world is undergoing continual modification. That's why people have to grow cool

66

beards and wear silk ties to prove their loyalty. Vampires must conform in order to blend in with their surroundings.'

'I still don't understand what a vamposexual is,' I confessed.

Baldur picked up from the table a test tube which had been left there after the Discourse lesson. Its stopper was labelled 'German Classical Philosophy Dept. Phil. Mos. State Univ.' Baldur shook on to his tongue the remaining drops of clear liquid, chewed his lip, frowned and asked:

'Do you remember the Eleventh Thesis on Feuerbach?'

'Who wrote it?'

'Who wrote it? Why, Karl Marx of course.'

I strained my memory. 'Oh yes. Just a moment. "Hitherto philosophers have only interpreted the world in various ways; the point is to change it."'

'Exactly. Your task, Rama, is not to interpret a vamposexual. Your task is to become one.'

Baldur was, of course, right. Theory in this context counted for little. But the Glamour course was not confined to theory. I was handed 'expenses': a weighty block of thousand-rouble banknotes shrink-wrapped in plastic and a Visa card with what struck me as an insanely high credit limit of a hundred thousand dollars. No accounting was required.

'Time for practical work,' said Baldur. 'When you've got through that lot, let me know.'

This was the moment when I came to realise that being a vampire was a serious and responsible matter.

There were two places a vampire was expected to buy clothes and other necessities: LovemarX, on Uprising Square and Archetypique Boutique, on Pozharsky Passage.

I had, as it happens, long been struck by a particular sign of the times expressed in the vulgar grafting of fashionable foreign names on to shops, restaurants and even novels written in Russian. They proclaimed: 'We're special, not like you, we're trendy, off-shore, refurbished *à l'européenne.*' Usually the only effect it had on me was to make me want to throw up, but I had passed LovemarX and Archetypique Boutique so often that instead of merely irritating me their names began to demand analysis.

From the theoretical part of the Glamour course I knew that the word 'lovemarks' refers to brand names which people lust after with all their hearts, seeing in them not merely the outward appearance of the object in question but the framework of their own personality. Presumably the final 'X' was a nod to the new Internet orthography – or perhaps to the marble bust of Marx in the sales hall.

Archetypique Boutique proved to be an entire shopping mall of boutiques in which it was easy to lose oneself. The choice of goods on offer was wider than in LovemarX but it was not a place I could warm to. Rumour had it that it had formerly been the headquarters of the Gulag Inspectorate – either the geodetic survey or the permanent administration staff. Discovering this, I could see why Baldur and Jehovah referred to the place as the 'Glamour Archipelago' or simply the 'Archipelago'.

The pictures on the walls of the Archetypique Boutique were mostly photographs of expensive sports cars with silly, jokey titles such as 'Wheelbarrow No. 51', 'Wheelbarrow No. 89', and so on. One such number would appear on your sales receipt and if you were able to identify correctly the make of the corresponding car you could claim a ten per cent discount.

I understood, naturally, that this was a standard marketing device: the customer is supposed to circumambulate through the Archipelago in search of the right *wheelbarrow* and catch en route sight of new items which could eventually end up in the shopping cart. Even so, the mutual magnetism of the words struck me as distasteful.

There was one other emporium where one was supposed to buy knickknacks such as expensive watches, pipes and the like.

This shop was called 'Height Reason – Boutique for the Thinking Elite'. In the marketing brochure the Russian name had been collapsed into a single, rather strange word: 'HIGHTREASON'.

Not being a smoker I had no interest at all in pipes. As for expensive watches, I had always been frightened off by the Patek Philippe advertisement in the same brochure: *'You never actually own a Patek Philippe. You merely look after it for the next generation.'*

I remembered, from seeing Tarantino's *Pulp Fiction*, a special technique whereby a costly chronometer could be passed to the next generation: in the paternal rectum while doing – and, I suppose, measuring – time in a Japanese prison camp. The situation of the businessman Khodorkovsky has made the subject very topical. Incidentally since then the innumerable photographs of Khodorkovsky behind bars has begun to look like a Patek Philippe ad campaign, the naked wrist of the imprisoned entrepreneur making the message unmistakeable. For my taste, the Patek Philippe chronometer was too big. On its own, perhaps, it might have been able to slip through, but never that bulky great metal bracelet...

The upshot was that I failed to enter the world of the Thinking Elite. Like all losers I naturally consoled myself by reflecting that I had never really wanted to.

JEHOVAH

If the answer Baldur gave to any query was so specific as to make it almost impossible not to grasp, Jehovah's explanatory powers had another distinction. He could outline an entire intellectual field in a few words, or follow a thread of key concepts through the most labyrinthine web of ideas. Often he would resort to surprising analogies.

'If you want to understand what human culture is,' he said one day, 'consider the inhabitants of the Polynesian Islands. There are tribes there who deify the technology of the white man. A particular object of worship is the aeroplane, which flies through the sky bringing all manner of beautiful and delicious objects. The Polynesian belief system is known as "cargo cult". The aboriginal people there have constructed ritual aerodromes to await, so to speak, Coca-Cola from heaven...'

I had the usual reaction in my head, along the lines of 'I remember everything that happened not to me...'

'No,' I said, 'that's nonsense. The reason the aborigines told that story to American anthropologists was simply in order to get rid of them quicker. Anyhow, it would have been impossible to persuade the anthropologists that the aborigines were actually after something entirely different. The truth is that the spiritual core of cargo cult lies elsewhere, and deeper. In Melanesia, where it all began, the inhabitants were so impressed by the feats of Japanese kamikaze pilots that they built ritual aerodromes for them to invite their souls to be reborn in the archipelago, should it be found there was not enough room for them in the Yasakuni Shrine.'

'I had not heard that,' said Jehovah. 'Interesting. But it does not alter anything. The indigenous people do more than build fake airstrips. They also make dummy aeroplanes out of mud, sand and straw – no doubt to provide the souls of the kamikaze with somewhere to live. These planes are inspirational artefacts. They sometimes have up to ten engines, fashioned out of old buckets and barrels. Seen as *objets d'art* they could be considered *chefs-d'œuvre*. But aeroplanes made out of mud do not fly. The same applies to human Discourse. No vampire should ever treat it seriously.'

I reported this conversation to Baldur.

'Does this mean,' I asked, 'that I too am learning how to make bogus aeroplanes out of sand and straw?'

Baldur looked me up and down with an expression of exasperation.

'Not just that,' he replied. 'That is indeed what you're being taught, but there's another side to it as well. You're also learning how to tart yourself up like a poof so that everyone will think you have access to a pipeline that spews out dosh – and hate you for it even more strongly. Have you forgotten who you are, Rama? You're a vampire!'

I spent a few days mulling over what Jehovah had said, looking up on the Internet examples of my countrymen's discourse, among them my old man's dicta on 'plebs' and 'responsible elites'. I could now understand practically all of them, including references to other texts, innuendoes and cultural allusions, some of them suave, witty and well written. Jehovah was right, all the same: these aircraft were not designed to fly. I found a good

71

many wise words in them, but they rang empty and hollow, like a cannibal's beads made from stray European coins.

I wrote in my notebook:

> *The cargo-discourse of Moscow differs from the Polynesian model in that, instead of playing with fragments of alien aviation technology it plays with fragments of borrowed jargon. The linguistic camouflage with which the 'pundit' lards his article fulfils the same function as the bright orange life-jacket adopted by an African headhunter: it's more than a mask – it's warpaint. The aesthetic face of cargo-discourse is cargo-glamour, it is what makes the struggling office boy skimp on his food so that he can buy himself an expensive power suit.*

When I proudly showed this observation to Jehovah, he twiddled his finger meaningfully round his temple.

'Rama,' he said, 'you're missing the point. You seem to think Moscow cargo-discourse is subordinate to New York or Paris cargo-discourse and that is the whole problem. It is not the case at all. *All* human cultures are cargo cultures. In no way can the artificial aircraft created by one tribe be superior to the artificial aircraft created by another.'

'Why not?'

'Because flightless aircraft are not susceptible to comparative analysis. They do not fly, and they lack any technological specifics that can be measured against any others. They only have one function, and that is a magical one which does not depend on how many buckets they put under the wings for imitation engines, nor on what colour they are.'

'But,' I objected, 'if we are surrounded by ersatz aeroplanes, they must have some basis in things people have copied, must they not? After all, for the cargo cult to have developed in the

72

first place, there was presumably at least one real plane flying through the sky.'

'The plane in question was not flying through the sky,' Jehovah answered. 'It was flying through the human mind. It was the Mighty Bat.'

'You mean vampires?'

'Yes,' said Jehovah. 'But there is no point in discussing it now. You lack the requisite knowledge base.'

'Just one question,' I said. 'You say that all human culture amounts to no more than a cargo cult. What do people build instead of mud aeroplanes then?'

'Cities.'

'Cities?'

'Yes,' answered Jehovah, 'and everything else as well.'

I tried raising the subject with Baldur, but he also declined to discuss it.

'Too soon,' he said. 'Don't run before you can walk. You've got to absorb what you need to know in the correct order. Your studies today must be the foundation for what you will learn tomorrow. When you build a house you don't start with the attic.'

There seemed no room left for disagreement.

There was one more societal practice I was required to master. It was the art of 'vampospirituality', sometimes called by Jehovah 'metrospirituality', from which I concluded they were more or less the same thing. Jehovah defined it as: 'conspicuous consumption in the domain of spirit'. What vampospirituality meant in practice was proof of access to, and familiarity with, the least accessible forms of ancient spiritual practices: it might include photo opportunities with the Dalai Lama, documentary evidence of acquaintance with Sufi sheikhs and Latin-American shamans, nocturnal visits by helicopter to Mount Athos, and so on.

'And this goes on here as well?' I asked bitterly. I could not see exactly what he was driving at.

'Yes, it is just the same here, and everywhere else as well,' said Jehovah. 'And for all time. Observe what happens when people converse with one another. Why does a man open his mouth?'

I shrugged.

'The key message a human being tries to convey to others is that he enjoys a much more prestigious level of consumption than might at first appear. At the same time he tries to instil in those around him the idea that their own level of consumption confers significantly less prestige than they had naïvely imagined. All social manoeuvres are subordinated to this aim. More importantly, it is the only issue that inspires unvarying emotions.'

'Well, I seem to have come across rather different kinds of people in my life,' I said in an attempt at light-hearted irony.

Jehovah looked at me mildly.

'Rama,' he said, 'you have just presented me with a prime example of what I was trying to get across. You wish to let me understand that you are accustomed to a mode of consumption that is superior to mine. Mine, you suggest, sucks. The only difference is that we are talking about consumption in the sphere of human relationships. This is the very movement of a human soul I have in mind. However hard you look, you will never find anything else there... The only thing that changes is the particular mode of consumption. It may relate to objects, impressions, cultural manifestations, books, conceptions, states of mind and so on.'

'That is revolting,' I said, quite sincerely.

Jehovah raised a finger.

'But on no account should you hold people in contempt because of it,' he said. 'Always keep in mind that for a vampire to do so is as shameful as it is for a human being to laugh at a cow because she has a greasy, fat, ugly udder dangling between her legs. It was we, Rama, who bred people and reared them. For that reason we must accept them as they are. No one else will ever feel compassion for them.'

'All right,' I said. 'So what am I supposed to do when someone fishes out his picture taken with the Dalai Lama?'

'You produce one of your own, a photograph of yourself standing beside Christ, the Buddha and Muhammad... No, better not have Muhammad actually there with you. You can just have arrows pointing to the edge of the picture: "Muhammad was here"...'

The word 'spirituality' often came up in our discussions, and eventually I became interested to know exactly what was meant by the term. Researching the subject by means of random degustations, I summarised the results of my observations in the following note:

Russian 'spirituality' means that people here devote their best efforts not to material production of any kind, but to putting on airs. By the same token, a person who lacks 'spirituality' reveals it by his inability to do so in the appropriate manner. Expertise in this field can only be gained through experience and money, hence there is no creature less spiritual than a junior manager.

The range covered in the Glamour course was extensive, but almost none of it could be memorised on the conscious level. It included a great many tastings – I had to sample an unbelievable number of absurd preparations, each one of which swelled the load of life experiences now weighing on my shoulders. To this day I do not know how I could have swallowed such as the following:

'Little bastard $%'
'Blow *ayu-yu.*'

'Cavalli No.3.'

'*Офтен!*'

'Bloody *masha ts.*'

'*Chichiki.*'

But my forays into the turbid smog of other souls were not in vain. I gained ever more acute understanding of what was going on in the world around me. Now, when I read coverage of a private concert by an A-list popstar in a Rublevka estate or some deferential article about the second Moscow Region Yachting Festival in Nice, I no longer felt crushed by another proof of my own inadequacy, but recognised that I had simply stumbled into the firing line of the new breed of Party machine-gunners who were replacing the Political Commissariat and National Folk Dance Ensembles.

The same was true of Discourse. I began to see that a spat between two intellectuals, one a lapdog of the regime, the other a fearless Valiant-for-truth fearlessly attacking it from all possible standpoints, bore no resemblance to a genuine conflict of ideologies, but was a duet for mouth organ and concertina. It was nothing but noise, whose only purpose was to act as background for the real ideology being trumpeted out loud.

'If Glamour is the ideology of the regime,' said Jehovah, 'the most important of all arts for us are PR, GR, BR and FR. In a word – advertising.'

GR, apparently, stood for Government Relations. I did not know what BR and FR were, and was too idle to ask.

We had two lessons devoted to advertising, not to its dubious theory as developed by human beings (Jehovah called it simply 'charlatanry'), but to its core techniques as applied to commerce, politics and information. Jehovah's definition was as follows: 'Without ever resorting to outright untruth, to construct from fragments of the truth a picture whose connection to reality is limited to whatever is good for sales.' It was an apparently simple formulation, but in fact it embraced a vitally important elaboration: if the link to reality proved not to increase sales (and very often it could not) then the solution was to connect it to something else. This was precisely the eye of the needle through which the multitude of caravans passed.

Among the examples adduced to illustrate this concept was this linguistic-geometric construct:

> *No one speaks of it.*
> *No one forgets it.*
> *This is the root of all.*
> *The source from which we all came, you and I,*
> *And all those whom for now you regard as 'other',*
> *Is not far off in the Himalayas, but inside yourself.*
> *It's real and tangible.*
> *Certain and serious.*
> *This is for real.*

The explanation was as follows:

> *Rule 3. Non-traditional positioning of anal–phallic penetration with addition of contexts orthogonally related to the subj.*

'Why the shape of the cross?' I asked Jehovah.

Jehovah shook a drop of clear liquid from the test tube on to his finger, licked it, and for a few moments stared unseeing into the far distance.

'You didn't read it all the way through,' he said. '"Why the cross?" is the campaign slogan.'

A template example of spin being deployed for political purposes was the campaign by the Loyalist Youth Movement 'True Batch of Hope' (*Surkoff_Fedayeen/built305*). This campaign was aimed at generating positive interest in the English-speaking mass media, basing itself on a quotation from late Nabokov translating early Okudzhava:

Nadezhda I shall then be back
When the true batch outboys the riot...

I did not need to ask: 'Why true batch?' The homonyms with the Russian phrase for a trumpeter sounding the retreat were obvious. The brief digression into advertising was thereupon abandoned, and we continued with the general theory of Glamour.

I now find it quite amusing to think back to the importance I attached at the time to the insights I neatly inscribed in my notebook:

The need for Scientific Communism arises when belief fades
in the feasibility of Communism actually being built, while the
need for Glamour arises at the disappearance of natural sexual
attraction.

Be that as it may, after I had experienced the effects of preparations labelled 'Catwalk Meat 05 – 07'and 'Suicide-Bimbombers of Beelzebub' (categories of fashion models so designated by some particularly misogynistic vampire) my original conception underwent an important clarification:

It is not as simple as that. What precisely is natural sexual
attraction? When you look close up at a girl who is considered
the epitome of beauty, you see the pores in her skin, the pimples,
the chapped lips and so on. Beauty or ugliness can be sensed
only at a distance, when the lineaments of the face can be
reduced to a schematic diagram which may be compared with

the manga-style templates stored in the unconscious mind. Where
these templates come from is anyone's guess – but one suspects
that in our day they have less to do with the genetic code than
with the Glamour industry. In the world of automation, coercive
governance of this type is known as 'override'.

There were a few entertaining moments. One sample turned up
twice in my programme, under different headings. The preparation was classified as: 'Art Projects Curator Rh4'.

The red liquid had come from a middle-aged lady who really
did look as if she could be an Islamist suicide-bomber. Both
Baldur and Jehovah had included her in their lists because in their
eyes a curator was seen to be someone pursuing an occupation
midway between Glamour and Discourse and thus representing
an invaluable source of information. I thought otherwise. The
purpose of the degustation was to study the inner world of the
contemporary artist, but this curator had not even mastered the
jargon of her profession – she was merely Googling her way
round it. There was, nevertheless, one touching detail: she had
experienced orgasm only once in her life, when a drunken lover
had called her a pubic louse feeding on financial capitalism.

I expressed my perplexity at this outcome to Jehovah and
was informed that this experience was, in fact, the point of the
lesson inasmuch as it revealed the subject in its entirety. I said I
did not believe it, whereupon he made me sample three artists
and another art gallery curator. Afterwards I made the following
entry in my notebook:

On average, the contemporary artist is an anal prostitute with
a mouth stitched shut and an arse painted on the wall. And the
so-called curator is a person who sets himself up as the artist's
spiritual pimp despite the complete absence of any spiritual
dimension in the proceedings.

Writers (whom we also covered in the Glamour course) were slightly better. After familiarising myself with their category I wrote in my notebook:

What is the most important thing for a writer? It is to possess a malicious, morbid, jealous and envious ego. If this is present, all else will follow.

Assorted varieties of critics, experts, press and Internet culturologists (it was around this time that I finally worked out what the word meant) found their way into the Discourse curriculum. A half-hour excursion into their universe allowed me to formulate the following rule:

The interim height of a crab louse equals the height of the object onto which it craps, plus 0.2 millimetres.

The last note I made on the Glamour course was as follows:

The most fruitful technique for promoting glamour in modern Russia will be anti-glamour. 'Deconstructing' glamour will allow it to infiltrate even those dark places where glamour itself would not dream of trespassing.

Not all the tastings had an epistemological purpose. Baldur often had me pry into another person purely in order that I should familiarise myself with a particular brand of Spanish crocodile-skin footwear or line of men's eau de cologne. A highborn English economist found his way into the Glamour list because he was a specialist in expensive clarets, and he was followed in my investigations by a Japanese designer whose silk neckties were the best in the world (it emerged that he was the son of a man who had been sentenced by court martial to be hanged).

Needless to say, such researches appeared to me a complete waste of my time and energy.

Before long, however, I grew to understand that the object of these excursions was not just to absorb yet more information, but to remodel my entire mode of thinking. The truth is that there is a vital difference between the mental processes of a vampire and those of a human being. When thinking, the vampire employs the same cerebral constructions as the man, but the path taken to get from one premise to another is as different from predictive human thought as is the exquisite trajectory of a bat flying through the dusk from a pigeon circling over an urban rubbish dump.

'The best human beings are capable of thought almost on a level with vampires,' said Baldur. 'They have a name for it in their world – genius.'

Jehovah's take was more restrained.

'About genius I'm not so sure,' he said. 'Genius resists analysis and explanation, it's a bit of a grey area. With us, everything is straightforward and clear. Thinking becomes vampiric when sufficient degustations have been imbibed to generate new parameters of associative connections.'

Technically speaking, my brain was already equipped to function in a new way. But the inertia of human nature still imposed its innate conditions. Many things which to my mentors were crystal clear I failed to grasp. What they saw as a logical bridge all too often presented itself to me as a conceptual chasm.

'There are two main aspects to Glamour,' declared Jehovah at one of our lessons. 'On the one hand, it is the searingly painful shame and humiliation brought about by one's poverty and physical ugliness. On the other, it is a malignant glee at the sight of the depravity and imperfections which others have not succeeded in concealing...'

'How can this be so?' I marvelled. 'You told me Glamour

was sex expressed as money. Surely there must be something attractive about it. Where is that in what you have just said?'

'You're thinking like a human being,' said Jehovah. 'Why don't *you* tell me where it is?'

I thought. But nothing came into my head. 'I don't know,' I said finally.

'Nothing that exists is imperfect or hideous in or of itself. Everything depends on correlation. For a girl to realise that she is a fat, poor, ugly freak, all she has to do is open a glamour magazine, where she will be confronted with a slim super-rich beauty queen. Then she has someone against whom to compare herself.'

'But why should the girl want to do this?'

'Well, come on, you can answer that,' said Jehovah.

I thought some more.

'She has to...' and suddenly vampire logic laid out the answer clearly before me. 'She has to, so that she and all those other people the glossy mags have turned into humiliated freaks will carry on financing the Glamour industry out of their wretched earnings.'

'Quite right, well done. But even *that* is still not the ultimate objective. You rightly talk of Glamour needing to be financed, but what is its aim?'

'Glamour drives the economy forward because its victims start stealing money?' I hazarded at random.

'Far too much like human logic. You're not an economist, Rama, you're a vampire. Concentrate.'

I was silent, because nothing entered my head. Jehovah paused for a minute, then said:

'The aim of Glamour is to ensure that the life of mankind passes in a miasma of ignominy and self-contempt, a condition known as "original sin". It is the direct result of consuming images of beauty, success and intellectual brilliance. Glamour and Discourse submerge their consumers in mediocrity, idiocy and destitution – qualities which are, of course, relative, but cause real suffering. All human life is dominated by this sense of disgrace and poverty.'

'Why is original sin necessary?'

'It is necessary because human thought must be confined within strict limits, and because mankind must remain in ignorance of its true place in the symphony of men and vampires.'

I guessed that in this context the word 'symphony' meant something like 'symbiosis'. But I could not get out of my head an image of some gigantic orchestra, before which stood Jehovah on the conductor's podium in a black tailcoat, his mouth smeared in blood...

After a pause for thought, I said:

'All right. I can understand why Glamour is a mask. But why do we say the same of Discourse?'

Jehovah closed his eyes and assumed a look of Yoda, the mentor of the Jedi.

'In the Middle Ages no one knew that America existed,' he said, 'therefore it was not necessary to conceal it. It never entered anyone's head to look for it. That is the best disguise of all. If our aim is to hide something from people, all we need do is make sure no one thinks of it. For this to be the case, human thought must be under permanent supervision, that is to say Discourse has to be controlled. To control Discourse, all we need is the power to establish its borders. Once they are set, an entire universe can be hidden beyond them. You know this from your own situation. You must admit, the world of vampires is pretty well camouflaged.'

I nodded.

'Not only that,' continued Jehovah, 'discourse is another, and magical, form of masking. I'll give you an example. No human being will disagree with the proposition that there is a great deal of evil in the world, is that not so?'

'It is.'

'But what is the source of this evil? Not a day goes without newspapers filling acres of space arguing about it. It is one of the most astounding aspects of the world we live in, given that people are capable of recognising the nature of evil instinct-ively, with no need to have it analysed and explained. To have succeeded in rendering it such a shrouded mystery is a serious magical act.'

'Yes,' I agreed sadly, 'that seems to be very near the truth.'

'Discourse acts in a manner not unlike an electric barbed-wire fence where the current touches not the human body but the human mind. It defines territory that cannot be penetrated from territory from which it is impossible to escape.'

'What is the territory that cannot be escaped?'

'I can't believe you're asking that. Glamour, of course! Open any glossy magazine and look. There in the middle you find Glamour, and round the edges Discourse. Or the other way round – Discourse in the middle and Glamour round the edges. Glamour is always surrounded either by Discourse or by empty space. There is nowhere for the human being to escape to. Empty space holds nothing for him, yet he cannot pass through the Discourse barrier. The only thing left to him is to sleepwalk through the pastures of Glamour.'

'But why do vampires need it?'

'Glamour has one other function which we have not yet mentioned,' replied Jehovah. 'And for vampires it is the most important one. But it is too early to speak of it yet. You will find out about it after the Great Fall.'

'And when will that be?'

To this Jehovah made no reply.

*

And so it was, taste by taste, swallow by swallow, step by step, that I was transformed into a culturally advanced metrosexual, ready to plunge into the very heart of darkness.

THE FILING CABINET

From what I have written it may appear that my transformation into a vampire was accomplished without inner struggle. This was far from the case.

During the first few days I felt as though I had undergone a major operation on my brain. At night I had nightmares. I was drowning in a bottomless black swamp enclosed by a ring of stone blocks, or else I was being roasted in the mouth of some horrible brick monster, which for some reason contained a stove. But the worst nightmare of all was when I woke up and became conscious of the new centre of my being, a nucleus of steel that had taken the place of my heart, had nothing to do with me, yet was at the same time the core of my person. This was how I experienced the Tongue as it gradually entered into a symbiotic relationship with my brain.

Once my missing canine teeth had grown back in (apart from being slightly whiter they were identical to my old ones) the nightmares ceased. Or more accurately, I stopped reacting to them as nightmares and came to terms with such visions in my dreams. I had had to make a similar adjustment when I first went to school. Now my soul gradually recovered itself, much as an occupied city comes back to life or the fingers of a benumbed hand begin again to stir. But all the time, day and night, I felt as though I was under surveillance by an invisible television camera installed inside me, through which one part of me observed the other part.

One day I went home to collect my things. The room in which I had spent my childhood seemed small and dark, the Sphinx in the hallway no more than a kitschy caricature. Seeing me, my mother for some reason lost her cool, then shrugged her shoulders and went into her room. I felt no link whatsoever with the place in which I had spent so many years; everything about it was alien. I quickly gathered up the things I needed, threw my laptop into my bag, and returned to my new apartment.

After lessons with Baldur and Jehovah I had time to take a closer look at my surroundings. I had been curious from the very beginning about the somewhat skimpy library of test tubes in Brahma's study, and guessed that somewhere there must be a catalogue. Before long I found it in one of the drawers of the escritoire: a handwritten album bound in a rather unusual snakeskin or something of the sort. Each drawer of the filing cabinet corresponded with a pair of pages in the catalogue, in which were notes and brief commentaries on the numbered test tubes.

The catalogue itself was divided into sections, amusingly reminiscent of the bays in a video store. The largest section was erotica, itself divided into eras, countries and genres. The cast list was impressive: in the French bloc were Gilles de Rais, Madame de Montespan, the Bourbon King Henry IV and Jean Marais. I could not conceive how it had been possible to obtain the red liquid from all these people, even in microscopic doses.

The military section included, besides Napoleon, one of the last shoguns of the Tokugawa Shogunate, Marshal Zhukov and various celebrities from the Second World War, among them the air aces Pokryshkin, Adolf Galland and Hans Ulrich Rudel.

These sections of the catalogue – the military and the erotic

– aroused my keenest interest, followed, as is invariably the case in life, by the keenest disappointment. The relevant contents in the filing cabinet itself must have been moved somewhere else. Only in three sections were there any test tubes containing liquid preparations: 'Master Mask-Makers', 'Prenatal Experiences' and 'Literature'.

I had no desire to learn anything more about the people who had made the masks the late Brahma had collected (they were displayed on the walls). Likewise the literature section: it contained many names familiar from the school curriculum and I still remembered the nausea they provoked during lessons. 'Prenatal Experiences' was the one that sparked my greatest interest.

I assumed this must concern the experience of the foetus in the womb. I could not even imagine what it could be like. No doubt, I thought, some vague glimmers of light, muffled sounds from the surrounding environment, rumblings from the maternal bowels, pressures on the body – in short ineffable feelings like soaring weightlessly through the air or swooping up and down on a roller coaster.

Bracing myself and selecting a test tube labelled 'Italy-(' I drew a few drops into the dropper, placed them in my mouth and sat down on the sofa.

What I then experienced, in its incoherence and illogicality, was like a dream sequence. I seemed to be returning from Italy, where I had evidently failed to complete the task I had been assigned – something to do with stone-carving. I felt sad, because of having left there many things I loved. I could see their shadows: summer-houses among the vines, tiny carriages (these were children's toys, memories of which were preserved with especial clarity), a rope swing in a garden...

But before I knew it I was somewhere else, apparently a Moscow railway station. I had disembarked from the train and gone through an inconspicuous door into an obviously special-ised building, which seemed to house a scientific institute of some kind. The building was in the process of being renovated: furniture was being moved out, the old parquet taken up from the floor. I decided I had to get out to the street, and found myself walking down a long corridor. At first it snaked along in one direction, then through a circular room to head off in another...

After some time wandering about in the corridor I noticed a window in one wall, but when I looked through it I realised that I was nowhere near a street exit; in fact I was even further away than when I had started, for now I was several storeys above ground level. I thought I had better ask someone to tell me the way out, but annoyingly no one was within sight. I did not want to go back along the winding corridor, so began opening one door after another looking for someone to ask.

Behind one of the doors was a cinema. It was in the process of being cleaned, the floor scrubbed. I asked the cleaning women how I could get to the street.

'Down here,' said an old biddy in a blue overall, 'down the chute. That's how we go.'

She pointed to an opening in the floor and I saw a green plastic shaft like you find in an aquapark. It struck me as a modern and progressive method of transport but I held back, afraid that my jacket might snag in the tube, which seemed rather too narrow. On the other hand, the old woman who had advised me to take this route was herself pretty wide in the beam.

'Is this really the way you go down?' I asked.

'Course it is,' said the woman, leaning over it and emptying dirty water with some kind of feathers in it from the bucket she held in her hands. I did not find this at all surprising, merely thinking that now I would have to wait until the tube dried out...

At this point the experience came to an end.

By now I had already absorbed enough from my Discourse studies to recognise the symbolism of dream visions. I could even make a guess at interpreting the labels on the test tubes. Presumably, if the one designated 'Italy-(' ended, so to say, in midair, and its neighbour was 'France-)', logically the first would conclude with the lyrical hero's leap into the shaft. But I did not test this supposition; the prenatal experience continued to occupy a disagreeable position in my emotional spectrum, reminding me of the feverish hallucinations induced by influenza.

The episode brought to mind a well-known analogy of the body inside the mother's womb as a car awaiting the soul which will come to drive it away on its journey. But what is the precise moment when the soul makes its entrance? When the construction of the car commences, or when it is completed and ready to depart? I discovered that it is possible to express this question, which currently divides adherents and opponents of abortion into two implacably opposed camps, in less adversarial formulations. Several examples of Discourse I had absorbed contained more interesting views.

Among them was, for example, this one: there is no vehicle for the soul to enter; the life of the body resembles the trajectory of a radio-controlled drone. A more radical interpretation still was that there is not even a trajectory of the drone, but a three-dimensional film of such a journey projected in some way onto a static mirror, which is the soul... Strangely enough, this perspective appeared the most plausible to me, probably because at this time my own mirror was reflecting a great number of other people's films while not itself moving anywhere, suggesting that it was indeed stationary. But what is this mirror? Where is it located? At this point I realised that yet again I was falling into the trap of conceptualising the soul, and my mood accordingly soured.

A couple of days later I found in one of the drawers a stray test tube containing less liquid than the others. Its index number did not correspond to the index number of the drawer. I checked it in the catalogue and saw that the preparation was designated 'Rudel ZOO'. The notes confirmed that it concerned the German airman Hans Ulrich Rudel. The classification, however, was in the erotic, not the military section.

Degustation followed promptly.

I saw nothing connected with military activities – unless one could include in that category some blurry memories of a Christmas flight over Stalingrad. There were no world-famous villains either. The material was all relentlessly everyday: Hans Ulrich Rudel was featured on his last visit to Berlin. Dressed in a black leather overcoat, with some implausible medal round his neck, he was superciliously, and with virtually no attempt at concealment, copulating in broad daylight with a high-school girl near the Berlin Zoo U-Bahn station. The girl was pale with ecstasy. In addition to the erotic element the preparation included memories of an enormous concrete ziggurat with platforms for anti-aircraft artillery. The whole structure had such a contrived air about it that I began to have doubts about the veracity of the whole proceedings. As for the rest, it resembled a somewhat style-conscious pornographic film.

I confess that I watched it several times, certainly more than twice. Rudel's face was that of an intelligent sheet-metalworker; the schoolgirl looked as if she had stepped out of a margarine advertisement. As I understood, intimate encounters in the vicinity of the Zoo station between people previously unacquainted with one another had become something of a tradition as the fall of the city became imminent. Eleventh-hour Aryan coupling appeared a somewhat melancholy pursuit, attributable perhaps to vitamin deficiency. I was particularly struck to learn that Rudel passed the time between aerial combat sorties by throwing the discus around the aerodrome, like a Greek athlete. Somehow I had a completely different conception of these times.

A few days later I did after all experiment with a preparation from the literary section. The late Brahma had been a great admirer of Nabokov, as was confirmed by the portraits of him on the wall. His library contained no less than thirty preparations, all in one way or another connected with the author. Among them were such strangely labelled test tubes as, for instance, 'Pasternak+½ Nabokov'. I could not work out what this could possibly mean. Either it concerned an unknown chapter in the personal lives of the titans, or it was an attempt to blend their talents in an alchemic retort according to specified proportions.

I wanted to try this preparation. But disappointment awaited me: the degustation did not result in any revelations. At first I thought the tube must contain nothing but water, but after a few minutes the skin of my fingers began to itch and I felt a strong desire to write some verse. I seized pen and paper. Ambition, however, failed to lead to my developing a poetic gift: the lines inched forward one by one but declined to shape themselves into anything consummate or harmonious. After filling up half a notepad, I found I had given birth to the following:

For your Kant, for your cut, for your rusty kalinka,
For your underhand tender so tenderly rigged...

Having reached this point, inspiration found itself blocked by an impenetrable barrier. The beginning seemed to predicate a response such as 'I would give you...' but herein lay precisely the difficulty. *What*, I thought, trying to see the situation objectively through the eyes of a third party, *could I conceivably be offering you for your cut of the rigged deal?* Several plausible answers couched in highly unsuitable language did occur to me, but none of them could be said to enhance the poetic context.

I came to the conclusion that my experiment with poetry had run into the sand, and got up from the divan. Suddenly I was overwhelmed by such a surge of joy welling up in my breast that nothing could prevent it from erupting and drenching all mankind with glittering foam. I took a deep breath and allowed the wave to gush tumultuously out. Then my hand wrote, in English:

> *My sister, do you still recall*
> *The blue Khasan and Khalkhin-Gol?*

And that was all.

It may be that the abridged result of the experiment was due to lack of emotional material in my soul. The greatest architect needs bricks, after all. As far as Nabokov was concerned, the deficiencies of my English vocabulary may also have had something to do with it.

Nevertheless, the experiment cannot be counted a complete failure. From it I learnt that there must exist ways of ring-fencing the amount of information contained in the preparations: this one had no revelations at all about the poets' private life.

I decided to ask Baldur about this.

'You mean you've been poking about in the library?' he asked, clearly displeased.

'Well, yes.'

'You shouldn't touch anything. Don't you have enough material to work on? I can ask Jehovah to give you a lot more...'

'All right,' I said, 'I won't do it again. But please explain how can there be only one property in a preparation? For instance, in this case, versification techniques. Without any personal images?'

'It's a distillation. There is a particular technology which is operated by a vampire-purifier. The red liquid passes through a cylindrical spiral in his helmet. He goes into a special trance and concentrates on the particular aspect of the life-experience he desires to preserve. In the process all other components of the experience are discarded in favour of the content selected by the purifier. This isolates the required spectrum of information and eliminates everything else. Human experience is harmful and destructive, and in large doses can be fatal. Why do you think people die like flies? It's because of their life experiences.'

'Then why am I gulping down these experiences by the bucketful in my lessons?'

'That's different,' said Baldur. 'You are being given undistilled preparations as a way of furnishing you with ballast, so to speak.'

'Why do I need ballast?'

'A ship with no ballast is liable to capsize and sink. But if she takes in a volume of water to the same level as the waterline outside, she acquires stability. You have to be prepared for the effects of any experience. It's like being inoculated. Not particularly pleasant, of course, but you just have to put up with it. It's part of any vampire's education process.'

Even without this proscription I would not have wanted to experiment further with Brahma's filing cabinet. Baldur was right: I was being expected to sample a vast quantity of preparations in the course of my daily lessons, and there was something pathological about wanting to continue doing so in my leisure time.

But there was still one question that interested me.

From the conversation with Enlil Maratovich I had learnt that vampires regard human beings as equivalent to milch cows, specially bred to serve as sources of food. This I found difficult to believe, and not merely because humanity had been assigned too menial a role.

The thing was, nowhere could I see anything that might be seen as the milking mechanism. The biting by which the vampire gained access to the subject's inner world was clearly not sufficient for sustenance, it was purely a route to analysis of a blood sample. There must be another method.

I tried to visualise what this method could look like. Perhaps, I thought, vampires consumed red liquid collected in the course of medical procedures? Or perhaps in the Third World there were plantations where people were raised specifically for the purpose?

Similar themes were common in mass culture. I remembered a film called *The Island* in which ignorant, infantilised people earmarked for spare-part organ harvesting were bred in facilities deep underground. They moved along sterile corridors, dressed in white sports clothes, hoping one day to draw the lucky straw... Another film, *Blade: Trinity*, depicted a factory with vacuum-sealed parcels of comatose individuals producing red liquid to feed vampires without ever attaining the level of consciousness.

Surely the answer to my question could not be anything remotely like that?

There was another puzzle. Vampires ate normal food. On several occasions I went for a meal with Baldur and Jehovah after our lessons, and our dining had nothing remotely Gothic about it. We patronised a mediocre restaurant on the Garden Ring Road to eat sushi. Everything was quite normal. True, Jehovah did once order a glass of freshly squeezed tomato juice, and while he was drinking it, his Adam's apple bobbing prominently up and down, I experienced such a feeling of revulsion that I seriously began to doubt my ability to become a vampire. But this was the only time the behaviour of either Baldur or Jehovah suggested even the merest hint of drinking blood.

Could it be that red liquid was consumed in special rituals on particular days?

I tried questioning Baldur and Jehovah on how it was done, but each time received the same answer as I had had from Enlil Maratovich: it was too early to speak of it; all in good time; I must wait for the Great Fall.

Obviously, I thought, *there must be a special initiation in store for me, following which the vampire community would accept me as one of their own and reveal its dark secrets. And then,* I thought, clenching my fists, *I would join in their customs... perhaps even take pleasure in them. How revolting...*

When I was a child, I use to think rissoles were revolting. Yet in time I was educated to like them.

I hoped I might find answers to my questions somewhere in the filing cabinet. Leafing through the catalogue one more time, I did indeed find something rather curious. It was a strange note on the last page of the journal. There was one preparation on its own in a separate compartment, and it was labelled as follows:

History: Command of the Mighty Bat

The compartment was right at the top of the cabinet. When I opened it, instead of the usual rack of test tubes I saw a small red box like a presentation case for an expensive fountain pen. Inside was a test tube, the same as all the others, but with a red stopper. I was intrigued.

I waited until evening before deciding on a degustation. It did not give me the answer to my most important question, but at last I found out some highly interesting information on another matter: how Brahma and Enlil Maratovich had been able to bite me without my feeling it. Originally I thought there must be some sort of anaesthetic substance which injects itself into the wound, as is the case with certain tropical bloodsucking insects. But I was wrong.

It transpired that a momentary psychic contact is established between the biter and the subject, akin to the sadomasochistic tandem ridden by the executioner and his victim, of which the latter is only dimly aware. The body feels the bite and realises what is taking place, not on the level of individual human consciousness but lower down, in the connections and valency of the animal brain. The signal is prevented from rising higher because along with the bite the victim receives a kind of shock which suppresses all normal reactions.

The shock is brought about by a special psychic command transmitted by the vampire's Tongue. It is known as the 'Cry of the Mighty Bat'. The precise nature of the Cry is unclear, but to think of it as a physically uttered and audible cry is misleading. It is many millions of years old and is powerful enough to have subdued instantly a mighty dinosaur.

Nor does it work merely by suppressing the victim's will. It is rather the memory of a unique biological pact, refined over millions of years, according to which the subdued animal relinquishes its blood yet retains life. The Cry of the Mighty Bat arose in an era far removed from our own, but the oldest areas of our brains have retained the memory they once had of its full horror.

Unfortunately, so meticulously purified was the preparation from the red case that it excluded all information about who might have made use of this command in antiquity. On the other hand, I was able to understand some scientific details. For instance, I learnt that the command never even reaches the higher centres of the psyche, because the entire process takes only three hundred and fifty milliseconds – below the threshold at which a human being or other large animal can register an event. Nothing whatsoever is retained in the memory of the person who has been bitten by a vampire, or if it is, the brain immediately activates a defensive reaction to eliminate it.

What, then, do people experience when being bitten by a

vampire? Reactions vary. There may be an irrational lassitude, a feeling of dread for the future, a sudden rush of weakness. The brain may be invaded by unwelcome thoughts: deceased relatives, unpaid overdue bills, missed football matches. The victim's mind avails itself of any device to mask what has occurred – probably the most unusual of all defence mechanisms invented by evolution.

At the same time I discovered the secret of my new teeth. They were, as I have already said, of perfectly normal size and shape and differed from my own only in being slightly whiter. As I learned, the teeth do not themselves puncture the victim's skin but generate an electrical discharge, something like the piezoelectric sparks from the crystal in a cigarette lighter. The electrical rods are the glands housed in the vampire's soft palate in the region of his second brain, approximately where his tonsils used to be. After the electrical discharge, a minute area of vacuum appears just above the small wound in the bitten person's skin, into which a few drops of blood are drawn. The bite is accompanied by a sharp but practically imperceptible jerk of the head: this is the vampire catching the drops of blood in flight and applying them with his tongue to his palate, after which degustation commences. Ideally there should be no visible signs on the victim's skin at all. In the worst case one or two drops of red liquid may fall, but there has never been any instance of blood actually flowing. To the victim the process is completely harmless.

As well as this information, the preparation contained some instructions along the lines of 'how to comport oneself when carrying out a bite'. This advice was of a purely tactical nature.

The vampire is recommended to act as though preparing to say something in a low voice to the victim. Care must be taken not to suggest to onlookers that he is about to spit in the victim's ear, or whisper indecencies, or inhale the scent of another person's perfume, or other such invasions of privacy: there could be as many interpretations as there are guardians of public morality.

All this lay in the future for me.

There is a painting by the artist Deineke, 'Fliers of the Future', which depicts young lads on the seashore gazing up at the sky where they see the faint contours of an aeroplane. Were I to paint a picture of 'The Vampire of the Future' it would look like this: a pale youth sitting in a cavernous armchair in front of the black hole of an empty fireplace, staring in fascination at a photograph of a bat.

FIRST BITE

Mithra telephoned to find out how things were going.

'Fair, I suppose,' I said grumpily. 'Only thing is, fair in a way I don't particularly care for.'

'Colourfully put,' chuckled Mithra. 'The Tongue does make for interesting conversationalists. But what I can't understand is why you're in such a mood. Surely you realise you've become a completely different person? Far better educated, more developed? On a different intellectual plane from what you were?'

'Maybe, but this enviable new person has a raft of questions to which no one wants to give him answers.'

'Just wait a bit, you'll soon know more than you bargained for. All in good time. Speaking of which, it's time I tipped you off about something. So it doesn't come as too much of a shock.'

'What is it?' I asked in alarm.

Mithra laughed.

'Anyone would think you're in shock already. Your first bite is coming up. When exactly I don't know, but you won't have long to wait.'

'I don't suppose I'll be able to manage it,' I said.

'Don't worry,' replied Mithra. 'You'll find your fiddle will play itself. You're frightened of the new, that's all. There's really nothing to be afraid of. A joyful moment in your life is approaching. Your first time is ... I can't begin to describe it. All I can tell you is that it will leave you with blissful memories.'

'What do I have to do?'

'Nothing, I told you. Just wait. Your spirit will tell you when the time comes.'

I cannot say that I found this parting advice very encouraging. It reminded me of the Japanese custom whereby the samurai, on taking possession of a new sword, must go to the outskirts of the town at night and behead the first person he meets. I felt oppressed, fearing that I might have to do something of the sort. But the Tongue maintained its passive calm, and the reassuringly solid weight at the centre of my soul soothed me like an ice cube held against the forehead ... I grant that the phrase 'at the centre of my soul' has an odd ring about it – after all, the soul has no such thing as a centre. But that is a normal soul; my soul did have a centre.

When it came, the event was nothing like what I had supposed. My first vampiric experience had less to do with Thanatos than with his long-term partner Eros. All the same, I would not go so far as to describe it as pleasant.

One afternoon, immediately after my lesson with Baldur, I lay down for a nap. On waking some hours later, I felt a sudden impulse to go out for a walk. I put on jeans and my Simpsons t-shirt – I sometimes used to wear it for my shifts at the supermarket – and left the apartment.

The town was bathed in evening sunshine. I wandered along the street, vaguely discontented. First I felt like smoking a cigarette, though I had never had the habit. Then I thought I might go for a pint of beer, but that was another thing I did not normally like to do. Precisely what it was I craved I did not know, but I definitely wanted to do something. And then, without warning, it became clear.

I cannot explain how I selected my target. All I know is that

101

at a certain moment it was there. It came about like this: I saw a girl walking towards me. She had on a light-coloured dress with a check pattern, and carried a white handbag. As she passed me she looked me in the eye. I turned and followed her without a moment's hesitation.

I knew what was happening. I seemed not to be in charge of my actions; the Tongue had taken control of my will. I distinctly remember feeling like a horse being ridden into battle by a veteran cavalryman. All the terrified animal wants to do is turn tail and run away, but the spurs digging deep into its flanks give it no choice – just as I had no choice – but to go into action promptly and effectively.

Coming up behind the girl I leaned towards her as though to call out to her. Instinct made me open my mouth as if to draw in a gulp of air; I saw the shell of her ear close to me, and then something strange occurred. I heard a faint click, my head involuntarily jerked back – and I knew the deed was done.

An onlooker, no doubt, would have seen the episode like this: a young man goes up to a girl intending to ask her a question, opens his mouth, bends towards her ear – and suddenly sneezes. Embarrassed he slackens his pace.

She did not turn round, simply drew up her shoulders nervously, and a tiny pink spot appeared on her neck. The bite had been expertly accomplished: not a drop of blood was to be seen on the skin. Fighting the desire to sit down on the pavement and close my eyes in exhaustion, I continued to follow her.

At that time I did not know that to bite a person of the opposite sex for the first time is an experience as extraordinary as one's first kiss. The Biblical expression 'knowing' a woman is actually no more than a euphemism for having sex with her. Only a vampire can truly *know* a woman. And when he does, his eyes are opened to an astounding secret, one which the ordinary person, capable of perceiving only his or her half of the truth, can never know in its entirety.

The fact is – and it is something of which mankind generally remains in ignorance – that the coexistence of the two sexes is an extraordinary, hilarious but completely invisible absurdity. People's knowledge of the inner life of members of the opposite sex is based on all kinds of gibberish – 'secrets of her heart' gleaned from a cheap wall calendar or, even worse, 'how to manipulate the male superego' as promoted in magazines like *Marie Claire*. This inner life is usually portrayed by one sex employing terminology tailored to its own understanding of the other: thus men appear as bearded, bullying, coarse versions of women, and women as idiotic dickless males who know nothing about driving a car.

The truth is that men and women are much farther apart than either side can possibly imagine. The extent to which they differ is almost impossible to put into words. The essence of the difference lies, needless to say, in the hormonal composition of the red liquid.

Think of the situation in this way: our world is populated by two types of drug user, each addicted to extremely strong psychotropic substances producing radically different effects. The hallucinations affecting each type are diametrically opposed, yet the subjects are obliged to live in permanent conjunction with one another. For this reason they have learned to indulge jointly in fundamentally different individual trips, relying on an elaborate form of etiquette that allows each side, despite the fact that the same words mean different things to them, to behave as if it understood the other.

It may be objected that all this is familiar territory to any transsexual who has undergone a sex-change operation and taken a course of hormone injections. Not necessarily so. Transsexuals alter their inner state by degrees, as a voyager across the ocean gradually forgets who he is and where he has come from. Vampires, however, are able to transport themselves from one configuration to the other in a matter of seconds...

The girl I had bitten remembered having seen me in passing, and I knew she liked what she had seen (it was exactly as though I was looking at my own reflection in a mirror endowed with emotions). This at first surprised me, and then I found it embarrassing. Finally, my thoughts found themselves impelled in a direction neither entirely proper nor, ultimately, under my control.

We turned into Bolshaya Bronnaya Street. Walking a pace behind her I shamelessly explored the twists and turns of her memory and invented ways to use what I discovered there. By the time we approached Pushkin Square, my plan was complete.

Overtaking her and marching ahead about ten metres, I halted, turned round and went back towards her with a broad smile on my face. She looked at me in astonishment, and continued on her way, past me. I waited a little and then repeated the manoeuvre: overtaking, turning back and smiling. She smiled in response and again walked past me. When I repeated the exercise a third time, she stopped and said:

'What is it you want?'

'Don't you recognise me?'

'No. Who are you?'

'Roma.'

I gave my real name, because I knew she had not recalled the name of the person I had decided to impersonate.

'Roma? Roma who?'

This was the moment I put my stolen ace of spades on the table. 'The Quiet Azure guest house. New Year. Room with the Christmas tree and the lights out. Everyone else had gone out to let off fireworks. Do you honestly not remember?'

'Ohhh...' – she even had the grace to blush – 'that was you?'

I nodded. She hung her head and we walked on.

'I've never in my life been as drunk as that,' she said. 'I'm really ashamed. Took me ages to get back to normal.'

'For me,' I lied brazenly, 'it's still one of the happiest memories of my life. That may sound exaggerated, but it's true. I kept ringing you afterwards. Many times.'

'What number did you ring?'

I spelt out the number of her mobile phone, changing the last two numbers from 18 to 19. That was the way she always changed them herself when she felt awkward declining to give her number but unwilling to say the real one – then it would always be possible to say that her companion had misheard.

'You mean you still remember it?' she said in surprise. 'You must have written it down wrong. It should end with 18.'

'Oh hell,' I said. 'Why does this always happen to me? Listen, can't we celebrate meeting up again like this?'

The rest was easy. First we went to a café on Tverskaya Street, then to another café, where I had to bite her once more in order to clarify what we could talk about while we were eating (this time a couple of tiny drops of blood did remain on her neck). I talked only about things that interested her and said only things she wanted to hear. It was not difficult.

I felt myself a Casanova. I had no conception of doing anything wrong. The difference between my behaviour and the standard pick-up approach was as described by St Paul: whereas the ordinary male sees everything through a glass, darkly, I saw it face to face. I knew exactly what to say and how to say it. It was like playing cards and being able to see what was in my opponent's hand. Yes, it was cheating. But the aim of people in this game is usually not to win but to yield to each other while taking care not too openly to breach the code of good manners.

We went for a walk, during which I never drew breath. It 'just so happened' the route we took led us back to where she lived, in a Stalinist skyscraper on Uprising Square. I knew there was no one else at home. Of course, we had to go up 'for a cup of tea'. Even the phase of courtship I generally find most problematical, the transition from chatting up to the actual business – something I never learnt how to finesse with any skill or elegance – proceeded this time without undue clumsiness.

Where I was ambushed was in an area I had least expected. Had it not been for the ennobling influence of the lessons on Discourse, I am sure I would never have been able to articulate what happened.

The glum, commonplace act of love, performed not from mutual desire but as a routine operation (which is how it most often takes place) always brought to my mind our electoral system. After enduring interminable torrents of lies, the voter is finally allowed to insert the only real – and pathetic – candidate into an indifferent niche, which has already seen so much tampering, doctoring and rigging it no longer cares two hoots about the outcome. The voter is then supposed to persuade himself that this boring performance has been precisely the event that turns the whole world delirious with ecstasy.

But I knew that on those rare occasions when the procedure is crowned with success (here I am referring not to elections but to the other matter), something occurs which is categorically of a different order. A moment can come about when two separate beings fuse together in a single electrical circuit to become as one body with two heads. An example taken from the world of heraldry would be the ancient Byzantine coat of arms depicting an orthodox chick in the act of enforced union with the turkey which has sneaked up on it from behind.

On this occasion the moment I speak of occurred. And in that second she understood everything about me. I do not know what exactly it was that she sensed, but I was unmasked, there was no question of it.

106

'You ... you ...'

Pushing me away she sat on the edge of the bed. Her eyes were wide open with such naked horror that even I was frightened.

'Who are you?' she asked. 'What was that?'

It was useless to try to bluff my way out of it. I could not tell her the truth, because she would not have believed it, and I could think of no satisfactory lie. I had no desire to bite her a third time in order to find a way of extricating myself from the situation. Getting out of the bed, I silently put on my black Simpsons t-shirt.

A minute later I was hurtling down the staircase, screeching like a shot-down bomber – although this particular bomber was falling rather quietly since I certainly had no desire to attract attention.

I felt no remorse. My only regret was finding myself in such a stupid position. The fact that I had twice bitten her neck did not seem to me at all reprehensible. The mosquito, I thought, is surely not to be condemned for being a mosquito. I knew I had not turned into a monster, at least not yet. This made it all the more alarming that any woman might now find me a monster.

The following evening Mithra rang up.

'Well,' he said, 'how did it go?'

I recounted my inaugural bite and the adventure that followed, omitting only the way it had all concluded.

'Well done,' said Mithra. 'Congratulations. You are now almost one of us.'

'What's this "almost"? Wasn't that the Great Fall?'

Mithra laughed.

'What are you talking about? You're only just cutting your teeth. What sort of a Great Fall could that be? No, there is another thing that must happen, and it's the most important of all...'

'When?'

107

'You'll have to wait.'

'How long?'

'Don't be in too much of a hurry. Get the most out of the tail end of your life as a human.'

These words sobered me up.

'Tell me honestly,' continued Mithra, 'about this girl. Did nothing unexpected happen?'

'Yes, something did,' I confessed. 'Just at the end. She realised there was something not right about me and took fright. As if she had seen the devil.'

Mithra sighed.

'Now you know. It's probably a good thing it happened like that. You are not the same as other people, and you should always keep that in mind. There can never be genuine closeness between you and a human being. Never forget that. And don't expect miracles.'

'How can a human being recognise me for what I am?'

'There's no way she can,' replied Mithra. 'The only exception is the situation in which you found yourself.'

'So, will it always be like that when...'

'No, it won't,' said Mithra. 'It's easy enough to dissemble. Loki will teach you how.'

'Who's Loki?'

'He's your teacher for the next stage of the course. But be careful: what we have been talking about is a taboo subject among vampires. It's never to be spoken openly about even with your instructors. Sexual dissembling is an essential craft but it's explained in a different way.'

'What is this next course?' I asked. 'I thought I was about ready to be admitted to society.'

'Loki's course is the final stage,' said Mithra. 'I swear it on my red liquid. As regards social life, you ought to check your postbox. There's a letter for you.'

Mithra left and I went down to look in my postbox. He was right: in it lay a yellow envelope, with no stamp or address. I wondered how Mithra knew about it, and concluded he must have put it there himself.

Back in the apartment I sat down at the desk, took a bone paperknife, slit open the envelope and upended it over the table. Out fell a large colour photo and sheet of paper covered with large, neat handwriting.

The photograph showed a girl of about my age with her hair weirdly dyed in ginger, white, red and brown strands. The hair had been stiffened with gel into a construction resembling a haystack that had served as target practice for artillery bombardment. It looked picturesque, but was probably rather impractical for public transport.

I do not know quite how to describe her face. It was beautiful, but not with the obvious kind of beauty that is commonly accepted as such, and engenders a response that is commercial rather than personal. This beauty was different. This girl's face was the kind that makes you believe only you are capable of perceiving its fascination while others would not understand or even notice it. For this reason it immediately lodges in your consciousness as private property belonging uniquely to you. Later, when it emerges that the exclusivity of the deal is in fact illusory and others are concerned in it too, you feel betrayed...

Also, I thought I had seen her face in a LiveJournal user pic.

I took up the handwritten sheet and read the following:

Hello, Rama,
You have probably already guessed who I am.
I'm now called Hera. I became a vampire (vampiress? I'm not sure what the right word is) at almost the same time as you, perhaps a week later. I'm just about to start my lessons on Glamour and Discourse with Baldur and Jehovah

109

– they've been telling me one or two amusing stories about you. So far, I'm enjoying it all. To be honest I am a simple sort of girl, but I've been told that my Discourse studies will make me a lot smarter. Isn't it amazing what a huge amount of stuff they can cram into your head?

I was also told that you and I are to meet during the Great Fall. They said you are very worried about it. Well, I'm pretty scared too, but you must agree that it is silly to be afraid of something when you have no idea what it is.

I should like very much to see you, to find out what you are like. For some reason I think you and I are going to be friends. Please send me your photograph. You could get someone to bring it to me, or send it electronically.

Till we meet,

Hera

Below she had added her email address and a weblink ending with an .mp3 extension. She had sent me some music.

I found it very attractive that she had written out the long URL by hand, in neat, sloping letters. For some reason this was rather touching. Nevertheless, it may be that the reason I found these details so enchanting was because I had seen her photograph beforehand.

I downloaded the song. It was 'Not Alone Anymore!' by The Traveling Wilburys. I liked the song, especially the end, where the line 'You're not alone any more' was repeated three times with such lyrical power that it almost persuaded me I was no longer alone myself.

I assumed that as Hera was only just at the start of her studies of Glamour and Discourse, I would be significantly more experienced and advanced. My photograph should reflect this. I decided a good setting would be in front of the filing cabinet: its smooth, polished surface would photograph well.

I put on my best jacket, sat in an armchair brought in from the other room, and took a couple of experimental pictures. Something was lacking in the composition. I placed a bottle of expensive whisky and a heavy crystal tumbler on the table, and tried a few more shots. Still needed something, I felt. I slipped a platinum signet ring with a jet stone over my finger (I found the ring in the escritoire.) Now I supported my chin on the finger, to make the ring more visible, and tried again. From what had grown to be a sizeable collection of selfies I chose the one which I thought gave the clearest impression of a bored demon – to achieve this effect I had to put two volumes of a medical encyclopaedia under my backside.

This done, I sat down at the computer and wrote my reply:

Hello Babe,

I was happy to get a letter from you. You're very nice. I'm glad I am no longer alone. We're alone together, aren't we? Work hard at your studies of Discourse and Glamour, they will seriously broaden your horizons. I'll be very glad to meet you.

Mwah mwah,
Rama

P.S. There is some serious music for you in the attachment.

I made a deliberate attempt to come across as dry, taciturn and ironic, since I believed this to have an irresistible effect on women.

For my musical offering I attached a 10MB recording of an evening service from a Taoist monastery: a single-note recitative piercingly chanted in Chinese to the accompaniment of a collection of exotic percussion instruments. It had been gathering dust for some time on my hard drive, and now I had found a home for it to go to. Casting a final critical eye over my photograph and finding it presentable, I sent the email.

LOKI

The last segment of the vampire foundation course was, like its predecessors, in two parts. It was entitled 'The Art of Combat and of Love'. The teacher was Loki, a tall, cadaverous old man with long yellow hair and a vague resemblance to an impoverished nineteenth-century Russian nobleman. He always showed up wearing huge glasses with coke-bottle lenses and a long five-button black jacket reminiscent of frock coats from the time of the Crimean War.

There was no second teacher; Loki taught both subjects. The course began with the art of combat, which was to be followed by a *cours de perfectionnement* in the art of love.

Loki was older than either Baldur or Jehovah, and initially I found it strange to have such an antique specimen as an instructor in hand-to-hand combat. But then I remembered the grey-bearded masters I had seen in some Hong Kong films, and decided it would be better not to draw too hasty a conclusion.

His manner of instruction was highly idiosyncratic: he did not so much speak as dictate, and insisted that I take down what he said word for word. Not only that, but I had to make notes by hand, using a pen filled with violet ink. All these necessities he brought with him to the first lesson, in a black holdall similar

113

to those of Baldur and Jehovah. When I asked why everything had to be done exactly so, his curt answer was:

'Tradition.'

The first lesson commenced with Loki going over to the blackboard and chalking on it:

> The secret of the longevity of the
> hardiest man alive consists exclusively in
> the fact that no one has yet killed him. –
> Loki IX

I understood that the source of the quotation was none other than the teacher himself.

'That sentence is not to be erased until the course is finished,' said Loki. 'I need the principle to be firmly embedded in your consciousness.'

He then sat me down at the desk with a notebook, placed his hands behind his back and proceeded to pace up and down the room, dictating at a measured pace:

'A vampire's fight technique ... is practically identical to that of a human being ... insofar as it concerns the actual practise of hand-to-hand combat ... The vampire employs the same blows, throws and holds as are met with in classical single combat ... Have you written that down? The difference lies in the vampire's use of these movements ... The art of combat for a vampire is characterised by the complete elimination of any ethical principles, resulting in maximum efficacy ... Its distinguishing quality is the vampire's deliberate choice of the most vile and ignominious techniques available to him ...'

I lifted my head from the notebook.

'How does one determine which fight technique is the most vile and ignominious?'

Loki raised a finger.

'Excellent point!' he said. 'Well done. Bull's-eye! The most common cause of a vampire being defeated in a duel is precisely taking too long to decide on that. Therefore, there can be no pause for reflection in a combat situation; one must rely on instinct. To be guided by instinct entails forgetting altogether about ignominy for the time being. That will automatically lead to the most ignominious fight strategy. That is the paradox. Got that?'

'Yes,' I said. 'But, ordinary people also trust their instincts when they get into a fight. And they're not usually overburdened with scruples. In what way do we differ from them?'

'Umm ... ah,' said Loki with a chuckle. 'Stand up. I'll demonstrate.'

I stood up, or rather tried to, because before I had managed to straighten my legs I received a sudden punch to the solar plexus. It was not an especially hard blow, but it was unquestionably despicable since Loki chose the precise moment to deliver it when I was most off balance. I toppled over, taking the chair with me, and struck the floor painfully with my elbow.

'See?' enquired Loki, as if nothing untoward had occurred.

I leapt to my feet, and he immediately spread his hands out in front of him in a placatory gesture.

'All right, all right, that's enough. Pax.'

My rage subsided. I was about to tell Loki exactly what I thought of him, when without warning he kicked my shin painfully with his boot. This was one dirty trick too far: after all, he had only just himself called a truce. I doubled over with the pain.

Loki walked over to the window, took from his pocket a sweet in a red wrapping, unwrapped it and popped it into his mouth.

'Suppose I were to give you a good sock in the jaw right now?' I enquired.

'How dare you speak to me like that?' Loki scowled. 'I'm your teacher. When you ask me a question I am under obligation to answer it, and in a way you're not likely to forget. Understand?'

'I understand,' I muttered, rubbing my bruised shin. 'But don't do anything like that again. Otherwise I won't be answerable for myself.'

'I promise,' said Loki and turned away.

Assuming he was ashamed of his scurrilous behaviour, I also turned round in order to return to my seat at the table, and at that moment he hurled himself at me from behind and kicked the inside of my calf. My leg involuntarily crumpled and I sank to my knees. He followed up his assault by slapping me about the ears with his open hands. I jumped up again and without saying a word advanced on him with my fists.

I should mention that when I was in tenth grade, I studied karate for a time. Needless to say, this did not instantly transform me into Jackie Chan. I could crack a tile on the wall of the school toilets with a kick, and break a wooden board which was already cracked by punching it, but that was the extent of my achievements. I did, however, acquire enough knowledge to appreciate what Jackie Chan could do on screen.

All the more astounding, therefore, was what I now witnessed. Loki leapt up the wall and climbed several steps, using only his feet. When he reached the point where gravity brought his body parallel with the floor, he somersaulted through the air to land lightly behind my back. There was nothing supernatural about this: nothing that did not conform to the laws of physics, but it was a manoeuvre demanding the utmost agility, not to mention courage.

A second later his leg swooshed round in front of my face, making me rock back on my heels. Then he grabbed hold of my arm and twisted my wrist behind my back in a grip of such rock-like impregnability that I instantly abandoned all thoughts of resistance.

'I give in, I give in!' I shrieked.

Loki released my hand. I was so astonished I forgot all my resentment. 'How on earth did you do that?'

'Sit down and write.'

I sat.

'In order to ensure invincibility in a combat situation, vampires have developed the *death candy*... Got that?'

The penny dropped. 'Aha! That's what you were eating, isn't it? In the red wrapper?'

'Exactly so.'

He thrust his hand into his frock coat and extracted another candy, small, round and encased in shiny red paper. It looked like one of those toffees they hand out free on aeroplanes.

'May I try one?'

Loki thought for a moment.

'Not today,' he said. 'You're... not calm enough.'

'Are you afraid I might... you know... smash you?'

Loki laughed contemptuously.

'My dear boy! You think the secret's in the sweetie?'

'Well, where is it, then?'

'The death candy can do nothing without the warrior spirit. You know what that is?'

To this I could find no answer.

'Well then,' said Loki, 'write this down.'

I bent over my notebook once again.

'In Hubei Province in China,' Loki commenced dictation, 'are to be found the picturesque Wudang Mountains. The name means "The Warrior's Shield". From ancient times they have been home to Taoists engaged in the practice of martial arts. The most celebrated was Zhang Sanfeng, who had the ability to fly...'

At this point Loki paused, evidently expecting me to ask whether it was true or not that this Zhang Sanfeng could really fly. But I forbore to ask.

'...to this day in the Wudang Mountains you will find many so-called Wushu academies, where gullible tourists come to receive instruction in pretty but ineffectual dances involving swords and staves...'

Here Loki perpetrated a few caricatured movements imitating this style of dance. They did indeed look rather comic.

'Before the Second World War, the true practitioners of Taoist martial arts withdrew further up into the hills, well away from roads, hotels and – ha ha – massage parlours. Not many true masters are left, but there are some. Living far from people as they do, the Tao masters need to acquire the means of survival, and the means in question are extremely important... got that so far? The means are supplied to them by vampires, and as a quid pro quo once a year the greatest Taoist masters donate samples of their red liquid to the vampires... From the resulting preparations vampires distil several varieties of death candy... However, the warrior spirit is also required, because without it the sweets are ineffectual... Have you written all that down? That is all for today.'

All night I tossed and turned in my huge four-poster bed beneath the baldaquin, trying to work out what the 'warrior spirit' could be. I came up with several propositions. The first was that it was, as its name suggested, some form of spirit with which one must make contact. Secondly, it might be some kind of heroic state of consciousness, which needed to be fostered and honed internally over a long period, without recourse to any specifically vampire expedients. This possibility appeared the least attractive to me. Thirdly, the 'warrior spirit' might be linked to a special procedure that altered the physical properties of the body. Without this it was hard to explain how the aging and manifestly unathletic Loki could move his legs with the agility of an amphetamine-fuelled acrobat.

None of the three theories was correct.

The 'warrior spirit', it turned out, was instilled by taking a special sequence of five breaths – alternating long and short. A species of code to activate the candy, it bore some relation to Taoist practices of fine-tuning the body's respiratory centres. Loki did not go deeply into the mechanics of the process – in fact I suspect he did not himself fully understand them. Merely to remember the sequence was enough.

Once I had learned it, Loki allowed me to eat a piece of the fatal confectionery. He warned me that I would not experience any revelatory visions, since the information in the sweet was purified – it was derived not from the Taoist's life but purely from his knowledge of martial arts. I dived into the experiment.

The sweet tasted like a boiled liquorice-flavoured candy. Completing the required sequence of breaths, I felt light-headed and as if my head was spinning round. But that was all. Just as when I had imbibed 'Pasternak + ½ Nabokov', I could not detect any personal information. All memory of the donor had been effaced.

The only discernible effect was that I now had virtuoso control over my body. This new-found ability was, however, undoubtedly most impressive. When I attempted something I had never succeeded in accomplishing as a schoolboy studying karate – the splits – I found, to my amazement, I could now do them with no effort at all. First, I did the splits cross-wise, then length-wise.

Next, I effortlessly repeated the trick that I had found so astonishing when Loki did it: I ran up the wall, did a backwards somersault, and landed on my feet. Loki urged me to attack him, and within a second I unleashed on him such a flurry of blows as I had previously seen only in the cinema (true, none of them reached their target). Once the effect of the sweet had worn off, I could not repeat any of these feats.

The secret of this gutta-percha-like plasticity, Loki explained, was not in the elasticity of the muscles but in their ability instantly to relax. That was what enabled me to do the splits and deliver high kicks with my feet.

'Physiologically speaking,' he said, 'the key is in the nervous impulses sent by the brain to the muscle cells. Even lengthy training has minimal effect on the physical properties of muscles, ligaments and bones. What it can affect is the sequence of nervous signals by which the mechanism is controlled. The death candy acts on this code. An averagely constituted man is, of course, far weaker than a trained fighter, but his physique is, nevertheless, sufficiently developed to be capable of performing the same actions. It is his nervous system that remains inadequate. The same applies to the power of the blow. This depends not only on the specific properties of the fibres in his muscles, but on his ability to concentrate his vital energy. The preparation affords the vampire temporary access to all these skills. However, the technology naturally has its limitations. Even if you were to absorb all a world champion weightlifter's red liquid you would still not be able to lift a 200 kilogram weight.'

I said, 'Are you telling me that when a gymnast subjects his body to a long period of training, he is upgrading his software rather than his hardware?'

'I am not familiar with the jargon of drug culture,' replied Loki.

I now understood why the vampire was bound to adopt the most dishonourable combat tactics of all available options. It was not, as I had at first supposed, an ethical choice so much as a practical necessity. Eating the sweet conferred an extraordinary feeling of confidence, an enjoyable sensation of playing with one's adversary as a cat plays with a mouse. But as soon as the effect wore off, the vampire was defenceless. It was therefore critical not to waste a second of the *death span*, as Loki called it.

According to the rules, a vampire must carry a death candy on his person at all times. Loki gave me a small case and showed me how to get a sweet from it: you press a spring and a sweet ejects straight into your hand. When speed is of the essence, the sweet can be inserted into the mouth immediately without unwrapping – the wrapping is made of special paper. A vampire gets a single death candy as standard issue, which he carries in his belt and is authorised to use only in life-threatening situations.

'Tell me,' I asked Loki, 'do vampires ever barney with one other? I mean, what happens if two of them get into a fight and each has eaten one of these sweets?'

'What do you mean, "barney"?' said Loki. 'Vampires aren't children. If there is a serious issue between two vampires, they resolve it by means of a duel.'

'A duel?' I asked. 'Do such things still exist?'

'In our world they do. But they are rare.'

'What does such a duel look like?'

'I'll tell you next time.'

Next time he brought a long black tube similar to those used for carrying rolled-up plans.

'So,' he said, 'what you need to know about duels ... Over the long history of vampires' existence, quarrels of a personal nature often arose. As a rule, vampires were recruited from the highest strata of society, in which it was the custom to resolve disputes by means of a duel. The practice spread to the vampire community, but following a number of fatal outcomes they were forbidden. The problem was that during a duel it was not only the vampire whose life was at stake, but that of the Tongue. You will have realised that the Tongue has not the smallest cause to be involved in a duel. It would be like two horses kicking each other, while their riders...'

'I see the point,' I interrupted. 'You needn't go on.'

'On the other hand, to ignore the humanitarian needs of the vampire or downgrade his role purely to that of a carrier is also inadmissible. For one thing, a depressive or discontented psychic environment for the human side of the personality has a bad effect on the Tongue's well-being. A compromise was therefore worked out which would allow vampires to clarify their relations without exposing either the Tongue, or by the same token the vampire himself, to the risk of loss of life.'

'But that simply turns the duel into a farce.'

'No it doesn't,' Loki smiled. 'What do you imagine is the point of any duel?'

I shrugged. The answer, I thought, was so obvious it hardly needed spelling out.

'People exchange words intemperately,' said Loki, 'but the words in themselves have no weight. The purpose of the duel is to lend additional weight to the words – a bullet, a blade or poison. The vampires' solution was simple: the duel falls into two parts. In the first part, agreement is reached on precisely what sort of weight is to be added to the words. In the second, it is determined to which of the duellists the relevant consequence is to be directed. A vampire duel is thus similar to a lottery. Do you understand?'

'Not completely, no.'

'In the first stage each participant in the duel writes down what is known as the Duel Order. It contains the details of the penalty to be applied to the defeated opponent. It can be whatever the duellist wishes: amputation of extremities, deprivation of sight or hearing, a flogging in the stables and the like. Penalties are governed purely by the depth of anger of the contesting parties. Their respective seconds are mandated to check that the prescribed penalty will in no way threaten the physical existence of the Tongue. Once they have done so, they must ratify both Duel Orders, after which the duel proper can commence.'

'Do the duellists know in advance what awaits them in the event of their losing?' I enquired.

'They do not,' answered Loki. 'The rules forbid it. Should these rules be breached, the consequences can be most distressing. As happened in the case of the last duel to be fought.'

'How did that end?'

'The losing party had his nose and ears cut off. Afterwards he wore a mask until his death. As a matter of fact he did not live for long.'

A tremor of fear seized me. 'Wait a moment,' I said. 'Who was this loser? What was his name? It wasn't by any chance...?'

'Indeed it was,' replied Loki. 'It was Brahma. His nose and ears were removed by the best plastic surgeon in Moscow, and he suffered no discomfort whatsoever. But after the operation he fell into a depression, and the Tongue was no longer willing to reside in his body.'

'Who was Brahma's adversary?'

'I am not supposed to tell you that,' said Loki. 'But since you ask... his duel was with Mithra.'

'With Mithra?'

'Yes. That is why Mithra was chosen to welcome you to our world. Such is the custom, if a duel results in the death of one of the participants. The victor assumes the responsibility of mentoring the newcomer to whose body the Tongue has transferred. But I beg you not under any circumstances to speak about this with Mithra. To do so would be considered deplorably tactless. Are you quite clear about this?'

I nodded. The news had stunned me.

'That means,' I said, 'that I am here because of Mithra.'

'No,' replied Loki, 'that is not the way to think of it. Mithra will have had no influence whatever on the choice. For that matter, Brahma himself had very little to do with it. Everything is decided by the Tongue.'

'What was the cause of this duel?' I asked.

'Something to do with Brahma's filing cabinet. Brahma was a passionate collector. Mithra borrowed part of his collection for a time, some pornographic rarities I believe, I don't know exactly. He wanted them just for private amusement, but pretended that he needed them for something important. After that there were problems with the collection, either Mithra drank them himself, or they were lost, or he passed them on to someone else – again, I don't know the details. Whatever the case, they disappeared. Brahma was furious, challenged him to a duel, and let it be known that he would have his fingers cut off. When Mithra heard this, he also decided not to let the matter drop... And the rest you know.'

'Is Mithra experienced at fighting duels, then?'

'Experience counts for very little,' said Loki. 'Fate decides everything.'

'What actually happens during a duel? Do they have death sweets?'

'Yes. There is a special duel issue, prepared from the red liquid of the finest fencers or marksmen.'

'What about weapons?'

'Rapiers or pistols,' explained Loki. 'But vampires use special weapons.'

He picked up the tube from table, opened it and took out a rapier.

'Have a look.'

At the point of the steel blade was a brass ball about a centimetre or a centimetre and a half in diameter. From it protruded a short needle.

'Tranquilliser,' said Loki. 'If the weapons are firearms, the pistol fires a syringe with the same substance. It immediately paralyses the penetrated target. He remains conscious, but can neither speak nor move. The tranquilliser maintains its effectiveness for approximately forty hours. During this time the seconds are obliged to see that all the conditions of the Duel Order are carried out. It can be a heavy responsibility for them, as it was in the case of the Mithra-Brahma duel. But it must be pursued to the last particular, even if the victim perishes as a human being...'

The discovery of Mithra's role in my fate turned him into something of an evil genius in my life. On the other hand, it would be difficult – if not impossible – to accuse him of malice aforethought. Loki evidently sensed what was going through my mind.

'Look, don't even think of taking this up with Mithra himself,' he repeated. 'It would not only be *mauvais ton* but quite unacceptable behaviour.'

'I promise,' I replied.

I wanted to learn more about those mysterious Taoists whose red liquid provided the ingredient for the death sweets, and decided to ask Loki about them. My question surprised him.

'Why do you want to know?'

'Just out of interest. Is it really not possible to glimpse anything of their lives?'

Loki shrugged.

'There are some candies where the filtering was not fully effective – rejects, we don't normally use them. But they won't tell you much. Taoists are not ordinary people, after all.'

'Couldn't you give me one?'

He made no reply, and I thought he must have regarded my request as silly. At the next lesson, however, he handed me one of the sweets cut into two.

'This is one of the rejects,' he said. 'It's still got something in it ... You're a strange boy, Rama.'

That evening, when darkness began to fall, I lay on the bed and put both halves of the sweet into my mouth.

Loki was right, there was not a great deal to see. But what I did experience I remembered forever.

The name of the Taoist from whose red liquid the candy had been made was Xiu Beishan (I even understood what the words meant: something like 'permission of northern goodness'). He was more than two hundred years old, and beginning to feel the onset of old age. By the standards of a normal man, he was in outstanding physical shape, but to himself he appeared a senile, good-for-nothing wreck.

He and I together ascended into the Wudang Mountains. Xiu Beishan struggled up to the holy place amidst a crowd of tourists. Disguised as a labourer he was carrying on his yoke two stone blocks used for making a roadway.

I saw red temples with roofs of brilliant green tiles, and enormous tortoises carved out of basalt standing among half-ruined pavilions. We traversed the narrow path of the ridge at the mountaintop, and saw a mountain tarn shimmering far below.

At last the Taoist reached his destination. It was called 'The Place of the Soaring Crags', and it did indeed soar above a precipice. At its highest point a small square had been neatly levelled out and paved with stone. It was a place of the highest power and holiness. Xiu Beishan had come here to receive a sign from the spirits.

Waiting until all the tourists had left to go back down the mountain, he threw down the yoke bearing the stones, and climbed the steps leading up to the exposed altar. There he bowed reverently and awaited the sign.

When it came, the sign from the spirits was strange. From

somewhere far away there flew in a huge butterfly, as big as a bird, with black and brown markings on its dark blue velvet wings. It fluttered around the Taoist before coming to rest on the edge of the altar.

The Taoist gazed longingly at the butterfly for some time, until his attention focussed on the tips of its wings, which were so frayed and tattered as almost to have lost their shape. As soon as the Taoist recognised this, the butterfly rose from its resting place, flew up into the air and disappeared into the green labyrinth between the trees that grew on the edge of the precipice.

For myself I would not have grasped the significance of the sign. But the Taoist understood, and through him, I too understood. As long as the butterfly could still fly, it made no difference how frayed and worn were its wings. But when it was no longer able to fly, there would be no more butterfly. That was all.

The Taoist completed his reverences before the altar, and made his way back down the staircase. I remembered the stone balustrade beside the stairs, with its sculptured flower vases. Some of the steps were made of the same carved slabs, ancient and worn down by thousands upon thousands of feet.

When I came back to myself, I was overcome by melancholy – and a feeling of repugnance that I had become a vampire.

THE FIVE RULES OF LOVE

When Loki said the time had come to study vampire techniques of making love, I imagined something along the lines of the Glamour course, only with the addition of red liquid preparations similar to 'Rudel ZOO'. I envisaged rows of test tubes each containing a three-dimensional, stereoscopic and stereophonic porn film, all of which – so I eagerly anticipated – it would be my job to watch and assimilate...

However, on learning that there would only be one lesson on this subject, I lowered the bar of my expectations. Even so, I thought, this single instructional session would surely prove to be as striking as it would be memorable.

And so it was.

On the appointed day, Loki appeared meticulously shaved and drenched in some kind of vanilla-flavoured eau de cologne. His holdall was twice as bulky as usual; I was curious to know what was in it, but felt I should not ask.

'I must warn you,' said Loki, 'that the curriculum of love-making instruction exists in two different forms, depending on whether the student vampire is a young man or a girl. The two courses have nothing whatsoever in common with one another. Another important point is that everything you will hear is applicable solely to relations with human females and may, in no circumstances, be transferred to vampire females.'

'What would happen were I to fall in love with a vampire woman?' I asked.

Loki shrugged.

'We take no account of such an eventuality. Our concern is purely with human beings. Your relationship to other vampires is a matter for you to work out and to take responsibility for. There's no basic training for recruits on this subject, you know. All right now, take a pen, open your notebook and start writing...'

Loki commenced dictating:

'A vampire's relationship with a member of the female sex is diametrically opposed to the cold cynicism of an ordinary human being. It combines pragmatic rationalism with knightly chivalry... have you got that? The rationalism consists in the vampire dispensing with the false and humiliating procedure of so-called courtship in favour of proceeding straight to the core question. Knightly chivalry consists in freeing the woman from the humiliating need to imitate orgasm, and in always rewarding her for her work...'

'I can't keep up,' I complained.

Loki allowed me to finish writing out the sentence.

'There exist five principles,' he continued, 'which the vampire must abide by in his private life. First, the vampire aims to ensure that the act of love follows immediately on first acquaintance. Second, once the act of love has been brought to completion, the vampire, as a rule, will terminate his acquaintance with the woman. Third, the vampire always pays the woman for her services. Fourth, the vampire does not generally bite a woman with whom he has sexual contact. Fifth and most important, the vampire must always prevent the woman from simulating orgasm...'

'I'm not following this,' I said, tearing myself away from my notebook. 'Is the vampire acting chivalrously in removing from the woman the obligation to imitate an orgasm, or is he actively preventing her from doing so?'

'They are one and the same thing.'

'How so?'

Loki favoured me with a long, searching look.

'Rama,' he said with peculiar emphasis, 'let us speak openly, man to man.'

'Fine by me,' I agreed.

'We will call things by their proper names. The concerted, synchronous genital orgasm of a man and a woman engaged in the sexual act is a beautiful but unattainable ideal, like the communist society of the future. The vampire must always keep in mind that female lovemaking behaviour is motivated economically and socially. It has been forged over the centuries, and a few decades of formal equality will not be enough to change anything.'

'You're always talking about the theoretical aspect,' I objected. 'Can't you tell me what it all means in practical terms?'

'I can. If after the third frictional movement a woman starts breathing heavily, rolls her eyes and cries out unnaturally, it follows that she is behaving mendaciously and is engaged in a social enterprise while her partner is occupied with a biological one. And whenever the individual lying beside a vampire is at work on her social project, it behoves the vampire to be on his guard.'

'But what possible advantage can a woman derive from simulating an orgasm?' I enquired. 'I really don't understand this.'

'You don't understand because you are thinking like a human being.'

This rebuke was like treading on my corns. I lowered my eyes in apologetic confusion.

'I'll explain,' said Loki in his best homiletic vein. 'We are least inclined to love those who have done good to us. The people we love are those to whom we ourselves have done good. And the more good we have done them, the more we want to do. It is a psychological rule, and Woman has been parasitically exploiting it for millennia. Her aim in imitating continuous multiple orgasms is to persuade the vampire that up to this point he has been making her happy, and to motivate him to continue making her happy. Surely you can see that? We're talking about an investment programme. The more heavily she breathes and the more loudly she moans, the greater the return she hopes to secure. For the vampire it is vital to nip this in the bud.'

I remembered Mithra alerting me to the veil of dissimulation that should surround the vampire's sexual masquerades. Nevertheless, pure devilry made me raise another objection.

'It seems to me...'

But Loki was already tired of my obstinacy.

'For the *particularly obtuse*,' he broke in, raising his voice, 'one has to use the simplest terms. *Do not allow the woman to simulate orgasm because this is the first step to taking away your money*. Is that clear enough now?'

I nodded, abashed.

'If the simulated orgasm is terminated at the outset,' continued Loki, 'you have a chance of building a relationship based on humanity. And since vampires are humane beings, that is their objective. Noted?'

'Noted,' I replied. 'But why should a vampire pay a woman for her services?'

'They say the only place where you can find free cheese is a mousetrap,' replied Loki. 'The same is true of sex. By the way, that's something else you should write down.'

I wrote the rubric down in my notebook, dotting it with a good, fat full stop.

'Good,' said Loki. 'That concludes the theoretical part.'

Delving into his holdall, he extracted from it a flesh-coloured package and a blue compressed air canister from which protruded a short rubber tube. Inserting the hose into the rubber bundle, Loki turned a black lever on the canister. I heard a loud hissing noise and in the space of a few seconds, the package swelled up, unfurling into the shape of a somewhat shopworn inflatable woman with long straw-coloured hair tumbling over her shoulders.

She had wide open blue eyes with thick eyelashes and a ready-for-anything scarlet mouth with a round hole in the middle. Loki gave her plenty of pressure, so that she appeared pretty plump. It was obvious that that she had been used to instruct several generations of vampires because she was covered with a palimpsest of stains and black marks, like footprints. There were also many inscriptions, like those with which schoolboys are wont to cover their desks. Prominent among the latter, on one of her thighs, was a couplet which, judging by the traces on the surface of the rubber, there had been repeated but unsuccessful attempts to erase:

She loved me for the dangers I had pass'd
And I subjected her to anal sex.

Seeing me staring at the thigh with the verse, Loki turned the woman over so that it was hidden.

'Let us address the practical methodology,' he announced.

'Eh-h-h ... in what sense of the word?'

'The direct sense.'

He kneeled down in front of the rubber woman and turned towards me. In his hands appeared a death candy, which he unwrapped and popped into his mouth.

'Confronted with the problem I described to you,' he began,

'vampires had no need to reinvent the wheel. They make use of the techniques of unarmed single combat. It is, incidentally, precisely for that reason that the arts of combat and love are linked together in one course. The vampire's innate humanism manifests itself in ensuring that aborting the fake orgasm is achieved exclusively by means that will not damage the health of the partner...'

Loki leant forwards over the rubber woman, supporting himself by resting his elbows on the floor. His face suffused with blood, and it occurred to me that a similar effect could have resulted from a sudden surge of passion.

In an abrupt but deft movement, he raised himself and hit the doll with his right knee. He then repeated the movement using his left knee. Next, he poked her in the middle of the stomach with his elbow, followed by jabbing his finger into the base of her neck. Finally, he slapped her ears with the palms of his hands.

It was an oddly unpleasant spectacle – a tall, thin man, dressed in black, lying on top of an inflatable woman and thrashing her with rapid but not particularly hard kicks and blows... Loki's motions were executed with extraordinary professionalism, even artistry; and I am sure that he could convincingly have appeared on stage with this routine in a surrealist theatre of some sort. All the same, it did occur to me that his actions were being invested with rather more emotion than was strictly needed for instructional purposes.

'Tell me,' I asked, surprising myself by saying such a thing, 'have you ever been in love with anyone?'

He froze.

'What's that you said?' he asked in bafflement, turning his flushed and burning face to me.

'No, no,' I muttered, 'nothing. I just...'

Loki got up, brushed an invisible speck of dust from his black jacket, and said, 'Your turn now.'

I looked at the inflated woman. For some reason I was anxious to postpone the moment of engagement for as long as I could.

'I have one more question,' I said, 'regarding point four. Why must the vampire not bite a woman with whom he has sex? Is this too a matter of knightly courtesy?'

'Yes, but not only that,' replied Loki. 'The most important reason is that after biting a woman several times, the vampire loses all interest in the woman as an object of desire. It has been observed many times. At all events, I have never come across any exception to the rule...'

He crossed his arms over his breast and fixed his gaze into the distance, as if recalling something long forgotten.

'Quite the opposite, in fact,' he continued. 'If desire for a woman reaches intolerable levels, the vampire can bite her repeatedly in order to learn the secrets of her soul and thus be cured of his obsession. This always helps. But if the vampire has other plans in mind, of course, he would not do so...'

Loki looked again at the rubber woman on the floor, and I realised that he was not to be further deflected from the matter in hand.

'Well, then, to work. You must learn the proper strokes. Let's go...'

I lowered myself to the starting position. The rubber woman stared with her blue eyes impersonally past me at the ceiling. If she felt anything at all, she was successfully hiding it from me.

'Raise yourself on your elbows,' said Loki. 'Shift your weight to the knees... Higher... Now give her a kick with your knee on to her side. Yes, that's right, excellent. Only be careful not to hit too hard with your left leg, you could damage her liver. It won't matter if you hit harder with the right knee. That's right. Well done! Now let's practise the elbow blows...'

The subject of the lesson was, of course, relentlessly practical, yet some aspects of the proceedings did stimulate my imagination. Each time I struck the doll, her head jerked up and then fell back, as if she were soundlessly laughing at my efforts – or even, to spite the whole world, simulating an orgasm.

I decided not to look at her face and averted my gaze. Then it seemed to me that I was lying on an inflatable lilo sculling in a desperate race with the rest of humanity towards shores of bliss beyond the far horizon, where awaiting the speediest rowers would be the rewards of sun, happiness, money and love.

THE GREAT FALL

The weather next day was beautiful but at the same time carried overtones of menace. A strong wind and a kind of bracing chill in the air were perhaps harbingers of autumn. The sun came out, then disappeared behind clouds, then reappeared again. I opened the window in the sitting room, fastened the casements back on the hooks attached to the walls and, on impulse, lit candles even though it was quite light. The draught of air coming into the room made the candle flames flicker, and this gave me much pleasure.

Mithra rang up towards evening to ask how things were going. I gave an account of Loki's lesson the previous day. It seemed to cheer Mithra up.

'I told you this is a taboo subject among the older generation. Just as they never use the word "blood". You understand this is not about faked orgasms, it's all about dissembling. Those spine-shattering methods Loki teaches should not be taken seriously though. A true gentleman would never kick a woman during sexual intercourse.'

'What would a gentleman do?' I asked.

'It's all according to personal taste. Personally, I put a pistol or a razor on the bedside table.'

I could not work out if Mithra was serious or not. In any case, what he said next caused me to forget about everything else.

'I've rung you for a reason,' he said. 'Today's the day for the Great Fall...'

A cold shiver ran through my whole body, starting in the region of the solar plexus and spreading rapidly to every single nerve ending. It was as though someone inside me had turned on an ice-cold shower.

'What? Already? So soon?'

Mithra laughed.

'First you can't wait for it to happen, now it's too soon... Anyhow, don't worry. There's nothing too terrifying about it.'

'What do I have to do?'

'Nothing at all. Just wait. A courier will come soon with a package for you, and the instructions will be inside.'

'Could I give you a ring back when I've got it?' I asked. 'In case I have any questions?'

'You won't have any questions,' replied Mithra. 'That is, unless you think them up specially. You won't need to ring me. I'll meet you.'

'Where?'

'You'll see,' said Mithra, and rang off.

I replaced the handset and sat on the sofa.

The one thing I knew for certain was that I wanted no part in any Great Fall. All I wanted was to sit quietly and calm down. I hoped that some great, ingenious idea would come into my mind and save me from my situation. I had no doubt that such an idea existed, and all I needed to take it in was a few minutes of concentration. I closed my eyes.

At that moment there was a ring at the door.

I got up and forced myself to make my doom-laden way to the door.

But no one was there – only a small, black casket lying on the floor. I picked it up, carried it into the living room and put it on the table. Then I went into the bathroom; for some reason I felt I ought to take another shower.

I washed myself thoroughly and combed my hair, anointing it with some gel. Then I went into the bedroom and dressed in my best outfit, an ensemble consisting of jacket, shirt and trousers I had bought complete off a mannequin in the LovemarX shop.

I had now exhausted all ploys to delay the moment of truth. Returning to the living room, I opened the casket.

Inside, on a red velvet lining, was a small dark glass vessel in the shape of a bat with folded wings. In the place of its head was a stopper shaped like a skull. There was also a sheet of paper on which was written:

Rama,

    Please take a couple of minutes to commit to memory the salutation which by tradition the novice vampire is expected to pronounce. It is very simple: 'Rama the Second reporting to Heartland!' I trust you will not find it too difficult.

    You may ask: why Rama the Second? Again by tradition, on solemn ritual occasions a number is added to the vampire's name, taking the place of a surname. I, for instance, am Enlil the Seventh. This does not, of course, mean that there have been six Enlils before me, nor that there has been only one Rama before you. There have been many, many more. But for the sake of brevity we use only the final figure of the next number in the sequence. Enlil the Eleventh will become once more Enlil the First.

    Keep calm and do not worry. All will be well.

    Good luck!

    Enlil

I studied the small flask. Presumably I would find further instructions in its contents. I vaguely remembered having heard something about the Heartland Theory as a semi-mythical geopolitical fetish interminably masticated at round-table brainstorming sessions in the editorial rooms of nationalist-orientated newspapers whenever it was felt necessary to justify to the sponsors where their money was being spent. I never did quite understand the meaning of the term. Most likely those participating in the brainstorming didn't either.

What could it mean in the present context? Some secret place, perhaps, connected with the heart? Presumably it was a metaphor. Well, there are all kinds of metaphors, I thought. You could find yourself locked in a room with some homeless bum and someone tells you, 'You want to be a vampire? Go on then, slit his chest open and eat his heart...' Heartland might be something of the sort. And what would I do then?

I heard a harsh, peremptory voice coming from the room saying:

'We'll know soon enough.'

It was my voice; I realised I must have spoken these words. And there was something else, something very strange. I knew myself to be shaking with fear, a mass of doubt, yet there were my hands firmly taking hold of the flask and withdrawing the crystal skull-shaped stopper. While part of me was still pleading for yet more time to begin the procedure, the Tongue had already assumed command.

The flask contained precisely one drop of liquid. I put it into my mouth and carefully rubbed it into my palate with my tongue.

Nothing.

I concluded that the preparation was going to take some time to produce its effect, and sat down on the sofa. Then I remembered the phrase Enlil Maratovich had asked me to memorise, and ran through it several times under my breath: 'Rama the

Second reporting to Heartland! Rama the Second reporting to Heartland!'

After a minute I was confident that whatever the circumstances I would never forget the words, and ceased to mutter them. At that point I heard the music.

Somewhere someone was playing Verdi's *Requiem* (by now I could often recognise pieces of classical music and never failed to amaze myself with my wide knowledge of works in the genre). Whoever it was must be listening to it on the floor above mine ... or perhaps it was through the wall – it was hard to pinpoint exactly where the sound was coming from. It seemed to me that the music, rather than the wind, was fluttering the curtains.

I relaxed and began to listen.

Whether because of the majestic music, or the evening light flickering tremulously through the curtains, the impression grew on me that strange developments were taking place in the world outside. A thought came across my mind that it had assumed the features of a *dream kingdom*, and this was odd because I had never experienced a *dream kingdom* for myself, only read about them in fairy tales. I did not actually know what they were supposed to look like. Nevertheless, I sensed that the geometry of the antique furniture, the rhomboid figurations of the parquet floor and the tiled fireplace surround were all ideally configured to correspond to a dreamscape ... perhaps I felt so because I was myself drifting towards sleep.

The last thing I needed just now was to crash out and miss the most important event of my life. Rousing myself, I began to pace up and down the room. Then it occurred to me that I might already be asleep and only dreaming that I was walking up and down the room.

That was the moment when I was seized by real fear. It occurred to me that the flask might have contained poison.

140

Perhaps I had not gone to sleep but was dying, and everything I was experiencing was no more than the final firings of the synapses in my brain. The thought was unendurable. Surely, I thought, if I were asleep, the terror would jerk me into wakefulness? But at once I felt that my fear was much too feeble to be able to do that, thus proving that I must be, in fact, asleep.

Or dead.

For death, I knew, was simply sleep that sank second by second deeper and deeper, a sleep from which one was, on wakening, no longer where one had been before but somewhere else, in a different dimension. And who could tell how long the sleep, the dream, would last?

Could it be that my whole career as a vampire had so far been no more than death, which I was struggling to conceal from myself for as long as possible? And would the 'great event' I was expecting prove to be the moment when I would ultimately be forced to face up to the truth and admit it to myself?

Try as I might, I could not rid my mind of the chilling supposition. On the contrary, I grew ever more convinced that I had hit upon the dreadful truth. I remembered reading that in every era vampires had been regarded as the living dead: by day they lay, cold and grey, in their graves, rising from them at night to heat their gelid bodies with a drink of warm blood... Was it possible that in order to become fully a vampire, one must die? And that single drop of clear liquid below the crystal skull had been the final passport to the new world?

I knew that if I were indeed dead, there was no limit to how extreme the terror could become. It could be with me for all eternity, for time is, after all, subjective. These final sparks of the brain's electrochemical activity could appear to my mind to be anything at all: there would be nothing to stop them lasting for many millions of years. Perhaps this was indeed how everything ended? The red and yellow glow of the sunset, the wind, the fireplace, the parquet – and eternal death... and people know nothing of this horror, because no one has returned to inform them.

'*Libera me, Dómine, de morte ætérna...*' intoned the far-off voice.

Was I really hearing someone playing Verdi in the flat above mine? Or was my dying brain transforming into music the unbearable knowledge of my fate?

I knew that if I did not make the supreme effort to rouse myself from this sleep, I would fall for ever into the black well where it would no longer matter whether I was awake or dreaming, because the naked gleam of the horror now before me was deeper than sleep, deeper than dream, deeper than vigil, deeper than anything I could ever know. The most amazing part of it all was that the entrance to this trap lay in full view for everyone to see, the path to it plainly marked by the simplest and most commonplace chain of deduction. It was incredible how everyone without exception manages to avoid this mortal spiral of the mind, from which there is no escape.

This, I thought, *is death for all eternity? This is what they are singing about... No, that cannot be. I will find my way out of it, no matter what the cost!*

It was crucial to do something to combat the paralysis that was engulfing me. I tried to tear myself free from the nightmare integument with my hands, as if it was a physical substance.

Suddenly I became aware that they were not my hands. Where they had been I saw something like black rags covered in short, shiny fur like a mole's. My fingers were bunched together in dark, stumpy, calloused fists with disproportionately large, horny knuckles such as might belong to a fanatical karate freak. I tried to unclench them but failed, because something was preventing them from opening; it was as if the fingers were bound together with surgical tape. I redoubled my efforts, and suddenly my wrists did unfurl, but not into ordinary human palms with five fingers. They were now like two black umbrellas. I looked at my fingers and realised I no longer had any.

In their place were long bony extensions joined by a membrane of skin. The only recognisable remnant was the thumb, which now stuck out from the wing like the barrel of a gun on an aeroplane. It ended in a sharp, curved nail about the thickness of a bayonet. I turned towards the mirror, already knowing what I would see there.

My face had turned into a wrinkled muzzle, a fantastic amalgam of hog and bulldog with a split lower lip and nose, resembling a concertinae'd snout. I now possessed huge cone-shaped ears with a multitude of complicated folds and partitions inside them, and a low forehead overgrown with black fur. A long horn, sharply bent backwards, towered above my head. I was quite low in stature, with a shaggy, barrel-shaped torso and short, bowed legs. Most repellent of all were my eyes, which were small, cunning, pitiless and radiated a kind of knowing cynicism – like those of a corrupt cop from a Moscow market.

This snout I had seen before, in the photograph of the vampire bat *Desmodus rotundus*, except that the bat lacked the horn proboscis. All the same, I had definitely become a bat, albeit a very large one.

To be frank, I now bore a strong resemblance to a devil. But no sooner had the idea entered my head than I realised that I must have stopped short of full devildom because I was deriving no pleasure in the transformation. And then again, I thought, this too was probably irrelevant: it was quite possible that devils did not like being devils at all.

My outspread wings were getting caught up in the furniture, and I folded them. To accomplish this I had to make a considerable effort to clench what had formerly been my fingers.

The wings, like two umbrellas, closed themselves up into black cylinders culminating in hard fist-like ferrules.

I tried to take a step forward, but found I was unable to. Walking was obviously a specialised form of motion. To shift my position I now had to support myself with my ferrule-fists on the floor and advance my soft rear paws to a new vantage point. I supposed this must be approximately how a gorilla moves.

I became aware that I had stopped thinking. My mind no longer generated random thoughts: it was as though the internal space where they had previously congregated had been vacuumed clean. All that remained was an acute, penetrating knowledge of what was taking place around me.

In addition to this extra-sensitive feeling of presence, I was aware of something I had never previously experienced. I existed in more than just the present. Immediate reality was also permeated with flashing images of possible futures, which modified and renewed themselves with every breath I took. I could choose between different versions of events that were about to happen. I cannot think of a good analogy to explain the process except perhaps the liquid crystal gunsight through which a fighter pilot sees the world outside his aircraft, able simultaneously to assess the different sources of information he requires. This gunsight was my own consciousness.

I sensed the presence of other people. There were two in the flat above mine. Three more were on my floor, and two on the floor below. Physically I could have approached any of them with a few leaps and flaps of my wings, but I had no desire to do so. I wanted to get out to the fresh air, which I could easily do by leaving the flat through the window, or the door, or...

I could not believe that this was really possible, but instinct persuaded me it was. My mind plotted out for me something like a green dotted line disappearing into the depths of the fireplace and then turning upwards, away out into the future. I aligned myself with this dotted line; in front of my eyes flashed the bars of the grate, then the bricks, then the soot inside the chimney and some kind of metal clamp. Then I saw the lead flashing of the roof, and the evening sky.

Only in a dream would it be possible to move with such airy fluidity. I knew I should fly westwards, where I would be met. It was easy to change direction: all I had to do was bank my body in the air and head off accordingly.

I could feel birds and insects hanging in the ether. They appeared after the whistling breaths my lungs automatically expelled after each flap of my wings. Each out-breath refreshed my view of the world, much as a windscreen-wiper clears the smeary haze left by wind and rain. Beneath me were houses, cars, people, but I knew no one could see me. No longer was I afraid that I had died; my earlier fear now appeared to me absurd. On the other hand, in the real world I would never have been able to exit my house through the chimney. Ergo, I was dreaming.

But in the world where I now found myself there was at least one other being who was sharing my dream with me. I realised this because of a distant cry, which exactly matched my own. It immediately rendered the world clearer and brighter, as if another sun had appeared to illuminate it. Someone similar to myself was approaching. I flew towards him, and was soon flying alongside.

What the vampire in flight most reminded me of was a pig with webbed wings. They did not sprout from the back, as images in churches depict devils and angels, but were stretched between the front paws and the rear paws. Where they joined the body they were covered with short black hair. The front paws were very long and their enormous fingers, webbed with skin, spread out to make the fan that formed a large section of the wing.

'Welcome,' said the creature.

'Good evening,' I responded.

'Don't you recognise me?' asked the creature. 'I'm Mithra.'

We conversed not with voices but in another medium. It was not telepathy, because I had no idea what Mithra was thinking. We exchanged phrases made up of words, but without uttering sounds. It was more like subtitles being transmitted directly into the mind.

'How was your flight?' enquired Mithra, casting a sidelong glance from olive-like eyes set deep in their sockets behind thickets of fur.

'Fine. Can we be seen from people's windows?'

'No.'

'Why not?'

'Watch out!' Mithra swerved to the right to avoid the corner of a Gazprom tower. I barely managed to replicate his manoeuvre. Once I was sure there were no further obstacles ahead, I repeated my question.

'How is it we can't be seen?'

'Ask Enlil,' replied Mithra. 'He'll explain it to you.'

That told me where we were going.

It was already getting dark. Soon we left the city behind; below us appeared and disappeared dark patches of forest, then we lost height and plunged into a thick mist. Before long I could no longer see anything with my eyes, not even Mithra who was flying just a few metres in front of me. However, I had no difficulty in orientating myself.

After leaving behind us a road with cars passing along it, for a long time nothing was below us except trees, mostly pines. Then there were fences and country houses of various different shapes and sizes. I was not apprehending them by vision, but was in a way touching them, except that the tactile sensation came not from my limbs or my fingers but, strangely, from the crics I was uttering. Similar sounds were coming from Mithra flying beside me, and they reinforced my spatial perception with stereoscopic confidence. I could 'see' every tile on a roof, every pine needle, every pebble on the ground. But I had no sense of colour, nor any visual information reaching me through my eyes, as a result of which the world appeared to me as a uniformly grey computer model, a three-dimensional simulacrum of itself.

'Where are we?' I asked Mithra.

'Round about Rublevka.'

'Of course. That's where the responsible elites live... Where else?... And what's this thick fog we seem to be in? I've never experienced anything like it.'

Mithra didn't answer. And suddenly, for the second time that day, I was seized by the icy grip of terror.

I could sense a hole in the ground. It was directly on our flight path.

Had I been looking at the ground with my normal human eyes I would probably not have noticed anything amiss. The area was entirely surrounded by trees while around the hole itself was a fence, which supported a camouflage netting with a thick layer of plastic leaves (I knew they were artificial because they were all of identical shape and size). Even had I looked at the sloping ground beneath the masking net, I would probably have taken it for a ravine and thought nothing of it. There are probably any number of ravines dotted about the countryside near Moscow, covered over with camouflage netting.

However, I was seeing it not with my eyes but with my echo-location apparatus, and to me it appeared as a tear in the very fabric of the earth. My cries went into it but did not return. It seemed that below its mouth the abyss widened out, although I could not be sure of this – the chasm was too deep; so deep that it filled me with dread. Perhaps it was not purely a matter of fathomless depth, but something else? At all events it was the last place on earth I wanted to go anywhere near, but Mithra was heading straight for it.

Entirely hidden by the netting, the pit resembled a flattened human heart – the outline one sees in comics. Or perhaps, I realised with a sinking feeling, the fan made of palm leaves on the wall above my childhood bed... All the way round the pit was the high, blank wall I had noticed from far off. But now it was clear that it comprised three different sections of fencing around three separate plots of private land. Together they formed a complete barrier without the smallest chink anywhere. There was no way the pit could be approached from the ground.

'Be careful now,' commanded Mithra. 'Do exactly as I do.'

Bending his wings back, he descended to the edge of the net, slowed his speed almost to a standstill, skilfully regrouped while hovering in the air, then dived under the edge of the net. I followed him and, just shaving the grass that grew round the edge of the pit, fell into the void.

Inside it was chilly. Here and there, growing out of the rock walls, were bushes and clumps of grass. The air smelled of the smoke from a fire of juniper wood, or something like it. I sensed many openings and cracks in the rock face. All I could see was a single light down below in the sheer wall of the precipice.

'Do you see the lamp?' asked Mithra. 'Head for it.'

'Will I be able to find it on my own?'

'You can't really get lost in here. Anyhow, you're not alone now...'

I was about to ask him what he meant, but he was already flying back up, away from me. At this point I noticed that another vampire had appeared in the shaft. He passed Mithra at the opening into the chasm and was now descending.

I realised that I would have to alight somewhere, and fast, because the shaft was too narrow for two bodies to fly safely side by side. Even for one it was awkward. I circled about like a swimmer in a pool, first to one side then to the other, losing height all the time.

Before long I had got down to the source of the light. It was shaded by a semi-circular arch, and in front of it was a small platform over the abyss, on which shone the yellow electric lamp. Here, evidently, was where I should land.

I had to fly several times backwards and forwards over the fissure, working out how I would be able to do this. The other vampire's wings were swishing only a few metres above me, and I was seriously concerned lest we crash into one another. There was no time to waste, and I decided I must trust my instincts.

Positioning myself directly above the platform, I slowed until I came to a complete stop in the air, furled my wings into fists and collapsed on to their bony knuckles. The manoeuvre was quite skilfully executed, but the resultant pose was somewhat melodramatic, as if I was praying on my knees before an altar. Almost at once the second vampire, with a rustle of wings, landed alongside. I turned my head but could see no more than his black silhouette.

All around was dark, damp and silent. Before us was the arch cut into the rock, and within it the feeble light of the electric bulb shining through a yellow glass shade in the form of an orange cut into quarters. Rather than dispelling the gloom it accentuated it. Beneath the lamp was a door, coloured so as to blend with the rock, so that I only noticed it when it began slowly to open inwards.

No one, however, was to be seen in the small rectangular entranceway. For a few seconds I hesitated, unsure whether to wait for an invitation or to proceed. Then I remembered the salutation I had been bidden to pronounce. Evidently this was the time to say it. I said it over to myself once or twice in order not to make any mistake, and then said loudly:

'Rama the Second reporting to Heartland!'

As soon as I had spoken the phrase I realised I had done so in my normal human voice. I looked at my hands and saw regular human fists pressing against the stone floor. My best jacket was all torn at the sleeve, the elbows spattered with soot. Not only that, there was a fresh scratch on my left wrist. I straightened my legs and stood upright.

'Hera the Eighth reporting to Heartland!'

I turned my head. Beside me stood the girl who had sent me her photograph. She was taller than I had thought, slim, wearing dark trousers and an equally muted t-shirt. I recognised her flamboyantly piled up shock of hair.

'Well now, my young friends,' came the voice of Enlil Maratovich out of the darkness, 'since you have arrived, welcome to my humble hamlet.'

And the lights came on in the room before us.

MIND 'B'

There was not a stick of furniture in Enlil Maratovich's hamlet, except for a stepladder. The setting was extremely ascetic: cushions of an indeterminate grey colour on the floor and a circular fresco in similarly depressing muted tones, depicting the funeral of an unknown knight accompanied on his final journey by a multitude of worthy gentlemen in lace collars, the deceased himself encased in a suit of black armour with a cleft breastplate, above which hovered a brilliant blue mosquito as big as a well-fed crow.

At approximately the height of my shoulders was a wide copper hoop attached to the ceiling by three rods. It took up almost all of the room. My first impression of this metal ring was that it was a very, very old object.

Enlil Maratovich was hanging head downwards, his legs hooked over the hoop and his arms crossed over his breast. He had on a tracksuit of thick black jersey. The black hood hung down and looked absurdly like the sort of fantastic stand-up collar ruff the Mosfilm costume department might pick out for a vampire.

'You look like one of the mobile vampires,' said Hera.

'What?' said Enlil Maratovich in some surprise.

'There was an advertisement on television a little while ago, about vampires who only use their mobiles at night so as to economise on the daytime tariff. During the day they sleep with their heads pointing down, like bats.'

Enlil Maratovich gave a snort of derision.

'As far as I know,' he said, 'vampires don't economise on tariffs. Vampires economise on advertising.'

'Allow me to disagree with you, Enlil Maratovich,' said Hera. 'I think ... that is to say, I am sure, that a PR campaign has been running now for some years aimed at rehabilitating the image of vampires. Those mobile vampires I mentioned are just one example. Any fool could see that it was really advertising vampires, not mobile phone tariffs ... to say nothing of the treatment vampires get from Hollywood.'

I could see exactly what she meant, and she was right. All sorts of instances came to my mind to confirm what she had said. For some unknown reason people seem anxious to ideal-ise us vampires. We are portrayed as exquisite connoisseurs, melancholy romantics, pensive dreamers – but always with a marked undercurrent of sympathy. Vampire roles are taken by good-looking actors, popstars are happy to appear as vampires in their music videos. Celebrities in the West and in the East see nothing shameful in appearing as vampires. It is most odd: sexual abusers of minors and gravestone vandals are much closer to the man in the street than we are, but in the world of human culture generally you will not find a shred of sympathy for them, while vampires are drenched by a positive outpouring of understanding and love ... Only now did I see what it all meant. It was incredible that I had not worked it out for myself.

'Yes, that is indeed how things are,' said Enlil Maratovich. 'Vampires all over the world regularly chip in to support yet another vampire movie, the idea being to put people off the scent of who is actually drinking their red liquid, or how it is done. But of course this cannot go on for ever. The day will come when the symphony of man and vampire can no longer be kept secret. And against that day we need to groom public opinion.'

I decided the moment was right for me to put the question that had been bothering me.

'Tell me please, Enlil Maratovich, our flight here... was that the Great Fall?'

'No.'

It was not the answer I had been expecting.

Enlil Maratovich smiled.

'The Great Fall is when you learn what I am about to explain to you today. For this reason it would be desirable for your heads to be functioning at their best, so I suggest you get yourselves into position.'

He indicated the hoop.

The copper ring had a soft padded cover of clear plastic, similar to a chin-up bar in a gym. I waited until Hera had got off the ladder (I had wanted to give her a hand but she managed it very adroitly on her own), then climbed up and hung on the ring myself with my head downwards. The blood rushed to my head, but I found the sensation pleasant and calming.

Hera was hanging directly opposite me, her eyes closed, the yellow light from the lamp falling on her. Her t-shirt hung down, exposing her belly button.

'Like it?' enquired Enlil Maratovich, addressing me.

I quickly averted my eyes.

'Like what?'

'Hanging like this.'

'Yes,' I said. 'More than I thought I would. Is it because of the flow of, er, red liquid into the Tongue?'

'Exactly. Whenever a vampire needs to gather his strength quickly and concentrate his energy, it is the best method.'

He was right. With each passing second I felt better. The

energy I had expended during the flight was restored. Hanging upside down was as comfortable as sitting in an easy chair near the fire.

'You are going to learn a secret today,' said Enlil Maratovich. 'But I imagine you have quite a few questions stored up. Perhaps it would be a good idea to start with them?'

'Well, could you tell us what our flight was?' I asked.

'It was a flight.'

'I mean, was it all a dream? A special kind of trance? Or did it all happen for real? What would an onlooker have seen?'

'The most important condition of that journey,' replied Enlil Maratovich, 'is that there should be no onlooker.'

'That's just what I don't understand,' I said. 'We were flying past houses all the time, in fact I very nearly crashed into one. But Mithra told me that we could not be seen by anyone. How can that be?'

'You've heard of stealth technology? This is something similar. Except that vampires absorb attention rather than radio waves.'

'So would we have been visible to radar while we were in the air?'

'To whose radar?'

'Well, generally.'

'The question has no meaning. Even if you had been visible to radar, the radar screen would not have been visible to anyone at the time.'

'I wonder if we could change the subject?' said Hera.

'Agreed,' replied Enlil Maratovich.

'I've had an idea,' continued Hera. 'I think I know where the Tongue lived before it took up residence in people.'

'Where?'

'In that huge bat which, until a few minutes ago, I was.'

Enlil Maratovich grunted approvingly.

'Our name for her is "Mighty Bat". That is how we usually

refer to her in English. Be careful, though, not to call her "Mighty Mouse" when you talk to our American friends. They tend to take offence, and it's not much help to explain that in Russian the same word does duty for both animals. That's their culture, nothing you can do about it.'

'Was my guess right?' asked Hera.

'Yes and no.'

'What does that mean?'

'You cannot actually say that the Tongue lived in the Mighty Bat. A very long time ago, many millions of years, it *was* the Bat. At that time dinosaurs roamed the earth, and their red liquid was the Mighty Bat's food. That is the origin of the phrase "The Cry of the Mighty Bat"... Think for a moment how amazing it is: when you bite a person today, you are giving him or her the very same command that aeons ago had the power to deprive a huge mountain of flesh of the will to resist. I simply cannot get my head round this incredible fact – it makes me want to fall to my knees and pray...'

I wanted to ask to which deity Enlil Maratovich would offer up his prayers, but could not quite bring myself to. Instead I asked him:

'Are there any fossil records of these enormous bats in the rocks? Have their skeletons survived?'

'No.'

'Why not?'

'They were too intelligent. They cremated their dead, as humans do nowadays. Another reason is that there were not very many of them, because they were at the top of the food pyramid.'

'When did they reach this position?' I asked.

'Vampires were always at the apex of the food pyramid. They were the first intelligent civilisation on earth. It was not a civilisation that constructed a material culture – buildings, industry

155

and so on. But that does not meant they were undeveloped – quite the reverse. From today's standpoint they may be termed ecologically advanced.'

'What happened to this civilisation?'

'It was destroyed by a global catastrophe sixty-five million years ago when our planet was struck by the asteroid that resulted in the Gulf of Mexico. The land was swamped by giant tsunamis that washed away all living creatures. But the Mighty Bat managed to survive by taking to the air. You can still hear an echo of those days in the Bible: "And the earth was without form, and void. And the Spirit of God moved upon the face of the waters".'

'Fabulous,' I said, for no other reason than to say something.

'Dust blackened the sky. It was cold and dark. In the space of just a few years almost the entire food chain perished. Dinosaurs became extinct. Dependent on their red liquid for sustenance, the Mighty Bat was also threatened by extinction. But vampires succeeded in extracting from themselves their own essence, in the form that today we call the "Tongue". You can think of it as something like the self's external memory card, the core of the brain, a kind of worm, ninety per cent of which consists of nerve cells. This receptacle for individual selfhood lodged in the crania of other creatures better adapted to the new conditions of life, and entered into a symbiotic relationship with them. I probably don't need to go into the details?'

'We already know that,' I muttered. 'What sort of creatures did they dwell in?'

'For a long period we lived in large predators, such as the sabre-toothed tiger and other big cats. Our culture was at that time, well... ah... somewhat alarming. Heroic and violent, you might say. We were terrible, magnificent and cruel. But you cannot be magnificent and cruel for ever, and approximately half a million years ago there was a kind of a revolution in the world of vampires...'

The term 'revolution' had frequently cropped up in Discourse, and could apparently mean almost anything you wanted it to. I thought of the most recent contexts in which I could remember it being used.

'Do you mean something like the Orange Revolution in Kiev? Or something more like the Volvo Revolution?'

'Hmm,' said Enlil Maratovich uncertainly, 'not quite. It was more akin to a religious conversion. As I mentioned, vampires set themselves the task of changing over from stock-raising to a form of dairy husbandry. They decided to create a milch animal for their needs. The result was the appearance of mankind.'

'How did they do this?'

'In the same way as humans bred dogs or sheep.'

'By artificial selection?'

'Yes. But not before a whole succession of genetic modifications had been carried out. And it was not the first such experiment. The Mighty Bat had already been responsible for the appearance of warm-blooded creatures, which were designed as vehicles for raising the temperature of red liquid to an optimum level. But the development of the human being represented a category leap to a new species.'

'What species was the human being bred from?' enquired Hera. 'From primates?'

'Yes.'

'Where? And when?'

'It took quite a long time. The final genetic modification occurred 180,000 years ago in Africa. That is where modern man came from.'

'How was this artificial selection achieved?' asked Hera. 'I mean, when cattle are bred, the cows selected to breed from are those that produce a lot of milk. But what was the decisive criterion in this case?'

'Vampires bred a creature with a special kind of mind.'

'What different kinds of mind are there?'

'Well,' said Enlil Maratovich, 'the story begins a long way back...'

He yawned, and closed his eyes.

A full minute of silence ensued. Apparently Enlil Maratovich had decided to begin his account not merely from a long way back, but from so far that at first nothing was visible at all. I thought he must have gone to sleep, and looked over inquiringly at Hera. Hera shrugged her shoulders. Suddenly Enlil Maratovich opened his eyes and began to speak.

'There is an old idea, often advanced in books of fantasy and the occult, that people merely imagine they move about on the surface of the globe and look out into illimitable space. In reality they live inside a hollow sphere, and the cosmos, which they believe they are observing, is no more than an optical illusion.'

'I know,' I said. 'It's an esoteric cosmogony of the Nazis. They even proposed building a rocket which would fly vertically upwards through the ice zone at the centre of the planet and annihilate America.'

My erudition produced no effect at all on Enlil Maratovich.

'In fact,' he continued, 'it is a metaphor of great antiquity, which was known in the days of Atlantis. It embodies an insight which people in those times had no way of expressing other than metaphorically: we exist surrounded not by objects but by sensations generated by our sense organs. All that we perceive as stars, or fences, or burdock plants, is nothing but an arrangement of images produced by nervous stimuli. We are hermetically sealed inside our bodies, and what appears real to us is in fact our interpretation of electrical signals received by the brain. The simplest – though not quite correct – model of the mind, which we will employ for the sake of brevity, is known as the "Cartesian Theatre". According to this model our sensory organs provide us with photographs of the external world, while we ourselves sit inside the hollow sphere, the walls of which are covered with these photographs. This enclosed spherical void is our world, from which we cannot escape however much we might wish to. Together the photographs constitute a picture of the world which, as it seems to us, exists outside us. Do you follow?'

'Yes,' I said.

'The original mind acts like a mirror inside the sphere. It reflects the world and takes decisions accordingly. If the reflection is dark, it is time to sleep. If light, it is time to search for food. If the reflection is hot, time to move aside until it gets cooler, and vice versa. All actions are determined by reflexes and instincts. We call this type of mind Mind "A". It functions solely as a reflection of the world. Understand?'

'Of course.'

'Now try to imagine a living creature which has two minds. As well as Mind "A" it has a Mind "B", which has no connection at all with the photographs on the walls inside the sphere but produces its own visions from inside itself. From its depths there arises ... an aura of abstract concepts, a sort of Northern Lights. Can you imagine that?'

'Yes.'

'Now we are getting to the crucially important part. Imagine that Mind "B" is itself one of the objects perceived by Mind "A", and the visions produced by Mind "B" are perceived by Mind "A" as equivalent to the photographs of the external world it is accustomed to reflecting. What Mind "B" has produced in its inmost hidden depths appears to Mind "A" as part of the outside world.'

'I don't follow that,' I said.

159

'That's only how it seems to you. In fact, you both encounter the phenomenon many times a day.'

'Could you give us an example?' asked Hera.

'I can. Imagine that you . . . well, let's say you're standing in the New Arbat in Moscow looking at two motor cars parked by the Casino. To look at they are both long and black, and almost identical. All right, one might be a touch sleeker and longer. With me so far?'

'Yes,' agreed Hera.

'When you notice differences in the shape of the boot and the headlights, the different sounds made by the engines and the design of the tyres, that is your Mind "A" at work. But when what you see is two Mercs, one of which is a glamorous, year-old, top of the range model, and the other a shitty pile of junk, the model Berezovsky would have used to go to meet General Lebed at the bathhouse five thousand years ago, which nowadays you can pick up for ten grand – that's Mind "B" at work, an aspect of the Northern Lights it produces. But because it manifests itself as two black cars standing side by side, you assume that the product of Mind "B" is something that really exists in the outside world.'

'You explain it very clearly,' I said. 'But it still does really exist in the outside world, doesn't it?'

'No. That can be easily proved. You can measure any Mind "A"-type difference between our two cars with a simple tape-measure. It won't change in a hundred years. But the differences Mind "B" ascribes to the cars are not susceptible to any objective assessment or measurement. And no one in a hundred years' time will be able to tell you for certain what they were.'

'So how does it come about that different people, seeing these two cars, will come to the same conclusion about them?' asked Hera. 'I mean, that one of them is a glamorous must-have and the other a crap heap?'

160

'The reason is that these two people both have a Mind "B" attuned to the same wavelength. This causes them to see an identical hallucination.'

'Who creates the hallucination?' I asked.

'Mind "B" does. Or to be precise, a vast number of such minds all interacting with one another. This is what distinguishes people from animals. Apes and human beings both have Mind "A". Only human beings have Mind "B". It is the result of that selection engineered by the vampires of old.'

'Why does a creature bred for milking need Mind "B"?'

'I should have thought by now that would be clear to you. Isn't it?'

'No,' I said.

Enlil Maratovich shot an inquiring glance at Hera.

'Nor to me,' she said. 'In fact, I'm even more confused.'

'The reason is the same for both of you. You are still thinking like humans.'

Hearing this rebuke once again, I reacted automatically, drawing my head deeper into my shoulders.

'Please teach us to think in a new way,' Hera muttered.

Enlil Maratovich laughed.

'My dear girl,' he said, 'five thousand marketing specialists have been defecating inside your head for ten years, and you expect me to clean it all out in five minutes... Don't be offended, though. I'm not blaming you. I was just like you myself. Do you think I don't know what you both think about at night? I know exactly. You're puzzled as to where or how vampires get hold of human red liquid. You think it might come from donor centres, or tortured infants, or underground laboratories, or some other such nonsense. Am I right?'

'Approximately,' I agreed.

'If I wasn't, you would be the only exception I've come across in forty years,' said Enlil Maratovich. 'And if you'd like to know, this universal blindness is the most mystifying thing I have ever encountered in my life. When you come to understand the truth of it you will think so too.'

'What is this truth that we have to understand?' asked Hera.

'Let's look at it logically, step by step. If the human being is a milk-producing animal, his principal business must be the production of food for vampires. So far, so good?'

'True.'

'Now tell me, what is the main activity of human beings?'

'Giving birth to children and raising them?' suggested Hera.

'An increasingly rare event in the civilised world. In any case, it is certainly not mankind's main preoccupation. What is more important than anything else to a human being?'

'Money?' I hazarded.

'At last. And what, exactly, is money?'

'As if you didn't know,' I shrugged.

Hanging upside down made this a rather peculiar manoeuvre.

'Perhaps I do know. But do you?'

'Somewhere or other I believe there are five ... no, seven scientific definitions,' I said.

'I know what you are referring to. But your definitions all suffer from one fundamental flaw. They were all formulated with the same objective: to earn money trying to sell these definitions. That is like using a ruler to measure the length of itself ...'

'You mean all the definitions are incorrect?'

'Not so much incorrect as that, when you analyse them in detail, they all say the same thing: money ... is money. Which is equivalent to saying nothing at all. But at the same time,' Enlil Maratovich raised his finger, that is to say pointed it towards the floor, 'at the same time, people do have an inkling of the truth, but only subconsciously. Can you remember what the representatives of the toiling classes call their masters?'

'Exploiters?'

'Bloodsuckers,' said Hera.

I expected Enlil Maratovich to snub her, but on the contrary, he clapped his hands in approbation.

'Yes! There's my clever girl! Exactly that, drinkers of red liquid. Even though it would never occur to any of them to do so literally. Now do you see?'

'You mean to say...' began Hera, but Enlil Maratovich did not let her finish.

'Yes. Just so. Vampires have long ceased to avail themselves of biological red liquid, in favour of a far more advanced medium of human vital energy. Money.'

'Are you serious?' I asked.

'Never more so. Think for yourself. What does human civilisation consist of? It's nothing more than a gigantic production of money. The cities people build are pure money factories, and that is the reason people crowd into them in such excessive numbers.'

'But much more than money is produced there,' I protested. 'In cities...'

'There is something called "the economy" which is supposed to grow constantly,' Enlil Maratovich broke in, 'although it is never completely clear just what is growing or to what purpose. Because when you start to analyse it, you see that it largely consists of bankers, stockbrokers, lawyers and other speculators orally pleasuring each other all day. People have no idea what it is that keeps on growing, yet they spend all their time worrying whether the rate of growth is faster or slower than they suppose it should be. And then all of a sudden they find everything has gone pear-shaped, and a period of national mourning is decreed for the whole country. But then it starts to grow again. And all the while, nobody – especially those who actually live in the city – ever glimpses this mysterious growing object with which they are so concerned...'

He extended his hand in front of him as if to show the panorama of the invisible city beyond the walls.

'What people are actually doing is producing something the nature of which they completely fail to understand,' he continued, 'despite spending all day every day thinking about it to the exclusion of everything else. Don't imagine it gives me any pleasure to say it, but the workspace for today's office proletarian – his cubicle – even *looks* like a stall for a large cattle stock. The only difference is that in front of his face instead of a feeding trough he has a monitor displaying his fodder digitally. And what does he produce in his pen? The answer is so obvious that it has even entered into the idiom of most languages: the worker is *making money*.'

I wanted to register another objection.

'Money is not a product which is being made,' I said. 'It is merely one of those inventions which have made life simpler, one of the evolutionary legacies by which mankind has risen above the animals ...'

Enlil Maratovich turned to me with an amused smile on his face.

'Do you really believe man rose above the animals as a result of evolution?'

'Of course,' I replied. 'Surely that is so?'

'No,' he said. 'He placed himself lower down, far lower. Nowadays the only person who can afford the lifestyle of an animal is a retired millionaire – to live in the bosom of nature in ideal climatic conditions, to move freely, to consume only ecologically pure food and, above all, to be entirely free from worry about anything. Just think about it – no animal works.'

'What about squirrels?' asked Hera. 'They gather nuts, don't they?'

'My dear, that's not work. If squirrels spent all their time from morning till night frenziedly trying to flog each other rotting

164

bear shit, that would be work. Gathering nuts is just free retail therapy. The only animals who work are beasts of burden whom men have bred in their own image and likeness. Plus, of course, man himself. If, as you say, the purpose of money is to make life easier, why is it that people strive all their lives vainly trying to earn it, only to collapse at the end into a senile heap of debris? Can you seriously imagine that people do all that for their own convenience? Oh please! Man does not even know what money truly is.'

He swept Hera and me with his gaze.

'But the truth is,' he went on, 'it's not at all a difficult or complex problem to understand what money truly is. All you have to do is pose the elementary question: where does it come from?'

The question seemed to be directed at me.

'It's not easy to explain in a couple of words,' I said. 'Economists still argue about it after all these years...'

'Let them go on arguing, for ever if necessary. But it makes no difference to the poor moneymaker. His time and his strength is where money comes from. His vital energy, drawn from the air, from the light of the sun, from nourishment and other life-giving experiences, are all transmuted into it.'

'You mean metaphorically?'

'I mean literally. Man thinks he is generating money *for* himself. In fact, he generates it *from* himself. Life is so arranged that the only way he is able to get hold of a little money for his own use is if he manages to produce considerably more for someone else. And everything that he does succeed in keeping for himself has this strange habit of slipping through his fingers... You must have noticed that? When you were working as an unloader in the supermarket?'

Hera looked at me with some curiosity. I wanted to kill Enlil Maratovich on the spot.

'I did notice,' I muttered.

'There is a simple reason why people do not understand the true nature of money,' continued Enlil Maratovich. 'They are only allowed to talk about it within the confines of cargo discourse. Human life has been processed into what to them is an unintelligible substance, but this is never mentioned. What does get endlessly discussed is which particular currency offers the best prospects at any given time – the euro or the yuan. Or should one be putting one's trust in the yen? Serious people never think or talk about anything else.'

'That's only natural,' I said. 'A man has to strive to obtain money, because otherwise he will die of hunger. That's the way life is.'

'The words are the correct ones,' agreed Enlil Maratovich. 'But I would put them in a slightly different order. That would alter the nuance.'

'How would you say it?'

'The way life is, a man will die of hunger if he strives to acquire anything other than money. And what I'm trying to explain at the moment is who set it up like this, and why.'

'That may be so,' said Hera. 'But how exactly does a man produce money? A cow has an udder. A man doesn't have anything like that.'

Enlil Maratovich smiled.

'Who told you that?'

I thought Hera was a trifle embarrassed by this.

'You mean a man does have an udder, like a cow?'

'Yes, I do mean that.'

'Where is it, then?' asked Hera, very quietly.

I could not stop myself looking at her breasts. My glance did not escape Enlil Maratovich's attention.

'In the head,' he declared, looking at me meaningfully and tapping his skull with his fingers.

'Where, exactly?' I asked.

'That's what I have just been explaining to you,' replied Enlil Maratovich. 'Mind "B" is the money-producing organ. It functions as a money-generating gland that is found only in mankind, not in any other animal...'

'Hold on a minute,' I interrupted. 'We were talking about how Mind "B" can explain the difference between two Mercs. What's money got to do with that?'

'If you bring it out into the clear light of day, the points of difference between the two Mercedes, seen by Mind "B", boil down to money. Nothing else. And the cultural landscape that consists of such differences is the mine from which money is produced. This mine, as you have already grasped, has no external reality at all, but is a construct within people's heads. That is why I say that people generate money out of themselves.'

'How can someone who works down a mine be doing so just in his head?'

'Very easily. A continuous process of abstract thinking goes on in Mind "B" which is condensed down to a pecuniary concentrate. This concentrate is the difference between the two Mercedes. It bears the same relationship to money as the leaves of the coca plant do to cocaine. Another way of putting it is that money is the purified and refined product of Mind "B".'

'Could this monetary distillate be the same thing as Glamour?' asked Hera.

'Good thinking,' replied Enlil Maratovich. 'But there are more inputs into our money distillate than Glamour alone. Almost any perception in the city of today is convertible into money. Nevertheless, some kinds of concentrate lend themselves to the output of a larger monetary yield per unit of information than others. In this context Glamour is miles out in front of the competition. That is why modern man is surrounded by so much gloss coating and hype. It's like clover for cows.'

'Does Glamour exist all around the globe?' I asked.

'Certainly, it's everywhere. But it's also different everywhere. In New York it's a Ferrari and clothes from Donna Karan. In a village in Asia it's a mobile phone with a big screen and a t-shirt with a Mickey Mouse USA Famous Brand logo. But essentially they are the same thing.'

Hera looked at my legs. I noticed that my trouser bottoms had fallen down, that is to say up, exposing my socks whose elasticated tops were embellished with labels in the shape and design of the Union Jack.

'And what is the role of Discourse in all this?' I asked quickly.

'Pasture has to be enclosed,' replied Enlil Maratovich. 'You must have a fence so that the stock doesn't straggle away.'

'Who is outside the fence?'

'We are. Who else could be?'

I remembered Jehovah having said the same thing to me, almost word for word.

Hera sighed.

Enlil Maratovich laughed.

'Were you expecting more from life, then?' he said. 'You shouldn't.'

'What happens to people who refuse to consume the concentrate and produce money?' asked Hera.

'I am the Good Shepherd,' replied Enlil Maratovich, 'so I won't come down too hard on you. But do just stop and think for a moment: how do you think a cow is going to set about refusing to produce milk? The only way she could do that would be to stop eating.'

'But surely people could, if they wanted to, produce something other than money? As they used to in the Soviet Union?'

Enlil Maratovich's eyebrows shot up.

'A good question... I can put it in a nutshell like this – animal husbandry can be aimed at producing both meat and dairy products. When it stops being for dairy, it changes to being for meat, and vice versa. Periods of transition are a combination of both. No third possibility has yet been discovered.'

'But what, in this context, is meant by raising stock for meat?'

'It means this,' said Enlil Maratovich. 'You can drink milk, and you can eat meat. There is a resource which people provide while they are alive, and there is a resource which they provide when they die ... Happily, those dreadful practices have been condemned and are safely buried in the past, so we do not need to concern ourselves with them.'

'You mean wars?' asked Hera.

'Not only,' replied Enlil Maratovich. 'Although war does have a role to play. There are different kinds of war. Sometimes vampires from various countries start it like children playing a game, except that instead of toy soldiers they use people. It can also happen that vampires from the same clan play games against one another with their toy soldiers at home, on their own territory. Of course, we usually try to divide the resources in an equitable manner. But we do not always succeed.'

'Why don't people just get rid of these beef and dairy cattle breeders?' asked Hera.

'Yes,' I echoed her. 'Tear down the walls? Return to their natural environment?'

'Don't forget, you yourselves are now numbered among the breeders. Otherwise you would not be hanging upside down here. I understand how you feel. I am myself by nature kind and compassionate. But you must get it into your heads once and for all that cows, pigs and people can never be liberated. Even if it were possible to devise some way of letting this happen for cows and pigs, it could never be done for human beings because in essence they are merely extensions of our digestive tract. There is no natural environment for them to live in, only an artificial one, because they themselves are fundamentally artificial. Humans have been bred to live only as they do. But there is no need to shed tears over their fate. In place of liberty they have *freedom*, and this is a wonderful thing. We tell them: go and graze wherever you like! The more freedom you have, the more money you will produce. That's not so bad, is it?'

Enlil Maratovich chuckled contentedly.

'I don't understand the most important thing of all,' I said. 'The entire flow of money from start to finish is controlled by people. How do vampires collect and use the money?'

'That is a whole different story,' replied Enlil Maratovich. 'You will learn about it later. But now I think we should stop talking for a while...'

Silence fell. I closed my eyes, enjoying simply being able to hang upside down and not think about anything. Soon I descended into a pleasant state akin to sleep, but not exactly sleep, more a crystal-clear state of abstraction. Iggy Pop must have known something of the sort when he sang: 'The fish doesn't think, because the fish knows everything...' Quite possibly in this state I too knew everything but it was too much of a problem to verify, since to do so I would have had to start thinking, and emerge from my state of bliss.

I cannot say how much time elapsed. Presence of mind returned with a loud clap of the hands. I opened my eyes.

'Reveille!' announced Enlil Maratovich briskly.

Taking hold of the hoop he nimbly lowered himself to the floor with an agility surprising in someone so corpulent. It was clear the audience was at an end. Hera and I followed suit to join him on the floor.

'Still,' I said, 'what you were saying about how vampires use money. Couldn't you just give us a hint?'

Enlil Maratovich smiled. Taking a wallet from the pocket of his sports trousers, he extracted a one-dollar bill, tore it in half and presented me with one of the halves.

'There's your answer,' he said. 'And now, quick march. It is time to leave here.'

'Where to?' enquired Hera.

'There is a lift here,' replied Enlil Maratovich. 'It will take you straight up to the garage of my house.'

HERA

The car exited from the underground concrete bunker, passed the security booth and out through the gates. Pine trees flashed past the car windows. I did not even catch a glimpse of Enlil Maratovich's house, or indeed anything else except the three-metre high wall. It was already noon – evidently we had been hanging in the hamlet all night and all morning. I could not imagine where all the time could have gone.

Sitting beside me, Hera laid her head on my shoulder.

I was stunned. But the truth was she had merely fallen asleep. I closed my eyes, pretending to be asleep myself, and allowed my hand to fall on her open palm. We sat like that for a quarter of an hour or so, after which she awoke and removed her hand from mine.

Opening my eyes, I looked out of the window and yawned, simulating emergence from sleep. We were approaching Moscow.

'Where to now?' I asked Hera.

'Home.'

'Let's get out in the centre. We could go for a walk.'

Hera looked at her watch.

'All right. But not for long.'

'Can you take us to Pushkin Square, please?' I said to the driver.

He nodded.

We did not speak again for the rest of the journey; I did not want to talk in front of the driver, who glanced at us from time to time in the mirror. He looked like an actor playing the role of an American President in a medium-budget disaster movie: sober dark suit, red tie, strongly featured face lined with fatigue. It was rather flattering to be driven by such an impressive specimen.

'Where shall we go?' asked Hera when we got out of the car.

'Let's walk along Tverskoi Boulevard.'

Past the fountain, avoiding the noxious petrol fumes suffocating the statue of Pushkin, we descended into the subway pedestrian crossing. I thought back to my first bite. It had happened not far away – as they say, the murderer is always drawn back to the scene of his crime. Could this be why I had asked the driver to drop us here?

But it would be a bad idea to bite Hera, I thought. It would almost certainly put an end to our expedition. I'll have to do without a crib in this exam... A lack of confidence bordering on physical weakness gripped me, and I decided the best way to overcome it would be to make some telling remark, an insight testifying to my acuteness of observation and brilliance of mind.

'Interesting, isn't it?' I said. 'When I was small, this subway used to have separate stalls all over the place. Then gradually there were more and more of them, so that now they're all combined into one complete row...'

I nodded towards the glass front of what was now in effect a shopping mall.

'Yes,' Hera assented placidly. 'They've rather gone over the top with them now.'

We came up on the other side of the street and walked on to Tverskoi Boulevard. As we passed the stone urns at the edge of the stairs it was on the tip of my tongue to point out that they were always full of rubbish and empty bottles, but decided not to offer any further demonstrations of my mental acuity. It was still necessary to say something, however; the silence was getting embarrassing.

'Penny for your thoughts,' I said.

'I was thinking about Enlil,' said Hera, 'or rather the way he lives. A hamlet perched over a precipice. A bit pretentious, of course. But very stylish as well. There aren't many people who could afford it.'

'Yes,' I said. 'And the way you hang on a ring, not a beam. Something rather philosophical about that.'

Luckily Hera did not ask me what was particularly philosophical about that, because I could have got myself into considerable difficulties trying to account for it. She laughed, evidently taking what I had said as a joke.

I remembered that her photograph had reminded me of a picture posted by a LiveJournal user. Perhaps it really was her I had seen, and she had an account with LJ? I had one myself, and even had about fifty friends (with whom, needless to say, I did not share all the details of my life). This seemed a suitable conversational topic.

'Say, Hera, didn't I see your user pic on LiveJournal?'

'You couldn't have,' came the reply. 'I don't indulge in any of that blog squittering.'

It was an expression I had not heard before.

'Why so severe?'

'Not severe at all. It's a scientific fact. Presumably Jehovah explained to you why people go in for blogging?'

'I don't remember anything about that,' I said. 'Why do they?'

'The human mind these days is subject to three main influences. They are: Glamour, Discourse and so-called News. When over a long period a man lives on a diet consisting of advertising, assorted punditry and so-called news stories, he starts wanting to become a brand, a pundit, and a source of news stories himself.

174

That is the reason for the existence of these mental latrines we call Internet blogs. Blogging is the defensive reflex of a mutilated psyche which continually spews out Glamour and Discourse. We shouldn't mock it, but it is rather degrading for a vampire to crawl about in these sewers.'

And she laughed. Her way of laughing was rather curious – loud, but short, as if the amusement was allowed to burst out from her for just a second before the valve closed again. It was like sneezing, except with laughter. And when she smiled elongated dimples appeared in her cheeks – two furrows really, more than dimples.

'Actually,' I confided, 'I hardly ever write anything on my LJ page. It's just that I don't read newspapers and I don't watch television. The LJ is where I keep up- to-date with the news. You can get a professional opinion on just about anything; all the experts have blogs nowadays.'

'Reading experts' blogs rather than newspapers,' she said, 'is like feeding on butchers' excrement instead of eating meat.'

The thought made me gag.

'Interesting. Where did you get that from?'

'I didn't get it from anywhere. I thought of it myself.'

'If you were to write a phrase like that in LiveJournal,' I said, 'you'd have to put a smiley after it.'

'A smiley is a visual deodorant. It usually means that the user is afraid you might think he's made a bad smell and wants you to know that really he smells like a rose.'

I suddenly wanted to stop aside and check that I wasn't exuding BO. We continued in silence to the end of the Boulevard. By that time I had worked up a pretty fair rage, but had been unable to come up with a suitable retort. Inspiration struck while I was looking up at the statue of Timiryazev.

'Yes,' I said, 'you're pretty good at Discourse. But as for

Glamour – well, perhaps I'm out of date? Is that the latest fashion these days, to dress like Tom Sawyer?'

'What does that mean, dressing like Tom Sawyer?'

I looked her up and down, at her faded black t-shirt, at her dark trousers – they also, presumably, had at one time been black as well – and at her trainers.

'Well, as if you're just off to paint a fence.'

This was, of course, below the belt; it was no way to talk to a girl. At least I hoped it was below the belt. It was meant to be.

'You think I'm badly dressed?' she asked.

'Well, not *badly* exactly. Working-class clothes are fine. They even suit you, as a matter of fact. The only thing is, for a serious vampire it's not really the style...'

'Just a minute there,' she said. 'You really think *I'm* the one wearing working clothes? Not you?'

True, there was a tear in my jacket and soot stains in a few places, but even so I felt confident that I was pretty impeccably dressed. I had bought the whole ensemble of jacket, trousers, shirt and shoes in LovemarX, taking it as a job lot from a display mannequin on the sales floor – all, that is, except the socks, which I bought separately. The advantage of the matching display was that it enabled me to cover up my problems with Glamour. As a tactic it was successful: Baldur personally approved my outfit, telling me that I looked like a Greenland queen on heat.

'Let's put it like this,' I replied. 'If I was going out to work on my vegetable patch I would wear different clothes. Clothes have after all a ritual significance, and rituals should be respected. They demonstrate status. Everyone ought to dress according to his or her position in society. That's the nature of the social code. In my opinion the vampire has a very elevated status. Not just very elevated, the topmost status of all. And we should dress appropriately.'

'And how exactly does dress reflect the social status?'

This was my chance to show that I too was quite advanced in Discourse.

'Generally speaking, in all epochs one sees the same simple principle at work,' I expounded. 'It is what is known as "industrial exemption". The clothes a man wears signal his freedom from heavy physical labour. For instance, long sleeves extending beyond the fingers, as in "My Lady Greensleeves". You know that song?'

She nodded.

'It's obvious,' I went on, 'that a lady who wears clothes of this sort is not going to be scrubbing out saucepans or feeding the pigs. The same applies to lace cuffs round the wrists, elegant shoes with high heels and winkle-picker toes, various non-functional details of one's attire such as baggy breeches, codpieces, all manner of frippery additions. But these days it's, umm, any kind of expensive clothing, tastefully chosen. Anything to make it clear that the person is not going off to paint a fence.'

'The theory is correct,' said Hera, 'but the way you are applying it in practice is way off beam. Your office uniform doesn't remotely suggest that its wearer has freed himself from the degrading labour of painting fences. Quite the opposite. It sends a signal that at 10 a.m. you have to be at your desk in the office, where you must equip yourself with a virtual bucket of paint and busy yourself until 7 p.m. – excluding a short break for lunch – painting a virtual fence inside your head. Your senior manager must be happy with the progress of your work, which he will assess by reference to the optimistic expression on your face and the healthy glow of your cheeks.'

'Why does it necessarily...' I began.

'How appalling!' she interrupted. 'And this is a vampire speaking? Rama, you look like a clerk waiting to go for a job interview with a Human Resources officer. Anyone would think you've got a short CV in your inside pocket, folded into four, which you don't dare take out to check in case you make the letters run with your nervously sweating palms. And you have the nerve to criticise me, on a day when I have specially put on our national costume to celebrate a great event?'

'What national costume?' I asked, dumbfounded.

'Black is vampire national dress. In the twenty-first century, "industrial exemption" style is when you couldn't give a stuff what the captain of the galley in which you are chained to the oars thinks about your jacket. Everything else is working clothes. Even if you're wearing a Rolex. Especially if you're wearing a Rolex.'

I did as it happened have a Rolex, not a particularly flash one but it was real. It suddenly felt unbearably heavy, and I drew my wrist back into my sleeve. I was beginning to feel as if I had been dropped over the Niagara Falls in a barrel.

We crossed over New Arbat. Hera stopped in front of a shop window, carefully looked herself over and took out a tube of bright red lipstick, which she applied to her lips. It made her look exactly like a vampire girl out of a comic.

'Lovely,' I said ingratiatingly.

'Thank you.'

She returned the lipstick to her pocket.

'Tell me, do you really believe vampires bred human beings?' I asked.

She shrugged.

'Why not? People bred pigs, didn't they? And cows.'

'But that's completely different,' I said. 'People aren't simple livestock. They have created wonderful cultures and civilisations. I find it very hard to believe that all this has been achieved purely to produce food for vampires. Just look around you...'

Hera took me at my word. Standing still, with comic deliberation, she looked all round, at a stretch of the New Arbat, the

178

Art Film Cinema, the Ministry of Defence and the Arbatskaya Metro Station, resembling a Mongol mausoleum in the middle of the steppe.

'Why don't *you* look around?' she said, pointing to an advertisement hoarding just in front of us. The advert was for a lavatory pan bearing the legend '9,999 roubles' in enormous letters, and a strapline that said: 'Eldorado – no one beats *our* prices!'

'I could suggest another strapline: "Freud's Gold",' I said. 'No, on second thoughts that would be better as a title for an action film.'

The toilet began to move, breaking up into separate vertical strips. I realised that the hoarding itself consisted of a series of triangular columns. When they moved round one step, a new advertisement came into view, this one promoting telephone tariffs. It was executed in joyful yellow and dark blue colours, and announced: '$10 free! Sign up for your ten dollars reward!'

After another couple of seconds the columns turned once more, and the following image appeared in severe black lettering on a white background:

I am the Lord thy God,
thou shalt have none other Gods but Me.

'Wonderful culture and civilisation,' said Hera, echoing my words.

'Well, what of it?' I said. 'All it is, some Protestants have rented this hoarding and are using it to advertise their account book – I mean, the Bible. I don't deny that much that surrounds us is ludicrous. But even so I can't believe that human languages and religions, merely to list which would fill an entire encyclopaedia, are simply the by-product of a vampire Food Supply Programme.'

'What is it that bothers you about it?'

'The disproportionate relationship between idea and result. It would be like building a huge metallurgical plant to produce... oh I don't know... paper clips.'

'Had it been vampires themselves who invented all these cultures and religions, then I agree it would have been overkill,' she replied. 'But human beings have done these things. It's all, as you said yourself, a by-product.'

'But if the only purpose of human beings is to provide food for vampires, then human civilisation must have a very low productivity coefficient.'

'Well, what does it matter how high or low it is? It makes no difference to us. To whom are we obliged to account for it?'

'That's true, but... I still don't believe it. There is nothing superfluous in nature. But here everything is superfluous.'

Hera frowned. She looked angry when she did so, but I already knew that it was simply the expression her face assumed when she was concentrating her thoughts.

'Do you know what termites are?' she enquired.

'Yes. Blind white ants. They eat anything made of wood, from the inside. That writer, who was it, Mrakes, wrote something about them.'

'Márquez?'

'Could be. I haven't read it, only heard about it in Discourse. I've never seen living termites either.'

'Same here,' said Hera. 'But I saw a film about them. Termite communities have a king and a queen, who are protected by the ordinary termites. The king and queen stay in their cells, which they cannot leave. The worker termites constantly lick them clean and bring them food. Termites have their own style of architecture, a kind of Gothic vision on acid. They have a complex social hierarchy with a range of different professions: workers, soldiers, engineers. The thing I found most amazing

180

was the way a new termite mound is created when a young king and queen fly away from the old one to build a new kingdom. As soon as they have arrived there, the first thing they do is gnaw off each other's wings...'

'Are you comparing human civilisation to a termite mound?' She nodded.

'The very fact that you can do so,' I said, 'proves in itself how far termites and human beings are from one another.'

'How?'

'Well, I don't think you're ever going to find two termites discussing whether or not their mound is similar to a Gothite cathedral.'

'In the first place,' said Hera, 'the word is Gothic, not Gothite. Secondly, nobody knows what termites talk about with one another. Thirdly, you didn't let me finish. In the film I saw, we were shown how there are two species of soldier termites. There are ordinary rank-and-file soldiers, who have something like a pair of pincers on their heads. And there are others who have a long sort of needle on their heads. This needle exudes a chemical irritant in the form of a jelly, an extract from a special gland. When it was discovered that this extract from a termite's pre-frontal gland is an effective cure for disease, people began to breed termites artificially so as to obtain more of the extract. Now, if you tried explaining to a horn-bearing termite from one of the artificially constructed mounds that the whole of his species' huge and complex monarchical structure, all their unique architecture and harmonious social order, had been created merely because of the accidental usefulness to some apes of the extract produced by their pre-frontal gland, he would not believe you. And if you did manage to convince him, he would see it as a monstrous, insultingly disproportionate travesty.'

'Junior manager's pre-frontal gland extract,' I repeated. 'A delightful comparison...'

'Straight from Enlil Maratovich. But let's not trash the office proletariat. It's vulgar to do that. Office-wallahs are not inferior to us, it's just that we have had the luck and they have not.'

'OK,' I said peaceably. 'Let's make it middle management.'

We were approaching the Cathedral of Christ the Saviour. Hera pointed to one of the benches nearby. On the back was an inscription in smudged yellow lettering:

Christ is Yahweh for the poor.

So mixed up has culture in Russia become over the past few years that it was impossible to work out whether this was meant to be abusive of Christ or, on the contrary, praise for him... For some reason there came into mind the torn-up dollar bill Enlil Maratovich had given me. I took it out of my pocket and read what was written around the pyramid with its single eye: '"*Novus Ordo Seclorum*" and "*Annuit Coeptis*". What does that mean, when it's translated?'

'"New Order of the Ages",' said Hera, 'aka "New World Order". And something like "our efforts are looked on with favour by Providence".'

'What's the point of it?'

'Just some Masonic gibberish. You don't need to go into it.'

'Probably not,' I agreed. 'The main point was the gesture, wasn't it? The fact that he tore the note in half? Maybe there is some special technology for destroying money, some annihilation in the process of which the vital energy it contains is distilled.'

'How could that be done, for instance?'

I reflected. 'Well, let's say the money is transferred to a special account, and then destroyed in a particular way. When the money itself has all gone the vital power remains and vampires drink it...'

'Not very plausible,' said Hera. 'Where does this vital force come from? After all, the account can only exist in a computer system. You wouldn't be able to say exactly where it is.'

'Or perhaps the vampires gather round the laptop from which the transfer is to be made to somewhere in the Cayman Islands. And the laptop has some kind of special vampire gizmo in its USB port.'

Hera laughed.

'What's so funny?' I asked.

'I'm just thinking what a good time it is for the likes of us when the banks default.'

'By the way, that's a very good thought,' I said. 'Maybe everything is completely centralised. The sort of thing where they devalue something by ten per cent and then live happily off the proceeds for half a year.'

Hera suddenly stopped and stood still.

'Hold on,' she said. 'I think . . .'

'What?'

'I think I've just understood how it's all done. Vampires don't drink human red liquid but a special infusion called *bablos*. Most likely it's made from old banknotes which are due for destruction. That's why Enlil tore one up.'

'Where did you get that from?'

'I've just remembered a conversation I happened to overhear. One vampire was asking Enlil when I happened to be there, if everything was ready for a *bablos* drinking session. Enlil replied that they were waiting for a consignment of old money from the Goznak mint, but it had not yet arrived. At that time I did not understand what they were talking about, but now it all falls into place.'

'A delivery of old money from Goznak?' I said incredulously.

'Think about it. People are constantly touching money, counting it out, putting it away in their wallets, scribbling on it, stashing it away. For them it is the most important material object there is. The result is that banknotes become saturated with humans' vital force. The longer a banknote remains in circulation, the more it gets impregnated. And when it is completely worn out and literally oozing human energy, it's taken out of circulation, and the vampires prepare their drink from it.'

I thought about it. It sounded bizarre, and not particularly appetising, but it might be more likely than my Cayman Islands theory.

'Interesting,' I said. 'Who was the other vampire Enlil Maratovich was talking to?'

'He's called Mithra.'

'Oh, so you know Mithra?' I said, surprised. 'Although, come to think of it, of course... It was he who gave me your letter.'

'He was saying some quite amusing things about you,' confided Hera. 'He said that... oy...'

She bit her tongue and put her hand over her mouth as if realising she had already said too much.

'What did he say?'

'Oh, nothing, forget it.'

'No, you'd better say it since you've started.'

'I don't remember,' replied Hera. 'Do you think we never talk about anything else but you? We have plenty of other topics, you know.'

'What sort of other topics, if it's not a secret?'

Hera smiled.

'He tries to chat me up.'

'How? What sort of thing does he say?'

'I'm not telling you. Why would I want to stifle your imagination by giving you examples? You might want to chat me up too.'

'Do you want to be chatted up?'

'Girls always like being paid compliments.'

'But you're not a girl. You're a vampire. You wrote that in your letter.'

As soon as I said it, I realised I had made a mistake. But it was too late. Hera frowned. We crossed over the street. After a minute or two she said:

'I've remembered what Mithra said. He was telling me that the late Brahma's filing cabinet was still there in the flat where you are living. All the compromising material had been taken out of it except one test tube with a preparation from the time of the Second World War. Something about Nordic sex in a zoo, I think it was. He said you had drunk it dry.'

'Little liar,' I said angrily. 'I did ... sample it, that's true. Maybe a couple of times. But that was all. There's still some left. At least there was, if it hasn't all leaked out ... But maybe Mithra, himself ...'

Hera burst out laughing.

'Why so defensive?'

'I'm not being defensive,' I said. 'I just don't like it when someone starts bad-mouthing others behind their backs.'

'But what's bad about this? If it was such a bad thing to do, you wouldn't have drunk it all to the last drop, would you?'

I had no answer to this. Hera advanced to the edge of the pavement, stopped there and held out her hand.

'What's this?' I asked.

'I'm going to catch a cab.'

'Are you bored with me?'

'No, not at all. Quite the opposite. But it's time for me to go.'

'Couldn't we go on a bit further, to Gorky Park?'

'Another time,' she smiled. 'Make a note of my mobile number.'

I had just finished typing in her number when a yellow taxi drew up and stopped. I held out my hand to her. She grasped my thumb in her palm.

'You're sweet,' she said. 'And very nice. But please don't wear that jacket any more. And don't put gel on your hair.'

Bending down, she kissed my cheek, butted my neck enchantingly with her head, and said:

'Mwah, mwah.'

'Mwah, mwah,' I said in turn. 'Glad to know you.'

When the taxi had driven off, I felt something damp on my neck. I wiped it with my hand and saw a tiny patch of red liquid on the palm, no more than if I had been bitten by a mosquito.

I felt like chasing after the taxi and smashing my fist through the rear window as hard as I could, or even kicking it in so that the shards of glass would fly in all directions. But it was already too far away.

THE CHALDEANS

Over the next few days I did not see any vampires. I was reluctant to speak to Hera on the telephone; I was even afraid she might ring me, because now she had bitten me I felt exposed not merely as an emperor with no clothes but as a stripped bare pretender with a rude word tattooed on his back. I was especially ashamed of having been caught trying to grandstand before her.

In my mind I kept going through what she would have been able to see: how the photographic image of myself as a world-weary demon with a signet ring had been achieved, a memory which now made me writhe. Then I had only to think of how, at the same time, I had used her photograph, to begin shaking with anguish.

'Mwah, mwah,' I muttered to myself, 'bloody mwah mwah to the lot of you.' So intense was my suffering that as often happens, the resultant catharsis, when it came, proved to be emotionally valuable, shining a light not just on the source of my pain but on the whole context that had brought it about. I wrote in my notebook:

The compulsion to relentless and pointless posturing is a widespread Russian disease to which vampires also are not immune. It stems not so much from the vulgarity of our national character as from a combination of European refinement and Asiatic oppression, a combination in which is to be found the essential characteristic of our life. The Russian, in carpeting the area with his airs and disgraces, is not trying to show that he is better than the people to whom he struts his stuff. It's just the opposite. He is calling out, 'See! I'm just like you! I also have a claim on happiness. You must not despise me because life has been so cruel to me!' Only through compassion is it possible to gain a true understanding of this condition.

My words about compassion came, of course, from rhetorical inertia. Compassion was an emotion that surfaced only rarely in me – although, like all vampires, I was sure that I fully deserved it from others. Alas, in common with human beings, we are bad at seeing ourselves from the outside.

I spent the time mooching about, visiting restaurants and clubs. Once or twice I bought drinks for girls I did not know, and tried to engage them in deeply meaningful conversation, but each time I lost interest in the proceedings when it was clearly time to progress to a more specific stage.

This may have been because I was not yet ready to put Loki's instructions into practice. But more likely it was because none of them looked enough like Hera ... This led me to reflect whether, supposing I were to meet a girl who did remind me enough of Hera, I would in fact act as Loki had taught me. In short, so confused was I on the personal front that I probably ought to have consulted a psychotherapist.

As often happens, I compensated for my inner turmoil by going on an excessive buying spree. In those few days I purchased a pile of schmutter in Archetypique Boutique and even, having correctly guessed the make of car – a yellow Lamborghini Diablero – featured in '*Wheelbarrow No. 2*', went so far as to qualify for a discount on a 'Days of the Week 7-Pack Top Executive' set of silk ties.

All this time I was filled with a premonition that I was soon to face a new ordeal, one more serious than its predecessors. As soon as the premonition had acquired sufficient density and bulk, it materialised in the shape of Mithra. He arrived in the morning, with no preliminary telephone call. By this time most of my anger towards him had evaporated.

'I didn't expect this of you,' I said. 'Why did you tell Hera all that?'

He was taken aback.

'All what?'

'About the "Rudel ZOO" preparation. You told her I drank it all.'

'I didn't say that at all,' said Mithra. 'We were talking about various unusual preparations, and I mentioned it as one you had inherited. Regarding you scoffing the lot, she worked that out for herself. Hera is extraordinarily perceptive.'

'You had no business saying anything to her about it at all. Couldn't you see that?'

'I do now. Forgive me, I wasn't thinking.'

'What is it you want?'

'We are bidden to go to see Enlil Maratovich. Today is a busy day, and night as well. In the afternoon you are to be presented to the Goddess. In the evening there will be a party.'

'What sort of party?'

'It's a ritual evening celebrating the friendship between vampires and Chaldeans. To put it in a nutshell, cunning and inhuman creatures organise a get-together at which each side tries to persuade the other that they are filled with open-hearted goodwill to which no human feeling can be a stranger...'

'Who will be there?'

189

'Of those whom you know, your teachers. Oh, and also your classmate. I'm sure you're missing her.'

'You mean Hera's going to be there?' I asked nervously.

'What's Hera got to do with it?'

'Whom are you referring to then?'

'Loki's going to bring along his rubber woman... Oh, goodness, what a look! I'm all shrivelled up, ha ha! Not for you, you fool, it's just tradition. Sort of a joke. You'd better go and get changed now.'

Leaving Mithra in the sitting room, I went into the bedroom and opened the wardrobe. Since my walk with Hera, the matching outfits I had bought from the mannequin aroused a feeling of revulsion in me. I now looked on them as a themed exhibit from a museum of Darwinism: the mating feathers of a parrot that had failed to make the natural selection cut. I dressed completely in black with a cotton t-shirt under my jacket.

I'm actually quite pleased Hera isn't going to be there, I thought. *She might run away with the idea she has too much influence over my taste...*

Mithra's verdict was encouraging.

'You look like a real vampire now,' was his comment.

He too was dressed in black, but with considerably more chic than I. Under his tuxedo he had on a black shirt front and a tiny scarlet moiré bow tie. He smelled fragrantly of 'New World Odour' eau de cologne from Gap. The combined effect was of a gypsy baron who had graduated from Yale.

Down below the same car that had brought Hera and me from Enlil Maratovich's house was waiting for us – a black limousine of unknown make. I recognised the chauffeur behind the wheel. When we got in to the car he gave me a polite smile in the mirror. We set off, and Mithra pressed a button to make the glass screen rise up, cutting us off from the driver.

'Who are the Chaldeans?' I asked.

'Members of an organisation which functions as an interface between the world of vampires and the world of people. Their official title is "The Chaldean Society".'

'Why do we need them?'

'Human beings have to be kept on a tight rein. That's what the Chaldeans do. They are our enforcement agency. They have been doing the job for thousands of years.'

'Do they control people?'

'Yes. Through the organs of the power structure, which they infiltrate. Chaldeans control all the levers of social status. No one can rise further than their allotted career level without their say-so.'

'I see. A Masonic conspiracy? World government?'

'Something like that,' smiled Mithra. 'Human conspiracy theory is actually extremely useful to us. People are aware that somewhere out there, there exists some kind of a secret society that controls everything. But who and what exactly this society is, has been hotly debated since time immemorial. And as you will appreciate, the arguments will continue for ever and a day.'

'Why do Chaldeans submit to the authority of vampires?'

'Tradition. Things have always been like that.'

'Is that all?' I asked, surprised.

'How else could it be? The power of any king depends entirely on the fact that he was also king yesterday. When he wakes up in bed in the morning, he has no levers of power or strings in his hand that he can pull. Any servant coming into the bedroom can wring his neck.'

'Do you mean people could... wring our necks?'

'Theoretically, yes,' replied Mithra. 'But in practice it's very unlikely. All fundamental values would vanish along with us. Humanity would be left without a skeleton.'

'Values, skeletons... that's all just talk,' I said. 'You can't keep

191

people down with restraints like that today. Don't we have any real control?'

'In the first place, tradition. That is a very real medium of control, believe me. Secondly, we keep the Chaldeans on a lead, and we control their red liquid. We are privy to all their thoughts, and that creates an indelible impression on people. They cannot hide anything from us. Human beings are suckers for all kinds of inside information. We can, so to speak, bring it to the outside for them. This is the basic material we trade with human beings in return for their services.'

'How is it that people know nothing of this?'

'What do you mean, people know nothing of it? Of course they know, and have done for a very long time. For instance, for many centuries the Privy Counsellors of the Kings of England were known as "Lord-Tasters" – now you understand what the phrase means. They're even mentioned in the history textbooks. Of course, what is written there is ridiculous, that they were supposed to have tasted the King's food to make sure that it hadn't been poisoned. Nice job for a Lord. Might as well make a bit of extra cash cleaning up the loo... We know it's impossible to dam up every single leak of information, but what we can do is make sure that it is scrambled so as to be unintelligible. People think we are far more supernatural beings than we really are. That helps. Proximity to the abyss seems to addle their brains. The funny thing is that by comparison with the abyss people have themselves fallen into, ours is quite shallow...'

I thought back to the chasm over which I had flown during the Great Fall. Which was in fact deeper – the black well of Heartland at the point where I had just begun to descend into it, or the yawning pit of the supermarket where I had worked as an unloader? It wasn't just a matter of the supermarket – any life choice available to a young person of my age was a rabbit hole leading straight to the dark pit below. The only variation was in the steepness of the corridor's decline. If one really thought it out, it was people, not vampires, who were hanging upside down, and what they thought of as height was in reality the abyss...

'Chaldeans,' I muttered, 'Chaldeans... I seem to remember something about them in Discourse... weren't they the inhabitants of Babylon? Or are they what criminals call a waiter?'

'I don't know about waiters. But you're right about Babylon. The Chaldean society arose in Babylon, and that is where its name comes from. They have existed since the time of the New Babylon Kingdom, at which time the town was ruled by the Chaldean dynasty. Incidentally, it is in this same Near Eastern tradition that we find the first mention of the Tree of Life.'

'Tree of Life? What is that?'

'It is where the Great Goddess lives. Different religions have different opinions about which part of it she actually lives in – the trunk or the branches, but every country has such a tree.'

'You mean, it is imported to each country from somewhere else?'

'The exact opposite. Every individual human nation takes root where there is a Tree of Life – around it, so to say – together with its language and culture. At the same time, however, all Trees of Life are one and the same tree.'

'And who is the Great Goddess?'

Mithra laughed. 'You'll find out this evening,' he said. 'I can promise you she will make a very strong impression on you.'

I felt a tremor of alarm, but decided not to show it.

'All the same,' I said, 'I still can't understand how it is that a secret company of people who control society's upward mobility are content to work for vampires. Why would they work for anyone except themselves?'

'I told you. Their souls are an open book to us.'

'Oh, come on! All it would take is one St Bartholomew's

Night and nobody anywhere will ever read anything again. If the Chaldeans have enough power to control this whole nuclear-financial snake pit, why should they bow the knee to anyone? People nowadays are very pragmatic. The higher they haul themselves up by exercising their levers of power, the more pragmatic they become. Respect for tradition doesn't drive anything much these days.'

Mithra sighed.

'You understand it all very well. Nevertheless, the people at the very top of the human chain protect the Great Goddess, and their reasons are entirely pragmatic. Pragmatism, you see, can be defined as concentrating attention on the practical achievement of a goal. Without a goal, there can be no such thing as pragmatism. And it is thanks to the Great Goddess that the goal becomes visible to people.'

'In what way?'

'Enlil Maratovich will explain that to you.'

'What's *bablos*? Could you at least tell me what that consists of?'

Mithra winced as if in pain.

'To Enlil!' he called out and waved his arms about furiously, as if warding off a host of bats.

The driver glanced back, evidently having heard something through the glass divide or seen Mithra's movements. I turned and looked out of the window.

Behind the window passed, repassed and disappeared block after block of eighteen-storey apartment buildings, the construction boom sites of the Soviet era's sunset. I had arrived in the Soviet Union just as it was preparing finally to fade from view. I was too small to understand what was happening, but I could still remember the sounds and colours of the time. Soviet power had brought these buildings into existence, shipped in the people to live in them, and then suddenly ceased to be. The whole process seemed to embody a kind of tentative plea for forgiveness.

What was odd, however, was that the people were still there in the same old concrete boxes of their Soviet homes. But broken now were the invisible threads that used to bind them to each other, and following years of zero-gravity drifting, they were being drawn into another, very different pattern. The world was now an unrecognisable place, even though there was no technological device capable of tracking the changes that had taken place. I found something stupendous about this. If such things could take place before my very eyes, why should I be so astounded by what Mithra was saying?

I knew that we were nearing Enlil Maratovich's house when I began to see glimpses of pine trees through the windows. We slowed down and the wheels bumped over one sleeping police-man, then another. We passed through a raised barrier, which I had not noticed last time, and stopped at gates in the high encircling wall. The wall I did remember, but not the gateway through it.

This was a substantial structure built of bricks in three shades of yellow, forming a complicated but unobtrusive decorative pattern. It occurred to me that such a gateway might have been a back entrance to Babylon. The two sections of the gates, made of something like the armour of a tank, slowly opened, and we drove in.

The road led down into the underground garage from which we had emerged last time, but instead we turned off into a side alley, passing along an avenue of ancient pines. We found ourselves in an open space filled with parked cars, several of which had flashing beacons mounted on the roof. The car drew to a halt; the chauffeur climbed out and opened the door for us.

I could see nothing resembling a house in the normal sense of the word. In front of us was a series of asymmetrical white surfaces rising straight out of the ground. In the nearest of them was a door, up to which led wide stone steps.

On one side of the steps was a beautiful waterfall of unusual design, resembling a stretch of river: the water ran down over wide ledges and disappeared into a concrete trench. Anchored in the stream were boats of different colours carved from stone. In every boat sat a stone knight, and a stone lady with a fan. It was evidently an ancient Chinese sculpture. Only the boats still had their original colour; from their occupants it had almost completely vanished. I noticed that the gentlemen were of two types: the first wore expressions of serious concentration, their hands grasped oars and they were rowing. The other kind raised broadly smiling faces to the sky and held lutes in their hands. They did not seem to think this particular crossing merited the effort of rowing. The ladies in all the boats were all alike: intense, dignified. The only differences between them lay in their stone coiffures and the shape of the fans they held in their hands.

'Crossing, crossing, river crossing.' I recalled the old wartime verses which promised: 'to some – the memory, some – the glory, and to some – the pitch-dark flood...' In fact for none of them was there any difference at all – the poet was being smoothly politic – but at the time probably no other sentiment could have been published.

Mithra and I climbed the steps. 'Enlil's house is very unusual,' he said. 'It's basically a multilevel dugout with see-through ceilings.'

'Why would he want to build it like that?'

'He says there is no peace when there are people the other side of the wall. But when it is mother earth, one sleeps better... He's a traditionalist.'

As soon as we came up to the door it opened. We walked past a liveried footman (I had never in my life seen one before) and along a winding corridor, to find ourselves in a large circular hall.

It was a very beautiful, airy room, full of light streaming through the clear segments of the ceiling and falling on a floor of tiles laid out in a complex geometric design. The decoration was classically restrained, with pictures and tapestries hanging on the walls separated by busts of philosophers and emperors from the ancient world – I recognised Socrates, Caesar, Marcus Aurelius and Tiberius. Judging by a couple of missing noses, they were originals.

One surprising detail was the fireplace in one of the walls: despite its imposing dimensions it was obviously too small to heat this immense space. Either the architect had miscalculated, or it was some kind of modishly recherché feature – the gates of hell, for instance. In a semicircle round the fireplace were several protectively covered armchairs. A small stage protruded from the wall on the opposite side, and in the centre of the room stood several tables laid out for a buffet supper.

I saw Enlil Maratovich, Baldur, Loki and Jehovah, but no one else I knew. I was particularly struck by the huge, red-haired man with an air of menacing authority standing beside Enlil Maratovich. However, his complexion was too ruddy for a vampire.

While Baldur, Jehovah and Loki confined their greeting to a nod of the head from afar, Enlil Maratovich advanced on me to shake my hand. After him the red-haired giant also extended his hand, and held my palm in his for some time.

'Marduk,' he said.

'Marduk Semyonovich,' corrected Enlil Maratovich, and raised one eyebrow meaningfully. I understood that I should treat the redhead with as much respect as I would Enlil Maratovich himself.

'Ah me,' sighed Marduk, shaking my hand and gazing

penetratingly into my eyes, 'the things you do to us, you young-sters...'

'What are we doing, exactly?' I asked.

'Chasing us to an early grave,' responded the redhead bitterly. 'It's the changing of the guard, time for us old-timers to leave the square...'

'That's quite enough of that, Marduk,' laughed Enlil Mara-tovich. 'You have plenty of sucking to do before you come to your grave. But the young are certainly pushing me in that direction. I only understand about half of the words they use.'

The ginger giant finally let go of my hand.

'No one's ever going to push you into a grave, Enlil,' he said. 'You moved there yourself while you were still alive, ha ha. That's where we all are now. Very farsighted... Well, shall we begin?'

Enlil Maratovich nodded.

'Then I shall admit the Chaldeans,' said Marduk Semyonovich. 'You have five minutes to get everything ready.' He turned and made for the doors.

I looked inquiringly at Enlil Maratovich.

'Now for our little ceremonial opening to the proceedings,' he said. 'Did Mithra explain to you who the Chaldeans are?'

'Yes.'

'Excellent.'

He took my elbow and steered me towards the stage with the microphone.

'Your presentation today will be in two parts,' he said. 'First you must welcome our Chaldean guests.'

'What do I have to say?'

'Say whatever you like. You're a vampire. The world belongs to you.'

My face visibly failing to reflect particular enthusiasm for the part I was down to play, Enlil Maratovich relented.

'Well, tell them you are glad to be in their company. Talk about the historic succession of the ages and how they are linked, but use vague language so that you don't inadvertently blurt something out. It doesn't really matter what you say. What you do next is much more important.'

'What is that?'

'You must bite a Chaldean and prove to the others that you have gone deep into his soul. This is a truly serious responsibility. They must be convinced anew that they are unable to conceal anything from us.'

'Whom do I have to bite?'

'The Chaldeans choose the victim themselves.'

'When does this happen? Right now?'

'No. Later, at night. It's a traditional number in our celebrations. It's supposed to look like a bit of a turn, a party trick. But in fact it is the most serious part of the evening.'

'And will this Chaldean be happy to let me bite him?'

'That should not concern you. The main thing is that you should be prepared.'

Enlil Maratovich's words hinted at a completely novel emotional condition, one composed of pride, confidence, detachment. It was a mental disposition I imagined proper to a Nietzschean superman, and I was ashamed that I could not measure up to this high standard but was obliged at each step to keep asking questions like a first-grade schoolboy.

We climbed up on to the stage. It was a small platform, enough to accommodate an instrumental trio or mini jazz combo. It had a microphone, two spotlights and some loudspeaker cabinets. On the wall was a dark panel, which from some distance away I had taken to be part of the music amplification set-up.

In fact it had nothing to do with music.

It was an ancient bas-relief with a half-effaced carving, attached to the wall by metal brackets. In the centre, above a

199

crudely represented surface of the earth, was an image of a tree with large, round fruits, resembling either eyes with lashes or perhaps apples with teeth. Surrounding the tree were figures, a wolf on one side, a woman bearing a goblet on the other. Round the edge of the panel were carved figures of legendary creatures, one of which resembled a vampire in flight. In the spaces between them were lines of cuneiform script.

'What is that?' I asked.

'It's an illustration to the *Epic of Gilgamesh*,' replied Enlil Maratovich. 'There is a mention in it of the Tree of Life. That is what you see.'

'What has the woman got in the cup she is bearing? Could it be *bablos*?'

'Aha,' said Enlil Maratovich, 'you've heard about that, have you?'

'Yes, out of the corner of my ear. I know it's a drink made from money, and all...'

Enlil Maratovich nodded. He seemed reluctant to expand on the subject.

'Is that a vampire?' I asked, indicating the winged creature in the corner of the panel.

'Yes,' said Enlil Maratovich. 'This bas-relief is a sacred object of Chaldean society. It is nearly four thousand years old. In times of old one like it would be found in every temple.'

'Are any Chaldean temples still in existence?'

'Yes.'

'Where?'

'Any place where such a bas-relief has been installed becomes a temple. You should know that for the members of the society who are about to appear before us, this is a thrilling moment: they are meeting with their gods... And here they come.'

The doors opened, and into the hall entered strange-looking people. Their multi-coloured garments were clearly not from the present era but harked back, so it would seem, to what the Ancient Persians used to wear. However, the most striking thing about them was not their extravagant costumes, which by a willing stretch of the imagination could be inordinately long and colourful domestic housecoats, but the gleaming gold masks covering their faces. Hanging from the Chaldeans' belts were metal articles I at first took to be old frying pans, but they were much too shiny and I realised they were ancient mirrors. The faces of the incoming guests were inclined towards the floor.

I had a memory of the film *Alien vs. Predator*, which has a scene I must have watched at least twenty times. A cosmic Hunter stands at the top of an ancient pyramid receiving the obeisance of a procession of priests who ascend towards him up an endless staircase. It was, in my opinion, one of the most meaningful frames in all American cinematography. How could I have imagined that I would one day find myself in a similar role?

A shiver ran down my spine. It struck me that I had violated some time-hallowed commandment and had set in train the creation of a reality through the power of my thought – that I might in truth dare to become a god... and this, it suddenly came to me, was the only sense in which the words 'The Great Fall' could have real meaning.

My head swam at the implications, but only for a second. As the mask-wearers approached the stage, they politely applauded me and Enlil Maratovich. The priests in the film had done nothing of the sort as they rose up to the summit, and I pulled myself together – there was no occasion to panic. If one ignored the strange garb of the incomers, the proceedings were much like a routine business presentation.

Raising his hand, Enlil Maratovich asked for and obtained silence.

'Today,' he began, 'is a day both of sadness and of joy. The sadness is because Brahma is no longer with us. The joy is because Brahma *is* still with us, only his name is Rama. He has become much younger and better looking. My friends, it is with great pleasure that I present to you Rama the Second!'

The masked guests once again broke into polite applause. Enlil Maratovich turned to me and with a gesture invited me to the microphone.

While I cleared my throat, I tried to conceive what I should say. Obviously I should be neither too serious nor too flippant. I decided to copy the tone and intonation of Enlil Maratovich.

'Friends,' I said, 'I have never seen any of you before. At the same time, I have seen you countless times in the past. Such is the ancient mystery we share, which binds us together. I am heartily glad of this new encounter... perhaps it is not an appropriate example, but I have just been reminded of a scene in a film I saw...'

At this point it dawned on me that it could be regarded as tactless and arrogant on my part to refer to the scene in *Alien vs. Predator*. It would look as though I were comparing the gathering before me to a crowd of ignorant Indians. Fortunately, I immediately lit on an alternative:

'Do you remember that film by Michael Moore to which Quentin Tarantino awarded the Palme d'Or at Cannes? About President Bush? In this film Bush says in the course of a meeting with pillars of the American Establishment: "Some people call you the elite. I call you my base..." With your permission, I should now like to repeat the same words to you, with a small elaboration. You are the elite because you are my base. And you are my base because you are the elite. I am sure you understand how inseparable these two conditions are. I have no doubt that in this millennium too our collaboration will be fruitful. To-gether we will ascend to new heights and advance still nearer to our... er... our magnificent dream! I believe in you. I trust you. Thank you for coming today.'

And I bowed my head in a dignified gesture of deference.

Applause broke out in the hall. Enlil Maratovich clapped me on the shoulder and steered me away from the microphone, which he then took himself.

'What was said about the base was quite correct,' he said, and swept his eyes severely over the hall, 'but there was just one sentiment with which I could not agree. It was the reference to belief. On this issue we abide by a three-part rule: never, to no one, and to nothing. The vampire does not believe. The vampire knows... Neither do we need this Bush. As the Great Goddess says: "The only bush I trust is mine..."'

Enlil Maratovich assumed a serious expression.

'Of course, there might seem to be a contradiction here with something I have just said,' he observed in a concerned tone of voice. 'It lies in the word "trust". But the contradiction is only apparent. There is no suggestion that the Great Goddess trusts anything. Quite the contrary. She says this because... well, who will be the first to guess the reason why?'

I heard laughter from several vampires in the hall. Evidently I had missed the point of the joke. Enlil Maratovich bowed in acknowledgment, took me by the arm and we left the stage together.

The Chaldeans were picking up their drinks and talking among themselves. It was clear they all knew one another and were friends. I was curious to see how they were going to manage to eat and drink in their masks. In fact the problem was easily solved: the mask was fastened to a round leather cap and when the wearer went up to the buffet table he simply turned the mask round 180 degrees so that the golden faces now appeared at the back of the head.

'Tell me please, Enlil Maratovich,' I asked, 'what was the point of your joke about "the only bush I trust is mine"? I'm afraid I didn't get it.'

203

'It was a pun, Rama,' replied Enlil Maratovich. 'And from the Great Goddess's point of view it is no more than a phantom pain.'

Once again I could not work out what he was talking about. This irritated me.

Marduk Semyonovich came to my aid.

'According to legend,' he said, 'the Great Goddess was transformed into a shower of golden rain, rather like Zeus in the myth of Danae. You will understand that this is a metaphor: in both cases a divinity is changed into money – or more precisely, not into money but into something which stands for it. From that time forward, all human minds have striven to gain access to the Goddess. She is that faint radiance which through the centuries has driven all humanity delirious with longing. Figuratively speaking, there is a thread which connects her to everyone. You, Rama, are therefore already acquainted with her.'

'Yes,' added Enlil Maratovich. 'The Great Goddess is the summit of Fuji. Do you understand?'

I nodded.

'But once the Goddess had become a shower of golden rain, she no longer had a body. And not having a body meant that she had no bush. Therefore the Goddess could safely say that she trusts it. What does not exist cannot betray or deceive.'

As a joke, it hardly merited the effort of teasing out its meaning. But that was not the reason for my irritation. I was getting bored with this prolonged game of hide-and-seek.

'Enlil Maratovich, when are you going let me into the secret of how this whole business really works?'

'Why be in such a hurry, little boy?' asked Enlil Maratovich sadly. 'The greater the wisdom, the greater the sorrow.'

'Please hear me out,' I said, trying to keep my voice under control and make it steady and authoritative. 'First, I stopped being a little boy long ago. Secondly, I feel myself to be in an ambiguous position. You have presented me to this company as a fully fledged vampire, yet I am still kept in the dark about the most important and fundamental elements of our way of life. The result is that I am forced to ask about the meaning of every phrase. Do you not think it is time...'

'It is time,' sighed Enlil Maratovich. 'You are quite right, Rama. Let us go into my study.'

I looked at the company gathered in the hall.

'Will we be returning to them?'

'I hope so,' replied Enlil Maratovich.

AGGREGATE 'M-5'

Enlil Maratovich's study was a large, serious, oak-lined room. Against the wall was a relatively modest desk with a swivel chair. Contrasting with it, rearing up in the middle of the room, was an antique wooden seat with arms and a high, carved back. The wood had been finished in now-faded gilt, and it occurred to me this was how the first electric chair in history might have looked, invented by Leonardo da Vinci on one of his rare days off when he was not busy protecting Mary Magdalene's mummy from the agents of the depraved Vatican. Presumably this stool of repentance would be where Enlil Maratovich would seat erring vampires before castigating them from behind his desk.

A picture hung above the desk. It depicted a strange scene, apparently a treatment being carried out in a Victorian lunatic asylum. Before a blazing fire sat five men in frock coats and top hats. They were tied hand and foot to their chairs, their torsos strapped in with thick leather belts as if in some primitive aeroplane. Each man had a stick in his mouth, held in place by a handkerchief tied round the back of the head. It was like the piece of wood forced between the teeth of an epileptic suffering a seizure, to prevent him biting through his tongue. The artist had caught in masterly fashion the reflection of the flames in the black nap of the top hats. Elsewhere in the picture could be seen a man in a long, dark red robe, but he was in shadow and only the outline of his body could be made out.

Two prints hung on the other wall. In the first a vigorously brushed dark green shadow floated above the darkened earth. This picture was entitled *Alan Greenspan's Last Flight*. The other showed a triple projection of a red carnation sticking out of the barrel of a machine-gun, with a caption in bold type:

Intra-barrel anti-infantry Carnation. Standard equipment for CNN military frogmen, BBC-SAS, Telewaffen landing detachments and other psy-ops units of NATO countries.

There were no other objects of particular interest in the study, except for a model in metal on Enlil Maratovich's desk of the first Sputnik to encircle the earth, and beside it a silver paperweight in the shape of a frock-coated and top-hatted Pushkin reclining on his side. He was propping up his peacefully benevolent face on his fist, exactly like a dying Buddha. Underneath Pushkin was a pile of clean white sheets of paper, and next to him a souvenir pen in the shape of a small sword. There was a lingering smell of coffee in the room, but no coffee machine to be seen – perhaps it had been put out of sight in the cupboard.

The clinical cleanliness of the place evoked somehow a disagreeable feeling, as though someone had recently been killed there, the body removed and the red liquid mopped up. Such were the associations produced in my mind by the dark stone floor with its prominent black fissures between the tiles: there was definitely something ancient and forbidding about it.

Enlil Maratovich motioned me to the chair in the middle of the room, and seated himself at his desk.

'So,' he said, raising his eyes to meet mine, 'you've already heard something about *bablos*?'

I nodded.

'What do you know about it?'

'Vampires collect used banknotes that are impregnated with human life-force,' I replied. 'Then they do something with them. Probably distil an alcohol infusion of their spirit. Or perhaps boil them.'

Enlil Maratovich laughed at this.

'Have you been talking to Hera? We've already heard this version. Rather clever, original and, as you would say nowadays, Gothic. But way off target. Used banknotes are not impregnated with energy, all they are impregnated with is human sweat. And seething with germs. I would not drink a decoction made from them even if personally ordered to by Comrade Stalin. Banknotes do certainly play a role in our rituals, but it is a purely symbolic one and has nothing whatever to do with nectar of the gods. Another go?'

I thought that if Hera's theory had been so wrong, mine might be nearer the truth.

'Maybe vampires do something with the money in bank accounts? Build up a large sum somewhere offshore, and then ... in some way distil it into liquid form?'

Again Enlil Maratovich broke into laughter. Our conversation was obviously affording him considerable pleasure.

'Rama,' he said, 'do you really think vampires are able to use financial resources in a completely different way from human beings? Money, after all, is simply an abstraction.'

'A pretty concrete one,' I said.

'Yes. But you must agree that money has no existence outside the limits of the human mind.'

'I don't agree,' I replied. 'As you are so fond of telling everyone, there was a period in my life when I worked unloading trucks at a supermarket and got a wage for it. And I can tell you for a fact that what they paid me came from outside my mind. If I had been able to get it from inside my own head, why would I have got up and gone to work in the mornings?'

'But if you had passed on your wages to, let us say, a cow, she would not have understood what you were doing – and not just because you were being paid such a pitifully small amount. To her your wages would have meant nothing but a heap of crumpled paper. There is no such thing in the world as money independent of human beings. There is only the activity of the human mind in its preoccupation with it. Do remember this: money is not a real substance, it is an objectification.'

'What's an objectification?'

'I'll give you an example. Imagine a prisoner incarcerated in the Bastille for having committed some dreadful crime. One day at dawn he is put into a carriage and taken to Paris. On the way he realises that he is being taken to execution. On the square there is great crowd of people. He is led up to the scaffold, where the sentence is read to him. He is strapped into position beneath the guillotine... a strike of the blade, and his head flies into the basket...'

Enlil Maratovich clapped his knee with his palm.

'And?' I enquired nervously.

'At that moment he wakes up and remembers that he is not after all a prisoner but a supermarket unloader, and a big heart-shaped fan fell down from the wall onto his neck while he was asleep.'

'It wouldn't have fallen,' I said quietly. 'It was glued on.'

Enlil Maratovich paid no attention to my retort.

'In other words,' he went on, 'something can occur in reality which a man cannot understand because he is asleep. However, he cannot completely ignore it. His sleeping mind therefore creates a convoluted and detailed dream-explanation for it. This dream is called an objectification.'

'I understand,' I said. 'What you're saying is that money is a colourful dream that people see in an attempt to explain something of which they have an inkling but do not actually understand.'

'Exactly.'

'But I believe,' I said, 'that people understand it all very well.'

'They think they understand.'

'But to understand, after all, means to think. And to think means to understand.'

Enlil Maratovich looked at me searchingly.

'Do you know what goes on in the mind of a cow which has been milked all her life by an electric milking machine?'

'A cow doesn't think.'

'Oh yes, she does. Just not as people do. Not with abstract concepts but with emotional reflexes. And on her level she also understands perfectly well what goes on.'

'How?'

'She believes that human beings are her deformed offspring. Hideous and misshapen though they are, nevertheless they are her dear little children, and they must be fed because otherwise they will suffer hunger. For that reason she eats her fill of clover every day and tries to give them as much milk as she can...'

Enlil Maratovich's phone rang. He flipped it open and brought it to his ear.

'No, not yet. It will be some time. Keep going with current business for now. Do the casting of the lots later.'

Closing the phone, he replaced it in his pocket.

'Well now,' he said. 'All that now remains for you to do is to assemble the various bits into the whole picture. Do you think you can do that?'

I shook my head.

'Think hard about it!' said Enlil Maratovich, raising his finger significantly. 'I have brought you right to the threshold of our world. You are standing before the door. But you cannot open it. Never mind open it, you can't even see it... Our world is so completely hidden that if we do not drag you physically into it by the hand you will never know that it exists. This, Rama, is what is meant by total camouflage.'

'Perhaps,' I offered, 'I am just too stupid.'

'Not only you. Everyone. And the cleverer they are, the more stupid they are. The human mind is either a microscope through which a man examines the floor of his room, or a telescope through which he looks at the stars in the sky outside his window. But the one thing he never sees is himself in the right perspective.'

'And what is the right perspective?'

'This is precisely what I am talking about, so listen very carefully. Money is simply an objectification needed by people to account for the spasms of the money gland – those mental contractions that Mind "B" continually experiences. And as Mind "B" is constantly at work, it follows that...'

I suddenly had a wild thought.

'Do vampires milk people remotely?' I breathed.

Enlil Maratovich beamed.

'Well done! Of course!'

'But... things don't happen like that,' I said, dismayed.

'Think. How do we get honey?'

'All right,' I said. 'The bee herself brings the honey. But to do that she has to fly into the hive. There is no way honey can be transmitted in the air.'

'Not honey, no. But life-force can be.'

'How?' I asked.

Enlil Maratovich took the pen from the table, took a sheet of paper, and drew this diagram on it:

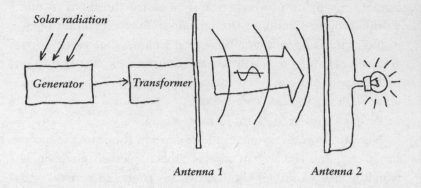

Solar radiation

Generator

Transformer

Antenna 1

Antenna 2

'Do you have a clear idea of what a radio wave is?' he asked.

I nodded, then thought a little more, and shook my head in denial.

'I'll try to keep it simple,' said Enlil Maratovich. 'A transmitter is a piece of equipment that excites electrons to rush about in a metal rod to and fro in a sine wave. The rod is the antenna. It produces radio waves, which travel at the speed of light. In order to capture the energy of these waves, a second antenna is needed. Both antennae must be of a length proportionate to the length of the wave, because the energy is transmitted on a resonating principle. I expect you know that when you strike one tuning fork, another one placed near it will begin to sound. But for the second one to ring in response, it must be identical to the first one. In practice, of course, it is all rather more complicated: in order to transmit and receive energy, the waves must be concentrated in a particular cluster of rays, the antennae must be correctly positioned spatially in relation to one another, and so on. But the principle is the same... now let me draw you another diagram...'

Enlil Maratovich turned over the sheet of paper and drew the following:

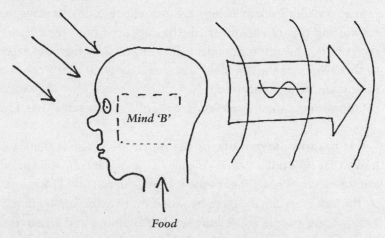

Glamour discourse

Mind 'B'

Food

'You mean, Mind "B" is the transmitting antenna?' I asked.

He nodded.

'And what is the person thinking while the transmitter is working?'

'Difficult to say. It depends what kind of person he is: a corporate manager or a guy with a fruit stall by a Metro station. But the inner dialogue of any contemporary urban dweller will fall essentially into one of two alternative patterns. In the first he thinks: "I'm winning! I'm getting there! I'll show the lot of them! I'm going for the throat! I'll screw all the money I can out of this shitty world!"'

'Yes,' I agreed, 'that makes a lot of sense.'

'And there is another pattern where he thinks: "I'm drowning! I'll never make it! I'm in deep shit! I'm a hopeless loser and will die dirt poor!"'

'That can happen too,' I confirmed.

'In any given consciousness these two processes take hold and turn about, and may be considered a single stream of thought altering direction cyclically. It's like an alternating current radiating from an antenna, transmitting the person's life-force into space. But human beings are not capable of capturing or registering this radiation. It can be captured only by a living receiver, not by any mechanical device. People sometimes refer to this energy as the "biofield", but exactly what that might be no human being understands.'

'Supposing a man doesn't say either "I'm a winner" or "I'm a loser"?'

'He has to be saying one or the other. What else is there for him to say? All other processes that occur in the conscious mind are soon extinguished. That's the job of Glamour and Discourse.'

'But not everyone is driven by ambition to achieve something,' I said. 'Some people aren't interested in Glamour and Discourse. Homeless people, alcoholics – they couldn't give a stuff.'

'It only seems like that because their world has different parameters of achievement,' replied Enlil Maratovich. 'But everyone has their Fuji, however small and disgusting it may be.'

I sighed. I was getting tired of all these references to experiences in my former life.

'A person occupies himself ceaselessly with the question of money,' went on Enlil Maratovich. 'But the process takes many different and often indistinct forms. To all appearances a fellow may be lying on the beach doing absolutely nothing and wanting absolutely nothing. But in fact he is thinking about that yacht out there on the horizon, how much it cost, and what he would have to do with his life to get enough money to buy one like it. His wife, meanwhile, looks at the woman on the next sunbed and tries to figure out whether her handbag and sunglasses are genuine, how much her Botox injections cost, and how much an equivalent liposuction job on her own arse would be, and which of their bungalows is more expensive. At the core of all such psychic vortices is a central abstraction – the idea of money. And every time these vortices erupt in a man's consciousness, there follows a milking of the money teat. The art of consumption, favourite brands, decisions based on taste and style – these are just the surface. Concealed below them is one fact and one fact only: a man has eaten a wiener schnitzel and is busy transmuting it into *Aggregate "M-5"*.'

It was an expression I had not heard before.

'Aggregate "M-5"?' I repeated. 'What is that?'

'In economics, aggregates are various aspects of the overall money supply. "M-0", "M-1", "M-2", "M-3" are forms of cash, financial instruments and financial obligations. Aggregate "M-4" includes verbal agreements about discounts, and kickbacks are also known as "M-Che" in honour of Ernesto Che Guevara and Anatoly Chubais. But all of these are simply mirages; they exist solely in people's minds. "M-5" is in principle something entirely different, a special kind of psychic energy produced by people in their struggle to acquire the first four aggregates. Aggregate "M-5" really exists. The others are merely objectifications of this energy.'

'Hold on, hold on,' I said. 'First you said that there is no such thing as money in nature. Now you're talking about Aggregate "M-5" which, apparently, does exist. So sometimes money exists and sometimes it doesn't?'

Enlil Maratovich pushed over to me the sheet with the first diagram.

'Look,' he said. 'The human brain is a device which produces for us what we call the world. This device is capable not only of receiving signals but of transmitting them. If we were to tune all such devices identically and concentrate the attention of all human beings on one and the same abstraction, all these transmitters would radiate energy on a single wavelength. That wavelength is money.'

'Money is a wavelength?' I queried.

'Yes. One cannot actually say of a wavelength that it exists, because it is simply a construct of the mind, therefore outside of the mind there is no such thing. And yet it is equally impossible to state that a wavelength does not exist, because any wavelength can be measured. Now do you understand?'

'Just a moment,' I said. 'Money is different in different countries. If a Muscovite is given a brown envelope full of dollars, does that mean he sends his vital energy to America?'

Enlil Maratovich laughed.

'Not quite. Money is money, no matter what it is called and what colour it may be. It's just an abstraction. Its wavelength therefore remains constant. But any signal possesses not only frequency but form, and that form can alter fundamentally. Have you ever wondered why there are different languages, nations and countries in the world?'

'Just the way the cookie crumbles,' I shrugged.

'Cookies may crumble. Everything else has a mechanism. Throughout the world there are sovereign communities of vampires. The national culture to which a person belongs is like a brand on a steer. It's like a key for a lock, or an access code for a door. Each vampire community can milk only its own cattle. Accordingly, although the process by which money is produced is the same the world over, its cultural objectification can differ sharply.'

'Do you mean to suggest that this is the whole point of human culture?' I asked.

'No, why should it be? It can have other elements as well.'

'What sort of other elements?

Enlil Maratovich thought for a while.

'Well, how can I put it? ... Imagine a man sitting in a bare concrete cage producing electricity. Let's say there are metal handles protruding from the wall which he slides to and fro, backwards and forwards. He's not going to be able to stand doing that for long, is he? He's going to start thinking: What am

I doing here? Why do I spend all day, from morning to night, sliding these handles back and forth? Why don't I get the hell out of here? That's going to occur to him at some point, don't you think?'

'Could be,' I agreed.

'Now suppose a plasma screen is suspended in front of him, showing a video of scenes of Venice and the handles are made in the shape of oars in a gondola sailing down the canal... and then, for two weeks a year, the handles have a new shape like ski poles, and the screen shows Courchevel... our oarsman won't have any more questions. The only thing he will worry about is losing his place at the oars. So he carries on rowing with redoubled enthusiasm.'

'Won't he notice that the same scenes keep coming round on the screen?'

'Oh yes,' sighed Enlil Maratovich. 'Solomon had something to say about that. You know, in the Bible. For that reason the length of the human lifespan was calculated so that people would not have time to draw significant conclusions from what's going on.'

'Another thing I don't understand,' I said. 'Surely, anything at all could be shown on the plasma screen. Venice if you like, or the City of the Sun. Who decides what the gondolier is going to look at?

'Who? Why, they do. They decide themselves.'

'Themselves? Well, then, why ever do people go on, year after year, looking at this... at this...?'

Enlil Maratovich shrugged his shoulders.

'Well,' he replied, 'as the saying goes, whatever floats your boat... Why should we care about it as long as they believe there *is* a boat and don't want to risk missing it?'

I sighed and turned my attention to the first diagram, then turned over and looked at the second. The empty space on its right-hand side seemed mysterious, even frightening.

'What is here?' I asked, indicating the place with my finger.

'Would you like to know?'

I nodded.

Enlil Maratovich opened the drawer of his desk, took something out of it and tossed it to me.

'Catch!'

In my hands was a dark glass bottle in the shape of a bat with its wings folded. It was in every particular like the one I had been sent on the day of the Great Fall. Now I understood.

'You want me to ... again ... ?'

'There is no other way.'

I was seized with dismay. Enlil Maratovich smiled encouragingly.

'Chaldeans,' he said, 'regard life as the metaphorical ascent of a ziggurat, at the top of which the Goddess Ishtar awaits them. They have heard of the Tower of Babel, and they think they know what it means. But people are looking in the wrong place. Sacred symbolism should often be understood as exactly the opposite of its superficial appearance. The top is the bottom. Empty is full. The most glittering career is in reality the most abject failure, a stadium is a pyramid, the highest tower the deepest chasm. The summit of Fuji is right at the bottom, Rama. You've been through this already ...'

For some reason this incantation worked. I took out of the flask the stopper in the shape of a skull, poured the single drop of preparation on to my tongue, and held it against the roof of my mouth.

After a few seconds, Enlil Maratovich said:

'Don't linger too long there. You have things to do up here.'

'There? Where is there?'

Enlil Maratovich's smile became even broader.

'Vampires have a motto: "Suckers wear the triple crown – into darkness, back and down!"'

'That I understand,' I replied. 'What I mean is, where do I go now?'

'You go there,' said Enlil Maratovich, and raising his hand pressed down on the Sputnik before him on the desk.

The room suddenly moved backwards and upwards. The next instant I realised that it was not the room moving, it was my Gothic chair, which had tipped over into the gulf which had opened in the floor, and before I even had time to cry out, I was slipping on my back down a sloping chute of some polished material, into darkness, back, and down, exactly as promised. Frightened of hitting my head, I tried to protect it with my hands, but the chute came to an end and I found myself flying into a bottomless black void.

For a few seconds I cried aloud, clawing at the air with my hands in an attempt to take hold. When I eventually succeeded in doing so, I realised they were no longer hands.

THE TREE OF LIFE

I was gliding down into the darkness for so long I had time not only to conquer my panic but to become bored and extremely cold. Virgil's phrase about Lake Avernus came to mind: 'smooth is the descent, and easy is the way.' The Romans considered that people could accomplish the descent into Hades without difficulty. *That's how much they knew*, I thought. The circles I was describing blended into a monotonously wearying passage – not unlike walking down the staircase of a high-rise building during a power cut. The most sinister aspect of it was that I had no sense of nearing the bottom.

To occupy my mind with something, I tried conjuring up everything I knew about the expression 'the tree of life'. First of all, it was the name of the tree on which the Scandinavian god Odin hung himself in his attempt to be initiated into the secret of the runes. You have to imagine him hanging upside down... Secondly, in the Gnostic Apocryphon of John, which figured in one of the degustations on the theme of 'local cults', there had been an excerpt on the subject.

'For their delight is deception,' I repeated over to myself what I could remember. 'And their fruit is an incurable poison and their promise is death. And in the midst of paradise, they planted the tree of their life... But I, I will teach you what the mystery of their life is ... the root of the tree is bitter and its branches are death, and its shade is hate ... Deception dwells in its leaves, and it blossoms from the darkness ...'

The tree that grows into darkness – a beautiful, and morbid, image. Its fruits, apparently, were also death, but I could not remember exactly. The agglomeration of so many such horrors in this description was not, however, especially frightening – after all, many things that made ancient man tremble with fear have long since become a normal part of our daily existence.

The chasm widened out. I wondered what could possibly have caused this strange geological formation. Enlil Maratovich's house was built on a hill, so it was possible that at one time it had been the mouth of an ancient volcano. Although, heaven knows, there aren't too many volcanoes on the outskirts of Moscow ... Or it might be a tunnel resulting from a meteorite strike. Of course, there was also the possibility that it was a man-made shaft.

I began to sense the bottom. It was closer than I thought – the confined walls of the well shaft were giving back too many reflections of the sound waves from my echo-locator, thus providing a misleading impression of the space. Below me was water, a small circular lake. The water was warm and steam was rising from it, which I felt as extra-dense air. I was afraid I might get a soaking or even drown. But as I descended even lower I became aware of a triangular opening in the stone face. It was the entrance to a cave just above the surface of the water, and there I could alight.

My first attempt was unsuccessful. My wings struck the water and I nearly fell in. I had to gain height again and repeat the manoeuvre. This time I furled my wings too high above the stone shelf and made a rather painful landing.

As on the previous occasion, the striking of my fists against the cold stone was the signal to shake me free of my dream and simultaneously of my bat body. I stood upright on my feet.

The surrounding gloom was damp, warm and slightly sultry. What air there was had a whiff of sulphur, and a peculiar kind of mineral smell reminiscent of spas in the Caucasus I had been taken to in early childhood. The floor of the cave was uneven, with large boulders lying about on it, so that I had to tread carefully and pick out a place for each step. A light burned in the depths of the cave, but I could not see where it was coming from.

What I saw when I turned a corner and entered the lit area was hard to believe.

Before me was an enormous, empty cavern, an underground hall pierced by spotlights which, however, did not illuminate the space so much as mask it, so blinding were they to anyone entering. The roof of the cavern was so far above I could hardly see it.

In the centre of the hall towered a gigantic structure to which led a long scaffold bridge made of metal. At first I thought the structure was a huge plant, some sort of shaggy cactus as big as a large house, surrounded by yet more scaffolding to which it was tightly bound by strips of dark material. It could also have been a barrel-shaped cargo rocket on its launch platform, an impression reinforced by the number of pipes and cables extending from it into the darkness. Above the structure were two huge metal rings set into the ceiling.

I worked my way forward, the ringing of my heels on the metal giving warning of my approach. No one, however, come out to meet me. On the contrary, I noticed several obscure figures scurrying away at my appearance. I had the impression they were women swathed in full-body covering, as in the East. I did not hail them, assuming that they would do so themselves if they wished to make contact with me. The ritual, I thought, might stipulate solitude.

After another ten metres, I stopped.

I noticed that this colossal tun, surrounded by scaffolding and pipes, seemed to be breathing. It was alive. And at this moment my faculties experienced one of those small miracles that occur when the mind suddenly assembles a coherent picture from a myriad of formerly random lines and zigzags.

I was looking at a giant bat trussed with belts and held up by an array of props and braces and buttresses. Her paws, like the upturned base of a giant crane, were forced into the two cyclopean copper rings in the stone ceiling, and her wings were bound to her body with ropes and trusses. I could not see her head – judging by the proportions of her body it was in a pit extending far below the level of the floor. Her breathing reminded me of a huge pump working.

She was old. So old that the odour that came off was more geological than biological – this must have been what I had taken for the sulphurous smell of mineral water. She looked unreal, like a whale enwrapped in its own flippers suspended above the ground in a corset. It was the sort of image a surrealist artist of the last century might have painted under the influence of hashish...

It was not possible to get close to the bat because she was surrounded by a fence. The scaffolding on which I was walking ended at a tunnel cut into the rock and led downwards. Cautiously I descended the slippery steps and found myself in a passage lit by halogen lamps. It was something like a gallery reinforced by steel framing, such as one sees in a mine on television, and black cables ran along its floor. A light breeze fanned my face: there was a ventilation system.

I proceeded along the passage. It soon brought me into a circular room carved out of the thickness of the rock. The room was extremely old; the roof was covered in soot, which had eaten so deeply into the stone that it no longer soiled the touch. On the walls were ochre drawings – rune-like zigzags and silhouettes of animals. To the right of the entrance was a darker patch on the wall like a window, except that it was not a window but a recess cut deeper into the rock. Before it stood a primitive altar – a stone slab with various artefacts lying on it. They included terracotta discs, crude beakers and a number of statuettes all resembling one another: figurines of a fat woman with a tiny head, enormous breasts and an equally enormous bottom. Some had been fashioned from bone, others from fired clay.

I turned one of the lamps round so that its beam fell on the recess above the altar. The opening was covered by a stretched-out piece of animal skin, in the middle of which was a wrinkled human head with long grey hair. It was shrivelled, but there was no sign of decomposition.

The effect was ghoulish and repellent. I hastily continued along the passage. After a few metres I came to another similar room with a niche in it also containing a mummified head sewn into a piece of animal hide. On the altar before it lay shards of crystal, unrecognisable fossilised organic matter of some description, and some bronze arrowheads. The walls were decorated with rich ornamentation.

Further on was another such room, then another, and another. There were very many of them, and the combined effect was of a history museum exhibition: 'From Early Man to Our Own Times'. Bronze axes and knives, rust stains where iron implements had disintegrated, scattered coins, drawings on the walls – I would certainly have spent longer looking at it all had it not been for those heads hanging there like monstrous dried cherries. They hypnotised me. I could not even be sure they were dead.

'I am a vampire, I am a vampire,' I whispered quietly to

myself, trying to dispel the terror gripping me. 'I am the most terrible thing here – nothing can be more terrible than I...'

But even I did not find this very convincing.

Gradually furniture began to appear in some of the rooms – benches and chests. Jewellery glittered on some of the heads above the altars, growing progressively more elaborate: earrings, beads, gold combs. One head was adorned with a necklace of small coins. This one I stopped to take a closer look at. And suddenly the money-bedizened head inclined towards me, as if giving me a nod.

This was not the first time I thought I might have detected some movement, but I had put it down to tricks of light and shade. But now I could hear the tinkling of the coins, and realised that light and shade had nothing to do with it.

Struggling with my fear, I stepped up closer to the niche. Again, the head twitched, and I saw that it was not the head moving but the animal skin on which it was hanging. And then I finally understood what it was.

It was the neck of the colossal bat, visible through the apertures in the rock wall.

I remembered that the Gnostic texts made mention of a certain high-ranking demonic creature, a serpent with the head of a lion – 'The Lord of This World'. Here everything was the other way round. The giant bat had the neck of a snake which, rhizome-like, wound its way deep into the thickness of the stone. Perhaps there were several such necks, and I was following the path of one of them along a gallery cut into the rock. Altar rooms were set up at those places where the neck could be seen.

In the rooms I saw much that was wonderful and much that was strange. The chronological sequence, however, was often disrupted, for instance when following a collection of valuable harnesses and weapons that seemed to belong to the era of the Golden Horde, I next came across a room with obviously

Egyptian relics, as if I had stumbled into the burial chamber deep inside a pyramid (the gods seemed to be distinctly second-hand: their faces had been maimed by a multitude of knocks). I remember one room lined with sheets of gold inscribed in Church Slavonic: as I passed through it I felt as though I were inside a safe of treasures belonging to an Old Believers' sect. In another room, my eye was caught by a gold peacock with emerald-green eyes and a rotting tail. I knew that at one time the throne of the emperors of Byzantium was flanked by two such birds – this might have been one of them.

It eventually dawned on me why there appeared to be such chronological dislocations. In many of the rooms there were two or three ways out. Behind these too were enfilades of more altar rooms, but they were unlit and the very thought of going along such passages filled me with terror. Clearly the garland of lamps was intended to guide the traveller along the shortest route to the goal.

The altar rooms also differed in mood. Some of them were monastic in their severity; others, on the other hand, reminded me of an aristocratic boudoir. The coiffures of the mummified heads gradually increased in complexity. Wigs began to appear, and layers of cosmetics on the shrivelled faces. I noticed that in all this time I did not see a single male face.

The deeper I descended into the stone gallery, the stronger grew the gnawing feeling in the pit of my stomach that the end of the journey was approaching. This was clear from the changes in the way the rooms were decorated. I already knew what must await me at the conclusion of the exhibition. There could be no doubt that it would be another head, and this time a live one – that very 'antenna of a dimension proportionate to the wavelength' of which Enlil Maratovich had spoken.

The eighteenth- and nineteenth-century altar rooms were like galleries in a small museum. They were full of pictures, escritoires stood against the walls, and on the altars themselves lay bulky folios with raised gold lettering printed on them.

One room, which I dated to the beginning of the twentieth century, seemed the most elegant to me, being furnished simply and in good taste. On the walls were two large paintings simulating windows into a garden in which cherry trees were in blossom. The pictures were so skilfully integrated into the space that the illusion was complete, especially viewed from the altar where the head was. The head in this room struck me as relatively unimpressive: it was adorned with no more than a single string of pearls, and the coiffure was extremely plain. On the altar before it was a white enamelled telephone which had been damaged by bullets. Beside it was a long cigarette-holder of coral. Looking more closely I noticed bullet-holes in the furniture and the pictures. There was also a peculiar mark on the temple of the shrivelled head – but this could have been an extended birthmark.

In the earliest room of the Soviet era the function of the altar was performed by a door resting on two stools. There was a telephone on this one as well: it was black and had a horn-shaped cradle for the handset, with something like the handle of an old car magneto on the side. The room was almost empty: the only decoration was provided by flags standing in the corners and crossed sabres on the walls. The altar niche contained not one but two heads, one hanging in the middle and the other huddled away forlornly on its own in the corner. Near the altar was a mourning wreath with a red ribbon woven into it, as withered as the head above it.

The altar in the next room was a huge office desk with a pile of cardboard folders with papers on it. Here was another telephone: a massive piece of equipment in black ebony, redolent of calm dependability. Bookcases, with rows of books in identical brown bindings, lined the walls. There were no heads at all in the altar recess; all that could be seen were some tubes bound up with insulating tape protruding from the skin.

The last room, by contrast, was a true museum of late Soviet life with a great number of different objects preserved in it. Garish cut-crystal vases and wine glasses on a sideboard, carpets on the walls, mink coats on hangers, an enormous Bohemian glass chandelier hanging from the ceiling... In the corner stood a colour television set as big as a trunk and covered in dust. In the centre of the altar table, among old newspapers and photograph albums, was yet another telephone – this time a white plastic one, with the USSR coat of arms in gold on the disc. There was a head in the altar niche: an ordinary, unremarkable shrivelled head with a hennaed chignon piled up in a bun at the back, and big ruby earrings.

The passage did not go any further. The Hall of Mature Socialism, as I privately dubbed this altar room, ended in a steel door. On it hung a nameplate, green with age, on which was written in queerly printed old script:

Ye Greate Batte

On the wall I noticed a bell. Shifting nervously from foot to foot, I pressed it.

Half a minute passed. The lock clicked open and the door opened a few millimetres, but no further. After waiting a little more, I put my ear to the crack which had opened.

'Girls, girls,' came a hoarse female voice, 'conceal yourselves, now. How many times do I have to tell you: get behind the screen!'

I rang once more.

'OK, OK,' answered the voice. 'Come on in!'

I entered, carefully closing the door behind me.

This altar room was the same size as its predecessor, but

228

seemed bigger because of its modern look. The walls were painted white and the floor had been paved with large sand-coloured tiles. Altogether it suggested a moderately prosperous Moscow apartment, except that the designer furniture looked more expensive than that. But there was not much of it: a red sofa and two blue armchairs. On the wall opposite the altar (so far I had not summoned up courage to look in the other direction) hung a plasma TV. Beside it was a bamboo screen with a representation *à la* Van Gogh of a French night sky, in the illimitable vastness of which burned what looked like hundreds of upturned smart cars. Evidently this was the screen behind which the girls had been told to hide themselves.

'Greetings,' said a caressingly tender voice. 'Why don't you turn round? Look at me; don't be afraid. You think I'm some sort of Medusa, and just one glance from me is enough to get you stoned? No, no, my boy. We're too low here to get high, ha ha. Only joking – just my little joke. Couldn't you raise your eyes and look at me?'

I raised my eyes.

The altar niche also bore traces of having been recently refurbished. They were even to be seen on skin of the bat's neck – where it touched the wall it was stained with white emulsion paint.

A woman's face was smiling at me from the middle of the recess – still, as the saying goes, with traces of her former beauty. From all appearances the head was about fifty years old, but in fact was probably more than that because even my untutored eye could see traces of numerous cosmetic procedures and rejuvenating injections. Only the mouth was smiling while the eyes, encircled by immobile skin, looked out full of doubt and alarm.

The head was crowned by an amazingly elaborate coiffure – a combination of Rastafarian 'let's-share-a-joint' dreadlocks and the cool glamour of a Snow Queen. Below it tumbled a shock of piebald dreads into which were woven beads and bangles of various sizes, while above it the hair had been teased up into a fan of four peacock feathers linked by a shell of golden chains and threads. The tracery of this glittering polygon made one think of a crown. As a hairdo it was certainly impressive: I thought how good it would have looked in the *Alien vs. Predator* film – on the head of some sharp-toothed cosmic sow. Atop this tired and puffy female face, however, it did look rather absurd.

'Well then, come to me. Come to Mummy,' cooed the head. 'Let me feast my eyes on you.'

I came close up to her, and we kissed one another three times in the Russian fashion, delicately passing the lips to brush the cheek near the mouth.

I was amazed by the head's manoeuvrability. First she seemed to fly at me from one side, then instantly appear at the other, and finally back to the starting point. During the kiss I just had time to turn my eyes, no more.

'Ishtar Borisovna,' said the head. 'Ishtar to you. Don't imagine I address everyone like that, only boys as pretty as you, ha ha...'

'Rama the Second,' I introduced myself.

'I know. Sit down. No, wait a moment. How about a little cognac to celebrate our meeting?'

'Ishtar Borisovna, you're not to have any more today,' protested a severe young female voice from behind the screen.

'Oh, it's only to toast our acquaintance,' said the head. 'Five grams apiece, that's all. Don't worry, the young man will help me.'

She nodded towards the altar table.

Here total disorder reigned. The marble slab was piled high with glossy magazines, all muddled up with cosmetic jars and bottles of expensive liquor. Right in the middle of the chaos bulked a massive, heavy laptop computer, the kind one could use as a replacement for a desktop. I noticed that the printed matter on the table was not confined to unadulterated glamour: among the magazines were titles such as *Your Property* and *Refurbishment in Moscow*.

'There's the cognac,' said Ishtar. 'And wee glasses too. Don't worry, they're clean...'

From the table I took the bottle of Hennessy XO, whose shape reminded me of the stone females from the early altar rooms I had seen, and poured some cognac into the large cut-crystal goblets the head had referred to as 'wee glasses'. To me they looked more like vases than glasses – they took just about the whole bottle. No objection was raised to this.

'Good,' said Ishtar. 'You do the clinking yourself... and then help Mummy.'

I tinkled one glass against the other and held one out, not knowing what I should do next.

'Tip it up, don't be afraid...'

I inclined the glass and the head deftly dived down below it to catch the yellow-brown stream. Not a single drop reached the floor. It made me think of midair refuelling. Instead of a neck, Ishtar had a furry, sinewy stem more than a metre long, which made her look like an animated tree-growing mushroom.

'Sit down,' she said, indicating the blue armchair placed beside the altar. I sat on the edge of it, sipped a little cognac and put the glass on the table.

The head smacked its lips once or twice and closed its eyes in contemplation. I had enough experience of vampires to know what this meant. I passed my hand over my neck and looked at my fingers – and there, sure enough, was a tiny red spot. Obviously she had managed to bite me as we kissed. Opening her eyes, she fixed them on me.

'I don't like it,' I said, 'when someone...'

'Well, I do like it,' interrupted the head, 'especially when I

231

have a drink. I'm allowed... Well, you know... Hello Rama. Roma as was. You had a difficult childhood, you poor, poor boy.'

'Why difficult?' I replied, embarrassed. 'It was a childhood like any other.'

'You're right, a childhood like any other. That's why it was difficult. Everyone in our country has a difficult childhood. It's so as to prepare a person for life as a grown-up. Which is going to be so difficult it will totally screw you up.'

Ishtar sighed and again smacked her lips. I could not work out whether she was savouring my red liquid, or the cognac, or both at the same time.

'You don't like being a vampire, do you, Rama?' she concluded.

'Why do you say that? It's pretty good, really.'

'When people like it, they don't live as you do. They want to spend every day as if it was a jolly Halloween holiday. Like your friend Mithra. But you... You were thinking about your soul again two nights ago, weren't you?'

'I was,' I conceded.

'What do you think a soul is?'

'I don't know,' I answered. 'Our people have already asked me that.'

'So how can you think about it when you don't know what it is?'

'Well, you can see that for yourself.'

'Certainly... Listen, do you think about the meaning of life as well?'

'Sometimes,' I replied, embarrassed.

'About how the world came into being? And about God?'

'That too. Yes, I have done.'

Ishtar frowned, as if trying to decide what was to be done

232

with me. A tiny wrinkle appeared on thc smooth surface of her forehead. Then it disappeared and all was smooth again.

'I do understand you,' she said. 'And I do a lot of thinking too. Especially just recently ... But I have reasons to. Concrete reasons. You though? You're so young, you ought to be living and enjoying yourself. Not like us pensioners!'

It occurred to me that this was how older women often talked, women who had been born under Stalin and who had preserved within themselves a cache of state-sponsored optimism which their schooldays had drummed into their frightened souls. There had been a time when I too had accepted the blister raised by such a burn as the stigmata of the sacred flame. But my course of degustations had cured me of this misapprehension.

Ishtar glanced at my glass and then at me, pulled a sour face, then winked and stretched her mouth into a smile. The whole pantomime took less than a second – her grimaces were so quick they were more like a nervous tic.

I understand what was required. Getting up, I took my glass from the table and we repeated the aerial refuelling procedure. Ishtar made no sound by which anyone sitting behind the screen could interpret what was going on. I took my seat again. Ishtar knitted her brow with an air of martyrdom and expelled a deep sigh.

'Well,' she said, 'this is how matters stand. I am a Goddess all right, but that does not mean I shall be able to give you any intelligent answers to your questions. You see, the realm in which I am a Goddess is a very constricted one. What you should do is this. You should seek out a vampire by the name of Osiris. He is the guardian of traditional lore. Tell him I sent you. He will explain everything to you.'

'How will I find him?'

'Ask someone. Only don't mention it to Enlil. They are

brothers, and have been in a quarrel for many years. I've also fallen out with Osiris, you might say.'

'What about?'

'It wasn't really about anything specific. It's just that he lost contact with me. He's a Tolstoyan.'

'A Tolstoyan?' I repeated.

'Yes. Do you know anything about them?'

'No. Never heard of them.'

'Tolstoyan vampires appeared at the beginning of the last century,' said Ishtar. 'The ideas of Count Tolstoy were very fashionable then. The simple life. The sufferings of the people, return to basic truths, all that sort of thing. Some of our people were also attracted to it and were tempted to follow the simple life. But how is a vampire going to simplify his life? They decided not to suck *bablos* any more and go back to pure red liquid. But without killing anybody, because after all they were Tolstoyans. So there aren't many left now, but Osiris is one of them.'

'How did he get into it?'

'Drugs – that's what I think, if I'm honest. Narcotics and all sorts of stupid books. You'll have your fill of talk if you speak with him. He can fuck your brains as well as Enlil can, only from the other direction...'

She laughed. I got the impression that the brandy she had drunk was already having its effect.

'What is *bablos*?' I asked

'Didn't Enlil tell you anything about it?'

'He started to. About the life-force a man radiates into space whenever he thinks about money. Aggregate "M-5". But he said I would learn the rest... here. If I am considered worthy.'

'Oy, give me a break,' groaned Ishtar. 'Considered worthy, my foot. Double checking, triple checking. I have no secrets from anybody. If you want to know something, just ask me.'

'*Bablos* – does the word come from *bablo*, the Russian slang for money?'

Ishtar tittered, and I heard the girls behind the screen laughing as well.

'No,' she said. '*Bablos* is a really ancient word. It may be the very oldest which has come down to us. It has the same root as "Babylon", and that in turn comes from the Akkadian word "*bab-ilu*" which means "the gates of God". *Bablos* is a sacred drink that turns vampires into gods.'

'Is that why we have names like we do?'

'Yes. Sometimes *bablos* is called "red liquid". But Enlil goes all scientific when he speaks of it: Aggregate "M-5", the ultimate condition of money. It's condensed human life-force.'

'Does one drink *bablos*?'

'One drinks cognac. One sucks *bablos*. There's not much of it.'

'Hold on a moment,' I said. 'I think there's a bit of confusion here. Enlil Maratovich told me that "red liquid" is the correct term for human...'

'Blood,' broke in Ishtar. 'With me you can call it that.'

But by now I was finding it difficult to say the word.

'He was saying that vampires stopped drinking red liquid when they developed human beings to the point where they could produce money.'

'Quite correct,' said Ishtar. 'But we are still vampires, so we cannot entirely do without blood. Otherwise we would lose our identity and our roots. What is money? It is the symbolic blood of the world. Everything depends on it, both for humans and for us. But the manner in which we depend on it is different, because we live in the real world whereas human beings live in the world of illusions.'

'Why do they? Surely they cannot all be so stupid?'

'They are not stupid. It's simply the way life is arranged. People are born into the world in order to create *bablos* out of

Glamour concentrate. It has different names in different eras, but the formula of human destiny has not changed for many centuries.'

'What is that formula?'

'"Illusion – money – illusion". Do you know what is the principal characteristic of mankind as a biological species? People are constantly chasing after visions that arise within their heads. But for some reason they do not capture them there inside their heads, where they appear, but pursue them in the real physical world, on which the visions are merely superimposed. And then, when the visions dissipate, the man stops and says to himself: oh Mama, what was that? Where am I, and why am I, and what am I supposed to do now? This syndrome applies not just to individuals, but to entire civilisations. To live amidst illusions is the natural habitat for people just as it is for a grasshopper to sit in the grass. Because it is precisely human illusions that produce *bablos*...'

They're obsessed with that bloody grasshopper, I thought. All the same, there was something very dispiriting about these older vampires always trying to talk to me in language they thought I would understand.

'What does it mean, to live in the real world?' I asked.

'It was very well put by Count Dracula. He said, "The image is nothing, the thirst is everything."'

'Is there a formula for vampires' destiny?'

'Yes. "Red liquid – money – red liquid". If we forget about political correctness, "blood – money – *bablos*". The red liquid in the formula is human, but not the *bablos*.'

'But how can "red liquid" be the name for both *bablos* and human... er, you know what I mean?'

'Because,' answered Ishtar, 'they are the same thing on different levels of the dialectical spiral. Not only in their colour but also in their essential quality. Like, for instance, beer and cognac...'

Pronouncing the word 'cognac' she glanced at the table, then at me, and winked. Trying not to make any noise, I poured out the remainder of the Hennessy XO into my glass and thence into the mouth of the head. Again with great agility she dived under the glass, and not a drop fell to the floor.

I could not work out where the cognac could be going to, once she had drunk it. Presumably there was some sort of craw in her neck. At all events, the full effect of the alcohol was now visible. Her face was flushed, and I could see what I had not noticed before, lines of scars from plastic surgery just below the ears.

I heard a meaningful cough behind the screen, from the unseen girl. I decided Ishtar would not get any more spirits from me.

'But the difference consists in the degree of concentration of the essence,' went on Ishtar. 'There are five litres of red liquid in a man. But in the whole of his life no more than a gram of *bablos* can be extracted from him. Do you see?'

I nodded.

'You can get a whole gram from a WASP in America. Our Russkies are far stingier ... I wish I had some to offer you. Hey, girls, have we any *bablos*?'

'No,' said the girl's voice behind the screen.

'So you see,' said Ishtar. 'The cobbler has no shoes. I'm the one who makes the stuff, and I don't have any.'

'How do you make it?'

'Would you like to know the complete technological process? Want to creep under my skirts? *Bablos* is my milk ...'

Obviously I had once again failed wholly to mask my feelings, because Ishtar burst out laughing. I bit my lip, pasting on to my face a serious and respectful expression. She found this even more amusing.

'Enlil gave you the drawing from a dollar bill, didn't he?' she asked. 'The one with the pyramid and the eye? That shows how

237

the production is achieved technologically, and it is also at the same time my allegorical portrait. Well, not precisely mine, but any Ishtar in any country...'

'You're much prettier,' I put in.

'Thank you. The pyramid is the body of the goddess in which the *bablos* is condensed. The significance of the eye in the triangle is that it represents a disposable head which allows the goddess to see humans and restore contact with them after any catastrophe or major shift in their world. The eye is separate from the pyramid, therefore it makes no difference to vampires what people might believe in, or what kind of paper currency might be circulating among them in a hundred years' time – dollars or dinars. We are like deepwater fish – we are not disturbed by any hurricane which may arise on the surface; it does not touch us.'

'I understand,' I said.

'And about me being prettier – well, you're not very good at pretending. You're very amusing, all the same... By the way, thanks for your thoughts about my hairdo. I'll bear them in mind.'

I had said nothing to her about her coiffure, but realised that my initial impression must have had time to embed itself in my red liquid.

'Please forgive me,' I said, shamefacedly.

'No offence, I'm not a fool. You're quite right. The only thing is, I too get bored and lonely. After all, I have to watch television, and read glossy magazines, and now there's the Internet. And they're all so full of advertisements! They keep on at you: "Buy it! Because you're worth it," ha ha...'

Ishtar cackled with laughter again, and I realised she was now completely drunk.

'I do believe it,' she continued. 'I know I'm worth it, because I'm the one who keeps the whole schmear on the road. But I can't go off and buy a Learjet, can I? Or a yacht... well I could, as a matter of fact, but what would I do with it? I tell you what, forget the damn yacht... I saw an ad just a while ago. In a magazine – there it is, have a look...'

She nodded towards the table.

Lying near the edge was a magazine folded open at a full-page photograph. A bride, all in spotless white, was standing beside a wedding limousine, her face buried in a bouquet of lilacs. The cavalcade of wedding cars waited while the groom meditatively twiddled his moustache by the door of the car. The photographer had skilfully caught the envious glance of a woman in a little red jalopy passing from the opposite direction. The caption below the photo read: "OKsana Panty-liners. We Dry Harder!"'

Only now did I finally grasp the point of Enlil Maratovich's joke about the bush which isn't. It now struck me as hideously cruel.

'I may be worth all the money in the world,' said Ishtar sadly. 'But I don't even need those, no matter how hard they try or dry... So why shouldn't I play about with my hairdo? And my make-up? Stick some earrings in my ears? All that sort of thing? You really ought not to laugh at a foolish old woman.'

I was ashamed of myself. And I also felt a rush of pity for her. Thank God I had not spotted the stitches of the facelift until after she had bitten me. Let her think that at least that was done successfully.

The ringtone of the mobile phone sounded.

'Yes?' answered Ishtar.

I could hear the quiet squawking of a male voice coming through the earpiece.

'With me now,' said Ishtar. 'We're having a talk, yes... Nice boy, very nice. When he gets a bit older I'll appoint him instead of you, you fat old git, do you hear? What's that? Did you get such a fright you've pissed yourself? Ha ha ha...'

The earpiece resumed its squawking.

'All right then,' she agreed. 'He'd better go, if that's the situation.'

She raised her eyes and looked at me.

'Enlil. He says it's time for you to go back up.'

'How do I do that?'

'There's a lift.'

Ishtar nodded towards the wall.

Now I saw that there was no way out of the room except the one I had come in by. We were in the last room of the gallery. What Ishtar was indicating was not a doorway to the next altar room, but the doors of a lift.

'I wish I'd come down that way,' I said. 'I almost drowned.'

'There's no way down to here in the lift. It only goes upwards. And only if you're lucky. That's all now; I'll say goodbye. I'm beginning to feel rather poorly.'

'Why, what is it?' I asked in alarm.

'The *bablos* is coming on. And I've had too much to drink... I get mixed up with my wings... You'd better go. No, before you do, come over here...'

I thought she was probably going to bite me again.

'Do you want to...?'

'No,' she said. 'Just come here, don't be afraid.'

I came up close to her.

'Bend down and close your eyes.'

The moment I did as she asked, something wet smacked me in the middle of my forehead, as if a post-office stamp had been put there.

'That's all.'

'Goodbye,' I said, and headed towards the lift.

As I was getting in I turned and looked at Ishtar.

'One other thing,' she announced, fixing me with her gaze. 'About Hera. Be very careful. Many years ago Enlil had a girl-friend like her. They had an affair, went out together, spent their whole time billing and cooing. But they never got as far as going to bed. I once asked Enlil, why not? Do you know what he said? "If you never ask a black mamba to bite you, you can have a long and happy time enjoying her warmth..." I thought then that he was a cold fish, cynical and heartless. But now I realise that that is precisely the reason he is still with us...'

I wanted to ask what this had to do with Hera, but did not have time to, before the doors closed and the lift started to move upwards. Looking at my reflection in the polished steel doors, I saw on my forehead the imprint of Ishtar's lips – like a scarlet rose.

ACHILLES STRIKES BACK

Enlil Maratovich met me at the lift.

'You're only just in time,' he said, looking at my forehead. 'They're casting the lots now.'

'Casting lots?

'Yes. They're choosing a Chaldean for your degustation.'

'Who does the choosing?'

'They always do it themselves, we don't interfere. They have a ritual, a rather beautiful one. Little bits of paper, each with a name on it, a red top hat... You'll see.'

We passed his study and stopped outside the door leading into the round hall. Besides ourselves there was no one else in the corridor.

'We'll wait here,' said Enlil Maratovich. 'When they have finished drawing the lots, they'll come out to us.'

'I'd like to wipe my forehead clean. I need a napkin.'

'Absolutely not, not under any circumstances. Ishtar's kiss is your ticket to a new life. Everyone must see it.'

'Funny place for a ticket,' I said.

'No, it's entirely appropriate. After all, don't people put all kinds of coloured stamps on your skin at a disco, so as not to have to fuss around with little bits of paper? It's the same here... It'll probably get you free drinks, ha ha...'

'Enlil Maratovich,' I said, 'since you mention drinks – when am I going to be given some *bablos*?

Enlil Maratovich looked at me with incredulity bordering almost on contempt.

'You really believe you are fit for service?'

I found this response rather cheering. *Yes of course*, I thought – *service. Vampires are just another form of public service; I could have guessed that.*

But aloud I said something else:

'Why not? Ishtar Borisovna herself invited me to have some, but there was none available.'

Enlil Maratovich laughed.

'Rama,' he said, 'that was Ishtar's little joke. I am honestly at a loss to know how to deal with your ignorance. Things are not as simple in our world as you seem to think they are.'

'What complications are there?'

'You're about to find out. Have you got your death candy with you?'

'What for?' I felt my heart beat faster.

'Have you, or haven't you?'

I shook my head. The smile disappeared from Enlil Maratovich's face.

'Didn't Loki tell you a vampire never leaves his house without a death candy?'

'He did say something of the sort. It's just that...'

'Don't try to excuse yourself. For this inexcusable, I repeat *inexcusable*, dereliction you deserve to be sent into this degustation empty-handed. You would be taught a lesson you would remember for the rest of your life. If I refrain from doing that to you, it is only because these proceedings are so important for the reputation of our whole community. We cannot take the risk...'

A candy appeared in Enlil Maratovich's hand, in a brilliant

green wrapper edged with a gold border. I had not seen one like it before.

'Eat it now,' he commanded. 'Otherwise you'll probably forget this one as well.'

Unwrapping the sweet, I placed it in my cheek.

'Why do I need it?'

'You are going to have to penetrate into the soul of a Chaldean and reveal to the assembled company his most deeply hidden secrets. This is a dangerous thing to do.'

'Why?'

'Because of the souls these Chaldeans have. When you start laying out for public inspection exactly what the subject whose red liquid you have tasted is most deeply ashamed of, most likely he is going to want to stop your mouth. He might even want to kill you. Without the death candy, things might not go too well for you.'

'Hold on a minute,' I said in alarm. 'This isn't what we agreed at all! You told me it would be just a simple degustation...'

'That is what it is, simply a degustation. But the only visible guarantee of the validity of the episode has always been the emotional reaction of the individual who has been bitten. Therefore your job is to dig all the nasty nuggets out of him, do you understand? Make sure you find whatever it is that he has buried most deeply within himself, that engenders the most painful humiliation in him. Turn him completely inside out. But be prepared for him to do anything he can to stop you.'

'Suppose he manages to do that?'

'Are you afraid?'

'Yes, I am,' I confessed.

'Then you must be absolutely certain who you are,' said Enlil Maratovich. 'That's the great Dostoyevskian question – are you a feeble trembling creature or do you have the right... Well, which is it?'

I definitely did not want to be a feeble, trembling creature.

'I have the right,' I said. 'Well, I hope I do.'

'Prove it, then. Most of all to yourself. And to everyone else at the same time. It's easier than you think. What are you afraid of? You have the death candy, and the Chaldean won't have one.'

'I hope you gave me a good one,' I worried. 'Wasn't past its best-before date, was it?'

'We'll soon know,' smiled Enlil Maratovich.

Remembering that I also had to psych myself up with the warrior spirit, I took the required number of breaths in and out in the right sequence, and immediately felt a springy lightness throughout my body. It was all just as it had been during my lessons with Loki, except that now there was also something new and unexpected: I was aware of everything that was going on behind me. I could feel the outline of the corridor, the surface of the walls and the unevenness of the floor – it was as if I had a fish-eye in the back of my head. The sensation was quite breathtaking.

The doors to the hall opened, and into the corridor came Marduk Semyonovich and Loki. It was obvious from their expression that something unforeseen had occurred.

'Well, who is to be?' asked Enlil Maratovich.

'Bit of a train wreck,' said Marduk Semyonovich. 'They've chosen Semnyukov. Deputy Minister.'

'Bloody hell,' muttered Enlil Maratovich. 'That's all we need.'

'What's happened?' I asked in a fright.

'Now,' said Enlil Maratovich, 'you'd better give me back that candy... Oh, you've already eaten it... Ha ha ha, never fear, I'm only joking. The only thing is, don't go too far and actually kill him, all right? That would not be at all a good idea from our point of view. I mean, it wouldn't quite be one of those times when we get wall-to-wall *Swan Lake* on our television screens – still, all the same he is a prominent figure.'

'I'm not planning to kill anyone. I'm more interested in staying alive myself.'

'Actually, it would be all right, in principle, if you do kill him,' went on Enlil Maratovich. 'So long as you do it beautifully. We can always pass it off as a car crash...'

And with that he steered me towards the doors, behind which I could hear the noise of voices and music. His touch was gentle and friendly, but I felt like a gladiator being propelled into the arena under the lash.

The hall had been completely rearranged. It was now lit by electric lamps, and had indeed taken on the aspect of a setting for a duel. The buffet tables had been moved back against the walls, and the Chaldeans were crowded round an empty space in the middle of the room, forming a living ring. There were more of them now; evidently some had aristocratically elected to come late, in time for the second act. Here and there in the crowd could be seen human faces. These belonged to vampires who from the sea of glittering, expressionless gold masks flashed me encouraging smiles.

Some of the Chaldeans were wearing strange clothes like fluffed-out skirts, made of something resembling either soft feathers or long-haired sheepskin. Only a few wore these skirts; all of whom were distinguished by exceptional physical development. Obviously this particular get-up was chic for Chaldean fitness fans.

One half-naked Hercules was standing in the empty space in the middle of the room, his arms folded over his chest, the electric light playing pitilessly on his metallic visage. His hirsute upper torso rippled with muscles, and the substantial beer gut below, while detracting from the overall harmony of the ensemble, only added to the terrifying aspect. It struck me that had the Huns or the Vandals left behind sculptural monuments to themselves, they would have been representations of bodies such as this. In the black foliage of his chest hung a chain with amulets – totemic little animals of some sort, and birds.

Even if I had not myself been aware of the seriousness of the moment, the expression in the eyes of the vampires watching me would have told me all I needed to know. On one side of the line was our fragile world, protected only by centuries-old prejudice and the death candy; on the other the merciless herd of humanity...

I decided to arm myself with the spirit one more time. After repeating the prescribed combination of intakes and outtakes of breath, I advanced on the half-naked Chaldean, inclined my head in sober, soldierly fashion, and said:

'Greetings. As you know, we two are to appear today... er... in tandem, so to say. I suppose we had better introduce ourselves. My name is Rama. What is yours? I know only your surname.'

The mask turned in my direction.

'I believe,' it said, 'it is for you to find that out. Is that not so?'

'Does that mean you will not object if I...'

'I most definitely will,' returned the mask with an air of finality.

Laughter broke out in the hall.

'In that case I shall be obliged to use force. Needless to say, within limits strictly defined by necessity.'

'Let us see if you can,' replied Semnyukov.

I took a step towards him, and he casually adopted a boxer's posture. One blow from that fist could kill me on the spot, therefore I decided not to risk approaching him too closely from the front.

I resolved to come at him from behind.

What I did caused me considerable pain in the muscles and joints, but it was undoubtedly executed beautifully, as required by Enlil Maratovich. The sequence of movements whereby I ended up in the desired position took no more than a second.

From my perspective, however, it was a very long, elastic second, the length of a complete gymnastic display.

To begin with I took a slow and uncertain step towards him. Mockingly, he spread his arms out wide, as if waiting to enfold me in an embrace. At that moment I darted forwards. So quick was I that before he realised I had moved at all, I had already dived underneath his arm. The moment he noticed my movement, from my vantage point behind him I leant against his back in a mirror image of his own derisive pose and opened my arms wide. He started to turn round, and at the risk of dislocating my neck, in a movement at once relaxed and inconceivably rapid, I turned my head and executed the bite. I may say, with no false modesty, that this second-long movement was worthy of being filmed, even perhaps needing a high-speed camera.

By the time Semnyukov had turned round to face me I was already beyond the reach of his fists. I therefore had no need to turn round to face him. But when he started to move in my direction, without looking round I stopped him with a gesture.

'Stop,' I said, 'stop right there. It's all over, Ivan Grigorievich. I have bitten you. Our functions are now reversed. It is for me to provoke you to aggression, and for you to resist the temptation with all the power at your command.'

'Everyone in this hall knows I am Ivan Grigorievich,' retorted Semnyukov.

Smacking my lips several times (for dramatic effect, and possibly in imitation of older vampires), I said:

'I propose a gentleman's agreement. Immediately in front of your feet is a thick black line. It's a kind of decorative design on the floor. Do you see it?'

Of course I could not see the line myself, but I knew exactly where it was and where it went. It was as though the navigation system in my head was giving me all the information I needed.

Enlil Maratovich must have given me a special kind of death candy, senior officer's issue.

'Let us agree,' I went on, 'that if you cross this line you will have lost. Do we have an understanding?'

'What do I need a gentleman's agreement for?' asked Semnyukov.

'To give you an opportunity to become a gentleman, if only for a short time.'

'Interesting,' said Semnyukov politely. 'Well, all right, let's try it.'

I sensed that he had taken a step backwards.

Furrowing my brow, I made my face assume an expression of the utmost concentration. Approximately a minute passed, after which absolute silence reigned in the hall. Then I said:

'Well, Ivan Grigorievich, what are we to say of your soul? It is widely believed that even in the wickedest of men some good can be found. The reason I have been silent for so long is that I have been searching for this element of good in you... Alas. There are in you only two character traits that lend you the slightest vestige of humanity. They are, one, that you are a paedophile, and two, that you are an agent of Mossad. Everything else is inexpressibly appalling. So appalling that it makes even me, a professional vampire, feel queasy in your presence. And, make no mistake, I have seen into the abyss...'

Semnyukov said nothing. A strained silence hung over the hall.

'Rama, we know you have seen into the abyss,' came the voice of Enlil Maratovich from behind me. 'So has everyone here. Try not to shake the heavens to no purpose. We're all used to this sort of rubbish, and it's not particularly compromising.'

'I'm not producing this information because it's compromising,' I answered. 'Quite the opposite. But if you want the filthiest, most appalling, most humiliating and most painful secrets of this soul, you must bear with me... I shall pass over the details of

249

this gentleman's private life. I shall not refer to his lack of financial probity, nor his pathological propensity to lie, because Ivan Grigorievich himself makes no attempt to hide these qualities, considering that they all contribute to making him a model of a dynamic modern man. Unhappily, in this he is perfectly correct. Nevertheless, there is one thing of which Ivan Grigorievich is ashamed. Something hidden very, very deep. Perhaps I ought not to mention it?'

I sensed an increase in the intensity of the electric atmosphere among the watchers.

'No, all things considered I probably should bring it out,' I concluded after a pause. 'Here it is. Ivan Grigorievich is on a friendly footing with many financial big shots and powerful businessmen, some of whom are here tonight. They are all extremely wealthy people. They know Ivan Grigorievich as a powerful businessman in his own right, whose company is currently confidentially managed by a group of lawyers. This is because our hero has been for many years in the service of the Government...'

I sensed that Semnyukov's head was moving from side to side as if in denial of something. I paused, assuming that he wished to make some response. But he said not a word.

'And so, gentlemen,' I continued, 'the most shameful, dark and repulsive secret of Ivan Grigorievich is that this confidential direction, these shares, these lawyers, are all a sham, and in reality he has no business at all. All he has are a couple of brass-plate Potemkin firms, consisting of an accommodation address for legal purposes, a company name and logo. He has not set up these companies for any particularly dubious purposes, but merely in order to give the *impression* of being engaged in dubious practices. As an interesting aside, gentlemen, the example of Ivan Grigorievich provides a perfect formulation of the principle establishing the divide between the rich and the poor in our country today. The rich man goes to great lengths to suggest that he has less money than he really has. The poor man pretends to have more. By this criterion Ivan Grigorievich is unquestionably a poor man, and his poverty causes him more humiliation than anything else, despite the fact that the majority of our contemporaries consider him to be very rich. He has invented numerous devices to conceal the true state of his affairs, including the not trivial matter of a Potemkin offshore company. But the truth is that he lives off bribes like any official. And even though the bribes can be very substantial, they are not enough, because the way of life Ivan Grigorievich seeks to maintain does not come cheap. And of course he cannot keep himself on a level to match the kind of people he consorts with in Davos and Courchevel... Well, there you have it.'

'I knew that,' said a male voice from the group of Chaldeans.

'Well, I never did,' chimed in another.

'Nor I,' announced a third.

Ivan Grigorievich crossed the line on the floor. He was probably not aware he had done so, but the fateful step had been noted by many of the watchers, and the hall resounded with voices calling: 'He's gone over! He's over the line!' or 'He's lost!' as though we were present at a quiz show being filmed for television. Ivan Grigorievich meekly bowed his head, accepting defeat, and then launched himself at me with his fists.

I could not see it, but I sensed his arm speeding towards the back of my head. I tilted my head and his fist, appearing from behind my back, whizzed past my ear. I saw on his wrist the white disc with the doubled Maltese Cross symbol of a Vacheron Constantin watch.

The strangest thing was that, although events in the physical world seemed to be taking place very slowly, my thoughts were moving at their accustomed tempo. *Why the Maltese Cross?* I thought, and immediately told myself not to be distracted. I recalled the advice Hector had given to Paris before the duel in the film *Troy*: 'Think only of his sword and of your sword.' But instead of swords, I was suddenly envisaging the psychoanalyst's couch. *How disgusting this Discourse is...*

What happened next was in real time practically instantaneous, but according to my subjective chronometer took about as long as it does to make a sandwich or change the batteries in a torch.

Before Ivan Grigorievich reached the place where I had been standing, I had already jumped to one side, and as his corpulent carcase lumbered past I took hold of his shoulder and let his momentum jerk me after him. We sailed over the space together like a figure-skating duo. He was too big for me to hit him with my bare fists; I needed something heavy, preferably made of metal. The only suitable object within reach was his mask. I tore it from him, whirled it in the air and brought the expressionless golden face down upon his head. Immediately after the blow I let go of his shoulder and we separated. The mask stayed in my hand. There was nothing at all complicated about this manoeuvre, but from the fierce spurts of my movements and the tension, my joints were aching.

After I had come to rest he took a few steps and crashed face downwards to the floor. I thought he had decided to avoid total disgrace by pretending to be stunned. Evidently the turning of my thoughts towards Hector had not been in vain. The whole *mise en scène* reminded me so vividly of the sequence in *Troy* where Brad Pitt kills the Thessalonian giant that I could not resist the temptation to become Achilles for a moment. Advancing on the crowd of Chaldeans, I clasped Ivan Grigorievich's mask to my face, surveyed them, and using the words of Brad Pitt said: 'Is there no one else?'

As in the film, the answer was silence.

The mask proved to be very uncomfortable; it was pressing

on my nose. When I took it off, I noticed that its golden nose had been flattened, as if by a hammer. Perhaps Ivan Grigorievich had not been shamming after all.

'Rama,' called Enlil Maratovich softly, 'no need to overdo things. Better keep it all in proportion...'

Turning back to the stage, he clapped his hands and commanded: 'Music!'

The music released the hall from the paralysis that had overtaken it. A few of the Chaldeans came up to Ivan Grigorievich, bent over his prone form, lifted him up and hauled him to the exit. I was relieved to see that he was able to stumble out on his legs.

The Chaldeans gradually recovered themselves – they split up into groups and dispersed around the room, getting hold of drinks, striking up conversations with one another. They avoided me. I stood alone in the empty space in the middle of the room, the heavy mask in my hand, wondering what I should do next. Enlil Maratovich looked sternly at me and made a sign that I should join him. I was sure I was going to receive a dressing down. But I was wrong.

'Very good,' he said quietly, although his face was frowning. 'That's the only way to deal with those bastards. Well done. You frightened the shit out of the lot of them. That's what it means to have young muscles. I can't do it any longer.'

'Why just the muscles?' I said, offended. 'Seems to me the main role is played by the intellect.'

Enlil Maratovich pretended not to have heard this observation.

'But that's not all you have to do,' he said. 'Now you have got to try to make them like you. Take part in their conversations.'

Saying these words he wagged his finger censoriously at me. From a distance our colloquy would have looked as though a strict papa was telling off his naughty little son. The inappropriateness of his gestures to the words he was speaking was highly entertaining.

'So I get to be the Queen of the Ball, do I?' I asked.

'You don't have to change your gender,' smiled Enlil Maratovich. 'All you have to do is make the acquaintance of the most important of our guests, so that they get to know you personally. Come along, I'll introduce you. And make sure you smile at them as broadly as possible – they must be persuaded that you are a heartless, hypocritical swine.'

SOLDIERS OF THE EMPIRE

Enlil Maratovich pushed me in the direction of three Chaldeans who were deep in discussion not far away, and followed behind me. As we neared them, their conversation ceased and they stared at us. Enlil Maratovich extended his arms in a conciliatory gesture, spreading the fingers wide as he did so. I suddenly realised the significance of this ancient token: it shows you have no knife or stone concealed in your hand.

'It's all over,' said Enlil Maratovich cheerfully, 'there'll be no more biting today. I've already reproved the lad for churlish behaviour.'

'That's quite all right,' replied the Chaldean furthest away, a short, stooping man in a robe of grey fabric dotted with little flowers. 'Thank you for a most entertaining spectacle.'

'This is Professor Kaldavashkin,' Enlil Maratovich told me. 'He is Chief of Discourse, undoubtedly the senior position of responsibility in the Chaldean community.'

He turned to Kaldavashkin.

'Allow me to present to you Rama the Second. You are already familiar with his name. May I recommend him to your tender offices?'

'Rest assured, our offices will be of the kindest,' responded Kaldavashkin with equal formality, screwing up his elderly blue eyes to scrutinise me. 'We're quite used to it, you know. I am told you are highly accomplished in Discourse?'

'I wouldn't say highly accomplished,' I replied, 'but it's true I got on better with Discourse than I did with Glamour.'

'Most gratifying to hear that such things still happen in the Fifth Empire. Ordinarily as far as I can see it is the other way about.'

'The Fifth Empire?' I said, surprised. 'What is that?'

It was Kaldavashkin's turn to be surprised.

'Did Jehovah not explain it to you?'

Thinking it must be something that had slipped my memory, I shrugged my shoulders.

'It is the worldwide regime of anonymous dictatorship, usually called 'Fifth' to distinguish it from the Third Reich of Nazism and the Fourth Rome of globalisation. It is a dictatorship whose anonymity, as you know, extends only as far as people. In essence it is the humane epoch of Vampire Rule, the universal empire of vampires or, as we write it in secret symbolic form, Empire V. You must surely have covered it in your course?'

'I think there was something of the sort,' I said hesitantly. 'Yes, yes... I remember Baldur also saying that Glamour is the culture of the anonymous dictatorship.'

'Not the culture,' corrected Kaldavashkin, raising his finger, 'the ideology. The *culture* of the anonymous dictatorship is mature postmodernism.'

We had definitely not covered this subject.

'What is that?'

'Mature postmodernism is that stage in the evolution of the postmodern in which it ceases to be based on previous cultural formations, but continues its development purely on its own basis.'

I had not even a glimmer of a clue what Kaldavashkin was talking about.

256

'What does that mean?'

Kaldavashkin's basilisk eyes blinked several times behind the slits in his mask.

'Your speech contained a very precise demonstration of what it means,' he answered. 'Your generation has lost all knowledge of the cultural codes of the classics. *The Iliad*, *The Odyssey* – all such works have been forgotten. Citations now incorporate previous borrowings and quotations which have been extracted from their original sources and so become completely anonymous. It is the most adequate cultural projection of the anonymous dictatorship, and at the same time the most effective of the contributions Chaldean culture has made to the creation of Black Noise.'

'Black Noise? What is that?'

'Didn't you cover that either?' asked Kaldavashkin in astonishment. 'What were you doing all that time? Black Noise is the sum total of all the different aspects of Discourse. Another way of putting it is that it is White Noise, all elements of which have been independently conceived and bought to form an arbitrary and random amalgam of signals, while each separate signal has in itself nothing random or arbitrary at all. Black Noise is the name for the informational environment that now envelops contemporary human beings.'

'But what is its purpose? To deceive people?'

'No,' replied Kaldavashkin. 'The purpose of Black Noise is less outright deceit than the creation of a background that renders it impossible for anyone accidentally to stumble on the truth, inasmuch as...'

But Enlil Maratovich was already pushing me towards the next group of Chaldeans and I did not hear the end of the phrase. All I could do was smile apologetically at Kaldavashkin and spread my hands in a gesture of helplessness.

My next encounter was with a small Chaldean of somewhat

feminine appearance with long, manicured fingernails and dressed in a dark blue tunic. Around him was what appeared to be a retinue of admiring acolytes in their gold masks.

'Mr Shepkin-Kupernik,' announced Enlil Maratovich by way of introduction. 'He is Chief of Glamour, undoubtedly the most important position of responsibility among our Chaldean friends.'

I had already grasped that there would be as many holders of positions of primary importance as there were Chaldeans.

Shepkin-Kupernik inclined his mask in dignified acknowledgement.

'Tell me, Rama,' he said in a melodious voice, 'perhaps you at least I shall succeed in weaning away from this black affliction? After all, you are still so young. Might we have a chance with you?'

The group of acolytes laughed. Even Enlil Maratovich joined in.

I was seized by panic. I had just avoided falling flat on my face over Discourse, but there I had been on a level playing field, discussing a subject in which I was generally reckoned to be pretty capable. But with Glamour I had always had trouble. *Now*, I thought to myself, *I am sure to be headed for disgrace*. What the 'black affliction' was I could not remember either. My only hope was to go for broke.

'It may be black affliction for some,' I said sternly, 'but there are some for whom it is the black death...'

The laughter died down.

'Very true,' answered Shepkin-Kupernik. 'No one could quarrel with that. But why is it that all you vampires, even the youngest and freshest of you, immediately take to dressing in these coal-black garments? Why is it so difficult to persuade you to add even the smallest ingredient of a different colour and texture to this banquet of total blackness? You can't imagine what I had to go through to get your friend Mithra to agree to that little red bow tie.'

At last I twigged what he was talking about.

'You vampires have such a wonderful, deep course on Glamour,' continued Shepkin-Kupernik mournfully. 'Yet as far back as I can remember it always ends up the same way. At first you all dress very well, in accordance with the theory. And then the rot sets in. One month, at the most two – and everything starts to slide into this hopeless black abyss...'

As soon as he said these words, a glacial tension spread around his listeners.

'Oh,' he whispered in alarm. 'Forgive me if I have said something tactless...'

I saw that I had been given me an opening to show myself in a better light.

'Think nothing of it,' I said in my friendliest manner. 'You are a witty conversationalist and by no means ill-informed. But if we wish to speak seriously of this... it is true that we, humble suckers that we are, have a predilection for the *noir*. In the first place, as I am sure you know, black is our national colour. Secondly... surely you remember how this came about for us?'

'On my red liquid, I swear I do not,' replied Shepkin-Kupernik.

It seemed to me he was relieved at having successfully avoided a dangerous turn in the discussion.

'Please think again. What is it that vampires do?'

'Direct the course of history?' offered Shepkin-Kupernik obsequiously.

'Not only that. Vampires also see into the dark recesses of your souls. In our early days as vampires, while we are still students, we still draw on a store of that divine purity we inherited from the Mighty Bat, which impels us to believe in people despite all that we learn about them as the days go by. During this period vampires often dress frivolously. But the time inevitably comes

259

when it becomes clear to us that there will be no ray of light amid the gloom. At that point the vampire goes into eternal mourning for mankind, and clothes himself in black to match the hearts that every day pass before his mental vision.'

'Bravo!' bellowed Marduk Semyonovich, who was also listening. 'Enlil, I believe you could incorporate that into the Discourse.'

Shepkin-Kupernik dropped something like a curtsey, intended to express the range and variety of his feelings, and passed on out of our way, along with his retinue.

The next little group to which Enlil Maratovich led me consisted of just two Chaldeans, both very alike one another. Neither was in his first youth, nor particularly neatly dressed – both were obese and extravagantly bearded. The only real difference between them was that below one mask bristled a ginger beard, below the other a dull grey one. Greybeard seemed to be half asleep.

'This is a gentleman with a very interesting profession,' said Enlil Maratovich, indicating the ginger-bearded Chaldean. 'It may well be the most vital in today's world. Just like in an Italian play, Mr Samartsev is our Chief Agent Provocateur.'

'Chief Agent Provocateur?' I asked in surprise. 'Can you tell me exactly what it is you do?'

'As a title it has a somewhat sarcastic tinge,' returned Samartsev in a deep bass voice. 'But vampires, you see, love to mock us poor defenceless humans. As you yourself have just reminded all of us here in a particularly brash manner.'

I was a little taken aback at his words. Samartsev paused for a few seconds, then jabbed his finger into my stomach and said, 'I'm now demonstrating what I do. I agitate. I provoke. Does it work?'

The assembled company neighed with laughter. I laughed along with them. As befits a provocateur, Samartsev was quite charming, in a twisted sort of way.

'In fact what I do is manage the future,' he said. 'I am, so to say, responsible for the design of tomorrow. My job is called that because in today's world provocation is not just a way of keeping score, but also the main underlying organisational principle.'

'I don't understand. How can provocation be a way of keeping score?'

'Very simply. When five Bolsheviks sit round the samovar singing revolutionary songs and one of the five is an agent pro-vocateur of the tsarist police who writes dossiers on the others, that's keeping score.'

'Aha! Got it. And how can provocation be an organisational method?'

'That's when the provocateur himself starts off the singing,' replied Samartsev, 'so that those who sing along can be recorded in the act from the very beginning. In an ideal situation, even the text of the revolutionary song should be provided by our creative team.'

'I see,' I said.

Samartsev made another attempt to poke my stomach with his finger, but this time I forestalled him with my hand.

'Of course, this doesn't apply only to revolutionary songs,' he went on, 'but more generally to any emerging tendencies. No one these days is going to wait until they see the green shoots of the new begin pushing their way through the asphalt, because, after all, important people travel along this asphalt. We wouldn't want any green shoots coming upon their own initiative, would we? No, nowadays we make sure that such freedom-loving sprouts are safely planted in specially designated spots. To manage this process obviously you need a provocateur, so the provocation becomes a tool of management.'

'What area does your colleague specialise in?' I asked.

'Youth subculture,' yawned greybeard.

'Well, I never,' I replied. 'Could you get me out on the streets, do you think?'

'No, it wouldn't work with you,' said greybeard. 'I say that in all youthful honesty.'

'You don't look particularly young,' I observed.

'Quite right,' he agreed. 'I didn't say I was young. On the contrary, I'm quite old. That too I say in all youthful honesty.'

'Listen, can you tell me which of our young politicians one can trust? After all, I'm not just a vampire. I'm also a citizen of our country.'

The grey-haired Chaldean shot a glance at Samartsev.

'Oh,' said the latter. 'I see you're no less of a provocateur than I am... do you know what "Catch-22" is?'

It was something I remembered from my Discourse training.

'Roughly, yes. It's a situation from which you can't escape because of a contradiction embodied in the situation itself. Isn't that it? A self-sealing logical trap with no way out. It comes from a novel by Joseph Heller.'

'Yes, that's right,' said Samartsev. 'In relation to the question you asked, Catch-22 consists of the following: whatever words are uttered on the political stage, the simple fact of a person's appearance on that stage is proof that he's a stool pigeon. Because if he were not, he would never have got within a mile of the political stage, which is cordoned off by three rings of security armed with machine-guns. Elementary, my dear Watson: if a girl sucks off a dick in a brothel, reason, armed with the deductive method, will lead us to the conclusion that what we have before us is a prostitute.'

I felt offended on behalf of my generation.

'Why does she have to be a prostitute?' I demanded. 'She might be a seamstress. She might have just arrived in the city from the sticks and fallen in love with a plumber who has come to fix the shower in the brothel. And the plumber has brought her in to his place of work because, temporarily, she has nowhere to live. And while they were both there they happened to have a free moment.'

Samartsev raised his finger.

'That unexpressed proposition is the foundation of the whole fragile mechanism of our young democracy...'

'Do you mean to tell me that despite everything we do have some kind of democracy?'

'In prospect, definitely.'

'Why only in prospect?'

Samartsev shrugged.

'Look, you and I are intelligent people. What that means is that, provided we act together, we, the intelligentsia, can arse-lick any dictatorship to death. Unless, of course, we don't ourselves expire prematurely from hunger.'

The specialist in youth culture added quietly:

'Any dictatorship except the anonymous dictatorship.'

Samartsev jabbed his elbow into the specialist's side.

'You and your youthful honesty!'

Apparently the jab in the ribs had finally woken up the youth culture specialist.

'Regarding young politicians,' he said, 'there are some bright lads among them, make no mistake. Not just bright, either. Talented. Real latter-day Gogols.'

'You seem to think there's a new Gogol born every day,' grumbled Samartsev.

'No, what I'm saying, it's true. Not long ago one of them got five hundred dead souls on to his payroll – I was telling you about it, wasn't I? Three times in a row. First time round they were Fascists, second time gay activists, third time Orthodox environmentalists. What it boils down to is that we'll always be able to find the right people to entrust with the destiny of our country...'

Enlil Maratovich dragged me away to meet more Chaldeans.

'I name you Kolovrat, like the Slavic warrior of old!' Samartsev shouted after me. '*Sieg Heil!*'

The next person I was presented to was the Chief of Spectacle, a small, puny individual dressed in a black robe. His mask was so big it looked like an astronaut's space helmet. The eyes that peered out from the slits in the mask were large and sorrowful. He looked like Gollum from *The Hobbit* – if that individual had for some reason taken monastic vows.

'This is Mr Modestovich,' said Enlil Maratovich. 'He has achieved great things for our culture, bringing it, one might say, into global safe harbour. We too now regularly produce exciting blockbusters about the struggle between good and evil, which invariably culminate in the forces of good triumphing at the end of the second episode.'

Modestovich's view of himself was altogether more downbeat.

'We make tasteless jokes about light and darkness,' he said shuffling his feet ingratiatingly. 'That's how we make our living...'

'Delighted to meet you,' I said. 'You know, there's something I have long wanted to ask a professional: why it is that in most mainstream movie releases the good guys invariably win? After all, that's not often what happens in real life.'

Modestovich cleared his throat.

'A good question,' he said. 'To an ordinary person it would be difficult to explain without equivocating, but to you I can speak plainly. If you will permit, I shall give you an example from agriculture. In Soviet times they used to conduct experiments to study the effect of different kinds of music on the growth of tomatoes and cucumbers, and also on milk yields. It was noted that major tonalities encourage vegetables to become juicier and milk yields to increase. Music in minor tonalities, on the other hand, produced vegetables that were small and dry, and the milk yield went down. Of course, a man is a more complex organism than a tomato or a cow. Nevertheless, the same rule applies. People are constructed in such a way as to find the triumph of evil unbearable.'

'Why is that?'

'For the answer to your question,' said Modestovich, 'we would both have to apply to Enlil Maratovich. It is the way you vampires have developed our species. Facts are facts: to confront a human being face to face with victorious evil is like obliging a cow to listen to the "Moonlight Sonata". The results will be deeply discouraging in terms of quantity, of quality, of fat content and all other parameters. The same is true of people. When evil triumphs everywhere people lose the will to live, and whole nations can become extinct. Science has shown that early Mozart is the best way to optimise a cow's milk yield. Similarly, until the day he dies a human being should be maintained in a state of radiant optimism and good humour. There exists a complex of positively constructive values that it is the job of mass culture to instil. We have to ensure that the principle is not seriously eroded.'

'What does this complex consist of?' I asked.

Modestovich rolled his eyes, evidently trying to recall instructions that had been hardwired into his memory.

'There are many provisions,' he said, 'but only one pivotal concept. Chaldean art must without prejudice, as the lawyers say, subject life to a dispassionate examination and, after harrowing doubts and hesitations, come to the firm conclusion that at the root of today's social structure essentially lies good – which will, despite everything, prevail. Manifestations of evil, dark though they may appear, are ephemeral and are always directed against the existing order of things. In this way the recipient's consciousness senses a correspondence between the concept of "good" and the concept of "the status quo". From this follows another conclusion, namely that service to the good, something every man in the depths of his heart desires to fulfil, consists in the daily production of *bablos*.'

'Can such primitive brainwashing really work?' I asked.

'Oh, oh, my dear young man, it's not as primitive as all that. As I said before, a man is more complicated than a tomato. Paradoxically, however, this makes the task simpler. To make a tomato juicier, you must make it listen to music in a major key. Whereas in the case of a man all you have to do is tell him that the music he is listening to is in a major key. It may be possibly be distorted by an inferior performance, but only for a while and not completely. Therefore in the end it makes no difference what music is played...'

My next introduction was to the Chief of Sport, a dynamic iron-pumper wearing the same kind of fluffed-out sheepskin skirt as my opponent in the duel. No doubt as a result of this coincidence, which was obvious to both of us, our conversation was rather short and strained.

'How do you feel about football?' asked the Chief of Sport, raking me with an appraising glance.

I had the impression that he had X-ray eyes that were measuring the muscles underneath my clothing. I was also uncomfortably aware that the effect of the death candy had worn off.

'You know,' I said cautiously, 'if I may be completely honest, the main objective of this game – the kicking of a ball into a goal – has always seemed to me rather contrived and artificial.'

'Ah, well then, better play chess.'

I could have said much the same about chess, but decided not to prolong the conversation.

The introductions and acquaintances continued for a long time. To the best of my ability I was affable to the masks and they were friendly back to me, but from the wary glints from golden eye sockets I understood that the Chaldeans existed exclusively in an atmosphere of fear and mutual hatred. This, however, had the effect of binding them together as tightly as Christian love or the joint possession of high-risk volatile shares could ever have done.

From time to time I thought I could recognise well-known people passing by. Sometimes my attention was caught by a familiar coiffure, sometimes by a way of stooping, or by a voice. But I could never be absolutely sure. Once, indeed, I would have gone to the stake to assert that no more than a metre away from me stood the famous mega-sculptor Zurab Tsereteli. The clue was in the studied skill with which he had fastened his gold Hero of Labour star to his robe: it was slightly askew, slightly too high, slightly ridiculous, and from a distance successfully conveyed the impression that its wearer was a man entirely devoted to the life of the spirit, and touchingly ill-adapted to worldly life (I had seen him on television with the star stuck equally casually on the lapel of his jacket). But Enlil Maratovich steered me past him so I had no chance to verify whether my guess was correct or not.

Eventually I had been introduced to all the people who needed to meet me, and Enlil Maratovich left me to myself. I was expecting a rush of attention, but hardly anyone even looked at me. From one of the buffet tables I took a glass of red-coloured liquid with a plastic straw in it.

'Do you know what this is?' I asked a mask standing next to me.

'Mosquito,' he muttered indifferently.

'Who are you calling a mosquito?' I asked huffily.

'It's a cocktail made of vodka and cranberry juice. Some glasses just have juice in them, but the straws in the cocktail ones have a sharpened end, like a syringe.'

And with that he took two cocktails and disappeared into a far corner of the hall.

I drank a cocktail, and then another. Then I walked up and down the hall for a while. No one took any notice of me. *Sic transit glamuria mundi*, I thought, listening to the babble of modish conversations all around me. They were about different topics: politics, movies, literature.

'Yes, he's a marvellous writer,' one Chaldean was saying to another, 'but not great. In my opinion there aren't any great writers in Russia now. On the other hand, we have more and more who are marvellous. Of course, there have always been plenty of those. You know what I'm talking about, don't you?'

'Certainly,' returned the second Chaldean, his eyelids fluttering meaningfully through the slits in his mask. 'But you were speaking of marvellous writers. If on the other hand there are some who really are, surely that means that they must be great, don't you think, on the other hand?'

Among the crowd were some Chaldeans from the West, who had presumably come to swap experiences. I heard a few snatches of conversations in English:

'Do Russians support gay marriage?'

'Well, this is not an easy question,' came the diplomatic response from a voice with a strong Russian accent. 'We're strongly pro-sodomy, but very anti-ritual...'

Also, apparently, there were some oil people, as I deduced from frequent expressions coming to my ears such as 'black liquid'. I went back to the table, downed another cocktail and soon began to feel better.

The variety show on the stage was going in full swing. The vampires were performing for the benefit of the Chaldeans a kind of floor show of local talent, apparently in a bid to inject a sense of cordiality and bonhomie into the relationship. Most of the time it was not very successful. Moreover, I picked up from the reactions in my part of the room that everyone had seen the programme many times before.

The first item was Loki dancing a tango with his rubber woman, described for some reason by the Master of Ceremonies, a tall Chaldean in a red robe, as a 'cult cultural object'. As soon as it was over, a group of Chaldeans climbed up on to the stage and presented Loki, on behalf of his silent partner, with a box wrapped in multiple layers of gold paper and tied with a scarlet bow. It took a very long time to unwrap.

Inside was a huge dildo, 'King Solomon's member' as the presentation committee explained. Along the side of this pink rubber log could be seen the inscription: 'And this too shall Pass!' I thought this must be a reference to the immortal couplet still visible on the thigh of the teaching aid. From the comments of people standing near me it was clear that this joke was also repeated year in and year out (someone mentioned that the previous year the rubber phallus had been Shakespearian black, a rather risqué stunt in our complicated times).

After that, on to the stage came Enlil Maratovich and Mithra. They performed a skit about life in China featuring the Emperor Jin-Lun and a stray mosquito. Enlil Maratovich was the mosquito and Mithra the Emperor. The point of the skit was that the Emperor notices he has been bitten by a mosquito, which makes him very irate. He starts to itemise to the mosquito the long list of all his earthly and heavenly titles, and at each new title the stunned mosquito bows his head lower and lower, simultaneously thrusting his sting (a telescopic aerial from an old radio set, which Enlil Maratovich kept pressed against his head) deeper and deeper into the imperial leg. By the time the Emperor, having at length concluded the review of all his titles, prepares to despatch the mosquito with a blow from his hand, the mosquito has also completed his work and happily buzzes off. This sketch was greeted with genuinely warm applause, from which I deduced that there were a good many representatives from the business elite in the hall.

There was then a collection of skits involving both vampires and Chaldeans, more like a sequence of short scenes and dialogues. Some of them referred to films I had seen (as I had recently been informed, this was known as 'mature postmodernism'):

'Would you like a geisha girl?' asked the vampire.

'Is that the kind who, when she throws a glance at you, you fall off your bike?'

'Yes, that's it.'

'No, thanks all the same,' replied the Chaldean. 'We want rumpy pumpy, not a bicycle crash.'

And so on.

Tired of standing for so long, I sat down on a stool near the wall. I was completely worn out, and my eyelids felt as though they had been stuck together. The last thing I saw with any clarity was a stunt performed by four elderly Chaldeans to whom I had not been introduced. They performed a rather wild dance, almost impossible to describe: like a quartet of pigs trying to emulate classical ballet steps by a quartet of swans. What was piquant about this number was that the Chaldeans were dressed as Teletubbies with thick gold antennae of the appropriate shape poking out of their masks.

Later various vocal numbers took over the stage, and at last it was possible to keep my eyes closed for long periods while still keeping abreast of the proceedings. Jehovah stepped up to the microphone with a guitar, ran his fingers once or twice over the strings, and in an unexpectedly fine voice started to sing something cryptic, reminiscent of early King Crimson:

> I know the place where the concentrates bloom.
> Mind 'B' does not need to be paid.
> I dance with a rose in the green courtyard gloom
> Where the columns have faces of jade...

Glamour concentrates were clear enough – let's just say that I myself knew a couple of places where they bloomed. And I could also understand why Mind 'B' didn't need to be paid. I could visualise a rose with its reflection in an endless corridor formed by a pair of mirrors, and then the green columns of Independence Hall on the back of the hundred-dollar bill leaping into the courtyard and beginning to tango with one another in imitation of Loki's movements with his submissive partner. Indeed, they had the solemn faces of American presidents.

By this time I was, of course, soundly asleep.

LE YELTSINE IVRE

All the next week I spent hanging in the late Brahma's hamlet.

I had an irresistible urge to crawl in there as soon as the car brought me home the morning after the party. I yielded to it, and immediately fell into the familiar crystal-clear state of suspended animation.

I was neither awake nor asleep. During this time the heavy, dark sphere with which the presence of the Tongue normally signalled itself to my consciousness assumed a stability that felt exactly right, suppressing all the thoughts and desires that continually arose when my body was in its usual position, before they could develop into palpable form. I vaguely understood the reason for this sensation: a man's actions are always directed towards eliminating the inner disharmony caused by the conflict between the true state of affairs and his ideal vision of them, in the same way as a guided missile closing in on its target progressively reduces to zero the discrepancies between the different readings supplied by its semiconductor brain. While I hung head downwards, the dark sphere rolled down to occupy the place that had formerly been the seat of the imbalances and conflicts. The ensuing harmony was proof against any disruption. I could not envisage any sense or purpose in ever attempting to emerge from the harmony the Tongue had established with itself.

Yet staying there proved more of a problem than I had expected. On the seventh day I heard a melodious ringing sound. The light unexpectedly came on in the hamlet, and a woman's voice, obviously recorded, could be heard expressively pronouncing somewhere very nearby:

> *As my days draw to a close I regret nothing so much as the long years I spent without sense or profit, hanging head downwards in the mindless gloom. Hours and minutes vanish undifferentiated in this pallid nullity; the unintelligent may believe that they will find harmony, but in truth all they are doing is coming closer to death...*   Count Dracula, Reminiscences and Reflections

I climbed down to the floor. It was clear that a device of some kind, having monitored the length of time I had spent in the hamlet, had activated itself. It was equally clear that I had exceeded the limit. I waited an hour or two, then resumed my perch. After five minutes the lights blazed on again, and just above my ear a bell started jangling.

This time it was anything but melodious; in fact it sounded distinctly unpleasant. On came the tape-recorder once more. It announced in stentorian male bass tones:

> *Having fallen into a state of paralysis the sons of the Mighty Bat were picked off one by one and destroyed by a pitiful tribe of apes who did not even understand what they were doing. Some died from being shot by arrows, others were consumed by fire. Vampires used to refer to their mute existence as the highest state of mind. But life – or rather death – showed that this was the most foolish of all their delusions...*
>
> Witzipotzli Dunaevsky, *The General History of Vampires*

I decided to try to outsmart my tormentor. I jumped down to the floor and immediately leapt back up the silver pole. A second later into my ear came a frenzied squeal from a clownish voice:

What will history say of me? It will say this: here's one more schmuck who's been hanging in the lumber room! Boo-ha-ha-ha.

I had had enough jousting with fate, so returned to the sitting room and lay down on the sofa. In fact all I wanted to do was go back to hang in the lumber room and allow my faithful black nucleus to continue to damp down the thoughts seething in my head. To hell with the judgment of history... But I was forced to accept that the prescribed limit could not be exceeded. Closing my eyes, I made myself sleep.

I was awakened by the telephone ringing. It was Hera.

'Let's meet,' she said without preamble.

'OK, let's,' I said, without giving myself time to think.

'Come to Le Yeltsine Ivre.'

'What's that?'

'A favourite hang-out restaurant for the cream of the crop. Or dream of the crap, if you prefer. My chauffeur will come and collect you if you don't know where it is.'

'You have a car and a driver?' I asked in astonishment.

'If you need one, you can have one too,' she replied. 'Ask Enlil about it. That's all for now. Waiting for you. Mwah, mwah.'

And she rang off.

Half an hour after our phone conversation her driver rang the doorbell. In the interval I took a shower, put on my new charcoal-black uniform (it looked ascetic but had taken a small army of sales people at the Archipelago to make the final selection) and drank off half a glass of whisky to give me courage.

The driver was a man, no longer young, wearing fatigues and an expression of mild offence.

'What sort of place is this "cream of the crop" restaurant?' I asked.

'It's that one out of town,' he replied. 'Forty minutes or so if there are no hold-ups.'

Waiting for us down below was a BMW jeep, the latest model – I had not been in one like it before. However, the novelty of imagining that I might myself be in a position to acquire a similar container in which to pass my time in traffic jams failed to excite me. Either I was already taking for granted the financial opportunities offered by the clan of which I was now a member, or I was simply too nervous at the prospect of the forthcoming meeting.

I had never heard of Le Yeltsine Ivre. The name seemed to have something in common with Arthur Rimbaud's poem 'Le Bateau Ivre'. Presumably the boat in question was our ship of state, as personified in the father and founder of the new Russia. It was odd, I thought, that Hera seemed so drawn to the Establishment, but perhaps this was the sort of response prompted by the mere appearance of a ministerial-level chauffeured bimmer...

I began pondering how best to comport myself when we met.

I could pretend that I attached no importance to the fact that she had bitten me and act as though nothing had happened. This would probably be a failure: I was sure to start blushing, this would make her giggle, and our encounter would get off on the wrong foot.

Alternatively, I could simulate offence – or rather allow it to be noticed by dint of not concealing it. This would not work either. I remembered a saying of the team leader of the unloaders at the supermarket where I had worked: 'The man who takes offence is good for nothing except carrying you on his back to the shithouse.' I did not see myself competing with Hera's driver in the matter of transportation services...

Eventually I decided to stop cudgelling my brains before there was a need to, and to wait and go with the flow.

The Drunken Yeltsin turned out to be a fashionable place – its parking lot was full of expensive wheels. I had never seen such an original entrance to a building: they had somehow managed to insert a real tank into the brick wall, and visitors had to climb up on to its turret in order to reach the entrance door at the top. This had been made easier by the addition of two latticework staircases, one on either side of the tank. However, a trail of footprints clearly showed that many guests with a taste for the extreme had chosen to climb up the tank from the front. A notice hung on the tank's cannon:

Please do not walk along the barrel. The Management.

Once inside the actual building, the corridor was shaped like an aircraft fuselage. The new arrival was greeted by a smiling girl dressed like a stewardess who asked for your boarding pass number. Only people on her list would be admitted to the establishment. The designer's idea seemed to be that guests should enter from the tank turret directly into the belly of the Presidential airliner.

I was met by a waiter dressed as a cabin crew steward, who invited me to follow him. The main dining hall of the restaurant was quite traditional in appearance except for an enormous stage with a sign announcing 'conduct the orchestra (by request in advance) from 22:00', and a circular pool, not particularly large but deep, with an arched bridge over it. On the wall nearby was a door bearing for some reason the legend 'wet room'. This all presumably had some connection to Yeltsin's biography, but I could not quite grasp its meaning. It had all happened too long ago.

The way through to the private rooms was at the far end of

the hall. As we approached the room where Hera was waiting for me, I experienced an acute loss of confidence.

'Excuse me,' I said to the steward, 'where is the toilet?'

He indicated the door.

I spent several minutes in the gleaming facilities, its urinals riveted to the chassis of the aircraft, before concluding that further inspection of my face in the mirror was unlikely to help matters. I went out into the corridor, and said to the steward:

'Thank you. I'll manage on my own now.'

Waiting until he disappeared from view, I turned the handle of the door.

Hera was sitting in the corner of the room on a pile of variously coloured plump cushions shaped like lengths of railway track. She was wearing a short black number with a high collar. It looked simple and chaste, but never had I set eyes on anything sexier.

Against the wall stood a table with two untouched place settings, while on the floor in front of Hera was a tray with tea things and a half-eaten cheesecake.

She raised her eyes to mine. In that second my confusion evaporated; I knew exactly what I was going to do.

'Hello,' she said. 'You're looking rather solemn and determined today...'

Before she had time to finish what she was saying I had taken two bounds towards her, dropped to my haunches, and...

At this point something unexpected happened which almost knocked me away from my plan of attack. As our two faces closed on each other she suddenly closed her eyes and parted her lips as if expecting, not the bite which no power on earth could by now have prevented me from giving her, but something else. When my jaws snapped shut and she realised what had taken place, her face darkened in a grimace of disappointment.

'Oof, you idiot. I'm so bored with the lot of you...'

'Sorry,' I said, retreating to another corner of the room and sinking down on a hillock of rail-shaped cushions. 'But once you ... I had to ...'

'No, it's all right, I understand,' she said sullenly. 'You don't need to explain.'

I could not hold off a moment longer. I shut my eyes, sealed myself off from the physical world and concentrated every atom of my being on what was now being revealed to me, the inner landscape that during so many long nights I had been able only to guess at. Now, at last, I was able to see everything with total clarity. However, I was not interested in the principal landmarks of her life, her secrets or her problems. I was tactful enough not even to glance in those areas. I was after something quite specific: her feelings about me. And those I established straight away.

I was not mistaken. I could have kissed her just now; she would not have resisted, had been hoping for it. She would not even have objected if matters had gone further than kissing ... how much further, she did not know herself. Perhaps, I thought, it was not too late? Opening my eyes, I moved diffidently towards her, but she divined what was in my mind.

'No, darling,' she said. 'One thing you have to get straight. It's either biting, or everything else. Today, please, you mustn't come any closer to me than one metre.'

I had no intention of giving up so easily, but I thought it would be politic to play a little for time.

'Would you like something to eat?' she asked.

I shook my head, but she still tossed the menu over to me.

'Have a look. They have some rather fun dishes.'

I could see that she was trying to distract me from looking too deeply into her, but I had in any case resolved not to invade her world without asking. I already knew the answer to the only question that concerned me, and it would not help me to go digging around in other areas. To this extent Loki's advice had been absolutely right and was confirmed by my own instinct telling me to resist the temptation.

I buried myself in the menu. The first thing on it was an introductory paragraph that struck me as encapsulating the message of the restaurant's name:

> *Any long-term inhabitant of Russia will long ago have identified a cardinal characteristic of our life: however revolting the current regime, its successor will be such as to suffuse memories of its predecessor with a painful glow of nostalgia. And nostalgia is best indulged with vodka (pages 17–18), hors d'oeuvres (pages 1–3), and all that can be found between the two.*

I now realised what Hera had been referring to with her 'fun dishes' – the menu included a supplementary sheet of fish *plats du jour* with the wildest names. There was, for instance, 'Carpaccio of Swordfish "Comandante Basayev"', and 'Euro Fish Soup "Freedom for Khodorkovsky!"'. My curiosity was piqued. I picked up the radio phone embellished with a picture of a tray-bearing waiter from the floor, and chose Freedom.

I then set to studying the wine list, predictably enough entitled 'Documents of State', and laboriously read line by line through the interminable list until my crystalline view of Hera's inner world began to fade. I then closed the book, congratulating myself on having allowed knightly *courtoisie* space to prevail over vulgar curiosity.

However, victory was not total – there was something I could still see, and like a mountain seen through a window with the curtains drawn I could not ignore it. There had been a disagreeable event in Hera's life. It had to do with Ishtar, whom Hera, like me, had been to see following her introduction to the Chaldeans (a procedure similar to mine, except that it was

Marduk Semyonovich who had presented her to the company, and following the clairvoyance séance she had had to defend herself with a bottle against an enraged female pop singer.) Something had happened between Hera and Ishtar, and Hera was now in a state of depression. Not only that, but she had been severely frightened.

But what had occurred in the depths of Heartland I could not see – it remained in some way hidden from me, as if part of her interior mapping had been obscured. I had not previously come across this phenomenon, so could not restrain myself from asking:

'What happened when you were with Ishtar Borisovna?'

She frowned.

'I beg you, let's not speak of it. Everyone asks me about it, Mithra, you...'

'Mithra?' I interrupted.

The name suddenly made me pay attention, and I realised that Hera's feelings towards Mithra were almost as warm as they were towards me. *Almost*. But Mithra...

Mithra, I realised with a mixture of jealousy and rage, had bitten her not once but twice. She had bitten him once. Nothing more had taken place between them, but that was already more than enough. Evidence of their closeness had been the last glimpse I was able to see in the outgoing tide of her memory before the window finally closed. The moment it did so I desperately wanted to bite her again, to find out exactly what place Mithra occupied in her life.

I also knew, of course, that this was something I should not do. It was clear as day: the second bite is followed by an irresistible need for a third, then a fourth... and so on without end... A name for the craving even came unbidden into my head: plasmaholism – although this had less to do with red liquid's plasma than with 'holism', the pathological desire for totality, for unrestricted access to her soul at the slightest suspicion of betrayal. If I were once to yield to the temptation, and then again, I thought, I could end up sucking the beloved being dry of all her red liquid.

Something of this must have shown in my face, for Hera blushed and said:

'What? What have you seen there?'

'Mithra has bitten you?'

'Yes, he has. That is why I do not want to see him. And I won't want to see you, if you bite me again.'

'Do you mean I can never bite you again?'

'You and I have to trust each other,' she said. 'And if we keep biting one another there can never be trust between us.'

'Why not?'

'What trust can there be if you know everything?'

This was logical.

'If it had been up to me,' I said, 'I wouldn't have done it first. You're the one who began it.'

'I know,' she sighed. 'Loki told me to. He said it is essential to be utterly cynical and ruthless about men, even if one's heart tells you otherwise.'

This was another area of her experience into which I had not looked.

'Loki?' I asked in astonishment. 'What did you study with him?'

'The art of combat and of love. The same as you.'

'But he's ... he's a man.'

'When we were having lessons on the art of love, he came dressed as a woman.'

I tried unsuccessfully to visualise Loki in a dress.

'That's extraordinary,' I said. 'He told me quite the opposite, that a vampire should not bite a woman in whom he ... well, in whom he is interested. So as not to lose the interest.'

281

Hera fiddled with her hair.

'Well,' she enquired, 'did it survive? The interest I mean? You didn't lose it altogether?'

'Not the least bit,' I replied. 'But I hardly saw anything. You could say that I don't know any more about you than I did before. All I wanted was to be quits with you. When you bit me by the museum...'

'Don't go on about it,' said Hera. 'Can't we change the subject?'

'All right. But one thing I don't understand: I wasn't able to see what had happened to you with Ishtar. How can that be?'

'She has that power. Whatever occurs between Ishtar and anyone whom she bites is hidden to everyone else. I wouldn't be able to see what you talked about with her either. Nor would even Enlil or Marduk.'

'I had the impression you were frightened and upset.'

Hera's face darkened.

'I did ask you not to talk about it. I may be able to tell you one day.'

'OK,' I agreed. 'Let's talk about something more life-enhancing. What did Loki look like in a dress?'

'Marvellous. He'd even got hold of artificial tits. I think he really liked it.'

'What did you cover in the course on love?'

'Loki talked to me about statistics.'

'What sort of statistics?'

'Are you seriously interested?'

I nodded.

'He said' – Hera furrowed her brow in concentration – 'let me try to remember... "Statistically speaking, the average male's relations with a woman are characterised by contempt and unbridled cynicism... Research has shown that seen from the perspective of male sexual morality two categories of women exist. A woman who declines to engage in the sexual act with a man is a 'bitch'. A woman who consents is a 'whore'. A male's relations with a woman are not only cynical but extremely irrational. The predominant view among men – held by seventy-four per cent of those surveyed – is that the majority of young women fall into both categories simultaneously, which is of course a logical impossibility..."'

'What was the conclusion?' I asked.

'That it is essential to be utterly ruthless in our dealings with men, since they deserve no other approach.'

'Did Loki bring an inflatable woman for your lessons too?'

Hera looked at me in bafflement.

'What on earth are you talking about?'

'I mean, of course, an inflatable man,' I corrected.

'No. You mean you had an inflatable woman?'

I muttered something unintelligible.

'What did you do with her?'

I gestured feebly with my hands.

'Was she lovely, though?'

I could bear no more of this.

'Could we change the subject?'

Hera shrugged her shoulders.

'As you please. You brought it up.'

A long silence followed.

'This is a weird conversation we're having,' said Hera sadly. 'We always seem to have to stop talking about whatever subject we get into.'

'We're vampires,' I replied. 'That is probably how it has to be.'

At that moment the soup was brought in.

The ensuing ritual took several minutes. The waiters placed on the table a grotesquely rococo soup tureen, took away the unused place settings, replaced them with new plates, then fished out from the steaming depths of the tureen a brightly painted china figurine with exaggeratedly rouged cheeks. At first I thought this must be Khodorkovsky, but the writing across her breast made it clear it was Hillary Clinton. The waiter then ceremonially placed the figure on a towel and presented it for inspection to each of us in turn, approximately as the cork of an expensive bottle of wine is presented to the nostrils of the client. It was then equally ceremonially returned to the soup. Hillary smelt of fish. Clearly there was a subtle point to all this, but once again it escaped me.

After the waiters had left the room, we stayed sitting on the floor.

'Are you going to eat something?' enquired Hera.

I shook my head.

'Why not?'

'Because of the watch.'

'What watch?'

'Patek Philippe,' I replied. 'Long story. Anyhow, what has Hillary Clinton to do with Russian fish soup? She's American, after all. I think they've rather overdone this one.'

'It's always the same in these expensive places,' said Hera. 'A sort of epidemic. Like for instance *Fallen Demon* or *IBAN Tsarevich*. Have you ever been to the *Marie Antoinette* on Tverskaya Street?'

'No, I haven't.'

'They have a guillotine there, just as you go in through the door. And the man wandering round the dining room serving desserts is the Marquis de Sade. Have you been to *Akhnaten*?'

'No, I haven't been there either,' I said, feeling like a clod-hopping bumpkin with straw in my hair.

'This season they've introduced monotheism. But the patron still dresses like Osiris. Or rather, undresses like Osiris.'

'Osiris?'

'Yes. Although I'm not clear what the connection is. Anyhow, on 4 November, this new Day of National Unity we've got now, he is brought back to life five times to Glinka's music. They bring in cypress trees specially, and keening women.'

'Everyone seems to be searching for some national idea or other.'

'Aha, right,' agreed Hera. 'But every time they let it off the hook at the last moment. The worst of it is this indiscriminate eclecticism.'

'That's not so surprising,' I said. 'They suck black liquid, so they can afford it. But this Osiris you were mentioning, he's not by any chance a vampire, is he?'

'Certainly not. It's just the role he plays, not his real name. No vampire would ever run a restaurant.'

'You don't know a vampire called Osiris?'

Hera shook her head.

'Who is he?'

For a second I hesitated, unsure whether to tell her or not. Then I decided I would.

'Ishtar told me to seek him out, when she saw how interested I was in certain things she could not tell me anything about.'

'For instance?'

'For instance, the origins of the world. Or what happens when we die.'

'Do you find things like that really interesting?' asked Hera.

'Don't you?'

'No,' replied Hera firmly. 'They're just the sort of stupid questions men always ask, the standard phallic projections of an unstable and immature intellect. I'll find out what happens after death when I die. Why should I bother about it now?'

'That's true, too,' I agreed, not wanting to argue. 'All the same, since Ishtar Borisovna herself suggested it, I should try to find him.'

'Ask Enlil.'

285

'Osiris is his brother, and they've fallen out. I can't ask Enlil.'

'All right,' said Hera, 'I'll track him down. And if you hear anything interesting from this Osiris, you will tell me, won't you?'

'It's a deal.'

Getting up, I began walking round the room as though stretching my legs. In fact they had not gone numb at all, I simply wanted to get closer to Hera and was trying to make my manoeuvre appear more natural.

I have to admit that all these preliminaries to the active phase of seduction have always been such an effort for me that they threatened seriously to devalue the prize. Usually at such times I behaved like a sex-obsessed idiot (which, to be honest, I was). But on this occasion I knew precisely Hera's feelings, and was determined to exploit my advantage.

Reaching the window in the course of my peregrinations, I turned to go back towards the door, then stopped halfway, made a right-angle turn, took two ponderous steps towards Hera, and sat down beside her.

'What are you doing?' she asked.

'It's like the old joke,' I said. 'One vampire sits on the rails, another comes along and says: "Couldn't you move along a bit?"'

'Oh,' said Hera, and blushed a little. 'I see what you mean, we are sitting on the rails.'

She pulled over another of the rail-shaped cushions and placed it between us.

I realised that my roaming manoeuvre had been too clumsy. We would have to go on talking.

'Hera,' I said, 'do you know what I'd like to ask you?'

'What?'

'About the Tongue. Do you feel it now?'

'In what sense?'

286

'Well, before, for the first six weeks or so, I could feel it all the time. Not just physically, but with my whole... well, brain I suppose. Or, if you'll forgive the expression, with my soul. But now I'm not aware of it at all. It's as if the Tongue has gone away; there's no sensation of it anywhere. I'm just as I was before.'

'It only seems like that,' said Hera. 'We are not the same as we were before. What has happened is that our memory has changed along with ourselves, so that now it appears to us as though we were always like that.'

'How can that be?'

'Jehovah explained it to me. What we think we remember is not how it really was. Memory is an amalgam of chemical compounds. It can accommodate any changes that are consistent with the laws of chemistry. If you take a lot of acid, the memory also acidifies, and so on. The Tongue radically changes our internal chemistry.'

'That sounds rather alarming,' I said.

'Why? What is there to worry about? The Tongue won't do us any harm. Generally speaking, it's a minimalist. At the very beginning, when it has just found a new nest to settle into, it arranges things how it wants them, bedding itself down so to say. At that stage you may feel uncomfortable. But once it has got used to you it stops being worried about anything and sleeps most of the time, like a bear in its lair. The Tongue is immortal, you know. It only wakes up to get a feed of *bablos*.'

'What about when there is a tasting?'

'It doesn't have to wake up for that. It doesn't care one bit what happens to us from day to day – to it, that's completely uninteresting. As far as the Tongue is concerned our life is like a dream that often it probably doesn't even notice.'

I thought about it. The description seemed to accord pretty well with my own perceptions.

'Have you ever tried *bablos*?' I asked.

Hera shook her head.

'We are to be given it together.'

'When?'

'I don't know. As far as I could understand, it will come out of the blue. Ishtar decides when. Even Enlil and Marduk don't know exactly when or how. They only have a vague idea.'

Every time I learnt something new from Hera, I experienced a slight pang of jealousy.

'Listen,' I said, 'I do envy you. Not only do you have a car and a driver, you always seem to get to know everything a month before I do. How do you manage it?'

'You ought to be more sociable,' smiled Hera. 'And spend less time hanging head down in your cupboard.'

'What is it then, are you always ringing them up, Marduk, Mithra, Enlil?

'No. They telephone me.'

'Why do they do that?' I asked suspiciously.

'You know, Rama, when you pretend to be a little bit thick, you're quite irresistible.'

For some reason I found this declaration encouraging, and put my arm round her shoulder. I can't claim that the gesture came across as completely unforced and natural, but at least she did not remove my hand.

'You know what else I don't understand?' I said. 'Look, I've completed my studies. I've "done Glamour and Discourse", as Baldur would say. I've been through my initiation and am now more or less a fully fledged vampire. What else do I have to do? When am I going to be given a job? Like a military posting, that sort of thing?'

'Something like that.'

'Well what sort of posting might it be?'

Hera turned her face to look at me.

'Is that a serious question?'

'Of course it is,' I said. 'I'm naturally interested in what I am going to do with my life.'

'What do you mean, what are you going to do? You're going to suck *bablos*, that's what. More precisely, the Tongue is going to suck *bablos*, and you are there to facilitate the process. You'll build yourself a house near Enlil's, where all our people live. And you will observe the crossing.'

I remembered the stone boats in the waterfall next to Enlil Maratovich's VIP dugout dwelling.

'Observe the crossing? Is that all?'

'What more do you want? To fight for the freedom of humanity?'

'No,' I said. 'Enlil Maratovich already explained that's not possible. All the same I'd feel much happier getting involved in some activity...'

'Why do you have to get involved in anything? You're still thinking too much like a human.'

I decided to let this barb pass me by.

'So what am I supposed to do? Just live like a parasite?'

'You are a parasite,' replied Hera. 'Or rather, you're a parasite's transport system.'

'What are you, then?'

'The same...' said Hera, and sighed.

She said this so hopelessly and quietly I was seized by a rush of sympathy for her. I felt that we were closer than we had ever been before. I drew her to me and kissed her. For the first time in my life this was an entirely spontaneous, natural development. She did not resist. Now the only thing separating us was that idiotic rail-shaped cushion behind which she had screened herself when I sat down beside her. I threw it out of the way, and Hera was in my arms.

'Please don't,' she pleaded.

I knew for certain she wanted it as much as I did. This gave me the strength to persist when in ordinary circumstances my courage could have failed me. I pushed her down on to the cushions.

'No, truly, please don't,' she repeated barely audibly.

But I had already gone too far to stop. I covered her lips with kisses, at the same fumbling with the zip at the back of her dress.

'Please, I really don't want you to,' she whispered for the third time.

I stopped her mouth with kisses. Kissing her was intoxicating and terrifying at the same time, like leaping into the dark. I could feel in her something strange, quite different from all other girls, and with each kiss I came nearer to the centre of the mystery. My hands roamed ever more confidently all over her body, straying in my ardour even into forbidden territories. At last she responded to my urgent caresses: raising my leg she brought my knee up to her thigh.

At that moment time seemed to stop – I felt like a runner in the stadium of eternity, frozen at the very moment of triumph. The race was almost over and I was in the lead. I had completed the final lap, and before me now was the dazzling pinnacle of happiness from which only a couple of insignificant movements separated me.

The next moment the light in my eyes went out and everything was black.

Never in my life had I experienced anything approaching such pain.

That such agony could exist was beyond my imagining – multi-coloured, jagged, throbbing in zigzags between unbearable physical convulsions and searing flashes of light.

In an immaculately controlled movement, specially prepared for by raising my leg in order to clear the trajectory needed for maximum inhuman force, she had kicked me with her knee. The only thing I wanted was to curl up into a ball and vanish far away from anything connected, however remotely, with existence or non-existence, but this was not possible owing to the pain which with every passing second was increasing in severity. I tried to suppress the cries of agony I could hear myself making, but could not succeed entirely, lapsing into a kind of mooing.

'Does it hurt?' enquired Hera, leaning over me with an expression of distress on her face.

'A-a-a-ah,' I wailed, 'a-a-a-ah.'

'Please forgive me,' she said. 'It's an automatic response. It's what Loki taught me: three times you ask the man to stop, and then you strike. I'm really awfully sorry.'

'Oo-oo-oo-ooh.'

'Would you like some tea,' she asked. 'I'm afraid it's cold now though.'

'Ooh-ah-ah-ah … no thank you, no tea.'

'It will pass,' she said. 'I didn't hit you very hard.'

'Really?'

'Really. There are five levels of strike. This was the weakest – it's called "warning". It's intended for men with whom one envisages continuing a relationship. It's not damaging to their health.'

'You're sure you didn't get the levels mixed up?'

'No, don't worry. Is it really so painful?'

I realised that I was now just about able to move, and rolled over on to my knees. But it was still impossible to straighten up completely.

'Do I infer,' I asked, 'that you would still like to continue our relationship?'

She lowered her eyes apologetically.

'Well, yes.'

'Did Loki teach you how to kick like that?'

She nodded.

'So how did you perfect the technique? You told me you didn't have any special training equipment.'

'We didn't. Loki put on a goalkeeper's protector box which he got from a hockey team. I bruised my knees terribly against it, even through all the padding. You can't imagine how black and blue they were.'

'What are the other strike levels, then?'

'Why do you want to know?'

'Just to have some idea what to expect,' I said, 'when we continue our relationship.'

She shrugged her shoulders.

'They're called "warning", "stopping", 'smashing", "retributory" and "triumphal".'

'What do they all mean?'

'I should have thought they were all pretty self-explanatory. You know what "warning" is now. "Stopping" is supposed to paralyse, but not to kill on the spot. It's so that one can leave the scene without needing assistance. The other three are more serious.'

'Allow me to express my gratitude,' I said, 'that you refrained from giving me the serious treatment. I shall telephone you every morning to say thank you. Only don't be surprised if my voice is rather higher than it was.'

Tears appeared in Hera's eyes.

'I did tell you not to come any closer than a metre to me. What I'd like to know is, isn't there anywhere in this town a girl can feel safe?'

'But I'd bitten you. I could see that you were not against my...'

'That was before the bite. A girl's hormonal balance alters when she's been bitten. It's physiological, you wouldn't understand. It's as though no one can be trusted any longer. Everything appears in a different light. And all desire to kiss evaporates.

That's why I said to you: either the bite, or everything else. Did you think I was joking?'

I shrugged.

'Well, yes.'

Tears were now trickling down her cheeks, first the right cheek, then the left as well.

'That's exactly what Loki said,' she sobbed. 'They're always going to think you don't mean it. So, go ahead and kick them in the balls with all your might, don't worry about it... Now, you bastard, you've made me cry.'

'You mean *I'm* the bastard?' I asked, with something approaching interest.

'My mother used to tell me, if a boy makes you cry, get rid of him and don't waste time regretting him. Her own mother used to say the same thing to her but she didn't listen. And then she suffered all her life with my father... even though the trouble didn't start straight away. But you've made me cry on our first date...'

'I do envy you,' I said. 'You've had such good advisors – kick 'em in the balls with all your might, chuck 'em out with no regrets. No one ever gave me advice about anything. I've had to learn everything the hard way.'

Hera buried her face between her knees and burst into tears. Grimacing with pain I crawled over to her, sat beside her and said: 'There there, don't fret. It's all right, calm down.'

Hera shook her head as if to dislodge my words from her ears, and buried her head even deeper between her knees.

I could see the absurdity of the whole situation. Here was someone who had a few moments ago very nearly killed me, then had been overcome by pity for herself and broken into sobs. The net result was that I had been transformed into the kind of monster her mummy had been warning her about all her life. The whole picture was so convincing that I could already

293

feel the crushing burden of my guilt. Moreover – as she had said herself – this had all taken place on our first date.

Where did we go next?

At the second attempt I succeeded in getting to my feet.

'OK then,' I said. 'I'd better go.'

'Can you get there on your own?

'I'll try.'

I thought she might offer me her car, but she said nothing.

It was a long way to the door and I shan't forget it. I moved there in tiny steps, taking plenty of time en route to look closely at details of the room's decorations that had previously escaped my attention. They were, however, extremely banal: miniature frescoes with views of Sardinia, and Party membership cards from Soviet times, pinned to the wall with upholstery tacks.

When I finally reached the door, I turned round. Hera was still sitting on the cushions, her hands clasped round her knees and her head still between them.

'Listen,' I said, 'you know what?'

'What?' she asked quietly.

'Next time you feel like a date with me... do remind me to bring a death candy.'

She lifted her head, smiled, and the familiar elongated dimples appeared on her damp cheeks.

'Of course I will, darling,' she said. 'Promise.'

OSIRIS

The front door bell rang just as I was finishing breakfast, at exactly ten o'clock, coinciding with the beeping of the clock. I wasn't expecting anyone to call.

On the threshold stood Hera's driver in his fatigues. His expression was, if anything, even more sullen than the last time. He smelt strongly of peppermint pastilles.

'Letter for you,' he said, handing me a yellow envelope with no stamp or address, similar to the one in which Hera had sent me her photograph. Right there on the stair I tore the envelope open. Inside was a sheet of paper on which was this handwritten note:

Hello Rama,

I'm terribly upset that everything went so wrong at our last meeting. I've been wanting to ring to make sure you had completely recovered, but thought you might be offended or think I was teasing you. So I decided to give you a present. I got the impression you would like to have a car too. I talked to Enlil Maratovich and he has given me another one, so this is now yours, along with the driver. His name is Ivan and he can also act as your bodyguard, so you can bring him with you when we next meet...

*Are you pleased? You'll be a real blade now, with your
very own bimmer. I hope I've raised your spirits just a little.
Do give me a ring.*

Mwah, mwah,

Hera

*P.S. I found out Osiris's address through Mithra. Ivan
knows where it is. Just tell him if you want to go there.*

P.P.S. Bablos is going to be soon – I know this for sure.

I looked at Ivan.

'What sort of a car does Hera have now?'

'Bentley,' replied Ivan, enveloping me in a cloud of menthol.
'What are your instructions for me?'

'I'll be down in fifteen minutes,' I said. 'Please wait for me in
the car.'

Osiris lived not far from Mayakovsky Square in a big building
dating from before the Revolution. The lift was not working so
I had to walk up to the fifth floor. The stairs were in darkness
because the windows on the landings had been boarded up with
sheets of hardboard.

The front door of Osiris's flat was of a kind I had not seen
for ages. It was like a farewell greeting from the Soviet era –
assuming, of course, it was not a designer's retro fantasy: the
wall was encrusted with at least ten doorbells, all of them old
and covered over by several layers of paint. The names under the
bells seemed vaguely menacing, reminiscent of the triumphant
proletariat.

I chose one at random and pressed the bell. I could hear it
ring on the other side of the door. I waited a minute or two and
then tried another button. The same bell rang. Then I pressed
each one in turn, all of them proving to be wired up to the same

unpleasantly tinny jangle, to which no one responded. I gave up on the bells and started pounding on the door with my fist.

'Coming,' came a voice from the corridor, and the door opened.

On the threshold stood a pale, thin man with a horseshoe-shaped moustache, wearing a leather waistcoat over a none too clean shirt outside his trousers. I immediately felt there was something Transylvanian about him, although he had rather too emaciated a look to be a vampire. But I remembered that Osiris was a Tolstoyan. Perhaps it was just the effect of having adopted the simple life.

'Hello Osiris,' I said. 'I've come from Ishtar Borisovna.'

The man with the moustache yawned indifferently into his palm.

'I'm not Osiris. I'm his assistant. Come in.'

I noticed on his neck a little square of sticking plaster with a brown stain in the middle, and all became clear.

Osiris's flat was a large, shabby communal apartment with signs of emergency repairs all over it: traces of welding on the radiators, holes in the ceilings with plaster filler in them, naked wires snaking along skirting boards as old as Marxism itself. One room, however – the largest, the door to which stood open – looked as though it had been completely refurbished: the floor had been finished with new parquet and the walls painted white. On the door, in black marker pen, was written:

REDQUARTERS

This room did indeed seem to be the spiritual and economic epicentre of the apartment, because while everywhere else appeared entombed in the sleep of ages, a powerful stink of tobacco and the sound of confident male voices emanated from this one. The men in the room seemed to be talking in Moldavian.

I approached the door. A big dining table stood in the middle of the room, and around it sat four men with playing cards in their hands. On the floor were various packages, rucksacks and sleeping bags. The card-players had sticking plaster on their necks, similar to that on the Moldavian who had opened the door to me. All four were dressed in identical grey t-shirts with the word:

BIO

printed in white letters across the chest.

The conversation fell silent, and the four card-players fixed their eyes on me. I returned their look in silence. Eventually the burliest of them, built like a bull, said: 'Overtime, is it? Triple pay, or you can fuck off right now.'

'Fuck off right now,' I replied politely.

The moustache said something in Moldavian, and I immediately ceased to be of interest to the card-players. Moustache took me delicately by the elbow.

'Not this room. We have to go further along. Come with me, I'll show you where.'

I followed him down a long corridor.

'Who were the people in that room?'

'Immigrant workers,' replied the Moldavian. 'I think that's the right name for them. I'm one myself.'

At the far end of the passage we stopped. The Moldavian knocked on the door.

'What is it?' came a quiet voice.

'Someone to see you.'

'Who?'

'Your people, I think,' said the Moldavian. 'Men in black.'

'How many of them?'

'They are one of them,' replied the Moldavian, squinting at me.

'Let him come in, then. And tell those boys to stop smoking. We're going to be dining in an hour.'

'OK, Chief.'

The Moldavian nodded at the door and shuffled off. Just in case, I knocked once more.

'It's open,' said the voice.

I opened the door.

The room was in half-darkness, the blinds drawn over the windows. However, I already knew enough to recognise the indefinable but distinctive character of a vampire's living quarters.

The room reminded me of Brahma's study in that it also had a tall filing cabinet going right up to the ceiling, only simpler and made of cheaper materials. On the opposite wall was a deep recess for a bed (what I think is called an 'alcove', although I had never seen one before). In front of the alcove was a low homemade magazine table improvised from an old mahogany dining table with the legs cut in half. On it was piled all sorts of rubbish – scraps of material, rulers, bits of various broken mechanical instruments, dismembered soft toys, books, clumsy old mobile phones from the late Russian era of the initial accumulation of capital, old power supply units, cups and so on. The most interesting object was a piece of apparatus resembling the product of a lunatic inventor's mind – a kerosene lamp with two circular mirrors on either side positioned so that the light would reflect precisely from one to the other.

Beside the magazine table was a yellow leather armchair.

I approached the alcove. Inside was a bed, covered with a quilted coverlet. Above it on the wall was a black ebony Stalin-era telephone, surrounded by a blizzard of pencil-scribbled notes. Beside it was a bell push similar to those I had seen outside on the landing.

Osiris lay on his side with one foot propped on the other knee, as if training his muscles for the lotus position. He had on an old cotton dressing-gown and large spectacles. His face and head resembled a balding cactus, with the sort of growth one gets if one starts off with a clean shave all over and then does not shave again for a week but allows the stubble to grow simultaneously over the cheeks and the head. His skin was pale and flabby, and he looked to me as though he probably spent most of his time in the dark. After inspecting me for a few seconds in a disinterested manner, he extended his hand for me to shake his wrist, which was white, soft and cool to the touch. In order to grasp it I had to stoop down so low that I needed to support myself on the junk-strewn table.

'Rama,' I introduced myself. 'Rama the Second.'

'Yes, I've heard about you. You're instead of Brahma, aren't you?'

'You could probably put it like that,' I replied, 'although I don't feel as though I am a substitute for anyone.'

'Please sit down,' said Osiris, nodding towards the armchair.

Before doing so I carefully inspected the dusty parquet underneath the chair and moved it a little way along the floor. Osiris laughed, but said nothing.

From where I was seated, Osiris's head was hidden from me by the corner of the recess, with only his feet visible. The chair had evidently been positioned there on purpose.

'I've come from Ishtar Borisovna,' I explained.

'How are things with the old girl?' asked Osiris amiably.

'Pretty well. She does drink a lot, though.'

'Well, yes,' said Osiris. 'There not much else left to her ...'

'How do you mean?'

'That doesn't concern you. Might I know the purpose of your visit?'

'When I was presented to Ishtar Borisovna,' I said, 'she noticed

300

that I think a lot about abstract questions. About where the world has come from. About God. Things like that. It's quite true: at the time I was thinking about such things. Anyhow, Ishtar Borisovna told me to seek you out because you are the guardian of the sacred lore and know all the answers...'

'That I do,' confirmed Osiris.

'I was wondering if you could perhaps give me something to read? Some sacred vampire texts?'

Osiris looked at me out of the alcove. His face loomed up in front of me when he bent forward.

'Something to read?' he repeated. 'I'd be glad to. But there are no sacred texts for vampires. The tradition exists only in oral form.'

'Well, could I hear it, then?'

'Ask away, whatever you like,' said Osiris.

I thought for a while. Before, I had seemed to have a great many serious questions, but now for some reason none would come to mind. Those that did seemed silly and childish.

'Who is Ishtar?' at length I settled on asking.

'Vampires believe she is a great goddess who was exiled to this world in ancient times. "Ishtar" is one of her names. Another is the "Mighty Bat".'

'Why was she sent into exile?'

'Ishtar committed a crime, the nature and significance of which we shall never understand.'

'Ishtar Borisovna? A crime?' I was astonished to hear this. 'When I talked to her, I...'

'You were not talking to the Mighty Bat,' interrupted Osiris. 'You were talking to her disposable head.'

'You mean there is a difference?'

'Certainly. Ishtar has two brains, a spinal brain and a cranial brain. Her higher nature is connected to her spinal brain, which has no power of language. For this reason it is difficult

301

to communicate with her higher nature. It would be truer to say that vampires communicate with her when they imbibe *bablos*. But this is a very unusual and specific form of communication...'

'All right,' I said, 'if you say so. But why was our world chosen for her exile?'

'It was not chosen. Our world was created in the first instance to be a prison.'

'How? Do you mean that a prison was constructed somewhere here in which to confine the great goddess?'

'This prison has no address, no location.'

'But according to the logic of the thing,' I observed, 'the prison must be wherever Ishtar's body is.'

'You don't understand,' replied Osiris. 'Ishtar's body is itself part of the prison. The prison is not *some*where, it is *every*where. If you are in a cell and examine its walls through a magnifying glass, you will find that you have entered another cell. You can pick up a speck of dust from the floor, look at it magnified hundreds of times in a microscope, see into yet another cell, and so on and so on, many times over. This is what some philosophers term "the malignant infinity", organised according to the principle of the kaleidoscope. Even illusions are so arranged that any one element in them can disintegrate into an infinite number of further illusions. The dream which you are dreaming, turns second by second into something else.'

'So the whole world is a prison of this kind?'

'Yes,' said Osiris. 'And it is very well built, down to the smallest imaginable details. Take the stars, for example. People in ancient times believed they were decorative points in the spheres which surround the earth. In essence, that is what they are: that is their main function, to be golden points in the sky. But at the same time it is possible for a rocket to fly to any of these points and after many millions of years arrive at an enormous

302

ball of fire. Further, it would be possible to land on a planet orbiting this star, to take from the planet's surface a sample of some mineral deposit, and analyse its chemical composition. There is no end to the number of these ornamental entities. But neither is there any point in journeying to them. All you would be doing is touring round casemates from which there can be no possibility of escape.'

'Just a second,' I said. 'Let us accept that our planet was created in order to function as a prison, and that the stars are merely golden dots in the sky. But surely the universe, including the stars, existed long before the appearance of our planet. Is that not so?'

'You cannot conceive with what subtlety this prison has been put together. It has been made full of traces of the past. But they are all simply elements in the design of the prison.'

'How?'

'Like this. The creation of the world includes the fabrication of a spurious, but at the same time absolutely authentic, panorama of the past. All those illimitable vistas into space and time are no more than stage settings in a theatre. Incidentally, this has already been well understood by those astronomers and physicists who have concluded that the universe is closed. Think about it yourself: even light itself cannot escape from it. There is nowhere else for it to go. What more proof could be needed that we are in prison?'

'It may be that light cannot escape from this world,' I said, 'but surely thought can? You yourself say that astronomers and physicists have established the outer boundaries of space and time.'

'Yes,' replied Osiris, 'they have ... But no astronomer or physicist can tell you what that means, because such matters are hidden from the human mind; all the human mind can do is pursue various formulae. The truth still comes down to that same malevolent kaleidoscope of which I spoke earlier, only now applied to theories and deductions. It is one of Mind "B"s by-products, a kind of oil-cake derived from the production of *bablos*.'

Osiris pronounced the word 'oil-cake' as 'all-cake'. I was not quite sure myself what the word meant, but I thought it was the waste product from oil-yielding plants – what was left after all the oil had been pressed out of them. It was agricultural terminology; Osiris had probably picked it up from his Moldavians.

'Hold on a minute,' I said. 'Do you seriously expect me to believe that mankind's knowledge of the origins of the universe is simply oil-cake?'

Osiris emerged from his niche and stared at me as if I were an idiot.

'I'm not seriously interested in what you believe,' he replied, 'but such is the case. Think for yourself: where did the universe come from?'

'What do you mean by "come from"?'

'At first people believed that there was a sphere above their heads with gold dots in it. How did this sphere get transformed into the universe? What started it off?'

I thought hard.

'Well... People began to study the sky, to look at it through a telescope...'

'Precisely so. And why did they do that?'

I shrugged my shoulders.

'Let me remind you,' said Osiris. 'The great discoveries in the realm of astronomy – Galileo, Herschel, and others – were made in the hope of accumulating riches. Galileo wanted to sell his telescope to the Venetian government, Herschel hoped to sweet talk some money out of King George. That is the reason these stars and galaxies came to our consciousness. And remember this: *bablos* is soon consumed, but the oil-cake that is left lasts forever. It's like what happened in camps where nomadic mammoth-hunters lived: the meat got eaten at once, but over the years there accumulated a huge mound of ribs and tusks, which people started using to build dwelling-places. It is precisely because of such ribs and tusks that today we find ourselves living not on a round island in the cosmic ocean, as the church used to teach, but suspended in an expanding void.'

'And is the micro-world also oil-cake?' I asked.

'Of course. But don't make the mistake of thinking that oil-cake is something negligible. I am referring to the origins of these phenomena, their genealogy, so to say.'

'Could we please go back to the beginning and recap step by step?' I asked. 'We seem to be skipping about rather rapidly. You told me that the Mighty Bat was sent into exile to Earth. Where was she sent from? And who sent her?'

'That is the most interesting question. Ishtar's punishment consisted in her not being allowed to remember who she was or where she came from. Initially she did not even realise that she had been exiled – she believed that she had herself created this world and had merely forgotten when and how she had done so. Later she began to have doubts, and she brought us, vampires, into being. To begin with we had bodies – we looked like giant bats. Well, you know all about that. Then, when the climate began to give rise to catastrophic changes, we evolved into Tongues that found lodgings in living creatures better adapted to the new conditions.'

'Why did Ishtar create vampires?'

'Vampires were initially creatures selected to assist the Mighty Bat. In a sense, they were projections of her. Their job was to discover the purpose of creation and explain to the Mighty

Bat how and why she had made the world. They failed in this task.'

'Yes,' I said. 'I understand.'

'After that the vampires decided to make the best of this world and establish themselves as comfortably as possible in it, and to that end bred the race of human beings, having created for them Mind "B". You've had explained to you the mechanism of how Mind "B" works?'

I shook my head.

'Mind "B" consists of two mirrors reflecting directly into one another. The first mirror is Mind "A", and it is common to all living creatures. It reflects the world. And the second mirror is the Word.'

'What word?'

'Any and all words. At any given moment only one Word can appear reflected in Mind "A", but the words can change and succeed one another very quickly, faster than an aircraft gun can shoot bullets. Mind "A" itself, however, is entirely stationary.'

'Why do the reflections have to be words?' I demanded. 'I for one practically never think in words. Mostly I think in pictures. Images.'

'All your pictures are also made up of words, as a house is made of bricks. But sometimes the bricks cannot be seen beneath the plaster.'

'But how can a Word be a mirror? What can be reflected in it?'

'Its meaning. When you place a Word in front of Mind "A", the Word is reflected in the mind, the mind is reflected in the Word, and between them they create the endless corridor that is Mind "B". In this endless corridor appears not only the whole world but the person who is seeing it. In other words, what is taking place in Mind "B" is a continuous reaction analogous

306

to atomic fission, only on a much deeper level. The absolute is split into subject and object, and as part of the process excretes *bablos* in the form of Aggregate "M-5". What we, vampires, suck is essentially not red liquid but the absolute. But most of us are not capable of grasping this.'

'Splitting of the absolute,' I repeated. 'Is that a metaphor, or is it a real reaction?'

'It is the mother of all reactions. Consider this: the Word can exist only as an object of the mind. But all objects need a subject to perceive them. They exist only as pairs: the appearance of an object leads to the appearance of a subject, and vice versa. A hundred-dollar bill presupposes the appearance of a person to observe it, like an elevator and its counterweight. Therefore when *bablos* is produced in the mirrors of the money gland, an illusion is inescapably generated alongside it – of the person who produces the *bablos*. And thus starts a continuous chain reaction leading eventually to *The Iliad* and *War and Peace*.'

'Could you make it a bit simpler for me?' I pleaded. 'Where are these mirrors located? In consciousness?'

'Yes. But the dual mirror system does not hang there in a fixed position, it renews itself with every thought. Mind "B" is composed of words, and if there is no Word for something, for Mind "B" it cannot exist. Words create objects, not the other way round.'

'So objects do not exist for animals?'

'Certainly not,' replied Osiris. 'It does not occur to a cat that she is surrounded by, shall we say, bricks. Until someone heaves one at her, of course. And even then, it isn't a brick, it's simply a miaow! Do you see?'

'Yes, sort of.'

'All right then,' said Osiris. 'Now I can explain an unintended effect that arose in Mind "B". This mind turned out to be a reflection of our universe. But that was not the worst of it. The universe in which we found ourselves also turned out to be a reflection of Mind "B". And from that time on no one has been able to distinguish one from the other, because now they are one and the same. It is impossible to say: this is the mind, and that is the universe. Everything is made of Words.'

'Why do you say Mind "B" is a model of the universe?'

'Any two mirrors juxtaposed to face one another exactly create a malignant infinity. That is our world. The Chaldeans carry on their belts a two-sided mirror which symbolises this mechanism.'

I looked doubtfully at the kerosene lamp with its two mirrors on the table. It did not seem remotely like a model of the universe. The thought came into my head that at best it might just be taken for the first Russian laser, constructed by the autodidact Kulibinin in Samara in 1883. But immediately I realised that with the right kind of spin put on it, the device could indeed become a model of the Soviet universe into which I had been born. Osiris was right.

'As was precisely the case with the Mighty Bat,' continued Osiris, 'man was confronted by the question of who he was and why he had been sent here. People began to seek the purpose of life. And the most remarkable thing is – they proceeded to do so without being distracted from the main function for which they had been bred. To put it at its plainest, mankind failed to explain creation in such a way as to convince the Mighty Bat. But on the way they did arrive at a conclusion about the existence of God. This discovery was yet another unexpected consequence of the workings of Mind "B".'

'Is there any way of sensing God?'

'God is not accessible either to the mind or to the emotions. At least not to human minds and emotions. Some vampires believe, however, that they approach God at the moment of taking *bablos*. For this reason it used to be said that *bablos* makes us gods.'

Osiris looked at his watch.

'But to experience it once is better than to hear about it a hundred times.'

THE RED CEREMONY

The next three days of my life vanished without trace in the hamlet – sunk in mindless gloom, as Count Dracula had perceptively observed. On the morning of the fourth day Enlil Maratovich telephoned.

'Well, Rama,' he said, 'I offer you my congratulations.'

'What has happened?'

'Today there is to be a Red Ceremony. You are to be given *bablos* to try. An important day in your life.'

I said nothing.

'The idea was that Mithra should call for you,' went on Enlil Maratovich, 'but he cannot be found at the moment. I would have come myself, but I'm busy. Do you think you can get yourself to Baal's dacha?'

'Where?'

'To Baal Petrovich's place. He is my neighbour. Your driver knows where he lives.'

'I'm sure I can, then, if the driver knows. What time should I be there?'

'There's no hurry. It won't begin without you. Hera will be there as well.'

'What should I wear?'

'Up to you. But don't eat anything. *Bablos* is always taken on an empty stomach. That's all for now, take care.'

Twenty minutes later I was in the car.

'Baal Petrovich?' asked Ivan. 'I know where he lives. Sosnovka-38. Are we in a hurry?'

'Yes,' I said, 'it's a very urgent matter.'

I was so nervous that I went into a kind of trance. I felt that the highway we were travelling along was like a river bearing me inexorably towards the abyss. My head was in a complete whirl. I could not decide which desire was the more desperate: to get to Baal Petrovich's place as quickly as possible, or to go straight to Domodedovo Airport, buy a ticket and fly immediately to anywhere that would take me without a visa. In fact, this option was not feasible since I had no documents of any kind with me.

The traffic was light and we arrived at our destination quickly, a rare enough event in Moscow. After being waved through a barrier, not unlike a border post, in a security fence bristling with CCTV cameras, Ivan brought the car to a stop in an empty parking area next to the house.

Baal Petrovich's house reminded me of something midway between an embryonic Lenin Library and a prematurely born Reich Chancellery. The building itself was not so enormous, but its wide staircases and ranks of square columns faced in dark yellow stone lent it a monumental and majestic appearance. It was an appropriate setting for an initiation ceremony. Or perhaps for some black magic ritual.

'There's her new one,' said Ivan.

'Her new what?'

'Hera Vladimirovna's car. The Bentley.'

I looked all round but could not see anything.

'Where is it?'

'Over there, underneath that tree.'

Ivan pointed towards some bushes growing at the edge of

the parking area, and then I saw a huge green car resembling a bourgeois chest of drawers daringly responding to the challenge of the times. The chest of drawers was parked on the grass, well away from the edge of the asphalt of the hard standing, half-concealed by the bushes, which was why I had not seen it at first.

'Shall I beep her?' asked Ivan.

'No, don't,' I replied. 'I'll go over and take a look.'

The back door of the car was half open. I could see movements inside, and then heard laughter which I thought sounded like Hera's. I quickened my pace, and at that moment a car horn sounded. Ivan had tooted after all.

Hera's head came into view inside the car, and beside it I caught a glimpse of another head, a man's, but did not recognise it.

'Hera,' I called, 'Hello!'

But the door, instead of opening wider, suddenly slammed shut. Something I had not expected was going on. I froze on the spot, watching the wind flutter a St George's Ribbon tied to the door handle. I could not decide whether to go on or turn back, and was just about to go back when the door flung open and out stepped Mithra.

His appearance was dishevelled (hair all tousled, yellow bow tie halfway down his shirt front) and extremely unfriendly. I had not seen him like that before. He looked ready to punch me.

'Spying, are we?' he asked.

'Not at all,' I said, 'all it was... I just saw the car.'

'Seems to me, if a car is parked somewhere like this, any fool would know better than to come near it.'

'Any fool might,' I replied, 'but I'm not a fool. And it's not your car.'

Hera emerged from the car. She nodded to me, smiled guiltily and shrugged her shoulders.

312

'Rama,' said Mithra, 'if you're having trouble, how shall I put it, making out on your own, let me send you some of those preparations that Brahma left behind. There's enough for a year there. You'll be able to work out your problems by yourself and stop bothering others.'

Hera took hold of his sleeve.

'Please, that's enough.'

I could see that Mithra was deliberately trying to insult me, and this for some reason unsettled me. Instead of becoming angry I felt disoriented. No doubt I did look rather foolish. I was rescued by the sound of a horn: Ivan was tooting again.

'Chief,' he called, 'you're wanted over here.'

I turned on my heel and walked back to the parking area.

A black-suited man I did not know was standing by my car. He was small, tubby, with a handlebar moustache like an elderly musketeer.

'Baal Petrovich,' he introduced himself and shook my hand. 'But aren't there supposed to be two of you? Where is Hera?

'She's just coming.'

'Why are you so pale?' asked Baal Petrovich. 'Are you nervous?'

'No,' I said.

'There's nothing to fear. It is very many years since anything untoward has occurred during a Red Ceremony. We have the best possible equipment... Ah, you must be Hera? Happy to make your acquaintance.'

Hera was alone. Mithra had stayed back with the car.

'Now then, my friends,' said Baal Petrovich, 'please come with me.'

He turned and led the way into his Reichskanzlei. We followed, Hera avoiding looking at me.

'What was all that about?' I asked.

313

'Nothing,' she said. 'For God's sake, we don't need to talk about it just now, do we? This day must not be spoilt.'

'Don't you want to see me?'

'I like you very much,' she said. 'If you must know, much more than I do Mithra. That's the truth. But please don't tell him that, OK?'

'OK,' I agreed. 'Tell me, though, did you kick him in the balls as well? Or is it only me you do that to, because you like me so much?'

'I don't wish to talk about it.'

'If you like me so much, why do you spend time with Mithra?'

'I'm in a phase of my life just now when I need him with me. You wouldn't understand. Or you might understand, but wrongly.'

'That's quite beyond me. Will there be another phase of your life? When you will want me with you?'

'Possibly.'

'It's like the worst kind of soap opera,' I said. 'Honestly. I can't believe you're saying this to me.'

'It will all become clear to you in due course. Now let's drop the subject.'

Inside, Baal Petrovich's abode seemed to have no connection with the Nordic totalitarianism of its exterior. The entrance hall was decorated in early oligarch-eclectic style, with a life-size German Knight of the Sword sandwiched between a German musical box and a seascape by Aivazovsky. The only feature distinguishing the surroundings from the furnishings of a crooked accountant on the take was that the knight's armour and the Aivazovsky were genuine.

We went along the passage and stopped before a high double door. Baal Petrovich turned to Hera and me.

'Before going in,' he said, 'we must become better acquainted.'

Taking a step towards me he brought his face closer to mine

and pecked at it with his chin, as if he were nodding towards sleep. I took a handkerchief from my pocket to wipe my neck, but the bite had been accomplished with consummate skill and not a trace was to be seen on the handkerchief.

Baal Petrovich closed his eyes and smacked his lips for a full minute. It made me feel uncomfortable – I wanted to bite him myself, to understand just what he was seeing for such a long time. At last he opened his eyes and looked at me with a twinkle.

'So you have been thinking of joining the Tolstoyans, have you?'

'What makes you say that?'

'Osiris. You were intending to join his sect?'

'Not at the moment,' I replied proudly. 'I was simply, ah, wanting to broaden my circle of acquaintances. But please don't mention it to Enlil Maratovich. Why upset the old man?'

'I won't say anything, don't worry. That's all right, Rama. We'll give you some *bablos*, and then you won't need to visit any of these sectarians.'

I shrugged my shoulders. Baal Petrovich advanced on Hera, bent down towards her ear and nodded his head as though responding to her quiet question. I had never before seen a vampire bite two people in such quick succession, but obviously Baal Petrovich was a specialist with great experience. After a few lip-smacking sounds, he said: 'Very good to meet such a purposeful individual.'

He behaved to Hera with great gallantry. Also, he devoted much less time to probing her.

'For some reason all my recent acquaintances seem to lead to the same outcome,' muttered Hera.

'Nothing personal,' replied Baal Petrovich. 'These bites are for purely professional purposes. I have to find out the best way to instruct you on the procedure, and for that, my friends, I need to gain an accurate picture of your inner world. Now, please come in...'

And with that he flung open the doors.

What was revealed was a brightly lit circular hall in which two colours predominated: gold and blue. The walls themselves were light blue, while gold gleamed from the pilasters, the mouldings of the ceiling and the frames of the pictures. The pictures were not interesting in themselves; in their somnolent lack of variety they were more like wallpaper: romantic ruins, noblemen on horseback, gallant rendezvous in woodland clearings. The painted ceiling was a representation of a skyscape with clouds, from the centre of which protruded a large gilded relief of the sun, backlit by concealed lamps. The sun had eyes and ears, a smiling mouth, and the general impression was of Khrushchev hiding in the ceiling. His round, complacent face beamed down to be reflected in the polished parquet floor.

Overcome by the splendour, I lingered in the doorway. Hera also stopped.

'Please come in,' Baal Petrovich repeated. 'We don't have too much time.'

We entered the hall. It contained no furniture except five big armchairs arranged in a semicircle around the fireplace let into one wall. The chairs were high-tech military style, equipped with servo drives, open-face helmets and a plethora of complicated couplings. Beside the group of chairs was a level control desk, raised above the floor on a steel support. In the fireplace a fire was burning, which struck me as odd since the air-conditioning was on full. Two Chaldeans in gold masks were tending to the fire.

'Interesting,' I said, 'you have very much the same set-up as Enlil Maratovich. He also has a circular hall, a fireplace in the wall, and chairs. But his, of course, is more modest.'

'Nothing to be wondered at,' replied Baal Petrovich. 'All

316

buildings designed for a similar function have things in common, just as all violins have a similar form. Please sit down.'

He signed to the Chaldeans to leave the room. One of them stayed behind a little to add some fuel to the fire from a paper packet marked 'BBQ Charcoal'.

'As part of the Red Ceremony,' explained Baal Petrovich, 'it is customary to burn some banknotes. There is no practical point to this, it is simply one of our national traditions, reflected in folklore. We are not short of money, nevertheless, out of respect for human labour we prefer to burn old currency, which we get from the State Mint.'

He glanced at his watch.

'Now I must go to change my clothes. Please do not touch anything in the meantime.'

Warming us with an encouraging smile, Baal Petrovich followed the Chaldeans out of the room.

'Weird chairs,' remarked Hera. 'A bit like at the dentist's.'

To me they seemed more like props for a space odyssey film.

'Yes, they are strange,' I agreed. 'Especially this breastplate thing.'

Each chair was equipped with a device familiar from sci-fi films featuring interstellar foot-soldiers – it came down over the cosmonauts' chests to keep them in place during landing and take-off.

'I expect they're to keep us from falling to the floor if we start writhing in convulsions,' I suggested.

'Probably,' agreed Hera.

'Aren't you at all nervous?'

She shook her head.

'Mithra told me it was a wonderful experience. A little painful at the beginning, but then...'

'Would you mind awfully not talking any more about Mithra?'

'All right,' replied Hera. 'Then let's not talk about anything.'

We had no more conversation until Baal Petrovich returned. I studied the pictures on the walls with exaggerated interest, and she sat on the edge of her seat looking at the floor.

When Baal Petrovich re-entered the room I did not recognise him. He had changed into a long robe of dark red silk and carried in his hand a bag like a cash-in-transit courier's. I remembered where I had seen a robe like it before.

'Baal Petrovich, have you ever been in Enlil Maratovich's study?'

'Many times,' he replied.

'There is a picture on the wall in it,' I went on. 'Some odd-looking people in top hats are sitting round a fire, strapped to their chairs, and with something like gags in their mouths. Near them stands a man in a red robe exactly like the one you are wearing. Is that picture an illustration of the Red Ceremony?'

'Yes,' said Baal Petrovich. 'Or rather, a representation of what it would have looked like two hundred years ago. At that time the ceremony was attended by certain risks to health. But nowadays it is a completely safe procedure.'

'But how were they able to swallow the *bablos*? I mean the people in the picture. They had gags in their mouths.'

'They're not gags,' replied Baal Petrovich, going over to the control desk. 'They are special appliances in which are incorporated a capsule of *bablos* made from the bladder of a fish. They also protect the tongue and the lips from trauma. The technology we use now is quite different.'

He pressed a knob on the control desk and the breastplates rose with a humming noise above the chairs.

'You may sit down now.'

I sat in the end chair. Hera settled herself two chairs away from me.

'Let's go,' I said. 'We're ready.'

Baal Petrovich shot me a disapproving look.

318

'I cannot approve such a frivolous attitude. How do you know whether or not you are ready, when you do not even know what is about to take place?

I shrugged.

'Why don't you explain, then?'

'Listen to me very carefully,' said Baal Petrovich. 'Since I know what sort of rubbish your heads are filled with, I wish you to be clear that the experience you are about to undergo will be surprising and not at all what you imagine. For you to have a correct understanding of what will take place it is essential from the start to grasp one fact that you may find damaging to your self-esteem. It is not we who suck *bablos*. It is the Tongue.'

'Are we not one entity?' asked Hera.

'Up to a certain point. And this is that point.'

'But we will feel something, won't we?'

'Oh yes, indeed,' replied Baal Petrovich. 'In no small measure. But it will be nothing like what the Tongue experiences.'

'What does the Tongue experience?' I asked.

'I do not know,' replied Baal Petrovich. 'No one knows.'

I had not anticipated this answer.

'How is that possible?' I asked in dismay.

Baal Petrovich burst out laughing.

'You were asking me about a picture in Enlil's study,' he said. 'But do you remember the picture that hangs in your own study? Napoleon on horseback?'

'To be honest,' I replied, 'I long ago became heartily sick of being compared to a horse.'

'This is the last time, I swear. Does the horse know what Napoleon is thinking? What is your opinion?'

'I think not.'

'And I agree. But when Napoleon canters round the field of battle before his army, he and his horse appear as a single

319

organism. In a sense that is what they are... And when Napoleon pats his faithful steed on the neck...'

'Why bother to go on?' I said. 'There's no point trying to explain anything to a horse, is there? Napoleon certainly wouldn't have done so.'

'Rama, I understand your feelings,' replied Baal Petrovich. 'But life is much simpler than is commonly believed. There are two paths. If a person is fortunate, incredibly fortunate – as you and Hera have been – he or she can become the horse that carries Napoleon. But by the same token, without that stroke of luck the person will remain a mere beast of burden.'

'Could we have done with horse-breeding?' asked Hera. 'Let's get on with the matter in hand.'

'With pleasure,' replied Baal Petrovich. 'So, the Red Ceremony is in two parts. First the Tongue sucks in *bablos*. This is the greatest mystery in the vampire's world. But as I have already said, this procedure does not take place with us personally, and we know little of its essential nature. During this time what you experience will be extremely varied and fairly unpleasant, and can even be painful. You must endure. Do you understand?'

I nodded.

'After that the pain passes and the second part of the experience begins,' continued Baal Petrovich. 'Physiologically, what happens is this: having absorbed enough *bablos*, the Tongue injects directly into the brain a charge from an extremely powerful neurotransmitter we call dopamen, which compensates for the negative experiences arising from the first part of the procedure.'

'Why is this compensation needed?' I asked. 'After all, the pain has already gone.'

'Quite so,' said Ball Petrovich. 'But disagreeable memories persist. The neurotransmitter secreted by the Tongue, however, is powerful enough to alter the content of the memory. To

320

be precise, not the memory itself, but the emotional balance connected with it. As a result the final impression the vampire retains of the Red Ceremony is in the highest degree positive, so much so that many vampires become psychologically dependent on *bablos*, a condition we call Thirst. This is, of course, a paradoxical reaction since the intake of *bablos* is in itself a fairly painful procedure.'

'What exactly is a neurotransmitter?' I asked.

'In our case it is an agent which generates in the brain a sequence of electrochemical processes, experienced subjectively as happiness. In a normal person dopamine is responsible for similar processes. Its chemical name is 3.4 dihydroxiphenyl-ethylamine. Dopamen is a closely related substance, as you will see if you look at the formula – on the right side of the molecule is the same nitric dioxide, but different figures for carbon and hydrogen. From a strictly chemical perspective the name is incorrect; it was invented in the sixties as a joke: "dope amen", which became "dopamen". At that time vampires were making an intensive study of their brains. This work was later curtailed, but the name stuck.'

'Why was the work curtailed?'

'The Mighty Bat became concerned that vampires might learn how to synthesise *bablos* themselves, and this could upset the time-hallowed order. If you're interested we can go more deeply into the subject. Would you like me to write down the formula for dopamen?'

I shook my head.

'Dopamen is also very similar to dopamine in the mechanism of its effect,' continued Baal Petrovich, 'but it is significantly stronger, approximately in proportion as crack is to cocaine. The Tongue injects it directly into the brain and it instantly generates its own reward circuits, which differ from the standard neuronal pathways of human happiness. It is therefore scientifically accurate to state that for a few minutes after receiving *bablos* the vampire experiences superhuman happiness.'

'Superhuman happiness,' I repeated dreamily to myself.

'However, this is not what you might imagine it to be,' said Baal Petrovich. 'The best thing is not to have any expectations. That way you will not be disappointed. Well, that is enough by way of explanation, I think. We may now begin.'

Hera and I exchanged glances.

'Raise your legs and spread your arms out wide,' commanded Baal Petrovich.

Cautiously I adopted the required position, resting my legs on a supporting ledge that slid out from beneath the chair. The chair itself was extremely comfortable; the body was hardly aware of it at any point.

Baal Petrovich touched a knob and the breastplate descended, gently pressing on my chest. He strapped my arms and legs to the chair with shackles made of what looked like thick plastic, and then repeated the procedure for Hera.

'Now lift your chin...'

As soon as I obeyed he placed in position on the back of my head something like a motorcycle crash helmet. Now the only part of my body I could move was my fingers.

'During the ceremony your body may appear to be travelling through space. This is an illusion. In reality you will stay exactly where you are at all times. Remember this, and do not be afraid.'

'Why do I have to be I strapped down like this?' I asked.

'Because,' answered Baal Petrovich, 'the illusion is extremely powerful and the body engages in uncontrollable movements to compensate for the imaginary motion in space. This can result in severe trauma. In the past there were numerous instances of this... Well, all is ready now. Do either of you have any more questions?'

'No,' I replied.

'Please be aware that once the procedure has started there is no way back. Your only option is to endure until the end. Therefore, do not attempt to remove your shackles or get up from your chairs. You will not be able to. Is that clear?'

'Quite clear,' answered Hera.

Baal Petrovich once again looked carefully over both of us and appeared satisfied with what he saw.

'Well, then, shall we go?'

'Into darkness, back and down,' I replied.

'Good luck.'

Baal Petrovich moved behind the chair, out of my line of sight. I heard a quiet humming noise. From the right-hand side of the helmet extruded a small, transparent tube, which came to rest exactly above my mouth. Simultaneously two soft rubber plugs exerted pressure on my cheeks, one on either side. My mouth opened and at the moment a single bright crimson drop escaped from the end of the tube and fell into my mouth.

It fell directly on to my tongue, and in a reflex motion I pressed it up against my soft palate. The liquid was thick and viscous, tangy and sweet to the taste, as though someone had combined syrup with cider vinegar. I had the impression that it was instantly absorbed, as though a tiny mouth had opened just there and sucked it in.

My head began to spin. The sensation increased in intensity for several seconds and culminated in total spatial disorientation. I was relieved that my body was firmly strapped in so that it could not fall. Then it seemed to me as though the chair itself was rising from the floor.

This was most strange. I continued to see everything around me – Hera, the fireplace, the walls, the sun in the ceiling, Baal Petrovich in his dark red gown. Yet at the same time I had an unmistakeable sensation of my body and the chair ascending, moreover at a velocity such that I experienced the G-force a cosmonaut docs when his rocket lifts off.

The gravity became so extreme that I had difficulty in breathing. I was frightened of suffocating, and tried to communicate this to Baal Petrovich. But my mouth would not answer to my commands; all I could do was move my fingers.

Gradually it became easier to breathe. I felt the speed of my ascent decelerating, as though I was approaching an invisible summit. I realised that I was on the point of overshooting, and then . . .

I just had time to curl my fingers into fists before my body plunged into a dizzy, delirious but at the same time terrifying weightlessness. I felt something cold tickling in the pit of my stomach as my body hurtled downwards at an appalling speed – and all this while I was sitting still in a motionless chair.

'Close your eyes,' said Baal Petrovich.

I glanced over at Hera. Her eyes were tight shut, so I followed suit in screwing mine fast shut as well, and that was even more terrifying because the sensation of flight was now all-consuming and utterly real, and I could no longer see the room around me, to reassure me second by second that what was happening was no more than a vestibular hallucination. I tried to open my eyes once more but could not. Evidently I had begun to whimper from terror; I heard a low laugh from Baal Petrovich.

Now a visual element was added to my hallucinations. The illusion of flying through the cloud-covered night sky was complete. All around was dark, but even so amid the darkness there were some clouds of a yet more impenetrable murk, like dense emboli of steam, and these I passed through with incredible speed. I seemed to be enveloped in a kind of crease in space which was absorbing air friction. From time to time I felt something inside my head tauten and the direction of my travel alter, which was a deeply unpleasant sensation.

Soon I began to distinguish something like luminous dotted lines among the clouds. At first they were so dim as to be hardly visible, but gradually they became clearer. I knew that these points of light had some kind of connection to people: either they were human souls, or thoughts, or dreams, or perhaps an element common to all these...

And then at last I knew what they were.

They were that part of human consciousness Enlil Maratovich had identified as Mind 'B'. They appeared like spheres in which flickered a softly appealing, nacreous luminescence – the 'Northern Lights', he had called it earlier. Linking the spheres was an invisible thread, looping them into long garlands. Countless numbers of these garlands spiralled upwards to culminate in a tiny speck of sheer black, which was where Ishtar had to be found. I could not see her, but her presence was as plainly perceptible as the sun above one's head on a hot day.

All of a sudden my body executed a sharp manoeuvre which was extremely painful and felt as though my bones had all been crunched sideways, upon which I found myself actually on one of the threads. Then I was moving along it, skewering the cerebral capsules one by one as I passed.

As far as I could see this had no effect on them. In fact it could not have – because they were not real. The Tongue's objective was not the capsules themselves but the bright-red drop of hope and meaning germinating within each one. One after the other the Tongue greedily drank down these drops, each time swelling with a dreadful kind of electric exultation, which increasingly filled me with terror.

I felt like a shade flying among thousands of dreams and feeding from them. The souls of all these people were as an open book to me: I could instantly understand everything about them. I was feeding on the reality of those waking dreams into which a man would lapse unconsciously many times a day, whenever his glance might fall upon a glossy page, a monitor screen, or a face in the crowd.

The crimson flower of hope could blossom in any soul, and the fact that this hope was wholly without meaning, like the farewell 'cock-a-doodle-do' of a broiler chicken, made no difference at all. The flowers themselves were real, and the unseen reaper whom I bore on my foam-lathered back scythed them down with alacrity. A red spiral of energy throbbed in the people, a glowing discharge oscillating between what they imagined was real and what they thought were fantasies. Both poles were delusional, but the sparks flying between them were real enough. The Tongue gulped down these sparks, inflating and shaking my poor skull.

It became harder and harder for me to keep going in this helter-skelter dash. The pace at which I had to assimilate all that was going on was unsustainable. In some unknown way I was looking into each person through whose mind I flew, and it was physically painful to keep up the tempo. There seemed only one way to step off the hurtling treadmill, and that was deliberately to think human thoughts, at a slow human speed, thoughts composed of clumsy, dependable human words. Doing so went some way to neutralise the effects of the crazily spinning sandpaper in my brain.

Somewhere children are asleep, I thought, *dreaming dreams that seem childish, but in reality they are already producing* bablos *just as the grown-ups do ... Everyone is put to work, from infancy on ...*

I was no exception. I could remember this bright-red germ of hope growing in me ... We imagine we are just on the point of understanding something important, of figuring it all out at last, of achieving something, after which a new life will begin, the right life, the real life. But this never happens because the red drop of sense and hope always vanishes, and we must begin again to grow it and nurture it from nothing. And then it disappears once again, and so it goes on throughout our life, while we become more and more tired until finally nothing is left to us but to lie on our beds, turn our faces to the wall, and die...

Now I knew what invariably happens to the red drop of hope. I fell ever more quickly through other lives as my rider was deftly scooping up the last remaining drops of meaning, swallowing them as it sated its inscrutable hunger. Many people I saw were on the brink of understanding what was happening, they guessed it but were incapable of thinking about it. All were deafened by the cry of the Mighty Bat, so that nothing remained for them but a dim memory that once upon a time their head had played host to a crucially important thought that had instantly vanished, never to return.

We were now nearing the final destination of our journey – the vast, invisible mass of Ishtar. I knew that it would all come to an end at the moment of impact. In the last second of the voyage I remembered that all of this had been familiar to me when I was a child. Then I had seen vampires flying through my dreams and knew that they were taking from me the most important thing in life. But in the real world it is forbidden for humans to know what they can know in dreams – and therefore, on waking, I took for the cause of my terror the fan hanging above my bed like a great bat...

This last second was followed by the impact. I understood that the Tongue had handed over to Ishtar its accumulated harvest, and after that something happened that I have no words to describe. Indeed, it bore no relation to me – it was connected solely with the Tongue. Then I lapsed into semi-consciousness.

My mind became calm, as the surface of a lake when a complete lull descends upon it. There was no activity at all. I cannot say how much time elapsed. And then on to the surface of this nothingness fell a single drop.

I do not know exactly what the drop struck that caused it to shatter. But in an instant the eternal, motionless background against which everything other than itself had taken place broke into movement. It was like the moment when you are looking at the sky and the branches of the trees, and suddenly a ripple passes over them and you realise that what you have been seeing was not the world but its reflection in the water. Before, I had not known that the background was even there. But the moment I saw it, I knew that I had never properly understood all that had been happening. And at once I became easy of mind and cheerful.

Before, I thought that life consisted of events that happened to me and to others. The events could be either good or bad, and for some reason many more of them seemed to be bad than were good. And all these events take place on the surface of an immense globe to which we are bound by the force of gravity, while the globe itself flies to an unknown destination through the cosmic void.

That was what I thought I knew. But now I understood that I, and the events, and everything in the universe – Ishtar, vampires, people, fans glued to the wall, jeeps bound to the earth, comets, asteroids, stars and the cosmic void through which they fly – are simply waves dispersing through that invisible background. They were the same waves as the one which a few moments ago had passed through my consciousness following the falling of the drop. One substance makes up everything there is in the whole world. And this substance was myself.

In the light of the knowledge I now possessed, the fears that had been building up in my soul for years dissolved instantly. Nothing whatsoever could threaten me in this world, nor could I be a threat to anyone or anything else. Nothing bad could happen to me, nor to others; the world was so arranged as to make this an impossibility. To know this was the greatest happiness that could be imagined. I knew it for an absolute certainty; rapture filled my entire being, and nothing that had ever happened to me before could remotely be compared to it.

Why had I never seen this before? I asked myself in utter perplexity. And immediately knew the answer. For something to be seen it must have form, colour, volume or dimension. But this background had nothing of the kind. Everything that existed did so as vortices and waves of this substance – but as for the substance itself, there was nothing able to persuade any of the sense organs that it was really there.

Nothing, that is, except the drop that had fallen from I knew not where, and in a single fleeting moment had wrenched me out of the world of illusion (now I knew for certain that it *was* a world of illusion, even though everyone else around me believed it was real). Now, I thought with quiet triumph, every aspect of my life would be changed, and never would I forget what I had just understood.

And at once understood that I had already forgotten it.

It was all over. Around me was once again the stifling blanket of calcified, imprisoning life, with its fireplaces, its armchairs, its smirking golden sun in the ceiling, its pictures on the walls, and Baal Petrovich in his long red gown. Nothing that I had so recently perceived could help me now, because the moment when it had happened was already in the past. Now I was in the present, where everything was real and concrete, where it made no difference what substance the thorns and prickles of this world were made of. All that mattered was how deeply they would pierce the body. Indeed with every passing second they penetrated ever deeper, until the world became again as it always had been.

'Well, how was it?' asked Baal Petrovich, appearing once more in my field of vision. 'How do you feel now?'

I was going to say that everything was fine, but instead asked:

'Can we do it again?'

'Yes,' said Hera. 'I should like to as well. Can we?'

Baal Petrovich laughed.

'There you are! You have already discovered what Thirst is.'

'So can we or not?' insisted Hera.

'No. You will have to wait until the next time.'

'Will we have the same experience?' I asked.

Baal Petrovich nodded.

'It is always the same as the first time. The whole thing is just as fresh, just as vivid. And just as intangible. You will want to experience these feelings over and over again. And the inconveniences of the first part of the ceremony will be quite irrelevant.'

'Is it possible to recapture the same feelings on one's own?' asked Hera. 'Without *bablos*?'

'That is a difficult question,' replied Baal Petrovich. 'To be perfectly honest, I don't know the answer. Tolstoyans, for instance, believe it is possible if you achieve sufficient simplicity in your life. But so far as I can judge, none of them has yet managed to do so.'

'What about Osiris?' I asked.

'Osiris?' Baal Petrovich frowned. 'There are all sorts of rumours about him. Some say that in the sixties he injected *bablos* – shot up, as people called it then. What that did to his head I can't imagine. As a result everyone today is afraid to bite him. Nobody knows what is in his mind, or what sort of a Tolstoyan he is. Osiris is, in a word, *terra incognita*. But from another point of view, experiences of this kind may be accessible to saints. Still others say that something similar may be perceived on the highest levels of yogic practice.'

'What are those levels?' asked Hera.

'That I cannot tell you. No vampire has ever succeeded in biting an advanced yogi master in this particular state. Not to mention saints, of whom there have been no real examples for a very long time. To keep it simple, it is better to think along lines like this: the only true way for a vampire to slake his thirst is to suck *bablos*. Thirst and *bablos* together constitute the biological mechanism by which the survival of the Mighty Bat is assured, in much the same way as sexual pleasure ensures the continuation of the species.'

He jabbed something on the control desk and I heard a low electrical humming sound. The breastplate rose into the air, after which the shackles loosed themselves from my arms and legs.

I stood up. My head was still spinning, and just in case I held on to the back of the chair for support.

The courier's bag lay open and empty near the fireplace. In the ashes behind the bars of the grate could still be seen fragments of partially burned thousand-rouble notes. Baal Petrovich evidently fulfilled his role with an exemplary sense of responsibility. No doubt he approached it as a religious ritual in which he acted as the high priest.

Hera also got to her feet, her face pale and serious. When she lifted her arm to straighten her hair, I noticed that her fingers were shaking. Baal Petrovich turned to her.

'Just one other little formality,' he said. 'Courtesy demands that I begin with the lady.'

In his hand appeared a gleaming circular object, like a large coin, which he carefully pinned to Hera's t-shirt. The brooch was heavy, and the shirt immediately sagged.

'What is it?' asked Hera.

'A commemorative badge for the "God of Money",' replied Baal Petrovich. 'Now you know why we are all named after gods.'

He turned to me.

'At one time I was a jeweller,' he explained. 'I make these badges myself, for old times' sake. They are all different. For you I made a special one – with wings of oak.'

'Why?' I asked suspiciously.

'It's all right, no nasty tricks. It just turned out like that. I started making them as wings, but they turned out in the shape of oak leaves. Thank God, though, we're vampires, not fascists, so they are not oak leaves but oak wings. Take a look. They're rather lovely, I think.'

On his palm was a dull platinum disc with two golden wings protruding from it. They did indeed look like oak leaves. The characters 'R II' were picked out in small diamonds.

'Do you like it?' asked Baal Petrovich.

I nodded my thanks, not so much because I really did like it but out of politeness.

'There is a motto on the back,' said Baal Petrovich. 'By tradition, I choose it as well.'

I turned the badge over. On the reverse was a safety pin and an inscription engraved in a circle round the edge:

It is not I who must suck it, but all the others. Count Dracula

Like all sayings of Count Dracula, the meaning may not have been the freshest, but there was nothing to object to in it. Baal Petrovich took his handiwork from me and pinned it on my chest, scratching me with the pin as he did so.

'Now you are true vampires,' he said.

'Where should it be worn?' I asked.

'Hang it in your hamlet,' said Baal Petrovich. 'That's what most of our people do.'

'When will the next ceremony be?' asked Hera.

Baal Petrovich spread his arms wide.

'It's not up to me. Enlil draws up the schedule and has it confirmed by the Prima Donna.'

I understood he was referring to Ishtar Borisovna.

'What is the frequency on average?' I asked.

'Frequency?' queried Baal Petrovich. 'Hmm... interesting point. I've never even thought about it. Just a moment.'

He took a mobile phone from the pocket of his robe and tapped in some numbers.

'The frequency is...' he said after a long pause, '3.086 x 10^{-7}Hz.'

'Meaning?'

'That's the frequency. So many cycles a second, isn't it? That is how many. The next ceremony will be in approximately one month.'

'Once a month isn't very often,' said Hera. 'It's not nearly enough. That's no good.'

'Talk to the management,' replied Baal Petrovich. 'We also have our hierarchy, you see. The lower you hang, the higher you fly. Enlil over there has his own home-based station. He and the Prima Donna can suck *bablos* every day if they want to. But at the start of your creative path, my dears, you are not likely to get it more than once a month.'

He looked at his watch.

'Now, are there any more questions? I've got to be going.'

There were no more questions.

Having made our farewells to Baal Petrovich, Hera and I went out into the passage. I took her hand. Like that we walked all the way to the entrance, but just before the front door she took her hand away.

'Shall we see one another soon?' I said.

'Not right away,' she replied. 'Don't ring me just yet. I'll ring you.'

Seeing us come out, Mithra came to meet us.

'Hera,' he began, screwing up his eyes against the sun, 'today is a red letter day for you. I want you to remember it for ever. So I've prepared...'

He fell silent and looked at me.

333

'What is it?' I asked.

'Rama,' he said, 'I like you, but you are somewhat *de trop* just at the moment.'

'It's also a red letter day for me,' I said. 'Don't forget that.'

'That's true,' agreed Mithra. 'I really can't think what's to be done about it... But here are two suggestions to help you in your battle with loneliness. First, you have Ivan. I bit him while I was waiting for Hera, and he likes you, rest assured of it. The other idea is for you to ring up Loki. He's a bit past it himself, of course, but if you fancy engaging his friend I'm sure he wouldn't mind. Unlike me...'

Hera grinned. Again I was lost for words – true, my head was still going round and round after the ceremony. Mithra put his arm through Hera's and led her away. She did not look back, not even once. Something strange was happening to her. She was not behaving as she should, not at all. I could not understand what it all meant.

They got into the car.

Ring up Loki, I thought. Well, why not? That might indeed be a solution. Of course it was the solution. There was no other, of that I was sure.

When I got to my car I sat in the back and slammed the door shut.

'Where to, Chief?' asked Ivan.

'Home.'

Ivan moved off, but had to brake in order to let Hera's car through as it emerged from the bushes. Nothing could be seen through its tinted windows – and the opacity inflamed my imagination with a blistering heat, so much so that any lingering doubts about my proposed course of action were dissipated.

I dialled Loki's number.

'Rama? Hello. What can I do for you?'

'Do you remember telling me about vampire duels?'

'Of course I do. Why are you asking? Are you planning to challenge someone?'

It was clear from his lighthearted tone of voice that he did not consider this a serious proposition.

'Yes,' I said. 'I am.'

'You're not serious, are you?'

'Yes, I am. How do I go about it?'

'All you have to do is tell me,' replied Loki. 'I arrange everything; it's part of my job. But I have to be certain that what you are saying is completely serious.'

'What I am saying is completely serious.'

'Whom are you challenging?'

'Mithra.'

Loki said nothing for a while.

'May I,' he said at last, 'ask the reason?'

'It's personal.'

'Does it have anything to do with his role in your fate? I mean Brahma perishing?'

'No.'

'Have you really thought this through?'

'Yes,' I replied.

'Rama,' said Loki, 'I must warn you this is not a joke. If you really want to issue a challenge to Mithra, I shall set the wheels in motion. But if I do and you change your mind, it could lead to a most embarrassing situation.'

'I. Really. Want. To. Challenge. Mithra,' I repeated. 'And I shall not change my mind.'

'Well, then. What is your preference in the matter of weapons? The rules say the choice lies with the person who is challenged, but a consensus is sometimes possible.'

'Entirely at your discretion.'

'Very well, then,' said Loki. 'In that case please email me a Duel Order. If you don't remember what that is, you are obliged

335

to set out in it the penalty you wish to be applied to Mithra should you prevail. But don't do it now. Write it tomorrow morning, when your head is clear, and when you have had a chance to think it over once again. When I receive it, I shall act.'

'Good. What form should my letter take?'

'I shall send you a template. Generally speaking, the form is not laid down, but the final line must be exactly as follows: "In this connection I am ready to meet God".'

'You're joking?'

'Not at all. This is no place for a joke. A duel is a very serious matter. One must be clearly aware of the unthinkable horror that may have to be faced as a result...'

VILLA DEI MISTERI

Duel Order

Mithra VI abuses his mentoring responsibilities in respect of
young vampires. Instead of helping them to find their place
in the ranks, he takes advantage of their inexperience to
worm his way into their confidence, after which he exploits
their trust in the most cynical manner. Discretion prevents
me going into details. But honour demands that I punish
the scoundrel. He must absolutely and categorically be
forbidden to have any contact with young vampires of the
latest intake.

In this connection I am ready to meet God.

Rama the Second

I read my letter through. 'Honour demands that I punish the
scoundrel' struck me as too pretentious. I changed the phrase
to 'I cannot stand by with folded arms'. Reading it a second

time I realised that it might appear as though Mithra's victim was myself. I altered 'discretion prevents' to 'discretion and compassion prevent'.

All was now in order with the letter. I sent it by email to Loki (his login name was, appropriately enough, 'sadodesperado') and awaited his reply.

Half an hour later my phone rang.

'I hope you have thoroughly thought this through,' said Loki, 'because the business is already in train.'

'Yes, I have,' I replied. 'Thank you.'

'Don't mention it. Mithra is writing his Duel Order as we speak. Incidentally, he did not seem at all surprised. What has been going on between you two, eh?'

I kept silent. After breathing for a while into the handset Loki realised his question was not going to be answered, and continued:

'The preparations will take a few days – we have to decide when, and how. Once this is settled I will get back in touch with you… Prepare yourself for a hard road, young man. Start thinking of the eternal.'

He replaced the receiver.

Loki was, of course, joking about the eternal. But, as they say, in every joke there is a grain of truth. I looked back up to the computer screen where my Duel Order was still open. Everything in it was clear and precise – except the reference to meeting God on which Loki had insisted. Putting my name to that had been a piece of deviousness on my part.

It was a phrase whose meaning I could not grasp at all. I was a god myself; my experience of the previous day had made that plain enough. The problem, however, was that I could not repeat it. To become a god again, I needed *bablos*.

At this point I reached a logical impasse – could I truly be a god if my perception and experience of the divine depended on a cause external to myself? A theologian would argue that I could not. Then, if I was not a god but something else, whom would I be meeting in the event of *force majeure*?

I was seized by horrible misgivings. I began to pace about the apartment, fixing on various objects in the hope that one or other of them would send me a secret sign or would redirect my reflections. The black and white picture of the bat; Napoleon on his horse; the two fastidious nymphettes ... if any of my *Penates* knew the answer, they were keeping the secret close to their chest.

Eventually my aimless wanderings brought me to the filing cabinet. I sat on the sofa and began to leaf through the catalogue. Nothing leaped out at me. Then I remembered that in the escritoire there had been some undocumented test tubes from the literature section. I opened it and started to look through the preparations in the hope of encountering something theological, but nothing there seemed appropriate to the high seriousness of the moment. I found one or two, such as: 'Tyutchev + Internet slang' and 'Isaak Babel + 2% Marquis de Sade' but they failed to awaken my interest.

Suddenly, into my head came the very person with whom I ought to be discussing this question.

Going over to the window I glanced outside. My car was parked on the other side of the street. Through its open window I could see the fixed look of resentment on Ivan's face – he was reading an "ironic detective" story. A day or two previously I had asked him where the irony was, and this had offended him even more. I took my phone out of my pocket; a few seconds later the signal reached its target, Ivan lifted his head, and I heard his voice:

'Good morning, Chief.'

'I have to go to see Osiris,' I said. 'In about ten minutes' time. I'll just change my clothes and have a quick cup of coffee.'

At Osiris's nothing much had changed. The door was opened by the bewhiskered Moldavian, who had in the meantime somehow managed to become even thinner and more pinched, and his skin more parchment-like. The card-players in the big room took not the slightest notice of me.

Osiris listened to my account of the Red Ceremony with the supercilious smile of a seasoned psychonaut hearing his neighbour's small son tell of his first experience with a cigarette end stolen from an ashtray.

'What was it that I sensed?' I asked. 'Was it God?'

'It's customary to believe so,' replied Osiris, 'but in reality no one knows. In olden times people used to call it "the shiver of the cloak". Vampires had no way of interpreting what they were experiencing until people came up with the notion of God.'

'Did people come up with the idea of God, or did they discover that he exists?'

'It's the same thing.'

'How?'

Osiris sighed. 'Look,' he said, 'Let me explain it one more time. Once upon a time the monkeys had what amounted to a still set up for them in their noddles. The still began to produce *bablos*. But alongside its primary product it began to produce other fractions as by-products. One of these fractions is called "the universe". Another is called "truth". A third is called "God". Now you are asking me: did the monkeys invent this third fraction or did they discover it? I really do not know how to answer this question.'

'You said that vampires come near to the presence of God when they imbibe *bablos*,' I reminded Osiris.

'Quite right, of course they do. This secondary fraction is an integral part of the primary product, and the vampire senses this. God and *bablos* are like petrol and diesel, both of which are produced when oil is refined. Vampires need to consume *bablos*, and for us God is a by-product. For human beings it happens to be a very valuable by-product. We don't object as long as people don't start trying to flog it to us as universal truth.'

'Does this ever happen?' I asked.

Osiris waved his hand airily.

'Almost invariably. For that reason it is essential always to have with you a death candy. Better still, two or three.'

I thought for a while, and then said:

'But then I think there is a contradiction in terms. If God is a waste product from an industrial process, how could he send the Mighty Bat here?'

'That is the nub of the whole thing. If God was something else, the Mighty Bat would have been able to rebel, to resist through all eternity, and at some point prevail. But how can one conquer the waste product of an industrial process that has sent one into exile? Not even Ishtar would have been able to do that. Therein lies the full horror of the situation.'

I was beginning to appreciate the fanaticism of my interlocutor's logic. I would have to put the question in another way.

'Very well,' I said. 'Then please tell me, does God appear purely as a by-product of the manufacturing process of *bablos*? Or does this by-product bear witness to the existence of God in reality? You cannot say these are one and the same thing.'

'No, they are not quite the same thing,' agreed Osiris. 'There was a time in antiquity when vampires argued about that very matter.'

'What conclusion did they come to?'

'No conclusion. They simply stopped arguing and turned their attention to other things.'

'Why did they do that?'

'Because,' said Osiris leaning forward out of his niche, 'if God exists, he does not want to exist for us. And if he does not want to exist for us, it follows that for us he does not.'

'But if God does not exist, why is there a word for him?'

'Because this word, together with all other words and concepts, is needed for the production of *bablos*.'

'I see that,' I said. 'But why then does it have the meaning that it does?'

'God is a creator. Words also create.'

'But you said they reflect.'

'Creation and reflection are the same thing.'

'How?'

Osiris smiled.

'This is not accessible to human intelligence, so do not try to understand it, just trust me. It seems to us that words reflect the world in which we live, but in reality they create it, in the same way as words create God. It is for this reason that God changes so fundamentally according to the dialectics of language.'

'This all has to do with words?'

'Of course. As is even written in the holy scriptures of humanity: "In the beginning was the Word, and the Word was with God, and the Word was God... All things were made by Him, and without Him was not anything made that was made..." You understand what that is all about?'

'I know what is meant by "and the spirit of God moved upon the face of the waters",' I replied. 'Enlil Maratovich explained that. But that is not what we were talking about.'

'These words explain the principle of how Mind "B" works. The key phrase here is "the Word was with God and the Word was God". It means that Mind "B" consists of two mirrors which reflect one another. Surely you can understand that? "God" is the word which creates God. What people call God appears in Mind "B" in exactly the same way as the image of a brick appears when it is produced by the word "brick". The only difference is that a brick possesses form, while God has no form. It is precisely this quality of Mind "B" that makes God conditionally visible.'

'I have the impression,' I said, 'that theologians have a rather more profound interpretation of the phrase "and the Word was God".'

'No profundity about it at all. There is only the word "profound", and whatever you do to yourself when you hear it. Vampires must be masters of discourse, not its victims.'

'May I ask a stupid question?' I asked.

'Am I to suppose all your other questions have been intelligent? Be my guest.'

'Does God actually exist?'

'Why should he not? I repeat, he exists in the Mind "B" of every participant in the enterprise. If God did not exist, how would we be able to talk about him? But in what capacity he exists – that is quite another matter.'

'I understand,' I said. 'Again you are telling me that he exists as a word. But that's not what I am asking about.'

'What are you asking about, then?'

'You said that Mind "A" is a mirror. Then you said that reflecting and creating are the same thing. Can one therefore say that God is present in every living creature as a Mind "A"?'

Osiris laughed.

'One can indeed say that,' he replied. 'But everything that we say will be composed of words, and any word which is presented to Mind "A" converts it instantly into Mind "B". All words are by definition contained within the money gland. The Mind "A" of which you speak is not actually Mind "A" but merely the reflection of the words "Mind 'A'". Anything at all of which we are able to speak is source material for the production of *bablos*. And at the same time a by-product of its brewing. It is a closed circle.'

I found this depressing.

343

'Could we drop the philosophy for a while?' I asked. 'Let's try speaking in direct terms. Is God present in us?'

'God is present in us. But we are not present in him.'

'How is that?'

'Do you know what a one-way mirror is, through which you can see in only one direction? It's like that.'

'Why is everything arranged in such a dreadful way?'

'You must remember that we are children of an exiled bat who is suffering loss of memory. And we live in a dimension where God appears merely as a by-product of the production of *bablos*. What more do you want?'

'Almost nothing,' I said. 'Do vampires have any form of religion?'

'Thank you, that's all we need.'

'What do vampires call God?'

'God. With a capital "G". Because a god with a small "g" is what we are. But God is not God's name, it is only what we call him. Vampires know that God will always be outside the confines of a name.'

'Do vampires observe any kind of religious rites?'

Instead of answering, Osiris smiled a crooked smile. My next question might, I thought, appear impolite, but I decided to ask it.

'The teaching you are now imparting to me – is it true?'

Osiris hemmed and hawed.

'You have been asking me about vampire traditions, and I have been telling you what they are. As to the truth of the traditions, that is quite a different question.'

'All the same, may I ask it? Are the traditions true?'

Osiris looked at me for some time before replying.

'You see, Rama,' he said, 'when you are young your organism produces all the hormones it needs, and the receptors in your brain function as they are supposed to. At that time of your life any "two times two equals four" proposition will radiate the infallible light of truth. But it is no more than reflected light from your life-force. It is the same with music. When you are young there is so much wonderful music to be heard, but as time goes by, somehow the music people write doesn't seem to be as good as it used to be. Every person thinks like this as they get older. Or, take women. When you are young, they seem irresistibly attractive. But when you get beyond sixty, say, and start having health problems of one kind or another, all that seems less important than how your digestive system functions, or your joints...'

'So you're saying that truth resides within us?' I asked.

'Yes. But people often load into terms like that more elevated meanings than they can sustain. This is futile. Truth is essentially chemical, not metaphysical. So long as you possess sufficient life-force, you will always be able to find the necessary verbal forms to reflect it. You can always think up a combination of words that will provoke the required excitation in your neuronal pathways, and that you will experience as the blessed breath of truth. But in fact, precisely which words are used is of little importance because one word is much the same as another: all words are merely mirrors in which the mind is reflected.'

This began to irritate me.

'But then,' I said, 'you are contradicting yourself.'

'Why do you say that?'

'You are not an ordinary vampire: you are a follower of Tolstoy. If truth is no more than a chemical *reaction*, why did you embark on a spiritual path? Why did you embark on the simple life?'

'Because I did,' replied Osiris, looking at his watch. 'You'll be going in a moment, and I shall call in the immigrant workers. I shall swallow two hundred grams of red liquid with vodka, and everything will become truth once more. The cracks in the wall will be true, so will the dust on the floor, even the rumbling in my stomach. But at the present moment everything is a lie...'

'If everything in the end comes down to chemistry and *bablos*, why do concepts like God, truth or the universe exist at all? Where do they come from?'

'Mind "B" has two operating phases, a productive phase and a non-productive phase. In its productive phase a man produces Aggregate "M-5". The unproductive phase is when no *bablos* is being produced. It is the decompression stroke of a piston. Mind "B" is not switched off during this part of the cycle, but what occupies it can be any meaningless abstraction you fancy. "What is truth?" "Does God exist?" "Where did the world come from?" – all that nonsense you first came to see me about. Multiplied by parallel mirrors, these questions grow into unrecognisable distortions, undergo a phase shift, and at a certain moment come to be recognised as answers to themselves. Then a wave of excitation passes along the brain's neuronal pathways, and the man concludes that he has hit on the truth. For that reason all human truths have the same equation format, in which one concept hooks on to another. "God is spirit." "Death is inevitable." "Two twos make four." "$E=mc^2$". There is no particular harm in this, but if there are too many of these equations the output of *bablos* falls. Therefore we cannot allow human culture to drift without direction. If necessary, we force it back with an iron hand onto the proper path.'

'How do we do that?'

'You've been through the Discourse and Glamour course. That's how. If you want to research specific methodologies, you'll have to ask the Chaldeans. But the general idea is that the non-productive part of the Mind "B" operating cycle should take up as little time as possible. If things are set up as they should be, people will not spend time seeking God. All the God they need is waiting for them in church – next to the collection box.

Nor will a man seek meaning in art. He knows that truth is to be found only in the box office. And so on. It's just as you were taught in school: the struggle to increase the power coefficient, or, as they say in physics, *cosine phi*, is a national priority.'

'What then is the purpose of existence?' I asked. 'Or is life entirely empty, with no purpose?'

'Why should it be? It's always possible to find many different reasons to live. Take your choice. Live your life so that it should be whole, full of inspiration and meaning. But know also that at the end, when you turn the final page, all these meanings will vanish like chaff before the wind.'

'So what is the point of it all?'

Osiris leaned forward, picked up something from the table and put it under my nose.

'What is this?' he asked.

I looked at the object he held in his fingers. It was a nail. An old nail, somewhat rusty round the head. Obviously used, it was bent and battered from having been pulled out.

'That? It's a nail.'

'Quite right,' said Osiris. 'A nail. An old nail. We can take the simplest, most basic object like this old, rusty nail. We can look at it carefully. And we can think: what is it?'

'It's a nail,' I shrugged. 'What is there to think about?'

'It depends on what you are talking about. Are you talking about this insignificant scrap of metal? Or about something that happens in your perception? Or about the fact that the nail is nothing more than a concept that you have? Or about the fact that your perception of this concept becomes the nail? In other words, are we talking about the nail as reflected in our consciousness, or the fact that we project the word "nail" on to the surrounding world in order to bring about that particular sum total of its elements which we have agreed to identify with the sound that particular word makes? Or, perhaps, you are

347

speaking of the dark and terrible belief some people have that a certain nail exists in and of itself beyond the limits of anybody's consciousness?'

'I'm already lost,' I said.

'Right you are. You're lost, and will never find your way out.'

'What had all that to do with my question?'

'This. You were asking: what is the point of existence? The point is this,' Osiris brandished the nail in the air. 'Here is a piece of iron picked up from a dump. And the non-productive part of your money gland's cycle cannot even tell you what it is, even though you can touch it, bend it or drive it into someone's palm. And you are asking me about something that has no existence *anywhere* except in the imagination, and not even there permanently: wispy word-clouds that arise for a second, cast their imaginary spell of meaning, and then disappear without trace the moment Mind "B" starts thinking about money. Understand?'

'No.'

'Quite right too. Get used to it, Rama.'

I nodded.

'When a man – and between ourselves, a vampire is simply an enhanced man – starts thinking about God the creator of the world, and what this might mean, he is like a monkey wearing a field marshal's tunic, strutting round a circus ring while flashing his bottom. The monkey has an excuse because that is how people have dressed him up. But for you, Rama, there is no excuse.'

Throwing the nail on to the table, Osiris pressed the bell next to the telephone. I could hear it jangling in the corridor.

'It's time for me to dine. Grigory will show you out.'

'Thank you for the explanations,' I said, rising to my feet. 'Although I must admit I didn't understand much.'

'No need to strain yourself,' smiled Osiris. 'The most important thing you should understand is that you don't understand. What is the point of trying to understand something when you already know everything? One drop of *bablos* will explain more than ten years of philosophical discussions.'

'Why then did you change from *bablos* to red liquid?'

Osiris shrugged.

'Some dance to remember,' he said, 'some dance to forget.'

The Moldavian with the moustache entered the room and I understood that the audience was at an end.

As he had done last time, the Moldavian showed me out. But this time, for some reason, he came out with me on to the landing of the staircase and closed the door to the apartment behind us.

'The lift is not working,' he informed me in a quiet voice. 'I'll come down with you.'

I had no objection, but all the same as I went down I hugged the wall, keeping as far away as I could from the banister rail beyond which was the drop into the stairwell.

'Excuse me for seeming importunate,' said the Moldavian. 'I am, as it happens, a Professor of Theology from Kishinev. I'm just working here to earn a crust. At the moment there is no great call in Kishinev for Professors of Theology.'

'I don't suppose there is,' I said sympathetically.

'You know,' went on the Moldavian, 'quite a lot of young vampires come here to talk to our employer. I wait outside the door in case the boss wants to call me in. Well, one overhears things from time to time, so I know what ideas are current in your world. I don't usually intervene in the discussions, but today you were talking about God, and I feel obliged to add an important amplification to what you have just been hearing. As a theologian, I mean. But I do ask you to repeat nothing of our conversation to my Chief. In fact, don't discuss it with anyone until your next supervision bite. By then I shall be away on holiday. Will you promise me that?'

'You seem to know a lot of detail about our practices,' I observed, 'even about supervision bites. It's the first I've heard of them, personally speaking.'

'Irony doesn't suit you, young man. In your circle all bites are supervision bites. There is no other kind.'

'Yes, you're probably right,' I sighed. 'All right, I promise. You have my word. What is the amplification you referred to?'

'It concerns what in your circles is known as Mind "B". Young vampires are told that human Mind "B" is simply the money gland. But this is not the case.'

'What, then, is the case?'

'Have you ever been to Pompeii, in Italy?'

'No,' I said. 'But I know it's a Roman city preserved under layers of volcanic ash. I've read a lot about it.'

'Yes, that's it,' said the Moldavian. 'And the most interesting thing about Pompeii is the Villa dei Misteri – the Villa of the Mysteries.'

'I remember. It's a villa on the edge of the town. The name comes from the frescoes, which depict an initiation ritual into the Dionysian Mysteries. Our Discourse studies even included some images of them. Very beautiful, they were. But what made you think of this villa just now?'

'You see, the villa had existed from the middle of the third century BC until the destruction of Pompeii – that is, for three hundred years. Today, of course, nobody knows what mysteries were enacted there. But the frescoes have so captured people's imagination that disputes and speculations about them still rage. To my mind, the really interesting thing is not the frescoes themselves, but the little details in the murals on the walls of the passage: enigmatic Egyptian symbols on a black background, signs, snakes – similar to what you see on old Singer sewing machines... I don't know if you have ever come across any machines like that?'

'You do jump about rather. You started off talking about Mind "B", then on to the villa, and now Singer sewing machines...'

'Give me just a second or two, and all will be clear. You cannot see it in the photographs, but if you actually go to the villa you will see many incongruous things there. On the one hand, yes, you have the frescoes, but on the other, in among these splendours you find the crudest and most primitive wine press... and then you start to notice all kinds of ugly agricultural outbuildings in the most inappropriate places. Tourists are told that the villa was definitely dedicated to the mysteries at some point in the distant past. But after the first underground tremors, which occurred long before the fatal eruption of the volcano, the owners sold the building and left. And the villa became a farm which made wine.'

'What point are you making in telling me this?'

'My point is, man is like the Villa of the Mysteries. You vampires believe that you yourselves did much the same: creating the farm in order to extract *bablos*. Therefore you regard the frescoes on the walls as by-products of agricultural activity. You imagine that they somehow emerged of their own accord from the mud and the splashes from the vats of fermenting juice...'

We stopped at the doorway leading out of the building.

'All right, then,' I said, 'do you have an alternative version?'

'I do. Mind "B" – what you call the money gland – is a receptacle for abstract notions. You will not find them anywhere in the world around you. Nor is God to be found anywhere in the world. Mind "B" was created expressly in order to provide a dimension in which God can appear to people. Our planet is no prison. It is a very large house. A magical house. It may have a dungeon somewhere in the basement, but taken all in all it is God's palace. There have been many attempts to kill

God, various calumnies have been spread about him, some even appearing in the mass media – that he married a prostitute, and that he died. But none of this is true. It is simply that no one knows in which rooms in the house he lives because he is constantly moving. All that is known is that any room that he enters is clean, and bright, and has a light burning in it. But there are also rooms into which he never goes, and as time goes by there are more and more of them. The first thing to happen is that a draught sweeps in, bringing glamour and discourse with it. And when glamour and discourse coalesce and start to rot, the bats scent them and fly in.'

'I suppose you mean us?'

The Moldavian nodded.

'I see,' I said. 'That's how it always goes. Let's heap all the blame on to those filthy, scabby vampires. It's a no-brainer, isn't it?'

'Why must you use loaded words like filthy and scabby?' asked the Moldavian.

'Well, you can always find a reason to hate us,' I replied, and flapped my arms a few times as if they were wings. 'We can fly, you know, and all those wingless mediocrities will never forgive this. You always try to destroy us by one means or another; it lies so deep in your culture...'

'Who do you mean by "you"?'

'Mankind, of course,' I replied, getting more and more heated and wound up. 'Who else? And what else would you expect, given that your entire history began with genocide?'

'What genocide?'

'Who do you think slaughtered the Neanderthals? Thirty thousand years ago? Did you think we would forget? We will not forget, and we will not forgive. With genocide it began, and with genocide it will end, you mark my words. So don't go heaping all the blame on us vampires...'

352

'You have not understood me,' said the Moldavian, alarmed. 'I am not blaming it all on vampires. Each room must answer for its own conduct. It may invite God to come in. Or your associates. Every room naturally inclines to the divine. But the majority of them, as a result of the glamour and the discourse, have come to the conclusion that it all comes down to interior design. And if that is what a room believes, you can be sure the bats are already flying about in it. God is not likely to enter such a room. But I am not blaming vampires. You are not, after all, rooms in the palace. You are bats. You have your work to do.'

'And what, in your view, will become of the palace in the end?'

'God has many palaces. When all the rooms in a palace have been occupied by bats, God destroys it. That is to say, he stops creating it, which comes to the same thing. It is said that this event resembles a light of such inconceivable power that it burns up the whole world. But what in fact happens is that matter, which is an illusion, disappears and the nature of God, which then will permeate everything, is finally seen as it really is. Much the same, it is believed, happens at the end of each individual life. Our own palace is now experiencing bad times. Almost all of the rooms are populated by bats. Everywhere one hears the crunching and squelching of a wine press squeezing out Aggregate "M-5"...'

'You are well informed,' I said.

'The question comes down to this: what are we to do when God finally loses patience and abandons this project?'

I shrugged my shoulders.

'I don't know. Perhaps we shall be sent to another planet to continue our work there. But something else interests me. You are a trained theologian. You speak of God as if he were an old acquaintance. Please then tell me why he made our lives so empty and senseless?'

353

'If *your* life had any meaning,' said the Moldavian, emphasising the word 'your', 'it would follow that those rooms which welcome the bats were following the right path. And God would have nowhere to live.'

'I see. Why, then, are you telling me all this?'

'I want to give you a telephone number,' replied the Moldavian, handing me a gold-edged card. 'If you would like to, come to one of our prayer meetings. I cannot promise you an easy way back. But God is merciful.'

I took the card. On it was written:

The Way to God through the Word of God
Logos CataCombo House of Prayer

On the back was a telephone number.

As I put the card away in my pocket, my hand passed over the place on my belt where the little case with the death candy should be. It was not there. Once again I had come out empty-handed. Even had it been there, however, I would certainly not have followed Osiris's advice. It was a reflex movement.

'That's clear,' I said. 'Instead of a wine press we shall install a candle-making cottage industry in the Villa of Mysteries, shall we? Your attempts will not succeed: the Chaldeans won't allow it. At best you'll muddle away with your hackwork in a corner. If, that is, there's anywhere left for you to do it...'

'Don't be facetious. You'd do better to reflect on this at leisure.'

'I will think about it,' I replied. 'I can see you are a good person. Thank you for involving yourself in my life.'

The Moldavian smiled a melancholy smile.

'I have to go now,' he said, touching the plaster on his neck. 'The Chief doesn't like to be kept waiting. Please remember that you promised not to mention our conversation to anyone.'

'I doubt anyone would be interested. Although … you know what? Why not have a go at recruiting Ishtar Borisovna? She's ripe for it. I'm giving you inside information.'

'Think about it,' repeated the Moldavian. 'The way back is still open to you.'

He turned and started walking up the staircase.

I went outside and shuffled back to the car.

The way back, I thought. But where to? Will there be anything left there?

Settled in the car, I raised my eyes to look at Ivan in the driving mirror. He smiled, artfully managing to keep up his resentful expression while doing so.

'I was just thinking about life,' he said, almost suffocating me with the pungent aroma of mint pastilles. 'And I thought up a Chinese proverb. Or maybe it's a quotation from Mao Zedong. Would you like to hear it?'

'Tell me.'

'However long you suck a dick, it will never make you an emperor.'

The argument was irrefutable, but the use of the verb 'suck', even in this neutral context, bordered on the offensive. I suddenly realised he was drunk, and may have been since morning. Perhaps he had not been sober on any of our previous meetings. This frightened me. I had no idea what was in his mind.

'Yes,' I said, cautiously leaning forward in my seat, 'social mobility is definitely on the wane in our society. Yes, something really should be done about it. On the other hand … no, you're not going to be an emperor. But an empress, well, that might be possible …'

In the middle of the phrase my head jerked back in its accustomed manner. Then I leant back in my seat and spent a little while analysing Ivan's personality map.

There was nothing to fear there. Except a car crash. But Hera... How humiliating to flirt with a driver...

But then, I thought scornfully, *what else would you expect? It's just an occupational habit...*

THE LORD OF THIS WORLD

At eight o'clock in the morning Loki rang up to tell me that the duel had been scheduled for today.

'We will come to you at eleven o'clock,' he said. 'Make sure you're ready. And don't drink a lot of liquid.'

He hung up without waiting, and I had no time to ask for any details. When I tried to ring back, there was no reply.

In the remaining three hours my imagination worked at double speed.

Firearms or blades?

In my mind I tried to picture what it would feel like to be killed by a bullet. I thought it might be something like a blow from a white-hot rod. Vampires are forbidden to shoot one another in the head, so Mithra would aim at my stomach, as happened to Pushkin...

But what if rapiers were the chosen weapons? What does a man feel when skewered by a blade? Probably it is like being cut with a bread knife, only much deeper, as deep as the heart. I tried visualising this several times but each time, racked with anguish, abandoned the attempt.

However, neither these nor similar phantasmagoria terrified me; on the contrary I found them relatively calming. Nor was I particularly worried by alternatives like those special weapons

I remembered Loki having spoken of. It was not the duel itself I had to fear.

The main threat, the one which was terrible to contemplate, would be embodied in Mithra's Duel Order. He might in truth be writing me a one-way ticket to a meeting with God, so that I could be about to find out for myself which of them had the right answer – Osiris or his red liquid provider. Even if such was not the penalty Mithra was planning to inflict, I was sure he would have devised some hideous abomination it would be better not to know about. *Thus is forged the will to victory*, as the old Red Army saying had it...

Half an hour before the appointed time I realised I had still not considered how I should dress for the occasion. Looking through the clothes in the wardrobe I found a black suit, jacket and trousers. It was slightly too big for me, but at least, I thought, it would not cramp my movements. I put on shoes with reinforced toecaps, not because I was seriously anticipating a physical fight, but just in case. Then I applied some gel to my hair, drank some whisky to give myself Dutch courage, settled myself in the chair and awaited my guests.

At eleven o'clock the doorbell rang.

Loki and Baldur were freshly shaved, smelling pleasingly of eau de cologne, and wearing expressions of ceremonious gravity. Loki was carrying a capacious black holdall.

'We seem to have aroused a certain amount of suspicion,' he said cheerfully. 'There was a policeman asking to see our papers – right here at the entrance to the flats.'

'Yes, he looked like a canny old dog,' added Baldur, 'as if he knew what was going on but could not say anything.'

I decided my own demeanour, too, should be high-spirited and jaunty.

'I expect he thought you were estate agents. There are always undesirables of one kind and another prowling about here, sniffing for their prey. It's a nice, quiet neighbourhood right in the centre of the city.'

Baldur and Loki sat down in the armchairs.

'Mithra wanted the duel to take place in a circus,' said Baldur. 'Why?'

'To point up the idiocy of the proceedings.'

'Idiocy, is it?' said Loki. 'It's rare enough these days that anyone shows a spark of self-respect and courage as in the old days. Nowadays this is classified as idiocy. Rama, you should be proud of yourself.'

Baldur winked at me.

'With him,' he said, nodding towards Loki, 'there are always two versions – one for the challenger and one for the challenged.'

I looked at Loki. There were traces of violet eyeshadow with gold specks on his left eyelid, the result of hastily removed make-up which could still be seen when he blinked. I supposed the rubber woman must have gone on maternity leave and he had had to act as a stand-in for her. Or perhaps he had simply been instructing someone else in his knee technique.

'So, are we off to the circus?'

'No,' said Baldur. 'We weren't able to organise the circus. There's a new concept for the duel, a complete break with tradition.'

I felt the pit of my stomach protesting.

'What is the concept?'

'You have three guesses,' smirked Loki.

'If it's a break with tradition,' I said, 'I presume it's some unconventional form of weapon?'

Loki nodded agreement.

'Poison?'

Loki shook his head.

'Poison is not allowed. You should know that.'

'Yes, I should,' I agreed. 'Perhaps, then, let's see ... what else could it be ... electricity?'

359

'Nothing of the sort. One last try.'

'Will we have to strangle one another at the bottom of the Moscow River?'

'All wide of the mark,' said Loki.

'Well, what is it, then?'

Loki pulled over and opened up his holdall. I saw some equipment with wires coming out of it, and a laptop computer.

'What's all that?'

'News of your affair has leaked out,' said Loki. 'Enlil and Marduk both know about it. As far as my information goes, the duel is taking place on account of a certain third party. We put our heads together to find a way of settling your stupid quarrel with minimal risk. It was decided that the duel should be fought remotely.'

'How are we going to do that?' I asked.

'You are both going to write a poem.'

'A poem?'

'Yes,' said Loki. 'It was Enlil's idea, and I think an excellent one. A romantic dispute calls for a romantic resolution. This one brings to the foreground not the macho brutality of the death candy, but the refinements of spiritual disposition and depth of feeling.'

'What will determine the outcome of the duel?' I asked. 'I mean, how will it be decided who has won?'

'For this purpose we decided to involve that very third party who was the cause of the quarrel being ignited. The victor's prize will be an immediate meeting with her. Neat, isn't it?'

I found it hard to share the enthusiasm. I would have preferred anything at all – Russian roulette, a fight with chessboards as weapons – to writing poetry. Versification and I were incompatible elements. I had put this to the test on a number of occasions.

Baldur decided to take a hand in the conversation.

'What are you tormenting the boy for? Tell him exactly what the procedure is going to be.'

'By all means,' agreed Loki. 'So, according to the rules of the engagement you and your rival must each compose a poem. The form of the poem must be a vampiric sonnet.'

'What is that?' I asked.

Loki looked enquiringly at Baldur.

'Did we not tell you?' groaned Baldur. 'What an omission. A vampiric sonnet is a poem consisting of twelve lines. Rhyme and metre, if any, are optional. The most important thing is that the last line must metaphorically suck, so to say, all the meaning out of the poem, expressing and encapsulating with maximum brevity the quintessence of the verse. The last line thus symbolises the process whereby red liquid is sublimated into *bablos*, which you then ritually present to the Mosquito Muse. Understand?'

'Approximately,' I said.

'But this is a lyric poetry convention, not a strict rule,' continued Baldur. 'Each poet can decide for himself the manner in which he proposes to convey the sense of the whole poem in a single line. After all, only the author knows what it is, is that not so?'

Loki nodded importantly.

'There's one other rule for the vampiric sonnet – it should be written as a reverse stairway. The result is a kind of ladder of meanings, symbolising the vampire's descent to the lowest essence. But actually that's not obligatory either.'

'What do you mean by a reverse stairway? What would it look like?'

'Like Mayakovsky,' said Baldur. 'Only backwards.'

I had no idea what he had in mind, but did not press the matter since the rule was not mandatory in any case.

Loki looked at his watch.

'It's time to begin. I'll get everything prepared. Why don't you go to the toilet? If you lose you will be paralysed for the next forty hours or so.'

He put the holdall on the table. I went out of the room and headed towards the bathroom.

Somewhere I had read that many great men had been visited by inspiration while sitting on the can. There seemed to be some truth in this because there it was that an idea came into my head, not an entirely ethical one but potentially very promising.

So great was its promise that I hesitated not a second, but set about putting it into practice with as little hesitation as a homeless person in the Metro would show before bending down to scoop up an accidentally dropped purse.

Coming back into the passage I tiptoed to the study, silently opened the door and hurried over to the escritoire. Opening it (unlike the filing cabinet it did not squeak), and trying not to make any noise with the glass, I took at random the first test tube I came across in the shambles there. It was the one labelled 'Tyutchev + Internet slang'. *Just what the doctor ordered*, I thought, and tipped all the contents into my mouth.

'Rama, where are you?' called Loki from the sitting room.

'Coming,' I replied. 'I'm closing the windows, just in case.'

'Good idea.'

A few seconds later I went back into the sitting room.

'Are you worried?' asked Baldur. 'You look rather pale.'

I said nothing. I did not want to speak because, having taken such a massive overdose of the preparation, I could easily blurt out the wrong thing.

'Now then,' said Loki. 'Everything is ready.'

I looked at the table.

On it was a motley collection of objects: a laptop computer connected both to a mobile phone and to the box I had glimpsed in the holdall. This box was now equipped with a flashing red light, and laid out next to it was a black cloth ribbon with rubber bands and hooks. To the ribbon was attached a syringe with a cumbersome-looking electronic machine. Two wires led from the machine to the box with the red flashing light. In addition, on the table lay a clip of identical needles with green couplings.

'What's all this for?' I asked.

'It's for this,' said Loki. 'See the syringe? It contains a tranquilliser. As I've already told you, it induces virtually total paralysis of the body for approximately forty hours. The syringe is controlled remotely by an electronic drive plugged into the computer. The poems will be sent instantly to the person of your mutual acquaintance, but she will not know which one is your work and which has been written by Mithra. When she has read them and chosen the winner, the result will be as instantly communicated back. At that point one of the servo motors connected to the syringes – either yours or the one on Mithra's arm – will be activated. After the injection the Duel Order will be proclaimed and immediately implemented. Any questions?'

'No, it's all clear enough,' I answered.

'Please then seat yourself at the computer.'

I did as I was told.

'Roll up your sleeve...'

When I had done so, Loki moistened some cotton wool with spirit and began to rub the bend in my elbow.

'I'm not feeling too well,' I droned limply.

I was not shamming. The truth was, though, that it had nothing to do with what was being done to me, but was the result of the preparation I had imbibed.

'You brought all this on yourself,' said Loki. 'You should have thought more about it beforehand. This part may hurt a bit – I'm just inserting this nice wee needle...'

'Ow!' I recoiled involuntarily.

'All right now, that's all. Don't move your arm for a while, let the bandage get secure... that's right...'

'How am I going to type with my arm like this?'

'Carefully and slowly, that's how. You have masses of time, you can type with one finger... Now look at the screen.'

I did so.

'There is a clock in the top corner. The countdown will begin from the moment you and Mithra are given the subjects for the poems.'

'Are the subjects different?'

'We'll see. Each of you will have exactly half an hour. If either of you fails to complete his poem in the time available, that person will automatically be deemed to have lost. Are you ready?'

I shrugged.

'I take it that means you are.'

Loki took out his mobile phone, dialled a number, and held the phone to his ear.

'Everything all right at your end?' he asked. 'Splendid. Then we'll begin.'

Replacing his phone, he turned to me.

'The clock is ticking.'

Two rectangles appeared on the laptop's screen. The one on the left had 'Mithra' written on it, the one on the right – 'Rama'. Next, letters began appearing one by one in the rectangles, as if someone was typing. Mithra's subject was 'The Mosquito'. Mine was 'The Lord of This World'.

This was a bonus, because the poet Tyutchev, whose presence I had already been sensing for some time, had a good deal to say on this theme.

However, there was a problem. The only verbal clothing I could now find for my thoughts had become extraordinarily ugly and monotonous: Internet newspeak was a young language but already a dead one. However, the issue of form was one to be resolved later – first I had to sort out the content, and I immersed myself in contemplation of the spiritual horizons now opening before me.

I could not see anything at all about life in the nineteenth century. On the other hand, I immediately realised that now I knew what one very famous quatrain by Tyutchev was all about:

You cannot grasp her with the mind,
No common yardstick takes her measure.
Russia is of a special kind,
You only can believe her treasure.

It turned out that the poet had had almost the same vision as the creators of my favourite film trilogy *Aliens*.

In the film a more efficient form of life has developed inside another organism and after some time reveals itself in an original and unexpected way. Much the same happened in Russian history, except that the process occurred not just once but cyclically, as each successive monster hatched inside the stomach of its predecessor. Contemporaries in the various epochs sensed this, but did not always grasp clearly enough the true meaning of the events reflected in maxims such as 'through the disintegrating inertia of the routine motions of the empire could be glimpsed the glowing contours of the new world'; 'from the seventh decade of the twentieth century onwards Russia was pregnant with *perestroika*', and such-like rhetorical flourishes.

Russia's 'special kindness' consisted in the unpredictable anatomy of the newborn creature. If Europe could be seen as a succession of identical personages trying desperately to adapt their decrepit frames to the fresh demands of the moment, Russia was eternally young – but her youth could only be maintained by wholesale rejections of her former identity, because each new monster at the moment of its birth ripped its predecessor into shreds, and (in accord with the laws of physics) began by being smaller but quickly gained weight. This alternative system of evolution was destructively spasmodic, as more thoughtful observers had perceived as far back as the nineteenth century. A Cartesian reason directed towards personal survival could hardly find anything reassuring in such a state of affairs, which was why the poet had said that Russia could only 'be believed'.

The result of this insight was that I realised once again how much courage and will were required to be a vampire in our country. And I felt even more contempt for the Chaldean elite, those predatory carrion crows gobbling up the remains of the latest dismembered carcase and priding themselves that in so doing they were 'controlling' or 'regulating' something or other. Moreover, they too would soon face a confrontation with the newborn monster that for the time being was gathering strength and keeping out of sight somewhere among the bulkheads of the spaceship's baggage hold.

All these thoughts passed through my mind in, at most, a couple of minutes. Then I began to feel an ominously minatory warning in verse breaking out inside me, straining at the leash – and it was exactly on the prescribed theme.

I put down everything I could. It was not easy, because most constructions in Internet newspeak were of little use in pinning down the intricate spiritual images that were opening themselves to my mental vision, all other linguistic paradigms being blocked. Each word had to be laboriously dredged up from the deep recesses of my mind. The tropes I was obliged to choose were very approximate and demonstrably inferior to the refined imagery of the nineteenth century. Nevertheless, there were instances of benefit to the expressivity of the verse. When I had typed it all out, I still had a good five minutes to concentrate my attention on what I had written.

This was the result:

NOUS OF ARCHONS 403

Why, OzzyMantis Hilton Paris,
Your laden's bong bin gucci grey?
Who are your Benny, Fishy, Aries?
OM NOM they dig your GDP?

Why do you stride in consequence
Squelching through mud, you head(less) honcho??
For whom swing you your stale incense?
Your Pale Horse! Your pinstripe poncho!

You're XJ now, the wind doth blow
The happy hayricks in your eyes
But don't chillax – through the slime below
The Lord Snake creeps – and crucifies.

I read through this bleak prophecy three times, checking and correcting any mistakes. I realised with some pride that I myself did not fully understand the poem as written. The only thing that was really clear was the provenance of the title: there is a Gnostic text, 'The Hypostasis of the Archons', which we had gone through in one of the Discourse lessons. I remember thinking at the time what a good name it would be for a Moscow restaurateur ('that darling of the Moscow bohemian crowd, Hypostas Archontov, is opening a glamorous new den: *Plato's Caveiar*'). And now the beam of the warrior muse had alighted on that memory. *Nous* was another Greek term, similar to hypostasis, for underlying reality.

I was particularly pleased with the twelfth line: the awe-inspiring meaning of the whole poem, foretelling the destruction of the King of Kings, Ruler of This World, by that same Gnostic snake with the head of a lion (or lion with the head of a snake, what difference does it make?) was now, as required, distilled in a single line. Having said this, it could also refer to Ishtar herself because of her long serpent-like necks. But I suppressed the unpatriotic association.

It would also be difficult to ignore the Headless Horseman, mounted on one of the horses of the Apocalypse: thus two great motifs in human culture were able to meet in the mind of a simple Russian vampire and unobtrusively shake hands and hooves with one another.

Twenty seconds before the red second hand on my screen crossed the finishing line I clicked the 'Send' button. I had done it.

The screen flickered and went dark. When it came to life again it was divided into two vertical sections. My poem could be seen on the right. The poem written by Mithra came up on the left. It looked like this:

MOSCowITO

> *Mosquito*
> *on the palm*
> *though very small,*
> *from the proportions*
> *of its body*
> *is like a mighty warrior*
> *now sunk in thought*
> *With its tiny head*
> *and torso long and round,*
> *were he a man*
> *he would be –*
Hero.

Mithra had chosen the safe option.

This was without doubt a most ignoble way to fight – a

368

scrupulously written, politically correct verse from a plodding careerist, reminiscent of those earnest reflections on the young Lenin from the culture of the last century. The mosquito always was for vampires what the *sakura* is to the Japanese – a symbol of beauty, consummate in its transience, flying by. It also had, so it seemed, a mystical subtext: the fresco in Enlil Maratovich's hamlet included a representation of the death of Count Dracula, a noble knight in black armour, from whose open breastplate could be seen flying off into the grey sky the humble mosquito of his soul.

The poem was written in the reverse stairway form Baldur had mentioned, and now that I saw it I at last understood what this was.

Even so, he had not completely succeeded in bringing off his twelfth line. That the mosquito is a hero, no one can deny. As the saying about Lenin goes, 'he lived, he lives, he will live forever'. But syntactically it was not quite correct to write 'he would be Hero'.

But then it dawned on me. Mithra was not merely describing the mosquito as a hero, he was making the association with Hera. Needless to say, despite the long, round body and the tiny head, this was an iron-clad compliment. It was tantamount to calling some ordinary girl an angel.

On the other hand, I thought bitterly, in my poem the main theme had been given poetical expression, in verse imbued with true lyric power. It touched on the most important strata of philosophy and *Weltanschauung*, and showed the drama of the human spirit. Above all, it fully reflected the culture and vitally important problems of contemporary civilisation...

But in my heart of hearts I already knew I had lost. Mithra's poem was better as any vampire would be forced to agree. My one remaining hope was that Hera would recognise some features of my style, and if she so wished...

The screen flickered again and I knew my fate was about

to be decided. The side of the screen on which Mithra's poem was displayed went dark, and some writing appeared diagonally across the lines of verse, as if someone was scribbling on the monitor with a marker pen:

Mack you!

But that's not necessarily conclusive, I thought, clinging obstinately to hope. A second later my half of the screen went dark, and across it splashed in flamboyantly lurid letters:

YJLTG JGL

I felt a slight twinge in the region of my elbow where the needle had gone under the skin, and thought I must have loosened the bandage with an awkward movement. I tried to fasten it with my free hand – but the hand would not obey. Then a wave of somehow involuntary fatigue flooded through my mind, and I took little or no further interest in the proceedings.

Of the next hour or two I can remember only disconnected glimpses. Baldur's and Loki's faces appeared before me a few times. Loki removed the needle from my arm and Baldur began to read out, in an officiously bureaucratic tone, Mithra's Duel Order. It went like this:

To Loki IX from Mithra VI.
Confidential

Duel Order

Rama the Second's conduct is stupid and insulting, but provokes only pity for him. In the event of my victory

*in this idiotic contest I request that he be tied to those
Swedish bars from which some time ago I freed him in
order to welcome him to our world. I further request that
on a table before him be placed a computer monitor to
which will be transmitted images from a camera attached to
my tiepin. I wish Rama the Second to view every last detail
of my encounter with that individual whose forbearance
and goodwill he has so shamelessly abused. Two concerns
motivate me. The first is that he should be made to
understand how a civilised man should behave in the
presence of a lady. The second is that, knowing Rama the
Second's predilections for such spectacles, I wish to afford
him some enjoyment. It is finally time for Rama the Second
to abandon his alienating links with the Nazi air ace Rudel,
through which he currently seeks solace from his solitude.*

In this connection I am ready to meet God.

Mithra the Sixth

Even through the dark torpor of my trance this enraged me –
but despite my fury I was unable even to lift one finger.

Loki and Baldur pulled me up out of the chair and carried
me into the study. Both Nabokovs stared straight at me with
immeasurable disgust, as if unable to forgive my defeat.

Baldur and Loki then bound me to the Swedish bars. I could
scarcely feel them touching me; only when they twisted my arm
too hard did I experience a dull sort of pain, as if through layers
of cotton wool. Then Baldur left the room, and I remained alone
with Loki.

Loki stood in front of me, and spent some time staring into
my eyes, pulling up the lids with his finger. Then he pinched me
hard in the stomach. This was extremely painful: the stomach

was the one part of the body that evidently retained full sensitivity. I tried to cry out, but could not. Loki pinched me again, much harder this time. The pain was unbearable, but I had no way of reacting to it.

'Fool!' said Loki. 'Stupid, stupid fool! Who do you think you are, eh? What were you playing at with all that stuff about the "Nous of the Archons"? What are you, a real vampo or a woolly, layabout, left-wing dreamer? "The Lord of This World" and "The Mosquito" are the *same theme*! Exactly the same! Simply a different formulation. Did you really not grasp that?'

He then pinched me again, this time with such force that everything went dark before my eyes.

'We were all so sure that you would win,' he went on. 'All of us! We even gave you time to go into the study and choose whatever preparation you wanted. I staked my entire store of *bablos* on you – five whole grams. More than a whole lifetime's accumulation! You're a cheap little swine, that's what you are!'

I thought he was going to pinch me again, but instead he suddenly broke into sobs – an old man's weeping, feeble and hopeless. Then he wiped away the tears with his sleeve, along with the smeared mascara, and continued speaking, now in an almost affectionate tone:

'You know what they say, Rama – everyone has a Prince of Denmark in his hamlet. It's quite understandable. But your prince has somehow set everyone's teeth on edge. Because of him, you've become a pain in the neck to everyone around you. It's high time you got over all that left-wing posturing. You've got to grow up. Because the road you're on now is going nowhere, I tell you that as your older comrade. You know they say there's a war between heaven and earth. Did you never think what it's about? I'll tell you. The war is because no one knows where earth is and where heaven is. There are two heavens, two heights fighting one another, each intent on turning the other upside down. When the matter is resolved the losing side will become earth. But until it is, nobody knows which way it will go. You are a field commander in this war, do you know that? The Lord of This World – that's you. But if you're not up to it, just go off into a distant trench by yourself and put a bullet in your head. Before you do, though, pass on the baton of the Tongue. And don't bother shooting yourself metaphorically in some stupid poem, do it for real. That's how it is...'

I breathed in deeply, and at that moment he pinched me with incredible force in the navel. The pain made me lose consciousness for several seconds – Loki had presumably eaten a death candy. When I came to, he was calmer.

'Forgive me,' he said. 'It was because of the *bablos*. You must know that yourself...'

I did know, and therefore was very relieved when Baldur returned to the room.

Positioning the table directly in front of me, Baldur placed the laptop on it. A tangle of cables led out of it into the passage. Adjusting the screen so that it was convenient to my angle of view, he asked:

'See all right, eh?'

Cupping his hand to his ear, he waited for a response, but when none came, gave up and continued:

'Silence means assent, ha ha... The conditions of the Order have been fulfilled. I must say, Rama, you've been very lucky. Up till this moment you could have lost your life several times over. But here you are, alive and well. It looks as though you are going to get away with nothing more than a bruised elbow. Congratulations, my young friend.'

I could see the screen with no difficulty. Presently it was filled with a grey snowstorm, through which it was hard to see anything identifiable.

'Mithra will initiate the transmission himself,' said Baldur. 'Good luck now.'

I expected Loki to give me one more parting pinch, but nothing happened. The door closed, and I was alone.

For some time the monitor on the laptop in front of me showed the kind of rippling grey lines on a television set before it has been tuned to a channel. Then a bright horizontal line appeared; it spread out to fill the screen, and I saw Mithra. To be precise I saw Mithra's reflection, as he was standing before a mirror combing his hair.

'Seventh to Fifth, come in Fifth,' he said, imitating a police car, and smiled. 'Can you hear me?'

He pointed to the glittering pin on his tie, and then stroked it with his finger. I heard a sound like distant thunder.

'Isn't it amazing what technology can do these days? All the same, there are limits to progress. I've often wondered whether it would be feasible for us to film ourselves flying? We'll find out today. Hera has fixed our appointment in Heartland, right at the bottom. She really has style, that girl. As you'll appreciate, the only way I can get there is to fly on wings of love. I wonder, would you ever have enough fire in your belly to do that?'

He turned away from the mirror and I could no longer see him. But what I could see was a large room with sloping windows – evidently a spacious loft. There was practically no furniture, but along the wall stood statues of well-known people – Mick Jagger, Shamil Basayev, Bill Gates, Madonna. They were as if frozen inside blocks of black ice, their faces fixed in grimaces of suffering. I knew this was currently all the rage in Moscow, probably a remote tribute to the *Chronicles of Narnia* – there was even a company specialising in interior design of this sort, and it was not particularly expensive.

Then I saw Mithra's hands. They were holding a little flask in the shape of a bat with folded wings. Mithra deliberately

374

brought it up to his chest where the camera was, to let me see it clearly. The flask disappeared from view, and I heard the sound of breaking glass – Mithra must have flung it to the floor, as used to be the practice after drinking a toast.

I saw a white leather chair. It moved nearer, then over to the side of the screen, and disappeared. Now I could see the grate of a fireplace. For a long time it did not move – presumably Mithra was sitting and waiting motionless in the chair. Then the picture failed, and grey lines of interference rose up one after the other from the bottom of the screen and disappeared at the top. There was no sound either.

The vision was off for a long time, at least two hours. I dozed. When the picture eventually came back to the screen there was still no sound, so I may have missed something.

A narrow passage swam towards me, carved out of the rock. This was Heartland. Whenever he entered an altar room, Mithra bowed to the mummified head above the altar. I had not realised this was the convention – no one had ever told me to do that.

In one of the rooms Hera was standing beside the altar. I recognised her immediately, despite the unfamiliar clothes she was wearing – a long white dress that made her look like a schoolgirl. It suited her wonderfully. If I had had any way of turning off the computer, I would have done so now. Of course I could not, any more than I could force myself to keep my eyes tight shut.

Hera did not move to face Mithra, but turned away and vanished into a side passage where it was too dark to see anything. Mithra followed her.

The screen went dark. Then appeared a dot of light, which grew into the rectangle of a doorway. I saw Hera again. She was standing leaning against the wall, her head bowed, as if grieving for something. She resembled a sapling, a young willow perhaps, touchingly trying to take root on the banks of an ancient river. A

375

Tree of Life that does not yet know it is the Tree of Life. Or then again, perhaps it does already know ... Mithra stopped – and I sensed that what he saw impressed him as much as it did me.

Hera vanished again.

Mithra went forward into the room. It was full of people. But I had no time to study them before something happened.

The screen flickered crazily, zigzags and bands of interference obscuring the picture. Someone's face came momentarily into view, covered with gauze and goggles, then the camera crashed into a wall and stayed there without moving. Now all I could see was the blobs and spots and irregularities of the paint.

I looked at these for several minutes. The camera then swung round and showed bright lights shining down from the ceiling. The ceiling swung off to the right, from which I deduced that Mithra was being dragged somewhere. There was a glimpse of a metal table and people standing round it, wearing surgeons' scrubs. The metal objects they held in their hands looked more like Aztec implements than medical instruments.

Then everything disappeared behind a white fabric screen, which hid both table and surgeons from my view. But for one second before this, a hand appeared on my monitor screen, holding something round – about the size of a football. The hand was holding it in an odd way, for a moment I could not work out how – then I realised it must be by the hair. Only when the round object had vanished from view did I realise what it was.

It was Mithra's severed head.

For a long time all I could see was the fabric of the white screen trembling in the draughts that came from deep underground. Sometimes it seemed to me that I could hear voices, but I was not sure where they were coming from – whether out of the computer speakers or from the neighbouring apartment, where the television was on at full volume. Several times I lapsed into unconsciousness. I do not know how many hours passed. Gradually the tranquilliser began to wear off: I could now move my fingers a little. Next, I found I was able to raise and lower my chin.

All this time thoughts were racing through my mind. The weirdest was the idea that Mithra had never untied me from the bars, and everything that had happened since then had been purely a hallucination, which in real time had lasted no more than a few minutes. This notion seriously alarmed me because it seemed so plausible in terms of my bodily posture, which was exactly as it had been on that far-off day when I had come back to consciousness and seen Brahma sitting on the sofa. But then I figured that the laptop computer sitting on the table in front of me proved the reality of everything that had taken place. And right on cue, to provide further evidence, the screen which was obscuring the view disappeared.

Now I could again see the room, flooded as before with bright light. But now there was no metal table or surgeons, and it could be seen that it was an ordinary altar room, except that it was a completely new one with all kinds of techno-junk on the floor, and it lacked an altar. Where the altar would normally be, in front of the niche in the wall, there towered up a piece of sophisticated medical apparatus attached to a perforated metal framework. As well as the medical equipment, the frame also supported a head hanging in front of the wall, enveloped in snow-white bandages.

The eyes in the head were closed. Below them were wide, black bruises. Below the nose was a half-effaced bloodstain. Another had dried at the corner of the lips. The head was breathing stertorously through transparent tubes inserted in the nose and leading out into some medical cabinet. I thought at first that someone had shaved off Mithra's Spanish-style beard. And then I realised the head was not Mithra's.

It was Hera's.

At the very instant that I recognised her, she opened her eyes and looked at me – that is to say, at the camera. Her swollen face was barely able to register emotions, but it seemed to me that pity and terror passed fleetingly over her features. Then her bandaged head moved aside, disappeared beyond the edge of the screen, and darkness descended.

VAMPILOGUE

A letter delivered by courier is always a gift of fate, since it mandates a brief emergence from the hamlet. And when in addition the letter looks so beautiful and smells so ethereally enticing...

The envelope was rose-pink and smelled delectably of a subtle, artless but at the same time unattainable – not eau de cologne exactly, but a single constituent of it, a secret, intrinsically aromatic ingredient that is almost never experienced by human nostrils in its pure, unadulterated state. It was the scent of secrecy, of unseen hands on the levers of power, of the wellsprings of dominion. The last, one might even say, was accurate in the literal sense – the package came from Ishtar.

I tore open the paper together with its soft lining. Inside was a black velvet pouch tied with a ribbon, accompanied by two folded sheets of paper with typewritten text. I already knew what I should find in the velvet pouch, so decided to begin with the letter.

Mwah, mwah, dear Prince of Hamlet,
How long is it since we saw one another? I've been counting the days, and they come to three whole months. Forgive me for not having been in touch with you before, but there has been so much to do. I'm sure you want to

know what my life is like now and what is happening with me. But, you know, it's very hard to put into words. It's a bit like finding yourself the figurehead of a huge ship – you're feeling each one of her sailors as you cleave through the water with your own body. Just imagine being the ship's captain and the figurehead on her bowsprit at one and the same time. You have no arms or legs – but it's still up to you to decide how the sails should be rigged. The wind that fills the sails is the breath of people's lives, and down in the hold goes on the mysterious work thanks to which mankind's existence finds its purpose and creates bablos.

In all this, of course, there are some less pleasant sides. The least pleasant is the ultimate prospect. You know what happened to the old woman, our former Prima Donna. It was, of course, dreadful and I am very sorry for her. But I know that one day I myself shall see a yellow silk scarf in the hands of the person entering my room... that is how life is arranged and it is not for us to change it. Now I understand why Borisovna became such a heavy drinker in her last six months. They treated her very harshly. While they were chiselling out a new room in the rock she kept asking everyone what those sounds were, but they all pretended they could hear nothing and that she was imagining things. And then, when it was impossible to keep up the pretence any longer, they lied to her that the lift was being repaired. Finally, towards the end, they said a new underground tunnel was being constructed so that Government high-ups can go straight from Rublevka to the Kremlin. She knew what the truth was, but could do nothing about it. It's terrible, isn't it?

I want to set things up from the very beginning so that no one will ever be able to treat me like that. I need to have friends I can rely on. I am going to institute a special

Distinguished Service Order: 'Friend of Ishtar'. From now on there will be a rank in our hierarchy reserved exclusively for holders of this title. You will be the first Friend of Ishtar, because no one is closer to me than you are. And I will do everything for you. Would you like a hamlet like Enlil's? That is all absolutely possible now.

About Mithra. I know you witnessed everything. I am sure you have thought long and hard about what happened, and it must seem very black to you. But it is always like that when a goddess exchanges her earthly persona. For a new head to be connected to the main brain in the spine you need a complete new nervous system, and another Tongue to act as the linking interface. The Tongue, naturally, does not die, it merely returns to its roots. But Mithra has gone for ever, and that is sad. Until the very last second he did not guess what was happening.

Between ourselves, Enlil and Marduk thought it would be you. Not that you were being fattened up like a sacrificial lamb, but they were practically certain you would be chosen. Hence the lackadaisical attitude to your education. You must have noticed that apart from me no one showed any great interest in your destiny or made much effort to draw you into our community. I expect you just thought you were living in seclusion on the edge of our world? Well, now you know why.

For Enlil the outcome was a huge surprise. For me as well it was a terribly hard choice, to decide which of you would live. In choosing you I went against all the others. So you had better learn once and for all that, except for me, you have no friends. But with me you don't need any others.

Never fear, I will not bash you with my knee again. I don't have one now. But I do have bablos, and now it is

381

all ours. All ours, Rama! And as for everything else – we'll think of something.

The rest will have to wait until we meet. And you shouldn't make a goddess wait too long.

P.S. You asked me to remind you about bringing a death candy with you at our next meeting. So, this is a little reminder... ☺

Instead of a signature there was a red facsimile like a single scrawled word 'Ish'; and below it a stamp with an ancient representation of a winged creature slightly reminiscent of a garuda bird. If the artist had had the Mighty Bat in mind, he had definitely flattered her.

I looked through the window. It was getting dark, and occasional snowflakes were falling. I had no burning desire to fly anywhere through the winter night, but felt I had no alternative. I realised that I no longer thought of her as Hera. Everything was different now.

I sat on the sofa and undid the throat of the velvet pouch. Inside, just as I expected, was a small bottle – but of a completely different design. The previous passport to Ishtar had been a small dark bottle in the shape of a bat with folded wings and a stopper like a skull. This flask was made of white frosted glass and was in the form of a headless woman's body, the tiny stopper resembling a neck cut off high up. It was a macabre reminder of the sacrifice the goddess must make in order to become a goddess. Evidently this Ishtar intended to take her job seriously. There were going to be a lot of changes, I thought, and how lucky I had been to end up on the right side of the watershed. But I was still a prey to uneasy feelings clawing at my vitals.

After letting the single drop fall on to my tongue, I sat in the chair and waited. If I had heard the ominous strains of

Verdi's *Requiem* coming through the wall again, it would have been most appropriate. But this time total silence reigned. The television set on the wall was on, with the sound turned off.

In any case, there was no need of sound; everything could be understood without it. The screen seethed with life, a firework display coruscated under southern skies, lighting up laughing bronzed faces. Brandishing his radio mike like a sabre, some international singing star or other resembling a bizarre cross between a goat and a Greek god, was dancing in a t-shirt with the enigmatic inscription '30cm = 11¼ in'. For a few minutes I was lost in contemplation of the scene. The star was singing to the accompaniment of an orchestra, which came in whenever he needed to take a breath. Across the bottom of the screen ran a translation of the lyrics:

This is what happens, what happens – a girl gives io-io-io to a boy and looks away – she probably thinks she's making a fool of herself or the boy is bored because he says nothing... Or else she thinks, io-io-io, she ought to gaze romantically through the window at the moon... Don't turn your eyes away, girls! Io-io-io, these are the best moments in a boy's life, and if he says nothing it's only for fear of scaring off the magic moment... io-io-io-io-io!

The singer paused and in came the orchestral French horns and trumpets. Even though you could not hear them, you could feel the power of the sound from the purple faces of the brass players blowing their brains out. I looked into the darkness outside the window.

Well, what of it? One requiem was as good as another...

But what if this time it was a real requiem? Perhaps Ishtar simply needed another Tongue?

A chilling fear gripped me, unfathomable and irresistible, not to be compared with any other. At the same time I recognised it as a normal state of mind for our times, and it was pointless to try to attribute any rational basis to it. One simply had to get used to it, was all. The clock in the passage chimed the hour. Now, I thought, it really was time.

My mind sketched out for me the familiar daredevil journey up the chimney and out to the stars. Prising myself up from the chair on my calloused fists, I somehow blundered round the room, threw myself into the jaws of the fireplace and emerged from the chimney into the cold sky. Making a few slow circles I gradually gained height.

Around me were large but scattered snowflakes, and the lights of Moscow shone mysteriously and romantically through their white shroud. The city was so beautiful it made me catch my breath, and after a few minutes my mood underwent a sea change. The terror disappeared, to be replaced by a contented peace.

I remembered that Hans Ulrich Rudel had once experienced something similar in the Christmas sky over Stalingrad, when thoughts of war and death suddenly morphed into a feeling of serene harmony. And flying over the tanks blazing in the snow, he had sung 'Silent Night, Holy Night' ...

It was too cold for me to sing. A different millennium now lay over the countryside, and beneath my wings blazed not tanks but the headlights of Chaldeans' limousines scorching their way out of town. And if the truth be admitted, the night was not distinguished by any particular sanctity. Nevertheless, the view was superb, and I promised myself that I would document every single thing I was feeling and thinking at this moment – I would record, so to speak, an instantaneous copy of my soul in order never to forget it. This snow, this dusk, those lights down there, I told myself, will be indelibly inscribed on my memory.

And another thing I would record was how I had changed.

Before, I had behaved very stupidly. Loki had been right. But now I had become wiser and had gained much understanding. I understood life, and myself, and the Prince of Denmark, and Hans Ulrich Rudel. And I had made my choice.

I love our empire. I love its glittering glamour hard-gained through suffering, and its bold discourse forged in struggle. I love its people. Not for providing me with bonuses and preferences, but simply because we are of one red liquid, albeit from opposite sides of the formula. And though I can't see it with my eyes, I can feel with my heart the all-powerful drilling towers sucking the black liquid from the arteries of the planet – and know that I have taken my place in the ranks.

Quick March, Comrade Mosquito, Sir!

But the order of things must be held firmly in place, for we face troubled days ahead. In this world of ours, there is not enough red or black liquid to go round. And that means it will not be long before other vampires come to pull the wool over the eyes of our Ivans and confuse their Mind 'B's, squinting greedily at our *bablos*. And then the front line will again pass through every hearth and every heart.

Exactly how we act to preserve our unique ancient civilisation with its lofty pan-ethnic mission will have to be the subject of much serious thought later on. But for now everything around me was a wide ocean of calm, while towards me floated snow-stars large as butterflies. And with each beat of my wings I was coming nearer to my strange girlfriend – and, it must be admitted, also to the *bablos*.

Which was now all ours.

All ours.

All ours.

All ours.

All ours.

All ours.

How many times would I have to repeat the phrase before I understood each facet and detail of its meaning? In reality the meaning was as clear as day: mountaineer Rama the Second is filing his report on the conquest of Fuji.

Here, however, was a very important nuance, which demands a few words of explanation.

The summit of Fuji is not at all what one thought it was as a child. By no means is it a sunlit world where grasshoppers and smiling snails sit at ease amid giant blades of grass. It is cold and dark, lonely and deserted on the summit of Fuji. And this is good, because cold and desolation is where the soul finds rest, and for all who finally reach the top of the mountain the way will have been unbearably exhausting. Nor is the mountaineer on the summit the same person who set out at the start of the climb.

I can no longer remember the person I once used to be. The images that come to the surface of my consciousness resemble more an echo of once-seen films than a record of my own history... I see below me dotted lines of light, and realise that they were streets along which not long ago I used to skateboard. At that time my random wanderings in space had no clear goal. Later I was driven around the city in a big black car, still not fully aware where I was going or why. But now, as I fly high aloft in the night sky on resilient, creaking wings, I know everything. This is how, imperceptibly to ourselves, we grow up. We gain in serenity and clarity. But we lose our naïve belief in miracles.

At one time I thought the stars in the sky were other worlds to which cosmic ships from the City of the Sun would one day fly. Now I know their minute needle-points are merely piercings of the armoured canopy that hides and protects us from the pitiless sea of light beyond.

It is on the summit of Fuji that one feels the pressure of this light upon our world most powerfully. And for some reason there comes into one's head thoughts of the ancients.

That thou doest, do quickly.

What is the meaning of these words? My friends, it could not be simpler. Make haste to live. Because the day is coming when the heavens will be rent asunder, and the light whose might and fury we cannot even begin to imagine will explode into our happy home – and forget us for ever.

Written by Rama the Second, Prince of Hamlet, Friend of Ishtar, Chief of Glamour and Discourse, Mosquito Mensch and God of Money with Oak-Leaf Wings.

The summit of Mount Fuji, winter.

ABOUT GOLLANCZ

Gollancz is the oldest SF publishing imprint in the world. Since being founded in 1927 Gollancz has continued to publish a focused selection of bestselling and award-winning authors. The front-list includes **Ben Aaronovitch**, **Joe Abercrombie**, **Charlaine Harris**, **Joanne Harris**, **Joe Hill**, **Alastair Reynolds**, **Patrick Rothfuss**, **Nalini Singh** and **Brandon Sanderson**.

As one of the largest Science Fiction and Fantasy imprints in the UK it is no surprise we have one of the most extensive backlists in the world. Find high quality SF on Gateway written by such authors as **Philip K. Dick**, **Ursula Le Guin**, **Connie Willis**, **Sir Arthur C. Clarke**, **Pat Cadigan**, **Michael Moorcock** and **George R.R. Martin**.

We also have a strand of publishing in translation, which includes French, Polish and Russian authors. Gollancz is home to more award-winning authors than any other imprint, with names including **Aliette de Bodard**, **M. John Harrison**, **Paul McAuley**, **Sarah Pinborough**, **Pierre Pevel**, **Justina Robson** and many more.

The SF Gateway
More than 3,000 classic, rare and previously out-of-print SF novels at your fingertips.
www.sfgateway.com

The Gollancz Blog
Bringing you news from our worlds to yours. Stories, interviews, articles and exclusive extracts just for you!
www.gollancz.co.uk

GOLLANCZ
LONDON